SISTERS
with a
SIDE
of
GREENS

MICHELLE STIMPSON

sourcebooks
landmark

Published by Sourcebooks Landmark, an imprint of Sourcebooks
P.O. Box 4410, Naperville, Illinois 60567-4410
(630) 961-3900
sourcebooks.com

Cataloging-in-Publication Data is on file with the Library of Congress.

Printed and bound in the United States of America.
WOZ 10 9 8 7 6 5 4 3 2 1

For sisters everywhere of every kind.
May we love ourselves and each other gently.

CHAPTER 1
Rose

Some days, you wake up, and you're supposed to feel different, but you don't. Take, for example, your birthday, your anniversary, the first day of the year. You want to be excited, but it's just another day, like all the days before it. I mean, it's definitely a blessing that most of the days in my fifty-nine years of life were just normal. No big, huge, breath-snatching tragedies, unless you count the day my husband left me for another woman, which I do *not* count as a tragedy because the truth is: my husband wanted a wife, but he didn't want to be a husband. Kind of like when you want to be fit, but you don't actually want to be one of those exercise-y people. And you want to eat dessert every night.

Dessert is good. So are wives. Really, who *wouldn't* want a wife? Somebody tending to hearth and home, somebody society says should be loyal, faithful, and respectful to you? Shoot, I want a wife, myself.

I know the ideal is for men to reciprocate for women. But that's not the everyday reality—especially not the faithful part, because we have an actual dictionary-word for a husband's other woman. Right there between "mistreat" and "mistrial" lies the word "mistress."

Wives, however, don't have a word for our "other" man in the entire English language. I'm not advocating for us to have a cheat-word. I'm just saying us not having one declares, "It's so unacceptable for a woman to do this, we ain't makin' a word for it, ma'am."

Maybe our word could be misteress?

Anyway. David leaving me was not tragic, nor was it unexpected.

Neither was my retirement day. Except it actually was a pivotal day, marking a line in my life's sand.

That morning, I got up, washed with my winter vanilla bean–scented scrub, whipped the bonnet off my head, moisturized my platinum-blond kinks, and let them point wherever they pleased. I pulled, zipped, buttoned, and buckled my uniform into place. The light-blue short-sleeve knit shirt bore the United States Postal Service logo, a white eagle on a darker blue square. How many times had I caught sight of this patch out of the corner of my eye and thought, "Is that a spot? No, it's the eagle."

I took one last look in my bathroom mirror and, mentally blocking out the bottles of beautifying potions strewn across my countertop, gave myself a once-over.

Not bad for fifty-nine and retired. Not bad at all.

I had beat the system a little by dyeing my short Afro blond before the gray could claim victory. My waistline was still present, aided by a standard-issue leather belt. Okay, the waist got exaggerated by the belt, but I was still glad to own one. That belt was the only "sexy" thing in my wardrobe, if one could count a black garrison belt as "sexy." My fashion preferences and penchant for jewelry died soon after I started working for the government. What hadn't suffered was my smooth, barely wrinkled skin. It brought plenty of speculation from strangers. I could tell by their age-related questioning. "Do you have kids? Or grand—"

I'd shake my head before they could finish, not offering an explanation. In my thirties and forties, the question about children gut-punched me every time. David and I never had children. We couldn't. Actually, *I* couldn't.

People need to mind their own business.

I slid balm across my full lips and gave them a solid smack. I smiled at myself. My dimples winked back. It was time to go to work one last time.

After warming up a frozen frittata and pouring coffee into a thermos, I breezed past the refrigerator and headed toward the garage door. I'm not sure exactly what happened, but somehow my knee caught the corner of the wall, and I swear it felt like an ax whomped my left kneecap. Glass broke. Time collapsed. I dropped the thermos and grabbed my knee, as though holding it would relieve the pain that became my entire existence in an instant.

Somehow—I must have hopped?—I made it to a chair in my dinette and sat, rocking back and forth, as I rubbed the throbbing knee with both hands. That's when I saw the picture of Momma on the floor. The glass protecting her airbrushed photo had split in three places, but her dark, beautiful face wasn't scratched. I'd get another frame. A better one, which was something I'd been meaning to do, anyway. Momma deserved to be remembered in something more than a cheap certificate holder moonlighting as a frame.

The thought that I'd be late to work tried to enter my consciousness. I was too busy rocking my knee and thinking about my mother. Besides, I'd been late to work before. What could they do to me today?

Ten minutes later, I'd recovered enough to free Momma from the broken glass and attempt to reset her picture in the frame.

That's when I saw the words written on back of her photo. *My Rose, Keep God first, family second, and you will bloom into all your dreams coming true.* If memory served correctly, my sister had given me the picture, already mounted inside the frame. So I had never seen these words before. It was a good thing I'd never seen Momma's handwriting, her demands, the promise she didn't have the authority to make, on the back of her picture.

For the thousandth time, I disagreed with my mother. I laid the picture and the frame on the dining table, unassembled. No time to ponder her presumptuous words.

I hobbled into my car and drove the seven miles from my home to the post office, something I had done for the previous fifteen years. Before then, I had driven twelve miles, back when I lived in the Oak Cliff area of Dallas. After the divorce, I moved into a smaller place and prayed I wouldn't get relocated due to all the cutbacks.

My prayers were answered. I'd remained at the closest post office most of my thirty-one-year career with the United States Postal Service.

Traveling the familiar—dare I say mundane—route to work, I wondered for the first time if I should have prayed that prayer to stay at the post office. Not just the location, the job itself. What if I'd gotten laid off, fired, or forced into early retirement? Would my desperation have driven me toward a different destiny?

Bloom into all your dreams coming true.

There's no way to change the past. I let the idea flitter out of my brain again as I pressed my badge against the sensor and entered the employee parking lot for the last time. I settled back into the heated seat of my five-year-old Honda SUV and watched the gate slide to the right.

Hmph. Appropriate. Been waiting all my life for an open gate.

The gate seemed more rickety, slower than it had ever been. *Why hasn't somebody fixed or upgraded it in all these years?* Surely the technology existed.

Yet I idled as I had done countless times, sitting in this identical spot behind the steering wheel of four different cars over the years. My knee still aching. Waiting for the gate to open. Wondering about the past and the future. What could have been if I hadn't spent the previous thirty years playing it safe with this good government job? What lay ahead of me without it? I hadn't envisioned myself after employment until that very morning. I had put off thinking about my future, fearful that I might find more of what I'd accomplished lay in the past. Nothing significant. Nothing worth filling a book, a diary, or even an interesting conversation.

A burst of heat reminiscent of perimenopause flashed over me. Anxiety wormed through my veins. I couldn't delay this internal conversation any longer. Today was my retirement day. The beginning or the end—or both.

The wood-paneled break room was decorated with exactly one wall of gold streamers, four black balloons, and a "Happy Retirement, Rose" banner. We had used the same one for every retiree for as far back as I could remember. The R, O, and S of my name were uniform stickers affixed to a rectangle. The "E" had been drawn onto its own rectangle with black Sharpie.

Those E's go quickly in a set of letter-stickers.

The room still smelled like the burning peppermint-scented wax someone had brought in to acknowledge the season. One can hardly go wrong with peppermint, but the scent was dangerously close to an arthritis-relieving cream my mother used to apply. So instead of suggesting a festive atmosphere, the scent brought a cryptic message at my retirement party: *You're old, and you probably need muscle cream, Rose. This is the beginning of the end.*

With my knee still experiencing aftershocks from my morning accident, I couldn't argue. Maybe retirement was like paying off a car note. As soon as you have the lien-free title in hand, your transmission conks out.

I thought I was ready for this day, but I wasn't.

Several coworkers brought store-bought dishes for the pot-luck/retirement gathering. None of them had actually dirtied a pot for the occasion, evident by the rip-away plastic packaging and the bright-orange "reduced price" sticker on a container of dried-out oatmeal cookies. As the celebrant, I brought nothing except my smile and my bootleg knee.

I sat at a table nearest the cake, carefully rising as people approached me. Their hands—some cold and chapped, some warm and damp—thrust into mine, one after another.

"I wish this wasn't your retirement party," my coworker Janie said, her head shaking in what appeared to be actual disappointment. Janie and I had worked together on a few projects over the last four years. She was sharp and wore thick glasses that made her eyes appear larger. People made fun of her behind her back, and I always felt bad for her, given what happened with my sister Marvina's eye.

Touched by Janie's sentiments, I said, "Oh, don't worry. We can always keep in touch. You *know* my address."

She shook her head even harder. "No, no! I was just thinking, it's a shame this is *your* retirement party, because you didn't bring anything for the spread."

"Oh. Well, alrighty then," I managed, adding a laugh so Janie wouldn't suspect she'd insulted me. Then I thought twice about it. Why was I trying to keep up *her* spirits when she's the one who'd offended me? I could take this opportunity to tell her exactly how I felt. Let her know I was a person who had worked somewhere for over three decades, and I didn't want to be remembered for whatever I brought in my trusty Crock-Pot. I wanted to be remembered for...well, for what? What marvel had I done other than show up every day and perform my job? Nothing memorable there. And there was no one left with whom I'd worked for more than five years to know that I had once been married, been through a divorce, lost both of my parents, took four weeks off for a hysterectomy, took a week off when my best friend died, big-chopped my hair three times, lost twenty-five pounds twice, and gained seventy-five over my tenure?

Yes, Janie could have used a lesson in manners. I wasn't in the mood to give it to her, though, because maybe she was right. Maybe the best thing I'd ever really done at the post office was cook. People hounded me in the hallways the day before Thanksgiving.

"What did you bring, Rose? What color is your container?" They always scraped—possibly licked?—my glassware clean after every break room banquet. Their satisfaction with my cooking, i.e. my mother's seasoning, always sent joy swirling through me, a swift, seldom, but sure snippet of happiness.

Then it dissipated. And I'd grab my empty glassware, rinse it, and pack it up until my next opportunity to cook for somebody else. A shame.

These facts stuck in my craw, because if my sister hadn't misappropriated my $40 and cheated me out of my destiny, I could have been more than a post office potluck princess.

My temples thumped every time I thought about Marvina. I forced myself to focus again. Janie had only told her truth, albeit one that didn't sit well with me.

My white cake with black and gold confetti sprinkles was identical to the one for Irene Rodriguez, who had retired three months earlier, and Mike Finley, who left a year ago. I despise black and gold together. The combination reminds me of our church choir robes—hot and scratchy and funky, depending on who wore it the Sunday before me. And here I was again, getting the second- or third-hand use of something with this color scheme. I hadn't expected anyone to go all out and buy linen tablecloths or anything, but thirty-one years deserved more than one wall's worth of used festoons, didn't it?

"Rose," Ken, my last supervisor, approached me from the side, laying a hand on my shoulder. He was young enough to be my son, and he always slathered enough gel goop in his blond hair to perform ten ultrasounds. Ken had never touched me. Ever. *Is he drunk?*

I quickly swiveled to the left, causing his hand to drop awkwardly. He slid it into a pocket.

"Yes, Ken?" Unsure of my facial expression, I took a sip of my juice, pressing the black plastic cup hard against my lip.

"Is anyone from your family coming?"

I swallowed my punch. "No. They're a few hours away."

He shrugged. "One road leads to everywhere."

I gave him a stay-out-of-grown-folks'-business stare.

He must have received my hint, because he changed the subject with, "So, what do you plan to do with yourself, now?"

Thick-soled nursing shoes padded across the linoleum floor to join our little group. Genevieve. Her long, postal-blue skirt swept the tops of her shoes. She would look ten years younger with a basic makeover. Working here, though, why bother? There was no one to impress. Practicality and comfort won every time.

I returned her smile and tried to think of an answer to Ken's question worth her shuffling over to hear. "I'm going to take a gap year."

Genevieve wrinkled her nose. "A gap year?"

Ken explained the concept and how the term usually applied to students taking a break between high school and college. "It gives them some time to contemplate, seriously, exactly what they want to do with the rest of their lives."

Genevieve laughed and spurted, "Then I must be having a gap *life*, because I still don't know what I want to be when I grow up."

We laughed, and they both waltzed away from what had become my short receiving line.

Genevieve's words clung to me. My throat thickened. *A gap life.* As in stuck between the clear, prescribed first leg of life and the ambiguous, limitless second leg and beyond, full of complexities and uncontrolled variables. You go from seeing your name on a name tag and someone whispering sweetly, "Rose, here's where you'll sit" in first grade to being presented with a list of over thirty fields of study and someone else barking, "Now, choose a college major to determine the rest of your life," only twelve short years later.

And then you blink. And thirty years later you wonder where the time went. *Who was I meant to be? Is it too late to be me? Did I miss my own life?* And you wonder why there's nobody at your job or in your life who cares enough—who loves you enough—to make a homemade dish to commemorate your departure.

I continued shaking hands and exchanged pleasant banter with a dozen more coworkers, shifting all my weight to the right side to keep my left knee from throbbing. I knew their faces and names, but not much more given the transient nature of employees recently. They called me an "old head." The folks I came in with and knew personally had long gone. The last one to leave, Edgar Lenear, had been employed at the post office when he died. In fact, we gathered in this same meeting room to hear the news of his heart attack and take up donations for his family.

This multipurpose room had seen a lot over the years.

We were nearing the thirty-minute mark for the official lunch-hour retirement ceremony. Ken, Janie, and our Postmaster shared a few generic words in my honor. A slide deck displayed the state of the world the year I started working at the post office. The president was George W. Bush, we were in the Gulf War, the Chicago Bulls won their first NBA championship. The average price for a gallon of gas was $1.14, and everyone gasped at the price of a stamp back then. Twenty-nine cents.

When we finished the slides, it was nearly time for everyone to return to work.

"Speech! Speech!" Someone began chanting, and the room chimed in.

At their insistence, I grabbed the podium and stepped onto the five-inch-tall wooden platform to speak.

I sound-checked the portable microphone with a tap on the side. "Um…hello. I would like to thank you all for coming to my retirement party. Ceremony. Whatever we call it."

Slight laughter from the dwindling audience.

"Working here for the past thirty-one years was the pinnacle of success, according to my parents. My father didn't have a degree, but he had a good-paying job at the steel mill. His work was hard, dirty, sweaty, sometimes deadly, back in my hometown,

Fork City." A few people glanced around, uncertainty written on their faces.

I added a little context so they'd know Fork City was only a few hours from Dallas. Head nods.

I continued my unrehearsed story. "The union strikes could send our family to the community food pantry. My mother had a few good jobs, but she lost them every time she got pregnant. Back then, there was no such thing as FMLA or paid time off for having a baby. Most of the time, a pregnant woman lost her job. Period."

Utter surprise registered on the faces of two thirtysomethings, Rebecca and Ashley, whom I recognized from a mandatory safety training session.

"When I got here, I was grateful. I put my head down, put my nose to the grindstone, and I did what I was asked to do."

Ken cleared his throat. A low rumble of laughter spread across the room.

I added, "For the most part." I took a deep breath, the term "gap life" still ping-ponging in my head. *Had these thirty-one years just been gap-filling years?* "I count myself blessed to have had steady employment. And…now… I guess that's it. Thank you."

Tears pricked my eyes. Emotion pressed hard on the lump in my throat, nearly suffocating me. *Why am I crying?* This was a joyous occasion. If not joyous, at least neutral, like the other lightly celebrated days of the year. Presidents' Day. Groundhog Day. Why couldn't my retirement day have at least brought a neutral straight line to my face instead of a frown?

These people. This place. This event. Not what I wanted then or now. A sudden rush of reality that twisted my gut something awful.

I didn't have time to evaluate my feelings, however, because the moment I stepped off the podium and my weight, for an instant, settled on that bad knee, it buckled.

The floor zoomed to my face.

Everything went black.

CHAPTER 2

Rose

Whispers whipped through the room. I recognized the soft voices. People from my job.

"I swear. I was like aaaaagh! First Edgar. Now Rose!"

Are they talking about me? I'm dead?

"I know. Rose was always so…dependable. Always at work. It's kind of like she didn't have a life. I heard she had, like, ninety days of vacation accrued."

"No way."

"Or whatever the max is. She just worked."

"Yeah. Sad. But you know what they say. Life is like a roll of toilet paper. You think you have so much left until you get down to the last few squares."

Am I in a casket? Is this my funeral? They're talking about me… and toilet paper…in the past tense.

"Rose? Rose, can you hear me?"

David's blurry figure towered over me, creating a bit of a time warp. I hadn't been this close to him in years.

A jackhammer pounded in my head. The light stabbed my eyes. I spread my fingers and felt the scratchy, cool, synthetic fabric spread across my thighs.

"Can you hear me, Rose?"

Slowly, my tongue began cooperating with my brain. "Yes."

"Stay still. Don't try to move. You're at the hospital. Your knee folded, you fell, and hit your head during your retirement ceremony. You're going to be all right. I got you."

I closed my eyes again as David ran his hand along my forehead. I wished I loved him more, because then I could have fully appreciated his touch.

The whispers continued. "She went down like lightning struck her."

David's warmth left my side. His shoes shuffled against the floor. The room fell silent. I knew he was giving somebody the Black Baptist church usher-eye for making unseemly commentary. There's no coming back from that arctic glare.

With David on guard to protect me from any harm, sleep began to swallow me again. As I drifted off, I wondered, would I ever get to live my dreams?

When I woke the second time, the last dregs of sunlight proved tolerable. I opened my eyes fully, and my pupils seemed to float around until they landed on the only other person in my room. David. He was still wearing black dress slacks and a blue button-down shirt with a colorful, paisley-patterned, loosened tie. He must have come straight from work, and that must have been several hours ago, judging by the sunset.

He smiled at me. His bushy salt-and-pepper beard rose an inch with the gesture. He'd put on a few pounds—I could tell from the extra padding on his neck. Other than that, he was as handsome as he'd ever been. Dark-brown skin, light-brown eyes, deep-set dimples carving shadows in his cheeks. I tried returning the smile. It was nice of my ex-husband to be there. I never took his name off the emergency contact list at work. He was a terrible husband, truly. A decent person, just as truly.

"Thank you," I croaked.

He waved me off. "I know you'd do the same for me."

I neither confirmed nor denied his statement. I would do the same for him if and only if he were certifiably in between girl-friends. No way would I show up to his hospital room, his ex-wife, and risk confrontation with his latest fling.

My hands found the bed remote. As I elevated my upper body, David jumped to his feet. "Take it easy, now. And don't lower your knee."

"Can I have some water?"

David presented me with a Styrofoam cup of water and glori-ously crushed ice. "Thank you." I crunched the cold jewels. Good ice gives you life.

"They'll dismiss you if you're feeling up to it," he said.

I nodded. "Yes. I want to go home." The brain fog lifting, I recalled nurses intermittently disturbing my sleep to check my vitals. A hospital is no place to rest.

"When the nurse comes back around, we can let her know."

He said "we" as though we were together. Perhaps going home together. I didn't like the sound of it. "Maybe I can stay the night. Get some sleep and Uber back to my car."

"Your car is already at your home. That guy, Ken, drove me to the post office. I took your car to your home, and I Ubered back here so I could take you home, take care of you tonight."

"Thank you, but you don't have to stay in the house with me," I said.

"Someone has to," he said. "You suffered a concussion. Your knee is unsteady. You could use help for a few days."

"I can *get* help."

David twisted his body to the left, then to the right, looking over his shoulders, bending down as though searching under a chair. "Who? Where they at?"

My lids shut tight again. "You're making my head hurt."

"I'm sorry." He stepped closer. "Stop being stubborn, Rose Tillman. Facts: No one from your job hung around long enough to make sure you were clear of all danger. Your nearest family member is two hours away, and I'm not even sure she'd come if you called her. Who you *do* have is me. I'm here, and I will help you if you'll let me."

He was right. My now former coworkers had resumed their normal lives. My blood kin… I don't know. She might care; she might not. I sighed. "You're such a realist."

"This is why I work with numbers. One and one makes two all over the world. What can I say?"

His analysis of the situation made perfect sense on paper. I was in need, and he was available and willing. However, I knew my ex-husband. David's dark eyes were twinkling with impossible delusions of a reunion. He was like Wile E. Coyote. No matter how many times his plans ended in disaster, he always built another ridiculous contraption to catch the Road Runner (i.e., me). It had been more than twenty years since our divorce, and David was still holding on to the bachelor dream. Between his women friends, that is.

Aside from his attempt for one-on-one time, David had whittled my life down to some simple, harsh truths. I was alone in the world. Now living on a fixed income.

If I fell and injured myself while at home, it would be days before anyone missed me, now that no one expected me at work. I'd overheard someone say, "I hope she has a speedy recovery." Isn't a "speedy recovery" something active people hoped for, so they could get back to their normal, fulfilling lives quickly? What did I need to speed up for?

Nothing. Nothing at all. Not work, not kids, or grandkids, not even a pet.

"David, before you come to my house, I need to ask. Do you have a woman right now?" I asked.

"I do."

"Is she mentally and emotionally stable?"

"Yes."

"Does she know that you and I are just friends?"

His face split into a wide grin. "It's nice to hear you say we're friends."

I rolled my eyes. The pain of exaggerated ocular movement took me by surprise. "Owww!"

"What?"

"My sockets hurt when I roll my eyes."

"Maybe you should stop rolling them, then, Rosey-Posey."

He'd started with our old pet names, now. The nickname caused an annoying prick in my psyche.

I sighed. "Let's stay focused, David. Is your current girlfriend safe? 'Cause ain't nobody got time for folks busting windows out my car, okay?"

"That was, what, ten years ago?"

"Eight," I corrected him. "What grown, fifty-something-year-old woman is busting out car windows, anyway?"

David's laugh softened my attitude. We could argue all day and then top it all off with a belly-aching laugh.

"Listen. I will let Ashley know—"

"Ashley? How old is she? Is she Black?"

He blinked slowly. "I will let Black, forty-nine-year-old Ashley know that I am your temporary caregiver. She will have to decide if she can live with the temporary arrangement or not. If she can, great. If not, she can bounce."

I took that to mean he wasn't heavily invested at this point in their relationship, which didn't surprise me. David was still David.

So there I was, riding shotgun with my ex-husband to my quaint two-bedroom home in a tucked-away neighborhood that no one ever visited unless they knew exactly where they were going. As soon as I walked inside, I reached for the scissors in the writing desk drawer and snipped off the hospital wristband.

David's hand pressed firmly against the small of my back, following me protectively as I limped to my bedroom. Our shoes shuffled along the carpet slowly. Patiently. We had done this dance before, with him fastened to my torso as I ambled my ailing body back to bed. David always knew what to do and how to show loving care during a crisis; his problem was with the everyday consistency of love.

We entered my bedroom, and I watched his eyes flutter over the layout. He seemed shocked by how much things had changed since he'd last been inside. His eyes traveled my four walls, taking in my faux exposed brick accent wallpaper, a full-length vintage mirror propped in a corner, a brown tufted velvet wingback chair, and several mounted pictures of powerful Black women, including Maya Angelou, Angela Bassett, and Aretha Franklin.

"Your bedroom feels like a café for the sisters. No men allowed."

Translation: *Are you sleeping with somebody in here?*

My head was pounding too hard to muster a sarcastic laugh at him.

I slipped off my shoes and laid face down on my damask comforter, sprawled out like somebody who'd gotten drunk and collapsed. "Thank you," I murmured into the pillow. If I shifted my weight a little to the right side, my left knee tolerated the position.

"Okaaaay. I'll just see myself to another bedroom?"

"Down the hall to the right."

"You just gonna lay there like that? Face down? Can you breathe?"

"Yes, yes, and yes. I just want to be alone right now. I'll straighten up in a second."

He clicked his cheek. "All right." Without asking, he reached past me and grabbed the two extra pillows on my bed. "Let's get you turned over and put these under your knee. Need to be careful with it. Keep it elevated."

I didn't protest him nearly lying on top of me to get the pillows. How could I? He was right. Everything he'd said tonight was right. I was alone. In addition to the fact I was alone, I now had a bum knee. I had to be "careful."

"I'll be back to check on you."

The authoritative tone in his voice brought consolation, calming the tension between us. Or maybe it was only within me.

He kept his word and returned to my room half an hour later holding a tray. By then, I had changed into a nightgown and tucked myself in bed again. I put on a half-smile and took three bites of the turkey sandwich he had made with too much mayonnaise. "Thank you."

"You're welcome. Are you okay in here tonight? Alone?"

"Perfectly."

He motioned toward the chair. "I could sleep there."

"That's nice of you to offer. Not necessary, though. I'll be fine."

I took a final bite of the sandwich, munched on a few chips, and drank a sip of sweet tea under his watchful eye. Then I gave him back the plate and set the tea on my nightstand. "I'm going to sleep again, now. I still feel a little woozy."

"Okay." He nodded. "But if you need anything, just call for me."

"I will." At that point, I was fighting to keep my voice steady because, behind my calm exterior, my emotions zigzagged like fifty goldfish swimming in a tiny glass bowl. My thoughts flopped against one another, thrashing and blending so I couldn't tell where one ended and the other began.

As soon as David turned off the light and shut the door, fears clawed at my arms and legs as tears flooded my face. *Is this the beginning of the end?*

And why did Ken have to imply that I was an insubordinate employee? And why did Janie think it was appropriate to tell me she'd miss my food more than she missed me? And why did my mom's amazingly flavorful seasoning—the secret ingredient to the dishes I brought to work all those years—cause me such pain?

Regret, fear, and uncertainty pumped a steady stream of tears down my face.

And no matter how much time had passed since my mother departed this world, even at my age, I also cried that night because I missed my Momma so hard.

David spent the next two nights in my guest room. By the third day, I was back to myself with the exception of a headache kept at bay with prescription-strength meds. The swelling in my knee also receded, and I'd say I was 70 percent recovered by mid-morning Saturday.

To thank David for his attentive care, even taking off a day of work to see about me, I pulled out my mother's special seasoning from its place high in my pantry and made his favorite meal. Fried chicken, macaroni and cheese, Italian green beans, and corn bread.

A batch of Momma's seasoning took several hours to prepare, not including the time shopping for fresh ingredients at the grocery store. Or even better, a farmers' market. Almost every smile-inducing childhood memory of mine was sprinkled with this seasoning on top. *Me, Momma, and Marvina.*

David's sacrifice gave me a good, solid reason to fry up some chicken using the spices. We had good memories together, too.

But this would have to be his farewell dinner, because, honestly, I couldn't have David hanging around my house much longer. The way he ran my bath water, rubbed Vaseline on my ankles, wrapped ice around my knee, and slid socks up my feet, I was starting to have hallucinations, like somebody applied a blemish-reducing filter to my memories. *Was it really that bad when he left for the other woman? Could I have forgiven him one more time? I mean, it was only, like, three affairs.*

"David, thanks so much for everything you've done," I offered as we sat at my dinette waiting for the corn bread timer to ding.

"It was my pleasure."

"I hope I never have to return the favor. But if I do, I will do it gladly."

He stuck out his bottom lip and gave a smug nod. "Good to know."

As he nodded, I noticed Momma's picture on the shelf behind him, the glassless frame surrounding it. "You put my mother's picture back together?"

"Yeah. I did. Good picture—you look just like her. And a nice message she wrote."

I glowered.

"Didn't mean to be nosy."

"That's what all the nosy people say."

The timer announced that the corn bread was ready. I got up and began loading David's plate with food.

I noticed for the first time that David was wearing a different set of clothes.

"Did you go home?"

"No. Ashley bought me a change of clothes and dropped them off yesterday."

I plopped a mound of green beans on his plate. "What? Now your new woman knows where I live! Do you realize the amount of potential drama coming from that bright idea?"

"I told you. She's perfectly reasonable."

"She has to be, bringing a fresh change of clothes for her boyfriend to his ex-wife's house. That's not normal, David."

"She's harmless," he declared, waving me off.

I clucked, "David Tillman, I have to give you credit. You know you a bad mutha shut-your-mouth when you got your new woman taking care of you for your old woman."

He grinned and stroked his mustache. "What can I say?"

"Oh, please. Nothing," I stopped him. More than likely, David hadn't told Ashley the whole truth.

Not my problem.

I presented him with his plate, flatware, a glass of sweet tea, and a napkin. I stood over him, waiting with excitement and a tinge of smugness, anticipating the moment he tasted the chicken. Watching people eat Momma's cooking for the first time, or the first time in a long time, was always a magical moment.

David feigned crying as he previewed his meal. "I can't tell you how much I miss this. You made this for me the day after we married. You remember?"

"Yes. I do." I pulled my bathrobe's belt tighter.

He blessed the food then bit into the chicken breast and tucked the overhanging meat into his mouth, no shame. He closed his eyes in bliss. Or not. A wrinkle appeared between his eyebrows. He swallowed.

"What's wrong?" I asked.

"This your mom's seasoning?"

"Yes."

He wiped his lips with the napkin. "I mean, don't get me wrong, this is good. But I'm just gonna say this and duck. It's not the same as I remember it."

I stared at him quizzically. "The people at my job *love* my cooking."

He reiterated, "That may be true, but people at your job probably never had the original recipe. Didn't you say most of them were new or new to your location?"

"Yes, but—"

"Well, they wouldn't know. This ain't it. I could *never* forget the taste of your mother's seasoning. I'm surprised you don't remember it."

"I *do* remember it. Mostly." *What did I forget? What did I measure incorrectly?*

"Nuh-uh," he insisted.

"Are you sure? My sister and I watched my mother mix those spices countless times. She fed half the community. She basically funded the building at New Harvest with her chicken dinners. And she left the recipe to me and Marvina." I heard myself rambling, but I couldn't fathom what he was saying. Forgetting that recipe would mean I'd forgotten my mother. I'd lost her all over again.

"Taste." He speared a chunk of chicken with his fork and thrust it toward me.

I tasted. Chewed. Swallowed.

The saltiness lagged. The heat swerved markedly toward too much pepper. The flavor spoke, "My grandmother cooks well." All proper and nice. But not, "Big-Mama-shole-put-her-foot-in-this."

My eyes watered, and this time I didn't try to hide my feelings. I couldn't. I let the drops slide down my face.

"I'm sorry." He shook his head. "I...I...why are you crying?"

I plopped onto the chair next to him. My hands flew to my face and I blurted out, "Because this seasoning is all I have left of my mother. My dreams. My life. And now you're telling me this is dead, too?"

"Wait. What? Your life isn't over, Rose, because of fried chicken."

"Yes, it is!" I slammed my hands on my thighs. My insides exploded in a volcano of red-hot grievances. "Don't you understand? I'm running out of toilet paper squares!"

"What?"

I gathered my thoughts by taking deep breaths. "All I ever wanted was to run my own business with Marvina, serving people good food, making money, enjoying life. I never wanted to clock in and out every day. I wanted an adventure. Important relationships with people. To trust my own abilities to succeed out there in the real world, not exist in the common rat race. But it turns out that's exactly what happened to me. Now I'm left with...this nothing, boring life to live. You understand, right?"

"No. I don't. I like numbers and facts and predictability. But that's me. I think if you still want the adventure, you should do it."

The air trapped in my lungs pressed out of me in a slow

sigh. I admitted to David as much as myself, "I do still want my adventure."

Allowing myself to speak the words lightened me. "But I'm almost sixty. It would take, what, five or six years to get things off the ground?"

He shrugged. "And?"

"I'd be sixty-five by then!"

He shrugged again. "Okay, so… These next five or six years are going to pass by no matter what. That's the constant. You could wake up on your sixty-fifth birthday and say, 'I am a business owner,' or you could wake up on your sixty-fifth birthday and say, 'I *wish* I was a business owner.' Either way, God-willing and the creek don't rise, you're going to wake up that day and say *something*. Might as well wake up with the outcome you want by then. Facts."

My eyes dropped to my lap as his words soaked into my spirit. Five years ago, I had been fifty-four, ticking off the days to retirement like a prisoner making tally marks on a stone wall. Five years before then, I had been forty-nine, wondering why the forties hadn't been the new twenties for me.

Oprah lied.

I stared at the improperly seasoned chicken again. The light-brown, flaky coating flecked with spices. The natural shred-lines. The slight glisten of grease.

Something had broken loose in me when I fell at the retirement ceremony. Little chips of my long-delayed desires rattled inside me like rocks inside a maraca.

Whether it was David's speech, the fact that I knew the recipe for perfect seasoning existed, divine intervention, Momma's words written on the back of her photo, or the remnants of pain medication for my knee and concussion, I don't know. All I did know in the moment was that this fried chicken staring back at me had not lived up to its potential. And neither had I. But I could fix this.

"Rose? You all right?"

I swiped the back of my hand across my face. "I'm fine. Never better."

"Really?"

"Yes. Really. I'm going to open my restaurant."

He poked his lips out and gave a sideways nod, speculation drifting over his features.

"What? You don't think it's a good idea?"

"It's a great idea. But first, you gotta get the right recipe for the seasoning, Rose."

"Is it too much pepper? Not enough garlic?"

"Don't ask me. You need to ask someone who knows."

My arms crossed my chest almost involuntarily. I cocked my head to the side and said to myself more than him, "Marvina."

CHAPTER 3

The smell of onions frying in butter for the spinach, the steam from potatoes bubbling in the pot, and the heat from a small kitchen stuffed with too many people tasting and stirring and sifting—this was life for Marvina Nash.

When Greater New Harvest Church remodeled ten years earlier, she had fought to keep the original gas stove and oven, even though it would mean more expensive repairs should something malfunction.

The remodelers had also warned her and Pastor Pendleton that the heat from the old-fashioned appliances made the entire area warmer than it had to be. She'd nodded and smiled. A little extra heat in the kitchen was a small price to pay for perfection.

Now, as she wiped sweat off her forehead with a paper towel, Marvina grinned again. At 5'9", two hundred pounds, she was a woman of size. She was thick-legged and broad-shouldered with a voice she sometimes softened to project more femininity than her endomorphic frame displayed. Momma had said that Marvina was "built for hard work," and Marvina had taken her words as a compliment. Sweating in a galley kitchen with classic red rooster decor suited her well.

The only drawback to the heat was that gel loosening at her hairline. Marvina had been wearing a signature French roll with a swoop bang since the '90s because it was convenient and because she'd lost depth perception when she lost sight in her left eye, making it quite treacherous to curl her long, thick hair. The classic, static style of wigs made life easier.

"Shake it some more," Marvina coached Ta'riq, the fourteen-year-old son of the church secretary, Eleanor, who often partnered with Marvina in the kitchen. Ta'riq always wore a hoodie on his head and a scowl on his baby face. People probably mistook his stern expression for anger, but after two weeks of cooking with him, Marvina knew that he was simply a serious, somber boy. Not a threat. Ta'riq was the kind of boy who, under Marvina's tutelage, quickly mastered the fine art of frying chicken on a gas stove in a cast-iron skillet.

Ta'riq wriggled the chicken strip. Clumps of flour cascaded from the meat to the foil paper waiting below. "How about now?"

Standing on his left side so she could get a good view with her good right eye, Marvina smiled and watched him work. There was nothing like cooking in the kitchen alongside the next generation. "It's ready. Now let's test your grease." Marvina patiently walked him through the process of dropping a grain of rice into the pool of oil. Two other children from the church's youth department, one barely tall enough to watch the experiment, crowded around.

"You see how it floated and sizzled?"

All three nodded.

"It's ready. Drop it in."

Ta'riq obeyed, and the magic of merging a thin coating of flour, vegetable oil, perfect seasonings, and chicken began. The low crackle was music to her ears.

"You catch on fast, Ta'riq. I expect to see straight As from you at the rate you soak up information."

Sasha Pipkins giggled. "Miss Marvina, be for real. Ta'riq stay in trouble at school ain't nobody giving him an A in class, except maybe PE."

"*You* get for real," Marvina countered. "Ta'riq can do anything he puts his mind to. You watch and see. Same for you, too, and a perceptive girl like you ought to be able to see more in him than what other people say he is."

Ta'riq piped up, "One hundred, Miss Marvina."

Pleased with Ta'riq's progress and having rerouted Sasha's sarcasm, Marvina wiped her hands on her apron. She left Ta'riq to repeat the process while she checked on Lil' Smoke's macaroni and cheese preparation. Good thing, too, because the child was about to overcook the pasta.

"Look here." She turned off the heat and removed a noodle with a fork. "Press this noodle up against the pot and feel." Experiencing was the only way he'd know for himself.

Lil' Smoke, dressed in skinny jeans, a Barack Obama T-shirt, and sporting a mohawk that made him appear three inches taller, took the fork from her and followed the directive. "It feels like there's a little bit of hardness left."

"Right. That's called cooking the pasta al dente. The noodle should be firm when you stop cooking it. By the time you bake in the cheese and everything, the noodles will be just right. You don't want your mac and cheese to stay in the pot too long. It'll have the texture of mashed potatoes if you do."

"Got it," Lil' Smoke said.

"I know you do. You're a smart one."

Lil' Smoke's eyebrows shot up like someone had called him

outside of his name. Marvina winked at him to reinforce the compliment. He softened, letting her words shape her picture of himself.

Marvina turned sharply to supervise Jasmine's sweet tea. The last time they trusted Jasmine to make the tea, she had created liquid diabetes. "Just remember, Jasmine, you can always add more sugar, but you can't remove it. Take your time. Ladle some in a cup and taste it. You're a patient person. You got this."

"Yes, ma'am. Thank you, Sister Nash."

"You're welcome."

It was nice to be on the receiving end of Jasmine's good manners. How this child got to be such a sweetheart despite her hell-raising parents was one of those odd sprouts that cropped up in families, like when two brown-skinned, brown-eyed parents created a light-skinned, green-eyed child. Sometimes genes reach back. Manners could, too, apparently.

Marvina watched as Jasmine stood on a stool and stirred the tea with a long-handled plastic spoon. Around and around.

Jasmine's grandmother, Vernetta Pendleton, had been the church's first lady and Marvina's aunt-in-law (i.e., her husband's aunt) back when Marvina joined New Harvest Church shortly after marrying Warren. Marvina had stayed with the Pendletons through the church split (hence *Greater* New Harvest) because of Vernetta's unconditional, genuine kindness, and friendship.

"No matter what folks say—even if those folk be my own nephew—I'm going to always treat you right because I have to answer for *myself*, not them."

Vernetta never wavered from that stance.

This child's demeanor mirrored Vernetta's. It was a shame Jasmine never really got to know her grandmother before she passed away.

"Sister Marvina?"

Marvina jumped at the sound of her name. She'd been lost in the rhythmic tea-stirring motion and her memories for a moment.

"Sister Marvina, may I see you in my office?"

"Oh. Yes. Yes, Pastor."

Marvina called across the kitchen to Sister Eleanor. "You got an eye on everything?"

"Yes. Go ahead."

Marvina hoisted the apron over her French roll, careful not to displace one hair, and looped it on a silver hook. The move caused a quick spasm in her neck, which she stretched a few times to loosen the ligaments.

She washed her hands and made her way down the church's back hallway to Pastor Jerry Pendleton's chamber.

He welcomed her into his slightly disordered office, leaving the door open for propriety. The smell of both dust and wood polish tickled Marvina's nose. How he managed to dust some parts of the office and miss others was beyond her. She wished he would let her and the other mothers clean his office, but Pastor had a stubborn streak sometimes.

Like the rest of the church, the glossy wood desk and matching bookshelf of Pastor's office had not budged an inch in fifteen years.

Marvina sat down in the butter-colored leather chair across from her pastor, straightening her skirt to cover her knees and re-adjusting the knit cardigan so that it brushed both sides of her neck in a high V. Momma had ingrained this etiquette into Marvina so that, even in the presence of a respectable man like Pastor Pendleton, Marvina still double-checked to make sure no parts of her body had slipped out from their hiding places.

Satisfied with her proper presentation, she looked up at Pastor again.

A picture of him with Vernetta hung directly behind his gold-tacked chair, sending a ripple of emotion through Marvina's heart. "I sure do miss her."

Pastor's eyes glinted with sadness. He raised his graying brows in exasperation. "You ain't the only one." His heavy glasses rested on his wide face again. "That woman was a gem."

"She sure was. Jasmine's got a personality a lot like hers," Marvina added.

"Skipped a generation, 'cause that son of mine...just pray for him," he voiced Marvina's thoughts exactly. "Listen, Sister Marvina, I know you really enjoy working with the youth. They adore you, and you're sharing life lessons that will stay with them forever. But...I don't know if you've heard... There's a move to, you know, get away from financing the church with chicken dinners. Greater New Harvest has depended on you a lot to do everything from selling plates to outright writing checks to keep us afloat."

Marvina felt a tingling in her chest, a locking of her jaw. She'd been prepared for a monetary request or an appeal for her to cater the next fundraising banquet free of charge. She might have even been ready for Pastor Pendleton to ask for her mother's recipes so future church members could carry the tradition forward. She knew that time would come sooner or later. But this?

Marvina tucked her lips between her teeth, constraining words she dared not unleash, though she was sure her flaring nostrils screamed, *Are you out of your mind?*

Pastor Pendleton's hands fanned open, as though trying to calm her down. "I know you do what you do out of your love and respect for the Lord and for my wife. You and Vernetta both poured your hearts into this ministry. But…it's a new day, Sister Marvina. Church attendance has plummeted since the pandemic. Not only here, but everywhere. We have to find new ways to attract and keep members while paying the bills at the same time."

This felt like he'd just hacked off her right arm and then tried to offer a Band-Aid.

Marvina straightened herself and spoke. "I of all people know what the pandemic took away."

His shoulders dropped. "I know, Sister Marvina. We all miss Brother Warren as well. But as folks who've lost our spouses, you and I both know how to move on after a change."

"And me cooking with the youth on Saturday mornings, us selling dinners to the community in the afternoon to raise money for the church, is standing in the way of us moving forward?" Marvina asked. The question came out more pointedly than she'd intended.

Pastor Pendleton was correct for believing her loyalty to Greater New Harvest stemmed from her connection to God and to Vernetta. Marvina's submission to Pastor Pendleton was an extension of her relationship to Vernetta. She didn't want to dishonor her deceased friend by disrespecting her husband. Still…

"It's a matter of how the church chooses to use its resources. Buying ingredients for food, for the special secret seasoning you bring—"

"I've never used the church's money to buy those ingredients," Marvina interrupted. She'd never written down the recipe, never bought them with the church's credit card, never asked for reimbursement because she never showed the list of ingredients to anyone, especially not in the form of an itemized grocery receipt.

Pastor Pendleton was dead wrong about that part. And he was wrong about the value of cooking in the kitchen with the youth, the value of speaking kind words to members of the community who bought plates, and the connections made across generations through that tiny kitchen.

"Well." He took a deep breath and straightened his back, though his eyes drifted from the direct line with Marvina's. "I have to make an executive decision. The church is going in a new direction. The leadership team and I have decided to join a network of churches. The Higher Works Alliance. We're pooling our resources and sharing our best practices to stay viable. We need to stay in line with the brand we're creating for the church, a brand that will attract the younger generation. Young congregants enjoy first-class music. They want to go on themed cruises together, not cook meals for the same people in the neighborhood week after week. We have to stay current, especially with the plans to build the new express line through Fork City in the next ten years. We need a more...polished presentation. With more...exciting attractions. I hope you understand."

"Is this an amusement park, a social club, or a church?" The words left her lips before Marvina could filter them.

"Please, Sister Marvina."

Cooking, being around people, serving others through food—this was her life. How could he take this away?

"I know how you must feel. I know how difficult it is to accept change, but the rebranding is for the better. I'll be preaching more on the importance of giving tithes and offerings. I know our members don't make much per household, but if we don't ask them to give willingly, we're not allowing an opportunity to sow seed and be blessed. You understand?"

Marvina didn't respond, because the math made no sense. Country folks who could barely pay their household bills didn't make enough to finance a flashy sound system and whatever fees this new network partnership would cost the church.

He continued, "We have to do it for Jasmine, for Ta'riq, for all the future leaders of this church. Or else there won't *be* a Greater New Harvest. And when I think of how much Vernetta loved this church"—his voice cracked, his gaze returned to Marvina—"I can't stand the idea that it might not be here in the future."

Marvina blinked back her own tears. Something in her wouldn't allow her to display her vulnerability. Not now, anyway. "With all due respect, Pastor. I don't believe Vernetta would have wanted Greater New Harvest to remake itself into some snazzy social club where people drink coffee in the pews and families don't worship together in the sanctuary."

He cleared his throat. "Sister Marvina, you're out of line. I believe Vernetta would have wanted the church to go on, to catch up to the times. I knew her longer than you and better than you."

Marvina sat an elbow on the armrest and covered her trembling lips with her hand. She took a sharp breath. She struggled to contain the fire bubbling in her chest. "I'm not going to argue with you, Pastor. You have to do what you believe is best." She hoisted herself from the chair. "Thank you for telling me."

"Yes." He stood as well. "You'll let the children and Sister Eleanor know?"

"No, sir. You can do that yourself." She couldn't bear to watch the children's faces melt with disappointment.

He huffed and yanked the bottom of his jacket. "Fine. I'll call a special meeting after service tomorrow."

Marvina dismissed herself from the conversation. She held

on to the walls so she wouldn't have to worry about running into one of them as she slipped into the restroom to compose herself. The single-stall lavatory on the west side of the church provided absolute privacy.

It always amazed Marvina how the bad eye still produced tears when she cried. She couldn't see from it, but she could blink and cry, and the eye moved in sync with her other eye so that most people didn't even know she might as well have a pirate's patch over it. And yet it received and responded to the message coursing through her whole body. Pastor wanted her to stop cooking at Greater New Harvest. He wanted her to stop bringing her mother's recipes and her special spices to the sanctuary to serve others. He wanted to change the church's "brand," whatever that meant.

But at the expense of Marvina's ministry, at the cost of her heart's purpose. Might have been easier to just stick a needle in her vein and drain all the blood from her body, because there wasn't much else to live for outside of serving others, in Marvina's opinion.

And he had this ridiculous idea that Vernetta would have agreed with him when Marvina was willing to bet the farm Vernetta would have advocated for the opposite. Marvina didn't appreciate how he was trying to hide his ambition behind his dead wife's desires any more than she appreciated him trying to make her the bearer of his bad news.

She was proud of saying, "No, sir," when he asked her to convey the message. Actually, she wished she had just said, "No." Alas, she had good home training and would respect her leader, whether she agreed with him or not.

After gathering her wits, Marvina straightened her face to finish the morning's cooking and then texted Sister Tessie to take her place during the afternoon plate sale, telling both her and

Sister Eleanor that she didn't feel good. It was the truth. Marvina felt awful after the conversation with Pastor Pendleton.

When Tessie arrived, everyone gathered around Marvina and prayed for her healing. Then Marvina grabbed the glass container of her secret seasoning and tucked it in her bag as she always did before leaving the church kitchen, because people had taken unauthorized helpings from the church pantry on more than one occasion. Marvina was reluctant to accuse people of stealing, but that's what it was. She could hardly blame them. The church folk weren't the first ones to lose their religion over Momma's seasonings. Her own sister, Rose, had done the same and worse.

Marvina couldn't finish her crying on the drive home because, with the impairment, she had to keep her vision as clear as possible. The loss of depth perception was bad enough. Blurriness would only make her trip downright dangerous.

Times like these, she wondered how differently her life might have gone if it weren't for Rose and her adventures.

Nothing she could do about it now.

She waited until she'd passed the front gate to her property, driven a few hundred feet to the carport, parked her car, and took the ignition from the key of her Buick SUV. Every time she beheld the ranch-style home with its wraparound porch, the dark shutters against light brick, the simple but intentional landscaping that welcomed her home, she had to be grateful. How many people paid cash for a brand-new house on three acres of land with a pool and a guesthouse? She had since had the pool filled with cement—it was more trouble than it was worth, and kids for miles around always seemed to find their way onto her property during the summertime. She wouldn't have minded if they hadn't been so unruly and destructive.

Thank you, Lord, for a roof over my head.

But after that conversation with Pastor Pendleton, Marvina wasn't trying to be all lovey-dovey with God. She had a bone to pick with Him because, while she was kind of sorry for bucking up to her pastor, she wasn't sorry for what she'd said. *That ain't how to run no church!*

Then she laughed at herself because she remembered something she'd overheard Sasha say one Saturday morning. Sasha had asked one of the youth boys three times to move out of her way, but he was flirting and remained blocking her path. So she barreled through him, stepping on his shoes in the process. "Sorry, not sorry," she'd sassed.

That was exactly how Marvina felt. Sorry, not sorry.

And in the middle of her prayer/fussing, she realized Pastor Pendleton had not once said he'd heard from on high about this. It was just one of them ways that seems right unto man, just like the Bible said.

Well, she wasn't in a position to tell that man how to run his church. But she didn't have to participate in his new scheme.

Now. How about that?

Marvina heard her phone vibrating in her purse. Most people still called her on the landline, because she wasn't glued to her phone, and everybody who knew her understood she was busy at the church all day Saturday. So getting a call early afternoon was unusual. She wondered if something had gone wrong with the food or the sales at church. Quickly, she fished the device from her cloth purse. Marvina did a double take and tilted her head a little to make sure she was reading the name correctly.

Rose Tillman.

Her chest froze. Rose calling couldn't be good news. Mentally,

Marvina ran down the list of possible disasters as the phone continued to ring. Their parents were already deceased, so there was nothing to be said there. Marvina's son, Warren Jr., was working in Seattle. He was one of those out-of-sight-out-of-mind adult children. Nothing concerning Warren Jr. would go through Rose first.

Whatever Rose had to say could go straight to voice mail. Marvina would listen, process, and return the call when she was ready. Or not.

She waited out the ringing and then held her breath until the ding signaling a voice mail came through. Then she rushed to remember how to retrieve the message and listened.

"Marvina, this is Rose."

The spike of distress in Rose's voice caused another hitch in Marvina's breath.

The message continued, "I need to talk to you. I'm on my way to Fork City to your house. I should be there in another hour or so."

Marvina tsked at the message. This was just like Rose, inviting herself to Marvina's home practically unannounced. If Rose was an hour away from Fork City, that meant she'd been on the road for an hour already. Why couldn't she have called and asked *permission* to visit before she left Dallas? No. That would make too much sense.

Plus, it was right in line with Rose's character to overstep boundaries and presume everybody agreed with her thinking, the same as she had done with the restaurant forty-dollar business registration foolishness all those years ago. Rose named the business after herself without so much as a conversation with Marvina. Where they do that at? *The Southern Rose Restaurant. Give me a break.*

Despite the decades and the opportunity to learn from her mistakes, the restaurant fiasco being one of many, it was clear that

Rose was acting like she was the homecoming queen of Marvina's life.

Still self-centered, if not selfish.

Marvina's first inclination was to call Rose right now and tell her to turn herself around and head back to Dallas. Conversations could take place by phone as easily as in person. Shoot, they could have even had a virtual meeting, for that matter.

But Marvina didn't follow her first thought because, truth be told, she was more worried than annoyed. Despite Rose's lack of manners, her voice didn't sound the same. A brief but sure wobble in her sister's pitch—like a warped vinyl record—had unsettled Marvina. She wanted to see her sister in person before sending her away. If nothing else, for Momma's sake.

CHAPTER 4

Rose

I was glad my sister didn't answer the phone. She didn't get a chance to ask me any questions, advise me to turn myself right back around, or call me rude for driving halfway to Fork City without asking permission first. I knew Marvina, and she knew me well enough to know I wouldn't be driving to her house for no reason.

We hadn't seen each other since the death of our mother's baby brother, Uncle Cleo, about six months earlier, the Wednesday after Juneteenth, to be exact. I remembered this because there was a big fuss in the family at a time when Black people should especially be on one accord. Some people thought Marvina should have volunteered to pay for the difference between having a funeral on a weekday and having one on a Saturday so more people could attend. Folks in Fork City were always bumping their gums about what Marvina ought to do with all the commas and zeros they *thought* she had sitting in a bank account.

When Uncle Cleo died, his oldest daughter, our cousin Sharon, called to ask my opinion about Marvina declining to help move the funeral to Saturday. "So people won't have to take off work and whatnot," she'd said. "Don't you think Marvina should honor y'alls dear mother this way?"

I replied, "No comment."

After which, Sharon promptly cussed me out and uninvited both Marvina and myself to our uncle's funeral.

Then Uncle Cleo's second wife, Aunt Farra—though not the one he was married to at the time of death—re-invited us. Then his first wife, Sharon's mother, called and uninvited us again, like she had authority in the matter. Marvina and I ended up bringing up the tail end of the family processional in the ceremony, walking right behind Aunt Farra. She and Uncle Cleo didn't have any children together, so I'm guessing that's why she was placed so far behind in the line. Marvina and I glided down the center aisle and sat down right next to each other. We stuck together, because it was kind of us against Uncle Cleo's first batch of a family, but my sister and I barely said a word to each other. Our silence was only broken because the preacher told us exactly what to say to one another.

"Touch your neighbor and tell 'em it's gonna be all right," and "Look at somebody and say joy cometh in the morning." In those brief directives, I stole a few head-on glances at my sister. The patch of gray hair around her temples had spread. She had picked up that same crease between the eyebrows that Daddy used to have. Not as deep, but close.

Other than that game of repeat-after-the-pastor, we didn't speak. In fact, I think she positioned herself so she *couldn't* see me out of her bad eye the whole time. She told me once that she sometimes arranged to sit on a person's right when she wanted to forget about them. Out of sight, out of mind.

I didn't forget about that trick of hers.

At the repast, one of Sharon's grandchildren—no manners at

all!—demanded that Marvina and I put our forks down, smile, and take a picture together. I mean, he said it just like that, "Y'all put your forks down and smile and get close together for a picture." No smile on his baby-smooth face, no "please" on that quick, commanding tongue.

So I got up and left because, for one thing, I don't do rude Gen Zers. Secondly, I just didn't feel like putting on a smile. My Uncle Cleo had died from pneumonia, the whole slew of Sharon's crew wasn't talking to us, and being around Marvina always made me cranky ever since the $40.

I left the old New Harvest church and drove myself back to Dallas. Uncle Cleo was the next-to-the-last bit of family I had still living in Fork City. Most of our cousins had moved out of the area altogether. Marvina was the only one left.

Before Uncle Cleo's funeral, I hadn't been to town in over a year. Marvina sent my portion of the rent for Momma's house quarterly. She also sent a standard-issue Christmas card every year. I envisioned her shaking her head as she hastily addressed, stuffed, and licked my envelope. Failure to sufficiently seal an envelope can lead to lost contents. I don't think Marvina ever cared one way or another if people received their card. She didn't mail cards for the recipient's joy; she mailed them out of habit and home training.

If nothing else, my mother taught us how to respect people because God had seen fit to give them life. Home training will do that for you.

About thirty minutes outside of Fork City, at the county line, I felt myself sliding down a nostalgic slope. Tall, naked trees, hidden driveways, one-lane roads, a wildlife crossing sign. They all whispered, "Welcome back, Rose." Suddenly, the tension of city life seeped out of my soul and flew out of my slightly open window. I'd basically entered a different era. A safer, slower time. Back when people knew not only their neighbors' names but their birthdays and anniversaries. We threw scraps over the fence for each other's dogs without worrying about getting sued because somebody's German shepherd was vegan.

Just good people in a small town with little opportunity, and some people liked it that way. Growing up, I couldn't wait to break free of Fork City and its country ways. But when I got to Bishop College, I missed home. My people. Not like a homesick college freshman. It was more like a disappointed traveler realizing they'd been bamboozled by the virtually staged pictures of their hotel. College was definitely harder and the city definitely had more than one McDonald's, but did that make it *better*?

My senior year of college was when I decided to bring all my city-college learnings back to Fork City and open a restaurant with my sister. That's why I sent her the $40, to register it in our home-town. Sure we could have opened a restaurant closer to Dallas, but who can resist a restaurant in a city named after an eating utensil?

I had a whole marketing plan mapped out, capitalizing on our home city's most fortunate name. And I conveyed all this informa-tion to Marvina in a very lengthy long-distance phone call. Despite our conversation and what I thought was a genuinely enthusiastic response to the idea, she put the money I sent home for the busi-ness toward the funds she needed to bail her then-fiancé, Warren Sr., out of jail for speeding tickets. He wasn't even a real fiancé, if you ask me, because he hadn't given her a ring at that point. Only a promise. And there she was wasting my $40, not counting the amount it cost me to print out the business registration papers, get an envelope, get a money order, and mail everything to her.

I know it was only $40 and some change, but it was my future.

My future was supposed to be *here* in Fork City a long time ago. Forty dollars ago.

Just before the home stretch, clouds began to gather overhead. Almost instantly, my knee started throbbing. It was time for another dose of pain medicine. I began rubbing my knee and realized it was swollen from sitting in one spot on the long drive. The weather didn't help. Neither did the fact I barely performed the exercises prescribed when I was dismissed from the hospital.

I needed to get out and stretch for a minute before I made the next turn down the eighteen-mile road to Fork City. Though the gas station on the corner of my last turn was abandoned, fond memories somehow made me feel safe, as though the memories hallowed the ground. I pulled off the road, stopped my car, and got out to give my knee a breather. My whole body needed a breather, actually. I raised my arms high and let the fresh air swoosh through my lungs. I imagined the stretching moves cleansing my body of all the residue from driving in city traffic, eating store-bought rather than home-grown vegetables, the sheer fact that my home was so close to my neighbor's, I could hear when he turned on his shower. All these factors combined must have meant something bad for my health. Too much shared breathing space.

But not here in Fork City. I faced the 6 o'clock sun, which would set soon, and appreciated my view of this barefaced beauty we call nature. I wasn't a fan of bugs, snakes, or moonshine, but the very air itself, purified by trees and unobstructed sunshine, settled over me and comforted me like a weighted blanket.

Too bad I couldn't live here. And too bad I wasn't the only one who'd decided this gas station made for an ideal pit stop. Two dogs, or wolves, or coyotes, or whatever they were, came around the side of the old gas station. They stopped. Sized me up. I wasted no time hopping back into the car. In my haste, I slammed that knee against the door's panel. If it hadn't already been messed up, it wouldn't have hurt so much.

By the time I reached Marvina's home and parked, the adrenaline from fear of the dogs had worn off, and I could have slapped a judge from the pain in my knee. I needed to get inside and get a bite to eat so I could take my medicine. I had packed an overnight bag, but there was no way I could twist my body around to grab it or walk extra steps around the car to retrieve it. The bag would have to wait until tomorrow. My coat would have to wait, too. No unnecessary movement.

I slung my purse over my shoulder and rocked myself a few times to gain momentum and push myself out of the car. I hobbled to the front door of my sister's home. Truth be told, it was a beautiful house. The kind of place people kept in a family for generations, and Marvina had obviously preserved the estate well. Fresh paint on the shutters, an intact screen door, light fixtures free of dead bugs. Even the air surrounding her home carried a sharp, clean scent.

She'd always been the neat one.

I rested myself against a pillar, regaining my strength from the shuffle between my car and the house.

Before I could knock, she opened the main door. Despite the zippy, bright flowers on her housecoat, her grave, appraising gaze swept up and down "What's wrong with you?"

"My knee."

"It's cold. Where's your coat?" she fussed.

"In the car. Are you going to let me in?"

Her scowl morphed from semi-annoyance to concern. My sister's plump, mellow-brown face stared back at me. With her bird lips, button nose, sullen glare, and thick, matronly arms—right down to the hard-working blackened elbows—she resembled Momma even more than I remembered.

Marvina unlocked the screen door and pressed it back to allow me inside.

I transferred my hand from the pillar to the doorframe, attempting to keep my full weight off the leg. "Can I get a piece of bread or something to take with my pain medicine? And I need to lie down for a bit."

When I saw the seven feet from the doorframe to the nearest couch, I suddenly wished I had a cane. Who would have thought I'd wish for a cane at the age of fifty-nine?

My sister smarted off, "You came all the way here on a bad knee to eat my food, take medicine, and go to bed?"

"Marvina, now is not the time." Still holding on to the door, I began a mental countdown to the next move. *Ten. Nine. Eight.* My master plan was to hold my breath through the agony. *Seven. Six. Five.*

"You need an ambulance?"

"Can't talk right now."

Four. Three. Two. I pre-winced and braced myself. *One.*

My sister's arm suddenly wrapped around my waist and she lifted my arm over her neck all at once, becoming my human crutch. "This is ridiculous. Don't make no sense. Why don't you just ask for help?"

We took a few steps toward the couch.

"Last time I asked you for help, we both know what happened."

Just when I went to lean on her for support with my knee, she jerked away from me, and I had no choice except to put my weight on that leg to keep from hitting the floor.

"Then carry on by yourself," she sassed, leaving me to catch myself on the arm of her leather love seat.

The only force stronger than the pain radiating through my limb was the anger coursing through my veins. I swallowed the howl that bellowed up from the center of my soul. I couldn't let her know she'd hurt me. Again.

As Marvina walked away, she barked, "Hawaiian rolls in the pantry. Take what you want. You know where the guest room is. Good night, Rose."

The Lord knows if I hadn't been fighting for dear leg-life, I would have told my sister where to go in her own house.

After I took the medicine, I slept in the guest room as Marvina instructed. Four hours later, I woke with my leg still aching slightly, but not as intense as before. More discomfort than distress.

I reached for the lamp I'd mentally noted before lying down and gave myself some light in the room that was large enough to make you feel welcome, small enough to let you know you couldn't stay too long, not with the tiny closet and the few feet to shuffle from the eyelet quilt-covered bed to the gray chest of drawers and finally the rocking chair. And no TV. A person could get claustrophobic in there.

I can't be here long.

I'd come to Marvina's house with the goal of asking her to refresh my memory about Momma's spice recipe so I could finally open my restaurant, the Southern Rose. As I lay in bed summarizing the mission, doubt swooped into the room. *Who do you think you are? You are way too old to be opening a restaurant? Are you trying to bankrupt yourself? What makes you think Marvina will give you anything?*

A jittery sensation flowed through me. Fear mixed with antici-pation, anxiety, and excitement all at once. It made me feel alive, as though everything I ever wanted might be right around the corner. I hadn't felt *this* alive since the day I graduated from Fork City Consolidated High School with my thirty-seven other classmates.

I remembered taking my proper place on stage as salutatorian, my skin tingling, a metallic taste in my mouth. Sadness tugged at my heart, too, because I realized I would probably never see these thirty-seven people all in one place again. We'd spent year after year together for more than a decade, and this was the end of the road.

"And now, we will hear from our salutatorian, Rose Yvette Dewberry."

Even as my body pressed into Marvina's cushy mattress, I could feel the old energy zipping through me, as though I was back in my high school gym, standing on wobbly legs and approaching the podium to give my speech.

Funny thing, here I was forty years later with one of my legs shaking just the same, and my throat tightening at the thought of my upcoming speech to Marvina. Good things happened to me when I got excited about the possibilities ahead.

Except with my sister. Excitement guaranteed nothing. It might take her days to come to a decision about what she was will-ing to share. Upstanding, churchgoing woman she might be, my sister was nothing if not the valedictorian of the class of holding grudges.

I couldn't outwait her in Fork City. I needed to set a time limit to tell her about my plans for a restaurant. The words "three days" popped into my mind. Sounded like a good limit to me. They taught us in Sunday school that Jesus stayed in the grave for three days, and when He got up, the whole world—past, present, and future—had flipped. If Jesus could change the world in three days, surely I could influence my sister in that much time or less.

Perhaps talking to Marvina this time would be like writing a five-paragraph paper. Introduction, three main points, conclusion. *Marvina, I need to get recalibrated on Momma's spices. Point one: So I can honor her properly. Point two: So I can open my restaurant. Point three: So I can live out my dreams.*

In conclusion, I need the seasoning recipe so I can live my real life.

CHAPTER 5
Rose

The next morning, Marvina filled the house with the smell of bacon. I could taste the thick slices already. I wondered if she'd gotten the bacon from a grocery store or the meat market and if she had sprinkled the meat with Momma's seasoning and honey.

Market-fresh, spiced, and honeyed bacon would be best, but I wouldn't put it past her to cook the scrawny slices for me and the fuller, more flavored ones for herself. After the way she left me struggling yesterday in her entryway, there's no telling what she might do.

I threw the covers off my legs and rubbed my knee, noting the diminished throbbing and swelling. Rain pattered on the window, and I wondered if bad weather might be contributing to the lingering ache. I swung to an upright position and let my socked feet touch the gray oval rug jutting out from under the bed.

Gingerly, I tested my strength. I was hoping for a slight limp day, but my joint dictated another day of waddling. I wished I could find those canines that scared me back to my car and…well, nothing. Animals do what they do by instinct. People, on the other hand, choose to betray.

I threw on a heavy duster from Marvina's closet and walked to retrieve my belongings from my car. After a shower, I donned a simple pullover house dress and joined Marvina in the kitchen expecting to see teeny tiny scraps of bacon saved for me.

But I was wrong. My bacon wasn't teeny tiny. My bacon was invisible, because Marvina hadn't cooked me anything at all.

Who does that? Who gets up in the morning and makes breakfast for themselves only? Our mother would have pinched her arm real hard for this level of foolishness, dirtying up dishes and turning on the fire for one person knowing somebody else was going to come behind her and do it all over again.

Marvina spoke, "Good morning," without looking up from her novel. Her hair was tied in a red scarf, her body covered in a plush terry cloth robe. Her 1980s-style kitchen, with heavy wood cabinets, tile countertops, and floral-patterned skylight, had not changed. The throwback setting only added to my throwback feelings, as though my emotions with my sister were also stuck in time.

"Morning. You mind if I make myself something for breakfast?"

"No."

Her tone made me question her response. "No you don't mind, or no I can't?"

She looked up at me over the rim of her glasses. "No, I don't mind."

"Thank you." I rolled my eyes once I turned from her. Then it hit me that if she was wearing glasses, one of the lenses must be plain glass, no prescription, because she was blind in one eye.

The realization still caught me off guard after all these years.

I rattled around her pantry and found instant oatmeal, dried cranberries, and almonds. I joined her at the table a few minutes later.

Marvina set her book face down on the table. "How long do you plan on staying here without explanation?"

"Not long," I replied. I began eating. Rather, stalling. Anybody who was petty enough to cook breakfast for one in a house with two people in it must be approached carefully.

Marvina picked up the book again just as the rain picked up outside. The crackle of distant thunder promised a significant downpour.

We sat with only the sounds of nature surrounding us while I figured out where to start. My daddy used to say that when you want something from somebody, you start out the conversation on a positive note. "You've kept the house up nicely."

"Thank you. This house is a blessing." She turned the page and angled her head sharply to see the page straight-on.

From where I sat, and given the tilt of her head, I could study her undetected. Her neck, like mine, had picked up a dozen or so tiny, dark moles. The condition was hereditary. Momma and her mother, Grandma Lewis, had them. People these days paid to have them removed, but because of how I first contextualized them as a child, like dainty little sprinkles on Momma's and Grandmomma's necks, I always thought of them as markers of wisdom and love, a rite of passage. Now that they dotted mine and my younger sister's neck, I was certain we'd crossed into another season of life together. Where were our wisdom and love?

Marvina turned another page. I suspected she wasn't reading; nobody reads that fast. It made no sense that we were sitting at the table playing childish games with all these senior citizen moles in place. I tried to converse again. "I don't know where to start."

She mumbled, "At the beginning."

"Duh," I sassed. "You sound just like Daddy."

A slight grin brought the first warm expression I'd seen on her face in I don't know how long.

"Marvina. I've been thinking."

She took a tiny bite of bacon, dog-eared a page in her book, closed it, and looked at me, chewing like she was bored. "Go on."

"You gonna eat all that bacon?"

"Probably not."

Carefully and slowly, I attempted to pinch off a piece of her bacon. The meat was too springy for a clean break.

Marvina stabbed her end with a fork. I tore off my portion and chewed, expecting the familiar, salty, smoky flavoring of my favorite breakfast meat. The fact that it was too rubbery should have been a clue. I pulled a napkin and spat out the morsel. "Tastes too piggy."

"It's *pork*."

"Yeah, but that tastes like he just oinked his last breath this morning," I tried to explain, hoping for another hint of humor.

"There's no such thing as bacon that tastes too piggy."

I pointed at her plate. "Yes, there is. Right here on this table. Fish can be too fishy, and bacon can be too piggy. Like wild game or something."

She sighed. "Rose. What do you want?"

Now was the time. My skin tingled. I rolled my shoulders back and inhaled a deep breath. "I would like to move forward with the Southern Rose restaurant."

She raised an eyebrow. "And?"

"And in order to do so, I need to perfect Momma's seasoning."

"Momma's seasoning is already perfect."

"Yes. I know," I stumbled. "But…according to David—"

She snarled and jolted up straight. "Goodness. David? As in your ex-husband, David?"

"Yes."

"What's he got to do with anything?"

She was peering into me now, searching for what I wasn't saying. "A few days ago, I injured my knee. Slammed it against a wall, straight out of the blue. At my retirement ceremony—"

"You're retired?" she interrupted again.

"Yes."

Her expression softened. "Well, that's good. Congratulations."

"Thank you," I said. "Like I was saying, at the retirement ceremony, my knee gave out, and I fell and hit my head. Got a concussion. David took care of me, and to thank him for his service, I made him Momma's fried chicken."

She tsked. "I wouldn't have made that rascal anything."

"Well, I did make it for him. And it didn't taste the same."

Marvina leaned in ever so slightly, bringing us a centimeter closer at the table. "Did you test the grease?"

"I did."

"Used the right amount of flour? Didn't cook it too fast?"

I nodded furiously. "I did everything right except the seasoning. I got it wrong."

Her eyes narrowed. "You got Momma's seasoning wrong?"

"I got it wrong."

"How could you get it wrong after all the times we—"

"I know, I know." I slapped both sides of my face and clawed my fingers downward, stopping at my clavicle. "I could hardly believe it myself, but it's the truth. I guess, over the years, I gradually added a little more of this and a little less of that until it wasn't the same anymore."

Marvina's eyes dropped to her plate again. She tore off another bite of her piggy bacon. Swallowed. "Listen, if you want the recipe for the seasoning, I'll show you again out of respect for the fact she was your mother, too. The recipe is like an heirloom she passed on to both of us. But I don't appreciate how you're using it, starting with cooking for David."

"Are you serious?" I laughed, though it sounded more like a desperate squeak. "What happened between me and David is between us. We were husband and wife for twelve years. How we ended, what we are now, and whether I choose to cook for him is nun-ya business."

"I wish it were that simple," she countered with a fake laugh of her own. "Do you remember when Daddy drove all the way to Dallas with his rifle to help you kick David out of y'all's house?"

"What Daddy did was not even called for," I said. "Let the record show, Daddy was dramatic, and you know it. Especially when Momma pumped him up with her fretful thinking."

"Be that as it may, I watched my father walk out of his house with a gun to confront another man. When he left, he was hot as fish grease. Scared the mess out of me. Momma, too. We prayed for the next six hours straight because all it takes is two men and one snide comment. Next thing you know, somebody's on their way to rot in an early grave, and somebody else is on their way to rot in the penitentiary."

"I didn't ask Daddy to come with a gun. I didn't ask him to come *at all*," I reminded her. It was ridiculous how she'd concocted this whole story about how David had threatened our father's life. "James Ray Dewberry is the one who rode into my town like he was Clint Eastwood's Black cousin. And all he did when he got there was sit in my living room with that rusty rifle while David carted his belongings to the car. It wasn't that serious. Daddy barely even said anything."

My sister used that same finger to point to heaven. "That's because Momma and I prayed up a wall of protection." She waved her hand and waggled her neck back and forth in a second of personal praise.

I wasn't sure how she could claim they'd prayed for God to stop something that was never going to happen, but whatever. "My whole point is, I need the right recipe again."

She took off her glasses and pinched the top of her nose.

Momma used to perform that gesture when we were getting on her nerves. "You girls argue so much, you should both become lawyers. Dewberry & Dewberry, attorneys at law," she'd say.

"I just…" she sighed. "All this blind ambition of yours. This seasoning recipe and all of Momma's cooking is nothing but dollar signs to you."

I read pity, anger, and disgust in the twitch of her upper lip. Maybe even a little pride of her own.

"That's not fair, Marvina. I wanted to open a *family* restaurant with that first forty-dollar seed—"

"Oh my Lord. Here it goes." She closed her eyes, clasped her hands, and pressed them against her chin, raised her eyes to the ceiling like she was posing for the cover of a Mahalia Jackson album. "Father God in heaven, lily of the valley, bright and morning star. Though we know You have already settled this in heaven and on earth, we come before You, once again, with the matter of the forty dollars."

"Do not bring God into this," I hissed.

"He's already here. And He wants you to forget it, Rose." My sister's sarcastic mask faded. The soft, gentle side of her prevailed again. "I ain't got the energy for this. Let it go. And stop blaming me for the things you didn't do in your life. I can't help that…so many things happened…all these years." She softened her tone, careful not to point her anger at the ways faith and hope had failed us.

I swallowed. "I trust that you will remind me how to make this seasoning, because I know it means everything to you, to both of us, to preserve Momma's legacy. What we do or don't do with the recipes is our own choice. Can we agree to that?"

Marvina stood and grabbed the edge of her plate. "I will honor our mother by recreating the seasoning with you. But not right at this moment. It's Sunday morning, and we're going to church."

I sucked my chin in. "Who's going to church?"

"Me and you." She rinsed her plate in the sink.

"Psshhh. I'm not going to church."

"House rules," Marvina declared. "I made a promise to God that I'd serve Him with this house by making sure there was no one left under my roof when I left for church on Sunday morning, unless they were physically unable to attend."

I raised my hand. "That would be me."

"No, ma'am. The way you just made your own breakfast, you got a reasonable portion of your health and strength to make your way to church." She set her breakfast dishes in the dishwasher.

Again, I stated, "I am not going to church."

"Well," Marvina shook her head, "you heard what I promised the Lord." She closed the dishwasher and faced me, leaning one hip against the counter and propping a fist on the other hip. "Now, if you want to sit outside on the porch in the rain until I get back, suit yourself. But you ain't gonna stay inside here so long as Sunday service is in session."

"Marvi—"

"Plus you could use some prayer for your legs," she added, pointing at my lower extremities.

"It's *one* knee. And I don't—"

"And!" she spoke over me again. "I can't show you the recipe while we're sittin' up here arguing. Momma always said nothing ruins good cookin' like a bad attitude."

My heart remembered how Momma phrased it. "We have to cook with love; it's the secret ingredient."

Without saying a word, I knew Marvina was replaying those same words in her head and heart as well. Not once had we ever stood on either side of Momma and watched her mix her seasonings with so much as an ounce of animosity between us. Sometimes our mother would sing and ask us to sing along. Sometimes she would talk in a low whisper so we'd have to lean in to one another to hear her explanations. The way Momma moved in a kitchen, everyone around her melded into one perfect machine.

"I'm gonna throw a roast and vegetables in the Crock-Pot and then get dressed."

"You putting carrots in the roast?"

She huffed. "I'm not a big fan of carrots with roast, but if you want some, you can add them yourself."

And just like that, we were back in the kitchen together. Her rinsing and seasoning the meat, chopping potatoes. Me preparing carrots and onions.

I sprinkled a dose of Momma's seasoning into my cupped hand and dipped my tongue into the tiny pool of memories I knew one taste would evoke. Salty, savory, smoky, full of earthy flavors that somehow blessed everything it showered.

As the flavor crystals and bits of dried herbs dissolved in my mouth, I closed my eyes and swallowed the heavenly fusion.

David was right. Marvina's batch—and all the batches Momma ever made with us—carried more kick than the one I'd used to make his chicken.

A hum of pleasure traveled back up my throat.

Marvina ceased chopping the onions. "You all right over there?"

"Perfect."

Roast was one of those dishes that only required a little bit of Momma's seasoning. I sprinkled as we both hovered over the pot, our heads nearly touching. The smell made my stomach flitter with fondness.

Ten minutes after we started, we accomplished what might have taken one woman half an hour to do alone. A knowing washed over me. I knew it as clearly as I knew my own name: I needed Marvina to partner with me for this restaurant. She had a way with people. I had a way of managing business. We both had a way in the kitchen that resulted in perfection every time. Somehow, I had to reverse the hands of time and get us back to the place where a business between us seemed logical and profitable and maybe even holy, in my sister's eyes.

Marvina hung her apron on the hook while I rinsed the dishes. "Can you be ready for church in half an hour?"

"I guess."

Not even a minute after Marvina left the kitchen, I couldn't articulate exactly what all we'd been arguing about, why we couldn't be together without verbally sparring all the time. Was it Daddy? David? Momma? The money? The carrots? Seemed like she and I had been going around in circles for years, arguing over something we couldn't name. At this point, I wasn't even sure if the forty dollars was the first breach or the last straw. I just knew somehow, someway, we'd gotten off track. It was up to me to pull us back together again, make it a win-win for both of us, and honor Momma's memory at the same time.

Might be easier to scale a skyscraper.

CHAPTER 6

The youth usher board was in service that Sunday, leading congregants to fill the pews from front to back. Sister Kingston, a longtime member of Greater New Harvest and also the church historian, doubled as the usher board president. She taught the teens well.

"Right this way, Sister Nash." One of the Jackson twins—Marvina could never tell those girls apart—escorted Marvina and Rose down the main aisle. The Jackson girl wore white gloves, a yellow blouse, and a navy-blue skirt hitched up by two safety pins to keep the garment from falling off her skinny frame.

As the choir sang its first selection, Marvina waved at her friends, smiling hard enough to make the skin crinkle around her eyes. She wore a flowery blue and purple skirt with a matching blazer and a white blouse underneath. Today, the wig she named "Diana," after Diana Ross for its long waves, swooped across her left brow, partially covering her eye, and cascaded down her back. Marvina wasn't much for makeup, but she couldn't stand a shiny face. A little matte base and powder to the rescue. Even with all that, Marvina knew her best asset was a smile.

Midway up the aisle was Sister Bettye Mae Lewis, who made the best sweet potato pie in all of Marion County. Bless her heart, she was raising all four of her grandkids, and two of them were having an arm-wrestling match right there in the sanctuary. A little farther up sat Brother Charles and Sister Raelynn in matching red and white outfits. Those two managed to find his-and-hers clothes every Sunday.

"Good morning!" Marvina said to all she passed by, though she knew they couldn't hear her over the choir's contemporary version of "Amazing Grace." Their hand-clapping and foot-stomping zapped all the holy reverence out of the song, if you'd asked Marvina. But obviously nobody asked her what should be happening at the church, so she moseyed on down the middle lane, doling out generous helpings of smiles and hellos.

Even with the misguided, up-tempo song, and even with arriving later than she normally would thanks to slowpoke Rose, the familiar smell of wood polish and musty carpet and the sweet faces of this congregation welcomed Marvina. Peace settled in her bones. This church was her home, too. For as long as God still met her there, her behind would warm that front pew every Sunday morning and most Wednesday nights, no matter what irreverent mishmash the choir sang.

After returning Marvina's genuine greeting, curious eyes flew from her to Rose, who hoisted a fake smile onto her face and barely wiggled two polished fingers as she followed the twin and Marvina toward the front. So far as Marvina knew, Rose hadn't been to church in decades except for family funerals. And she'd never set foot in Greater New Harvest because Rose all but disappeared from Fork City before the old church split.

In Momma's vernacular, Rose tightroped somewhere between

a heathen and a backslider, the latter being the worst state. Momma grew up strict holiness, and she'd tried her best to raise Rose and Marvina that way at the old church, too, but then Daddy came behind her and danced with the girls every Saturday morning while watching *Soul Train*. He barely went to church despite all of Momma's fasting and praying. Since Marvina loved both her sanctified mother and her groovin' Daddy—not to mention she didn't have a heaven or a hell to put anybody in—Marvina didn't speculate on whose soul was going where.

Nonetheless, it was good to see Rose in church again. Maybe being in the sanctuary would rub off some of that surly spirit.

Three rows shy of the front, the ushering twin slowed to a stop and held out a guiding hand to the second pew on the right side of the church. She pressed a cheek against Marvina's cheek and asked in her ear, "Sister Nash, is it okay if you sit here on the third row?"

The third row? Marvina wasn't sure she'd heard the girl correctly over the choir's singing. She turned her head ninety degrees to get a full view of exactly why this child would be asking her to relocate. The first row on the left side was filled with a pack of well-dressed visitors. The five deacons and their wives took up the second row, rather than occupying their usual row beside the pulpit. They only made this kind of move when there was a special declaration to behold. Why were these special guests so worthy of a change in seating arrangements? Were they a family reunion in town? Deep-pocketed historians visiting the historic homes of Fork City, Texas? Politicians vying for voters in the next election?

Far be it from Marvina to ask newcomers to get up off her usual pew, but they actually did need to get up off her row so she could see. Viewing the service from the right side, with her vision impairment, was like putting blinders on a horse for Marvina.

She didn't have the luxury of sitting any old where in the building, visitors or not.

"If you want, you can sit on the second row on the right," the girl offered apologetically. "Behind the missionaries and the first lady."

Marvina pulled the twin close, gripping her wrists, and said, "Baby, I can't sit on the right side."

"So, it's okay if you sit on the third row, then? I wasn't sure if it was more important for you to sit closer or to sit on a certain side. We have a lot of important people here today."

"*We're* important, too." Rose butted in sharply.

Good thing the choir was singing louder than a pack of hyenas, else the sisters and the bewildered usher might have become a spectacle.

"Never mind," Marvina loosed the girl, patting her forearm to let her know she wasn't upset with the messenger. "But I do need to sit on the left side. So the third row will have to do."

"Yes, ma'am."

Marvina felt her skin tingling with indignation as she squeezed between the tight pews and took her seat. It was downright claustrophobic. What if she'd been larger? What if she'd had crutches? A baby stroller?

It was one thing to be moved from her usual spot. If the child had said "I'm sorry, Sister Nash, I have to seat you here because you were late," she could have handled it. The twins were new to ushering, and they'd probably been told to fill each pew from front to back with no respect of persons. Sister Kingston would teach her later to reserve spots for the regulars. But it was a horse of a different color to be told she had been moved because she wasn't a VIP in her own church.

A dollop of bad attitude spread all over Marvina like butter on hot pancakes.

The choir brought that ridiculous and utterly disgraceful rendition of a classic hymn to a close, thank God. Sister Jovelette rushed through the announcements, and Deacon Williams only took up one offering, which made Marvina wonder what time the Dallas Cowboys played.

Rose placed a hand on Marvina's jumping knee, stilling the nervous motion Marvina hadn't been aware of. Rose tilted her body and whispered, "Sister, you all right?"

Marvina's throat was too dry to respond with words. "Mmm hmm."

Finally, Pastor Pendleton took the podium and solved the mystery. "Ladies and gentlemen, brothers and sisters, we are honored this morning to have in our midst a number of new members to our family." Pastor's eyes panned the entire congregation as he spoke. His gaze seemed to skip past Marvina. Or was it her imagination?

He continued, "Many of you know that we have had our fair share of struggles here at Greater New Harvest. In fact, many churches across the country and around the world have suffered since the pandemic."

The congregation gave a collective moan.

"Despite the lifting of ordinances and the vaccinations, all the science we now know, and all the time that has passed, people simply have not come back to church yet."

"A shame!" came from shiny-domed Deacon Scott, Pastor's lead commentator. If nobody else "amened" the preacher, Deacon Scott would.

Rose mumbled under her breath, "Here we go."

"I won't lie, church. We've been fighting to keep the doors of

Greater New Harvest open. We've only made it this far by the grace of God," Pastor Pendleton said in a deep, sad tone.

"And my lottery winnings and my chicken," Marvina thought. Of course, all her blessings came from God. But were it not for her generosity with the blessings and her diligence preparing and selling chicken and greens and other foodstuffs seasoned by Momma's spice recipe, the church would have shut down a long time ago.

Pride puffed like a balloon inside Marvina's chest. She recognized it. She didn't want to feel this way but she did. In fact, she didn't like the way she'd felt since being relegated to the third row. This wasn't the mindset she wanted to entertain in church. But as Pastor Pendleton went on to introduce the folks from the Higher Works Alliance to the congregation and formally announce what he'd told Marvina privately in his office, she couldn't stop her lips from pouting.

"We've got to keep up with the times and do what it takes to chase the souls we're called to reach," Pastor persuaded a ripe, applauding audience. "Can't keep financing the church on the youth cooking group's chicken dinners, as delicious as they are, young folk. Sister Marvina." He nodded politely, looking at her directly from the pulpit, trying to add a laugh to soften his jagged joke.

"No, sir!" Deacon Scott cosigned on Pastor's spiel, though Marvina wasn't sure exactly what he seconded—the part about the finances or the part about the delicious food. Either way, she wished he'd shut up.

Marvina felt the tension gathering in the joints of her finger. She spread her fingers apart to stretch them before a spasm took hold.

Pastor returned his gaze to no one in particular. "I've made some new appointments to help guide the changes. Deacon Willis will preside over the choir and the ushers. Deacon Eiffelway will work with the youth in all their affairs..."

Marvina didn't hear the rest. Deacon Eiffelway, of all people. He didn't even like young folk. And he was certainly not a fan of Marvina's since way back when she won the lottery. He was the main one saying she needed to go before the congregation and repent for gambling and accepting the check on television. In one breath, he said it brought shame on the church. In the next breath, he was gladly counting the tenth of her take-home winnings that she gave to the church, right off the top.

"Mother Jackson will head up the women's auxiliaries," he summed up the new appointments. Marvina was not among the chosen, and she had a good idea why. She supported her teams by cooking and selling dinners alongside her team members. Now that they'd moved on to bigger and supposedly better ventures, the whole community cooking-for-Jesus plan got vetoed. Or maybe voted down by the Alliance. Either way, Pastor Pendleton had just ripped the purpose straight out of Marvina's belly.

She noticed heads whipping toward her. The teens. Her youth cooking group. They seemed to understand what this meant for them, and their faces bore no smiles.

Didn't the adults realize what Pastor was saying? Did they understand what this would mean? Church as they knew it was about to be over, and each of their auxiliaries could be next on the chopping block. The ushers, the sewing circle, the men's retreat-slash-fishing-trip, and the robed, march-in choir, never mind their song selection. All of their unique, God-given passion projects could be gone just as easily as Marvina's youth cooking classes and plate sales once they started aligning to standardized Alliance practices.

"We have to make progress, especially with the new loop coming through town soon."

Rose elbowed Marvina. "What loop?"

"Extending 255 all the way around to 20."

"Hmmm," Rose perked up. "Maybe y'all will get a Sonic Drive-In or an IHOP out of the deal."

Marvina ignored her sister.

After ten minutes, Pastor Pendleton was finally able to put a bow on his speech. "We'll soon attract people from our surrounding towns. More businesses. New homes, more traffic, more opportunities, and more young families looking for a church. When they come here, we must be able to provide an experience they'll remember. But that takes initiative. And faith. And changes."

Marvina took a peppermint from her purse and sucked on it to relieve the lump in her throat.

Rose held out a hand, requesting a mint, too.

"Don't you have your own mints?" Marvina squeaked softly.

"If I did, would I be asking you?"

Marvina fished out another mint and pressed it into Rose's open palm. "A grown woman ought to always have something to freshen her breath."

"My breath is fine. I'm eating because I'm bored." Her face sagged accordingly.

Marvina rolled her eyes to a close and prayed silently. Between Pastor going on and on about how much better things would be in the Higher Works Alliance and Rose acting like an apathetic teenager sitting in adult church for the first time, Marvina was near tears. *Lord, help.*

Marvina surveyed the room, spotting tentative glances and raised eyebrows despite how they seemed to all verbally endorse the proposal. Though people's bodies shuffled in discomfort, no one would voice a dissenting opinion in this setting. Maybe not ever, after the picture of gloom and doom Pastor Pendleton painted about the sure failure to come if Greater New Harvest didn't make these changes.

Now that her throat had loosed and her mind tiptoed past her feelings far enough to process, Marvina had to admit to herself: the pews were not as crowded as they had been a few years earlier. She couldn't keep rescuing the church from its financial woes. She was, after all, a widow with one long-distance son, clear across the country. She needed to hold on to what financial security she could for as long as she could. And the last few times she lifted that cast-iron skillet, her wrist did quiver ever so slightly under its weight.

Shoot. Maybe it is time for a change. Not only for the church, but for me.

The very idea took Marvina by surprise. She couldn't remember the last time she considered her own state, her own needs above the church or the children she instructed. She felt worse than prideful. Selfish was the right word. One of the ugliest, least Christian-like traits one could possess, according to Momma.

What was she supposed to do now with Momma's spices? Cook for herself only? The very last entity that needed her was ending their relationship as sure as death did her part from her late husband, Warren Sr. Who would need her now?

A sense of rejection rolled from Marvina's head to her feet, flattening her spirit the way a rolling pin flattened dough. She couldn't take much more of this.

Rose poked Marvina's arm.

"What?"

"Is he going to preach, or is he going to give a campaign speech?"

Marvina could only shake her head.

Turned out that Pastor had found a scripture to combine his Higher Works Alliance pitch with his preaching. The message, though a bit out of context in Marvina's opinion, brought a somber sense of surrender to this morning, this sacred space. Even from the third row, she perceived the excitement in Pastor's eyes and the ambitious glow from the Alliance leaders. This was a done deal.

And, since she was not a natural fighter (except when it came to Rose), Marvina let go of her anger and focused on receiving what she could from the sermon. Two words resonated with her: *start over*. Not at all what she wanted to hear, so she pushed the phrase to the back of her mind.

No one answered the call to fellowship, and only a few folks went up for special prayer. Rose didn't budge when the minister petitioned for those with ailments to approach the altar. Her knee was still swollen, a fact on display due to the questionably short velvet skirt Rose had assembled with a black wrap shirt, tights, and ankle boots. Marvina gave her a pass, though, because she probably hadn't known she was going to church.

Plus, maybe it was God's way of allowing Marvina to bear witness to her sister's physical condition. All those years on her feet at the post office must have taken a toll on Rose's body.

Help her, too, Lord.

Marvina knew for sure, now, that the Cowboys had a noon kickoff, because Pastor joked about it as they rose for the benediction.

"I hope none of y'all are rushing out of here to check your numbers on the football pot," he half-teased.

With all minds clear, he dismissed the church.

Ta'riq swarmed to Marvina's side as she and Rose traveled in the reverse direction down the main aisle.

"What, we don't get to cook anymore?" he questioned.

Never the source of confusion, Marvina answered, "I taught you plenty, Ta'riq. If you can't cook by now, after all the hours we spent together, you must not have been paying attention."

"Yes, ma'am, but it's not the same without your special touch. And your spices. You ever gonna to pass it along to somebody?"

"Nuh-uh!" Sasha flanked Marvina's other side so quickly that Rose had to take a step back. Sasha apologized, but she continued confronting Ta'riq, "You trying to push up on her for the spice recipe?"

Marvina's heart warmed as the teens discussed exactly which one of them was most entitled to the secret ingredients. Their argument, which bordered on flirting, carried them out the sanctuary and into the parking lot, Marvina sandwiched between them the whole time. The energy passing between them invigorated Marvina. "Y'all know I have a son, right? And a sister."

Marvina thumbed toward Rose, who had made a beeline from the main entrance to her Honda and was unlocking the doors already. Good thing, too. With the children by her side and Rose hurriedly trying to leave the church grounds, Marvina avoided the after-church whisperings. People would be talking today. She didn't want to be accosted by other congregants, even the well-meaning ones, and bust out crying in front of them all.

"That's your sister?" Ta'riq asked like a kindergartner who'd just realized his teacher didn't reside in the schoolhouse.

"Yes. I had a mother, a father, a husband. I still have some family, too."

"I'm just sayin'," Ta'riq backpedaled, "you're at the church so much, I thought maybe you lived all by yourself."

She ignored the fact that Ta'riq was basically saying Marvina didn't have a life outside of the church, as far as he could tell. "My sister's visiting."

Sasha hummed, mischief in her eyes. "So, your sister knows the secret seasoning recipe, too?"

Marvina stopped at the rear of Rose's SUV. "Listen. I can't give you the recipe. It's a family heirloom. But you can keep cooking. Remember. The most important ingredient is love."

"Love and that seasoning," Ta'riq countered, his voice cracking from the perils of puberty.

"You can't leave us hanging like this, Sister Marvina," Sasha whined.

Hanging was the right word to describe how Marvina felt, too. Dangling, susceptible to the harsh, indiscriminate winds of progress.

"I think they're just trying to move a bunch of rich people into Greater New Harvest. Like church gentrification," Sasha sassed.

Cold winds lifted the ends of the Diana wig and swung the tips across Marvina's face.

Rose tapped the horn. She was ready to leave.

Marvina flung the hair aside with a flip of her head. "Let's all pray that God's will be done, you hear?" No matter how hurt or betrayed she felt, Marvina wouldn't disrespect an elder or question authority in the presence of children.

"Marvina, let's go!" Rose insisted through a lowered window from the driver's side.

"I have to skedaddle, now." She gave Ta'riq and Sasha hugs. "You can always join the choir or…or help out with the media team."

The teens' snarls and sneers, barely tempered by respect, spoke for their disinterest in her suggestion.

"Well. Pray and ask the Lord to show you how He wants to use you. Will you do that? For me?"

"Anything for you, Sister Nash," Ta'riq agreed, brandishing a bright smile.

His sweet response lifted Marvina's spirits a bit.

But they were soon dashed again when she got in the car.

"Let me guess. They're trying to move forward without you and the other women who actually run this church?" Rose surmised.

Marvina snapped her seat belt. "I don't want to talk about it. Let's drive home in peace." She didn't expect her sister to honor the humble request. That would be too much.

"All I know is, I wouldn't sprinkle another speck of Momma's seasoning there. After all you did for them?"

"I didn't do it for them. I did it for the Lord. He's pleased with my offering."

"Yeah. Well." Rose stopped talking long enough to back out of the parking space carefully. "Sounds like it's time for you to cast your iron skillet elsewhere."

"I repeat. I don't want to talk about it."

"Suit yourself. I've got plenty to say."

"You'll be sittin' here talking' to yourself, then."

Rose glared at Marvina. "You're just like Momma, you know that?"

Was that supposed to be an insult? "Thank you," Marvina replied.

Rose sighed, shaking her head.

Confusion piled another weight on Marvina's thoughts. She knew Rose and Momma had their disputes, but the way Rose shook her head, Rose was holding on to more than the memory of a few skirmishes. And yet, she cared about Momma's spices enough to be offended on Marvina's behalf.

She didn't have the emotional energy left to untangle the knots kinked up inside Rose. Marvina only hoped Rose would get whatever she came for soon so that Marvina could get back to her one-woman house and somehow nurse her own injured purpose back to life.

CHAPTER 7
Rose

The rain picked up again on our way home from church. Fitting. Marvina sat in the car sniffing and dripping her own personal raindrops all the ride home.

For as much as Marvina disparaged the situation, I saw a silver lining. A highway extension through Fork City, more potential patrons, very little competition. The picture was coming into view, one puzzle piece at a time. If Fork City was on the verge of an economic boom, I was poised to catch the fallout. Put it all together and—call it a miracle or a series of unfortunate events—but my sister and I could have a second chance at the restaurant dream if we stopped arguing long enough to make good decisions and if Marvina stopped pouting long enough to see the Pastor had done her a favor. Good riddance!

I considered making a U-turn more than once, heading back to the church and giving Marvina's Pastor a piece of my mind. Now, me? I hadn't been to Sunday service in years before that morning with my sister. Not because I didn't believe in God or because I was against religion. It was this particular *brand* of religion—Momma's kind of religion—that chewed me up, blew a big, pink bubble out of me, and then spat me out when I lost the sweet appearance of perfection.

What I did was wrong, technically, so I understand why Momma, the church, and I didn't get along.

But Marvina? If she was anything like our mother, which I suspected must be true, my sister sacrificed every bone in her body for that church. Giving, cooking, cleaning, serving. All with a genuine, hearty smile no matter how unreliable the other volunteers, no matter how little sleep she'd had the night before, say, the Pastor and wife's anniversary service. Marvina didn't deserve to have her cooking ministry cut off like a gangrenous foot.

My sister kept her promise to keep quiet in the car, and I kept to mine to keep talking out loud. "Don't make sense what they're doing. When people from the suburbs or the inner city move to a rural area, it's because they want a slower pace. They want to stretch out on a wide parcel of land and return to a simpler lifestyle. Roosters crowing first thing in the morning. Pitch-black darkness at night. They might need a little coffee shop or a shopping center to feel sophisticated, but the last thing they want is a highfalutin church that reminds them of where they came from. They want to go back in time. To fried chicken dinners and mashed potatoes, you know?"

She gave no response.

I inched my car close to the house so we could run inside without getting soaked. I parked. Pushed the button to unlock the doors. Marvina remained a statue. I waited. Rain pattered on the roof of my car and streamed down the windows and windshield. Smelled nice. Fresh.

Marvina cleared her throat. "When are you going home?" Her voice came out scratchy and uncharacteristically cold.

I looked at her as she stared ahead stoically with her eyes glazed over and her lips sucked in. Momma would have called her mood "stanky." This was not the time to hit her with my jolly good, half-baked let's-start-the-business-together idea. "Let's go inside."

"You really gonna drag this out until tomorrow or Tuesday?"

"I'm not dragging anything except *you* out of this car before it starts thundering and lightning. You can't sit out here complaining about the church all afternoon," I fussed.

"You're the only one complaining," Marvina snapped back.

I considered leaving her in the car and going inside until I remembered I didn't have the key to her house. "You coming in?"

"In a minute."

"Marvina. You can't let this get you down."

"I'm already down, and you being here ain't helping. Will you promise me you'll leave when I show you this recipe?"

"That's rude."

"I'm sorry," Marvina mumbled.

"Thank you."

It dawned on me that this was the first time in decades Marvina and I had been alone together. Sitting in the car, a few feet away from her, the hostile energy between us pulsed. I didn't like my sister, and she didn't like me.

But it hadn't always been this way.

As little girls, we were inseparable. People thought we were twins. Fraternal twins, mind you, but the way Momma combed our hair and matched our hair bows and clothes, it was a reasonable assumption. Me being the oldest, I was naturally protective of Marvina. Momma reinforced my proclivity to safeguard my sister by knighting me "Rose, guardian of Marvina." Charged with blazing the trail of purity and finer Christian holy womanhood for Marvina and all the daughters who might come behind her.

I never asked for that halo hovering over my head. When I fell short of being an angel via my unorthodox relationship with David, everything changed between my sister and me. I didn't know if she was angry with me, disappointed in me, afraid of me, or all of the above. All I knew was she stopped talking to me, and that was that.

People say time and circumstance have a way of healing things. I could not concur. The forty-dollar laceration between us showed no indication of clotting or scabbing or regenerating fresh skin.

"You know what hurts the most?" Marvina interrupted my thoughts.

"No. What?" I didn't know if she was talking about the church or about us, but I was listening.

"The *way* Pastor did it. I guarantee you, if Vernetta Pendleton was alive, she would have called a meeting for discussion about the new direction of the church. Decent and in order."

"Was today your first time hearing about the Alliance?"

"No," she said. "Pastor called me into his office last week and told me. It wasn't a conversation. It was an FYI type of situation. Like he's a dictator."

"Well, he *is* the Pastor," I reminded her. "The buck stops with him."

She twisted her body to face me. "But if Vernetta were here, she would have counseled him to talk to the congregation first. Not only the deacons, the *people*, the heartbeat of the church. Pastor Pendleton ain't no ignorant man. If he had talked to us, explained his reasoning, we might have come to the same conclusion he did about our next steps. It's just..." She shuddered as she turned away again. "I don't see how us cooking and selling plates is counterproductive."

Lightning flashed in the distance.

"Can we take this conversation inside?" I asked.

The way she grabbed the door handle and hustled out of my car, you would have thought I'd called her out of her name.

I swiped up my purse and followed her inside as quickly as possible, slowed a tad by my uncooperative knee. Sitting with my legs all cramped up in church did me no favors.

Marvina made a beeline to the Crock-Pot to check on the roast we'd started before we left for church. From the aromatic mixture of onions, carrots, and potatoes swimming in beefy broth with pitch-perfect seasoning and tender meat, I knew we were in for a treat in another hour or so. I also knew I'd blown whatever opportunity presented itself to reconnect in the car by abruptly asking if we could move the discussion inside. It was a practical suggestion, but Marvina had taken it the wrong way.

"I didn't mean to cut you off from talking about your predicament with your pastor."

She waved off my apology, then opened her spice cabinet to add pepper to the roast. Marvina still liked her food spicy-hot, which surprised me given our age. Had she not also inherited the late-night indigestion following a fiery meal? Shoot, I quit eating salsa after 8:00 p.m. ten years earlier.

"Don't make that roast too hot," I said.

Now she gave me the stank eye to match her stank attitude.

"I've got a stake in this roast," I claimed. Standing in her kitchen, surrounded by some of Momma's old utensils and plates, and thinking about the carrots I'd chopped, I had every right to ask for a reasonably tolerable roast.

"Rose, I know you don't mean no harm. And I know you came a long way to get Momma's recipe, which I have already promised I'd help you re-create. Let's change out of our clothes, make a batch of seasoning for you, and then I'll give you some roast in a take-home container and we'll call it a day. Okay?"

Now she was just plain acting silly. It was pouring rain outside, which made the road leading out of town tricky and treacherous, even in an SUV. The roast had another hour to go, probably, and I'd had enough of her taking out her church frustrations on me. We might not be besties, but I did not appreciate her kicking me out of her house for no good reason, not even giving me a chance to properly eat my lunch.

"I would like to sit down and eat my food in peace before I get on the road."

She held the ledge of her counter with both hands as though she were trying to keep her balance. "My, my, my. In all these years, you have not changed one bit."

I clutched imaginary pearls. "*I* haven't changed?"

"I said what I said."

"What changing do *I* need to do, exactly?"

Marvina straightened and counted off on her fingers. "For one, you need to stop thinking about yourself all the time. For two, you can't just invite yourself to my house and stay as long as you good and well please, Rose. Did you forget? You moved. You left us. We don't talk. We're not friends. We don't like each other." Her mean words soured the air.

"I never said I didn't like you," I countered. Heat pulsed through my body. "Don't put words in my mouth."

"You didn't have to say it. Your actions spoke for you."

How on earth my sister thought I had wronged her and not

the other way around baffled me. It's like she'd watched the movie and I'd read the book. Same characters, same settings, but the plot played out differently.

A rumble of thunder preceded another snap of lightning. A pop came from outside, and the house went completely silent. No power. Absent the buzz of electrical appliances and the whooshing of air-conditioning, the rain sounded heavier, more intense.

"Hmph. Might as well have a seat," she surrendered to divine intervention.

Together, we moved to the living room, where the large windows offered the most light. Marvina occupied the love seat. She grabbed her novel, clicked on the book light, and escaped into what appeared to be a romance.

I kicked off my shoes and elevated my swollen knee on the sofa.

Neither of us spoke. It felt right, almost sacred, to sit in the same space in peace and quiet together for the first time in years. I wondered if my sister was thinking the same. I couldn't be sure, but she must have had her mind on something, because she stayed on that same page for ten minutes.

My sister slammed her book shut. "You reckon I should go outside and flip the breaker?"

I started to ask her who died and made her a handyman. Then I remembered that her husband actually *did* die. That'll do it. When a marriage ends, a woman is forced to assume everything her husband used to do.

Nonetheless, we still had daylight, and with the mild, Texas winter temperature, there was no rush for her to go outside in the thick of the passing storm. "You want to wait until the rain dies down?"

"A little water never hurt anybody."

I warned, "A little *lightning* did."

She stopped. Cocked her head to the side. "You got something smart to say about everything, don't you?"

"Well, ain't that the pot calling the kettle black? We both got it honest. From Momma."

Marvina couldn't deny the truth. And somehow, this shared thread of memory connecting us in that moment signaled a temporary truce.

"If I put on my cloth gardening gloves, I should be fine."

"Fine," I gave in. "Let's go do it together, while I'm here. That way if one of us gets shocked, the other one lives to tell the story."

"Now you *really* sound like Momma." Marvina chuckled.

She was right. Momma had a way of connecting the dots between any situation and death. If you wanted a headband, Momma heard of girl your age who had died from lack of blood circulation due to a headband. No headband for you. If you wanted to join the chess club, Momma had read a story about somebody who had a heart attack from the stress of playing chess. No chess for you.

Marvina found a flashlight in the kitchen drawer. She retrieved two pairs of rain boots from her closet.

We still wore the same size shoe.

As I stuffed my feet into her extra boots, I said, "If it's all right with you, I'm going to take a pain pill for my knee and lay down for a bit when we finish. Then we can eat the roast, make the seasoning, and I'll be out of your hair afterward, per your request." It pained me to say those words because, dagummit, Marvina needed to start this restaurant in Momma's memory as much as I did. She just didn't know it yet. I didn't have another ten or twenty years to wait for her to cool off and stop playing the victim in our sisterly saga, but today clearly wasn't the day for her conversion.

I held the umbrella over both our heads with one hand and the flashlight with the other. Heavy rain slapped our arms, and winds pushed the water under the umbrella. We huddled close, trampling through mud together, and made our way to the side of her house. Marvina located the main switch, then, wearing her thick, purple gloves, flipped it to its normal position.

Suddenly, out of the corner of my eye, I caught a dark figure lurking in Marvina's guesthouse. It happened so quickly, it made me think of a ghost, which, of course, sent my heart to racing. I tapped Marvina on the shoulder and whispered, "Look."

Marvina turned her body so she could follow my line of sight. She squinted really hard. "What?"

"I just saw someone walking."

"Where?"

"In the guesthouse. Is someone staying there?"

"No." Marvina kept her focus trained on the front window of the house and, sure enough, the figure moved again.

She gasped when she saw it, too! Something moved behind a curtain.

"Shouldn't be nobody in there," she whispered, now.

"But there is," I said. "We need to call the police. Come on. Let's go back inside."

CHAPTER 8

The sisters linked arms and hightailed it back to the house. Marvina could feel Rose's hand shaking, and she knew Rose could probably feel her heart thumping through her chest wall.

Rose was the quickest with her cell phone. "The address is 2390 Wilkerson Road. There's a trespasser on our property. We need the police... Yes, we saw someone... No, no one has permission to be there."

Marvina rushed back to the dining room window for another look. No shadows. No movement. Had they both imagined it?

Her mind flashed back to the time she and Rose—they had to be about six and eight years old—beat on their parents' bedroom door, then rushed into their room sobbing uncontrollably.

Daddy sat straight up in bed. "What's the matter?"

"We don't want you to die!" Rose cried.

"No. We want you to stay with us. Don't die, Momma. Daddy, please, don't."

Momma and Daddy gave each other confused looks. "Who said we were dying?" Momma asked.

"We were talking," Rose whimpered, "about how one day, you

are going to get old and die. And then we'll be all alone." She let out a wail as though she were at the funeral right then and there. Marvina followed suit.

Momma and Daddy burst out laughing. Then she and Rose started giggling, too, for no other reason than seeing their parents laughing made them feel like maybe they were mistaken about the possibility of their parents dying. Maybe they'd fallen for another one of those childhood myths, like the nonexistent boogeyman, whom they could safely categorize in the never-gonna-happen or something-grown-ups-say-to-discipline-kids category. Already, as young girls, they had figured out Santa and the tooth fairy. Maybe this was along the same lines, and they'd worked themselves into a frantic frenzy for nothing.

In the present, Rose was almost arguing with the 911 dispatcher. Her nerves were getting the best of her. "Yes, we are the property owners. No, it's not a tenant." She looked at Marvina for confirmation that everything she'd relayed was true.

Marvina nodded. Then she went to double-check the lock on the front door, because the last thing they needed was for an intruder to enter this house after he'd gotten everything he wanted from the guesthouse.

There wasn't much in her eight-hundred-square foot pool house, but a thief wouldn't know that before breaking in.

While Rose held the line with the dispatcher, she grabbed the fireplace poker. Marvina looked around the living room for a suitable weapon.

Rose pressed her phone's screen, then asked her sister, "Don't you have a gun around here?"

"What in the world would I be doing with a gun?" Marvina countered.

"Because you're an old woman living in this big house off a side road all by yourself, that's why! You gotta start looking out for yourself more!"

"Are we really fighting right now? This very second?"

Exasperated, Rose pressed her phone again. "Yes, I'm still here. No, nothing has changed. How soon until the police get here?"

Marvina resumed her post by the window, making sure no one snuck up on them. *A gun.* Her late husband got her one, years ago, but she'd never learned to shoot the thing. She surrendered it in a countywide gun roundup to get guns off the streets, no questions asked. Marvina didn't think she had it in her to shoot anyone. Besides, she lived in Fork City, Texas. What were the odds? To date, her most dangerous trespassers traveled on four feet.

But the way Rose looked at her just now with that *Really?* expression, Marvina couldn't help but feel a little silly. A little naive. Warren Sr. had said these same words to her when he was heading out of town to visit his father's land for weeks at a time. He had spoken the words from a husband's protective love, a sense of duty.

Rose probably had those same feelings. And given the current situation, maybe they'd both been right. Maybe she should approach her safety, or her life, differently.

"Ooh!" Marvina shrieked as the figure passed behind the curtain again. This time, she'd been able to make out the person's slight build. "It's a child…or a small woman."

"What?!" Rose's unphoned cheek pressed against Marvina's as they stared through the same slat opening.

Marvina repeated, "A child or a woman."

"You sure?"

It was, actually, a fair question given her problems with depth perception.

Rose said, "Could be a little man."

The new context shifted Marvina's fear from herself to the person in the guesthouse. Police were en route. The rain came in sheets now, which always adds a layer of ambiguity for everyone from drivers to football players. What if the wrong officer came, gun drawn, and overreacted? Escalated the situation and shot somebody's baby on her property? She'd never be able to live with herself for calling the police when she could have just as easily gone out there and talked to the person.

"We need to go out there, Rose."

"No, ma'am. We will stand right here and wait for the police."

"But what if something terrible happens when they get here?" Headlines blasting questionable police shootings scrolled through her mind. Should they have called the police in the first place?

Marvina remembered the time her father and Uncle Cleo beat up Aunt Barbara's boyfriend after he put his hands on her. No police, no charges, no jail time, just street justice. And that old boyfriend didn't stalk Aunt Barbara, either, because he knew he'd get another beatdown if word got back to the men in Aunt Barbara's life that he was bothering her again. People didn't involve the police if they didn't have to, back then. Momma always said people were too quick to involve the law in stuff they could just as easily resolve with a little common sense. No need in putting somebody's name in the system for life over something temporary and petty.

"You've been reading too many books and watching too much TV," Rose fussed. She grabbed Marvina's elbow and yanked her around so they were face-to-face. She wagged an index finger before Marvina's nose. "You are not going to be a hero today. Let the officers do their job when they get here."

Her grip remained tight on Marvina's arm.

They both turned their heads toward the sight of the police cruiser rolling into the yard. Concerned more with the stranger's safety than getting wet, Marvina was the first to go outside and approach the long-nosed, short-statured policeman wearing a heavy-duty raincoat. She yelled over the sound of the rain, "Officer. Thank you for coming. Listen, we don't know who's back there. It could be a child. Someone who's lost, or looking for a place to stay dry. It's coming down pretty hard out here."

Rose added, "But it *is* a stranger." She stood next to Marvina and covered her with the umbrella now.

"Ladies, I'm going to have to ask you to go back inside the main house." He motioned toward the front door easily.

Marvina was glad to see his steady hand pointing. No shaking. She was glad they'd gotten an officer with a temperament more like Andy than Barney from *The Andy Griffith Show*.

Again, Rose gripped her sister. She dragged Marvina back to the house, where they watched and waited for this to unfold.

"Lord God, please protect the officer and the person in the house," Marvina whispered.

"Amen," Rose seconded.

The officer opened the gate to the pool area and approached the house in question. He knocked, like someone inside had sent him a paper invitation to come by. He called out a few times. His lips moved in conversation. He nodded a few times. Shook his head. Spoke again. Then stepped back into the rain a few steps. A small, dark triangle appeared where the intruder slid the curtain aside.

Rose gulped. "Okay. There is definitely someone in your house."

Side by side, the sisters scoped the scene as the officer stood in the rain seemingly coaxing the person into opening the door with gentle hand movements. Then, slowly, the door opened, and someone stepped out with raised hands. The officer immediately patted the person up and down. Apparently satisfied that they had no weapon, he cuffed them, then whipped a tiny umbrella from his pocket. With one hand on the cuffs and one on the umbrella, he led the person away from the house.

They trudged across the yard, faces looking at the ground to avoid the onslaught of rain.

The intruder was dressed in black pants and an oversized hooded camouflage jacket, making their face invisible from that angle.

"Is it a man or a woman?" Rose asked. "Black or white?"

"I don't know, Rose. I'm standing right here with you. We're seeing the same thing."

The officer then escorted the person to the back seat of his car and folded them inside. With the trespasser in custody, Rose and Marvina opened the door to the house and welcomed the officer inside.

He removed his hat as he crossed the threshold. In the process, he looked down at the puddle forming on the hardwood floor. "Sorry for all the water, ma'am."

"Don't worry about it," Marvina said. "What's happening? Who is it?"

"Not sure of her name. She's been in your house for a few days. Squatting. Says she can't go back home."

"Is it a teenager?" Rose asked.

He bowed slightly. "She looks to be maybe seventeen or eighteen. Depending on her exact age, I'll either take her to a shelter or to child protective services. But first I need to ask if you want to press charges for trespassing. If so, her first stop will be jail."

"No," Marvina and Rose insisted simultaneously. First time they'd wholeheartedly agreed in decades.

"Is she from around these parts?" Marvina asked.

"Can't rightly say. But she sounds like she might be, judging from her way of speaking."

"She's probably somebody I know, then. If not her, I'm sure I know her people. Is there any way..." Marvina swallowed the bulge in her throat.

"Can we talk to her first? Find out what's going on before you take her away?" Rose filled in where Marvina left off.

He bounced on his toes, bobbing his head a bit, narrowing his green eyes, as though he was annoyed now. "Ladies, you called the station and asked for help with an unauthorized person on your property. I came here, negotiated a surrender, and you want me to release the intruder to your care, now?"

Marvina confirmed with a nod. "I can get her back to wherever she belongs."

"What if I leave and she attacks you?" he posed. "You expect me to double back here to rescue you again?"

When he put it like that, Marvina understood why he seemed irked.

He continued, "I don't take kindly to people abusing the system. Are you sure you two don't know her?"

Rose jumped in, "Well, first of all—"

"Officer, what's your name?" Marvina intervened before they all ended up going to jail.

He stood tall. "McGillam."

"Officer McGillam," Marvina repeated in a sugar-sweet tone, "No. We don't know her. We appreciate your quick response and your bravery, going out there all by yourself, in the pouring rain, not knowing what or who was on the other side of that door."

Her compliment smoothed out the wrinkles on his forehead,

and the corners of his lips turned slightly upward. "I've been serving the people of Fork City twenty years now. It's my pleasure, Miss…"

"Marvina. And this here is my sister, Rose."

He tipped his head again. "Mighty fine to meet you both."

Rose's lips were as tight as a fist.

Marvina didn't wait for her sister to respond to the greeting. "Officer McGillam, now, we could really use your help in making sure this situation gets resolved peacefully. Why don't you stay a minute while we talk this out? I've got a fresh iced lemon pound cake sitting in my cake stand."

Surely, Officer McGillam hadn't gotten so pudgy eating salads and broccoli.

His brows jumped to attention, and excitement danced across his face. Then he cleared his throat to summon a professional demeanor again. "Well, like I said, I've been on the force for twenty years. I have a gut feeling that's never led me wrong, which is why I didn't draw my weapon. That girl in the car is probably more scared of us than we are of her. And I do think of myself as a keeper of the peace. I'm also a pretty good judge of when folks are lying. I think the young lady is telling the truth, especially the way she was shaking like a leaf. So yes, let's try to get to the bottom of things the good old-fashioned, small-town way. With communication."

"Sounds good to me," Rose agreed tentatively. How many times had their mother advised them: *You can catch more flies with honey than with vinegar?*

"All right, ladies. Let's give it a shot."

When Officer McGillam went back to the cruiser to get the intruder, Marvina chastised Rose, opening her eyes wide for the panic effect. "Look. We don't need your attitude right now."

"I don't have an attitude! He—"

Marvina tsked. "Listen. There is a young woman, maybe even a child, whose life pushed her to the point of living in my run-down guesthouse. I wouldn't send my dog out there to pee! Do not make today worse for her."

"I'm not trying to make things worse. I only want Officer McGillam to give us the same respect we've given him," Rose said. "His comment about us abusing the system was unnecessary."

"Might be, but—"

"No *might* to it!" Rose fussed.

"Just…just…help me get the cake ready," Marvina ordered.

Rose slid four saucers from the cabinet and pulled four forks from the drawer.

Marvina carefully lowered the cake from atop her refrigerator and lifted the glass dome. "Hand me a knife."

Together, they prepared four places at the table without a moment to spare. Officer McGillam entered the front door again and walked, with the suspect, toward the kitchen area. The girl's lowered face was hidden behind the hoodie. Her hands were still cuffed behind her back, which immediately broke Marvina's heart. Not once had she ever been in the presence of a handcuffed person. When a teenage Warren Jr. went to jail for public intoxication, Marvina had done what she had to do to free him.

She felt the same way now about this stranger.

Officer McGillam drew the hood off the girl's face, revealing her cornrows, a reddish-brown skin to her round baby face, and big brown eyes filled with tears.

"I'm sorry," the girl choked out. She was shaking like a wet dog. "I didn't have anywhere else to go."

All anxieties melted away as Marvina's servant-heart warmed

to attention. This was a child in need, right up Marvina's alley. She flipped her mental Rolodex of the Black folk in Fork City. The girl had a broad nose like the Munroes, a pronounced forehead like the Wrights, a reddish skin tone like the Redmonds—that family was part Cherokee. From the loopy stray curls that had escaped the braids, Marvina could see her hair favored the Redmonds, too.

"What's your name, sweetheart?" Marvina asked.

"Kerresha Smith."

"You some kin to the Redmonds?"

"A little."

Rose spat impatiently, "Officer, please free her hands. There's three of us and one of her."

His eyes met Marvina's, and she confirmed with a nod.

Rose smacked her lips, obviously upset that Officer McGillam was taking final orders from Marvina.

The click and slide of steel brought a sense of relief to the room.

As soon as the girl's hands were free, she swung them up to her belly and rubbed the roundness that had been undetectable beneath the oversized sweater. There was no mistaking the baby bump at that very moment.

"Woah," Officer McGillam remarked. "Did not see that coming."

Marvina and Rose stood dumbstruck as well. This homeless, squatting baby was having a baby.

CHAPTER 9

Rose

It's funny how one little detail changes everything. Kerresha's half-polished fingernails spreading across her stomach made my chest shrink. Even now, after I was well past what should have been my childbearing years, the sight of a pregnant woman still arrested me. Worse, the sight of a pregnant girl like Kerresha—ill prepared to take care of herself, let alone give a child what it needs—shook my sense of right and wrong and justice and fairness in this world. Made me question what was wrong with me that I shouldn't be a mother, despite me checking off all the boxes I was told led to easy, happy street.

"Let's all sit down and have some cake." Marvina piloted the path to the table. "Anybody want some milk? Tea?"

I turned the offer down and sat before my plate, but I didn't touch it. Adrenaline or cortisol or pure green jealousy pulsed through me with a fury that took me by surprise. I had talked myself out of this mental place years before. I made up a story that God knew David would leave me, so He spared me the hardship of being a single mother by making my womb incapable of carrying a baby full term. There was one less fatherless Black child in the world. I didn't have to worry about my son or daughter lashing out because of the rejection.

And yet, here sat this girl, wet, homeless, and darn near taken downtown for trespassing, carrying a ball of life inside her. If the baby looked anything like Kerresha, it would be adorable. In fact, Kerresha had the kind of face that probably had not changed much since she was a baby. Pudgy cheeks, big bright eyes, and a little extra helping of fat under her chin. She'd be the first one named in a "Guess who?" baby picture contest.

How is this fair?

Marvina calmed the situation with hospitality and pound cake. Forks clinked plates. Glasses full of milk clanked on the wooden table. The silence gave us all a moment to process.

"May I borrow a napkin, ma'am?" the girl asked.

Marvina slipped one from Momma's vintage peach seashell napkin holder and passed it to Kerresha.

Kerresha produced a phone from her pocket, wiped it off, and placed it face down on the table.

Officer McGillam chugged through a glass of milk in record time. Either that or we'd been sitting at the table longer than I reckoned, lost in thought.

"Kerresha, baby, what's going on with you?" Marvina started the investigation after the girl had scarfed down the cake.

She held a fist over her mouth and belched. "I'm sorry. I have heartburn and indigestion, now."

"When was the last time you saw a doctor?" I asked.

She shook her head. "Maybe like...two years ago?"

"Uh, she means for the baby," the police officer said.

"Oh," Kerresha said, "Never."

"Never?" I repeated.

She repeated her head-shaking gesture. "No. I didn't have the money or transportation."

"We've got to get you to a doctor," I stated. "Prenatal care is very important."

"I know it is," she agreed. "I have a book that tells me everything that's supposed to happen and when. So far, I'm doing pretty good. There's nothing unusual happening, or I would have gone to the hospital emergency room." Again, she palmed the sides of her belly like a basketball.

"How long have you been out there in the other house?"

She shrugged. "A few weeks, I think. Lost track of days all by myself like that."

"Well, who's been feeding you?" Marvina asked the question that was also on my mind.

"I walk to the Quick Shop, out the back gate when I need something."

"You have money for food?" Officer McGillam asked.

"Of course she has *some* money," I answered for her. "She's got an iPhone."

"It's a reasonable question." Marvina intervened with a smile, passing an unspoken warning to me, cosigning Officer McGillam's implied accusation of theft. She gave her attention to Kerresha again. "We just want to make sure you're okay."

"Thank you. I'm fine. And I'm really sorry about not asking for permission to stay in your house. I didn't have anywhere else to go."

Marvina exonerated Kerresha with a dip of the head. "No hard feelings. You can call me Miss Marvina. This here is my sister, Miss Rose."

Kerresha acknowledged me with a subdued glance and an

embarrassed press of her lips. Her gesture touched a soft spot in me. I wanted to hug her and fuss at her and ask her, "What were you thinking?" and take her shopping for what she needed all at the same time. I sighed for Kerresha and for the innocent baby inside her.

"What's your plan, sweetheart?" Marvina prodded gently.

The girl shrugged. "I don't have one, for now. I mean, I've already applied for housing, but I can't get help until the baby is born. I planned to wait in the house for a while, until..." Her voice trailed off like we were supposed to finish the rest of her sentence.

"Until what?" I had to know.

Kerresha's face bunched up around her eyes, nose, and mouth. Her bottom lip trembled. "Miss Rose, I don't know what I'm gonna do," she cried.

The way she said my name, all sweet and respectful and desperate, I won't lie, my heart swelled as big as her stomach. I swear, sometimes young people have no sense at all; I was definitely in that number at her age.

Marvina asked, "Where is the child's father?"

More tears escaped Kerresha eyes. "He's out of the picture."

"The hell he is," I squawked. "Here you are living in a vacant house while he's out doing God knows what."

"If I may speak, he needs to man up," the officer added.

Now he and I agreed on something.

Kerresha bowed her head and stared at her hands, which were perched on top of her bump. She rolled her lips between her teeth, barricading words inside herself. Made me wonder if she'd been assaulted. Or maybe the baby's daddy was married. In a small town like Fork City, such a scandal would be hard to outlive.

"Ooh wee!" Officer McGillam exclaimed. He blinked hard.

"This is one heck of a mystery. I do believe I'm gonna need another piece of cake to settle me."

This man was as irritating as a piece of chicken stuck between your back teeth.

As though we'd practiced our three-way nonverbal communication, Marvina, Kerresha, and I gave each other something's-wrong-with-this-man glances. I got up to cut him another chunk of cake.

I listened as Marvina asked more questions about Kerresha's family, and Officer McGillam inquired about her age and job status. I wanted to give him the benefit of the doubt. Maybe he was just doing his job, making sure she wasn't underage or a threat to me and Marvina. Still, I had a sense we weren't going to get the whole story out of Kerresha so long as he was sitting there. So I searched Marvina's pantry for plastic wrap and tore off a piece. I wanted to present his last piece of cake to-go.

"Here you are, Officer," I said. I dropped the swaddled slice into his open hand and held my place standing next to his chair.

He got the message and rose to his feet. With his free hand, he pulled his belt back up over his gut. "Well, ladies. How do we want to handle this?"

Kerresha kept her head down, waiting for the verdict.

"We can take it from here," Marvina said.

"You sure?"

"Yes," I confirmed. "We got this."

He surveyed all three of our faces again. "I don't mind leaving this young lady here. But I need you both to commit to keeping an eye on her and getting her to a clinic soon. I think the job's too big for one person. But you're both doing it together, so I feel better about breaking protocol this once."

Marvina's head bobbed up and down hard as she replied eagerly, "You have our word, Officer." She raised both eyebrows at me.

"Yes. Both of us," I agreed, realizing I had just signed up to stay in Fork City for way longer than I meant to. It was one thing to open a restaurant there, another to be under the same roof with Marvina and a wayward girl.

"Fine with me." He tipped his hat. "I'll check back soon, make sure y'all three are getting along well."

"Thank you, Officer," my sister said. "I'll do my best to keep a cake on hand for when you drop by."

He grinned wide. "Ma'am, you don't have to do that."

"It'd be my pleasure."

He silently accepted her offer.

Watching them was turning my stomach.

"Alrighty then." I ambled toward the front door. Mimicking Marvina's candied tone, I added, "All's well that ends well."

"Kerresha, I'm leaving you in these ladies' care. Don't make no trouble for them, you hear?"

She wiped under her nose. Nodded submissively.

"And if you want me to go have a word with your child's father, you let Miss Marvina or Miss Rose know. If he's from around here, I can sniff him out and put some pressure on him."

Okay, now he was doing the most. He might have been an officer of the law, but he wasn't a relationship expert. And I wouldn't send no officer to go harass a young Black man when he had no business there. I opened my mouth to tell him so, but once again, Marvina butted in. "I'll be in touch if we need your help."

Officer McGillam dismissed himself properly, cradling

Marvina's cake on his way out. With the door closed and locked, my sister and I both breathed a sigh of relief.

"Thank You, Lord," she muttered.

"Amen," I found myself agreeing again.

We locked eyes for a moment as the weight of what just happened settled on our shoulders. We had both committed to caring for a pregnant girl. Together. Questions suddenly pinged through my head: Is the baby healthy? Can we all get along? Do we have enough money for this? How on earth did I let Marvina rope me into this?

I followed Marvina back to the kitchen table built for four. Kerresha sat in the same spot drawing invisible circles on her stomach. She might have been soothing herself. Or the baby.

We sat down again.

"Sweetheart, the first thing you need to do is hold your head up," I started. I lifted the girl's chin with a finger. Kerresha's pouty lips flattened. "That's better."

"Thank you for saving me from jail and for telling the officer you would watch me. But don't worry. I can find someplace else to live."

"Nonsense," I said. "I meant what I said to him. You can't just wander around the streets looking for a place to stay. Not in your condition."

Marvina put a hand on Kerresha's. The circling motion ceased. "You said you're kin to the Redmonds, right?"

"I am. On my Daddy's side."

"Who's your momma?" My sister pressed.

"Lyla."

My sister's face tightened. "Lyla Phillips?"

"Yes," Kerresha murmured. "She kicked me out already."

"For being pregnant?" I asked.

"Yes, ma'am."

I know folks used to send girls away or kick them out to force them into marriage back in the day. But it had been a long time since I heard of somebody kicking their pregnant daughter out into the wild. Even decades ago, I wondered how on earth they figured mother and baby would survive. And after all I went through with my failed pregnancies, it amazed me when people couldn't understand what a miracle it was to conceive a baby, what has to happen in just the right window of time, how many times a person can try and try and still never get to hear somebody call them "Mom." Sure wasn't something to kick somebody out over.

Marvina stood. "Sounds like the rain slacked up. Kerresha, go on out to the guesthouse, get your things, and bring them back inside."

She obeyed, slinking out of the main house with another "Thank you."

Wrong as it was, I almost wished Kerresha would run away. We'd call Officer McGillam, and he'd go out and find her and take her on to whoever might be in a better position to help her. I mean, who were we kidding? My sister and I couldn't be running all over town trying to get this girl a doctor and do all the stuff it takes most people nine months to coordinate.

Marvina and I reconvened at the window and watched through opened blinds as Kerresha walked back to the guesthouse. The front window's sheer curtains tickled my nose. Marvina's warm shoulder pressed against mine.

"Lord bless this child," Marvina prayed out loud. My sister's breath still smelled like church usher peppermint.

Her compassion toward Kerresha, while admirable and needed,

had me feeling some kind of way. Where was all this compassion when I was young and in what I thought was love with David?

"How far along you think she is?" Marvina asked.

"How would I know?"

"Sorry."

Kerresha disappeared into the guesthouse.

I asked, "You know her momma well?"

"No, and from what I understand, I don't want to."

I waited for her to expound. When she didn't, I prodded, "Go on."

"It's not for me to repeat gossip about people."

"You've already crossed the slander border. Spill it."

Marvina poked out her bottom lip and shook her head. "They call her momma Lying Lyla." She whispered it like an old cowboy telling a tall tale around a fire pit.

I giggled. "I could think of worse things to be called, I suppose."

"She ain't the average liar. She's malicious. Mean-minded. And a thief, too. Lyla's the kind of person who'll steal from you and then go help you look for whatever she already stole, knowing the whole time you ain't gonna find it 'cause it's in her back pocket."

I jerked my head back and side-eyed her. "Did that actually happen, Marvina?"

"I told you it was gossip."

I clicked the inside of my cheek and turned again to find Kerresha returning across the wet lawn with a suitcase and a purse. Good thing her luggage was hard plastic.

"Even if the lying and stealing part is true," I reasoned, "that doesn't mean she kicked her own child out. Might be mother-daughter drama."

"Perhaps."

"Only one way to find out. I say we go talk to Miss Lying Lyla herself."

"You think? What we gonna say?"

"I'm sure you'll think of something holy and friendly." My voice dripped with sarcasm. "She'll be back living in her mother's home in no time, with you doing the talking."

"I'll take that as a compliment," Marvina chirped. "But what if it doesn't work?"

"I guess you will have to—"

"*We* will have to," she demanded the correction.

"I don't live in Fork City. I have a whole household in Dallas, two hours away. I came here for a recipe and got stuck here because of the weather, and now this child. I don't mind helping, but I can't just abandon my home for two, three, four months."

"You sure can't leave me here with her all by myself, either. I don't want you here any longer than you have to be, but there ain't no rush now that we're in this deal with Officer McGillam. This ain't no time for you to be a deadbeat sister. Again."

I gasped, "Deadbeat? *Again*?"

Kerresha dragged her suitcase up the steps, now.

"Absent. Estranged. Not present. Whatever you want to call it." The words erupted from her mouth like a geyser. She turned from me and opened the door.

"Marvina! I—"

A flicker of despair darted across Marvina's face, so deep and so intense my insides twisted painfully in response to her pain. The dagger in her glare cut my coherent thoughts to pieces.

Marvina quickly pushed the screen back to let Kerresha inside. "Come on, sugar." She took the handle of Kerresha's bag, and they moved toward another hallway in the house, a hallway I had never traversed, seeing as there was a whole other half of Marvina's house I'd never set foot on because I'd been seated in the open-space rooms the few times I visited her.

And apparently there was also a whole other side to Marvina I didn't know, either.

She threw words at me over her shoulder. "It'll take me a while to get her settled. You can go ahead and take your pain pill. And go to sleep."

They left me standing in the living room at a loss for words. If anyone had asked me three days earlier if I loved my sister, I would have said, "Yes. From a distance." And the reason I still loved her was because I *used* to love her fiercely. That sopping wet Sunday, though, her painful scowl confessed that her love for me had been equally as fierce. A long time ago.

It had been three days since I arrived. Three days was supposed to be my limit. But I had the feeling it was just the beginning.

CHAPTER 10
Rose

After Marvina called around town a bit Sunday evening, we got a better idea of what we were dealing with. Lyla had quite the reputation for how she mistreated the general public, but there was no consensus about who she was as a mother.

So we packed up Kerresha and headed out Monday morning to see if we could bring this situation to a close.

All the way over, Marvina darn near buried her face in the visor mirror, nervously tugging at her wig. I recognized the move. She was trying to make sure her left eye was covered by at least a few tendrils of hair, in the unlikely chance that someone might spot her disability.

That someone, in this case, would potentially be Kerresha's mother. Why Marvina cared what Lying Lyla thought of her was beyond me. I mean, we were not young anymore. By this point in life, every woman had something—wrinkles, varicose veins, thicker toenails—*some* kind of souvenir to show for all her trips around the sun.

"Stop all that primping," I told my sister. "You look fine."

"Leave me alone, please."

I ignored her.

"Kerresha, is this the right street?"

"Yes. Third house on the left."

Well, it wasn't actually a house. Not in the traditional wood and bricks sense. It was a small, sinking mobile home with a bowed skirt, as though the trailer had gotten tired and squatted down in the dirt.

The mailbox was missing a number between the third and fourth digit. No telling how many envelopes and packages got returned to senders on account of this negligence.

Someone had put a huge orange ceramic pot containing a cactus in front of the drain, presumably to cover the hole that still peeked around the pot anyway. And a sour smell permeated the air, like there was a habit of pouring out bad food right outside the front door.

This shed a whole lotta light on Kerresha's bleak living options. Marvina's guesthouse didn't seem so bad compared to this. Tiny as that trailer was, there might not have been space for anybody to sleep without rolling over on the baby. This sight put a leash on my judgments about Lyla.

Except for the stealing concept that Marvina planted in my head.

My tires crunched the rocks leading up to the wooden boards arranged as a staircase. Once parked, Marvina and I unclicked our seat belts. An orange and white striped cat scurried under the trailer's skirt. I hoped that cat devoured all other smaller critters in the vicinity.

Kerresha did not move.

"You ready?" I asked her.

"I told y'all. She's not going to let me back in."

Marvina nearly sang, "Don't be so pessimistic."

I glanced up at the rearview mirror and caught Kerresha rolling her eyes slightly. I felt her pain. Marvina could be irritatingly merry.

This child knew her mother. We didn't need optimism. We needed real talk. And maybe some good old-fashioned guilt to get this woman to take her child back in.

"How many kids does your mother have?" I asked.

"Three. I'm the baby."

"Okay."

Marvina's expression drew a question mark.

I ignored her. Opened my car door. "Let's do this."

She led the way. I stayed one step behind, holding on to the wobbly rails. I imagined the unsteady planks sliding and me falling on top of the cactus, piercing myself to death. *Should we even be here?* From the looks of things, Kerresha was better off with us. Still. A girl needs her mother in times like these.

Marvina knocked on the side of the metal screen frame. We stood in the chilly breeze waiting for an answer that didn't come.

So I opened the screen door and slammed on the door of the trailer like the police.

"Who is it?" a woman's voice yelled from inside the structure, loud and indignant.

I answered, "It's Rose and Marvina."

"I don't know no Rose and Marvina! Whatchu want?" The voice drew closer.

"We'd like to visit with you. We have your daughter, Kerresha," Marvina said in the same way I imagined social workers requested a mandatory interview.

"You can keep her."

Marvina's eyes grew wide. She hadn't expected that answer.

My sister, my sister, my sister. First of all, no one says "visit with you" anymore. Secondly, she wasn't used to folk back-talking her, I suspect because she never had a job, so far as I knew. Not just any job, one where you have to regularly interact with unstable public citizens.

Me, on the other hand? I'd been cussed all the way up and down and darn near threatened over Christmas packages delivered late, running out of Elvis stamps, and the rising cost of stamps themselves. As though I pushed the red button to raise the rates. After thirty years at the post office, I knew how to handle unreasonable people.

"Lyla, we need to talk to you about yo' child," I stated sharply, with authority I didn't actually possess.

Locks twisted and popped. The door swung open. Red-rimmed eyes and bruises covering her arms told me the rest of the story. She had been, I suspect, a beautiful woman once. Hazel eyes, high cheekbones, and a long neck. Kerresha took her good looks from her mother.

But Lyla was hooked on something potent now. There could be no reasoning with her. "Come on. Marvina, let's go." I pivoted to leave. A bad move, given my knee.

"Naaah. Uh-uh. You got me up out of bed, you have to give me something for my time, now."

"What?" Marvina asked.

Lyla held out hand. "Cash."

The trailer creaked in resistance to a sudden gust of wind.

I sucked my teeth at her. "Uh, I don't think so. *We're* taking care of *your* child, not the other way around. You got us messed up."

Lyla snarled at me.

I did not veer from her eyes. I hold a tenth-degree black belt in the staring game.

She finally broke our staring match and asked, "Why are you here?"

"Because Kerresha is pregnant, and she needs prenatal care," Marvina said. "Also because she's currently homeless."

"And? She's nineteen. She can figure it out. She's gonna have to. When you get yourself involved with grown-up activities, you become a grown-up in my book. There's only one woman shaking the sheets with a man in *this* house, and it's me."

Marvina softened her voice even more. "We understand she made a mistake, Lyla. Life as she knows it will come to an end in a matter of weeks. A lotta pressure. Stress. Responsibility. But this child's gonna be your grandbaby. Don't that mean somethin' to you?"

"Nope. Don't mean nothin' to me but another mouth to feed. Look around." She flicked her hand in the air. "I can't afford more food, clothes, electricity, water."

Yet, from the smell of her breath, she seemed perfectly capable of purchasing items in the alcohol category.

I tried not to judge, because I know sometimes people use alcohol and drugs to self-medicate. The way this country got our systems set up, it's easier to get cannabis than a counselor. So, judgment? No. Not on that part. But guilt? Yes. Plenty, on the Momma-carin' part. "Now, you know good and well this child needs her mother right now more than ever. You kickin' out your baby girl in her greatest time of need? That's cold as ice, Lyla."

She put her raggedy, chip-nailed finger in my face. "Listen. You keep my name out your mouth!"

I don't take kindly to people invading my personal space. "Get your sorry finger out of my face!" I raised my arm to push hers away.

Marvina grabbed my wrist. "Both of y'all stop it. We came here in peace, trying to get a solution."

A rooster crowed in the distance, calling an end to our verbal boxing round.

Lyla backed down. I retracted my claws and let my sister speak for the both of us again.

"We don't mind working with you to see to it Kerresha has what she needs starting off as a new mother. She's a sweet girl. She needs support."

Lyla's face fell slack. Her eyes watered. Her lower lip wavered. "I know she needs help. And I know she's a sweet girl. Quiet, too. Not sure where she got that kind spirit. Skipped a generation, I guess. But I'm in no state to give her or a baby anything right now."

For somebody known for lying, Lyla spoke her painful truth that day.

"Where is the child's daddy?" I asked. "You think his family would be willing to take Kerresha in?"

"I didn't even know Kerresha had a boyfriend, let alone where he might be now. She said he's in college. I think she's holding out for him to come back to her, but knowing men, he's moved on with his life, probably."

"Well, who's taking care of her? Who's paying her cell phone bill?" I asked, hoping for the name of someone who could take the girl in. Maybe Kerresha's paternal side.

"She pays the bill, when she can. It's pay-as-you-go."

I believed her. Kerresha wasn't one of those glued-to-the-phone kids. Not once had she totally occupied herself with her cell phone screen the way I'd seen most people her age, so engrossed they'd accidentally step in front of a speeding train.

Marvina sighed. "Understood. I'm going to leave you my number." She wrote her name and number on the back of a receipt plucked from her purse and gave it to Lyla.

Lyla tucked the slip of paper into her bra. She blinked back her tears. "Thank you." With that, she went back into her trailer and closed the door behind her.

"Well. That's that," Marvina declared. She turned on her heels and headed down the steps and to the passenger's side of the car again.

I proceeded down the shaky steps, careful of my knee.

I still had unanswered questions. *What about Kerresha's father? Grandparents? Where are her older siblings?* I couldn't imagine... Well, yes I could. When I thought about what happened between me and Momma, what happened between me and Marvina, I didn't have to imagine because I knew what it meant to disconnect from a family member. Different circumstances, same result.

We rode back to Marvina's in silence. I'm sure Kerresha heard the whole conversation through the windows. She didn't ask any questions, and neither did we. The whole thing was too sad to discuss.

Thankfully, the food rescued our minds. We returned to Marvina's home and sat down at the table to eat more of Sunday's after-church roast for Monday's lunch. By then, all the ingredients had melded into one another real good, the taste of every bite consistent with the one before it. And Momma's seasoning added the perfect flavor to it all.

"This is really good," Kerresha complimented.

Marvina and I both said, "You're welcome," at the same time.

"Oh. Y'all cooked it together?"

"You could say that," Marvina credited properly.

Kerresha shoveled the food into her mouth. It felt good to watch her eat, to know she was nourishing herself and the baby inside this nice, warm house instead of the place where she'd come from. The trailer. A day like today, where a cold front came through in the middle of the morning, must make a tiny mobile home feel like a walk-in freezer.

Marvina let out a light tee-hee. "You're definitely making sure the baby will have some meat on its bones! We'd better go ahead and set an appointment at the clinic," Marvina said.

Goodness gracious. This was really happening.

Kerresha swallowed. "I'll call tomorrow."

"Find out how much it costs," my sister added.

"I will. And I can pay for it."

"Where are you getting money?" I asked point-blank. I didn't appreciate Officer McGillam asking nosy questions because he was an outsider looking in. But now I had a dog in the fight, so to speak.

"I was in a program when I was in school. It was like a research grant study to see if money motivated student performance. They credited us money for perfect attendance, good grades, involvement in other programs. Counseling, too. When we graduated, they gave us all the money we'd earned along the way."

"Oh! That was nice," Marvina said.

A flicker of pride crossed Kerresha's face. "I made the second-highest amount."

"You must be one smart cookie," I affirmed.

"Thank you. I'm sorry my mother was so rude to y'all."

"No need to apologize for her," I said. "We're not responsible for what our parents do. They're not perfect people."

My sister raised an eyebrow at me. I was walking a fine line, and she wanted to shove me over to the safe side to protect her charmed memories of Momma.

"Well, it's the truth. Parents are prone to failure," I reiterated. "You and I know this better than anyone."

Marvina glared at me. "No one is perfect. Not mothers. Not *daughters*, either."

"I never claimed to be perfect. I made a mistake."

"No. A mistake is when you act without realizing those actions will have negative consequences as result. That's different from a lapse in judgment." She didn't mince words. The way she sounded all calm and collected while criticizing me—classic Momma move.

"Do you get a pass for being young? Naive? Inexperienced?"

Kerresha's spoon clacked against her bowl. "Ummm… Are we talking about me or one of y'all?"

"These are general understandings," Marvina deflected in a soothing manner.

"I call BS," Kerresha said. Her eyes darted between Marvina and I. "No disrespect."

I'm sure Marvina was fixing to express her disapproval of the term BS, but I swallowed my food a second faster and spoke. "You're right to call it, Kerresha, because she's definitely talking about me," I spouted off.

"You had a baby at my age, too?" Kerresha asked. Her eyes searched for compassion in mine.

"No. I never had a baby."

"Oh." Her gaze fell to her bowl of roast. Thankfully, she had the good graces to refrain from asking me why.

We kept eating.

"Sssss," Kerresha said, wincing. She shifted her weight and then I heard a slight thump.

"You all right?" Marvina asked.

"It's my feet. My shoes are too tight."

Immediately, my sister and I jumped to her side.

"Let us see," I ordered.

Kerresha turned her body toward us and extended her legs. My sister pried off the left shoe, me the right. Out popped plump, fluid-filled feet with fiery red indentations from her shoes. Fattened toes like hers must have been the inspiration for the *Ten Little Piggies* nursery rhyme.

"You need to be lying down and elevating your feet," I screeched. "Come on."

Marvina went straight into action, leading us all to what would be Kerresha's room for an indefinite amount of time.

As we helped her get situated in bed with strategically placed pillows, we peppered her with questions.

Do you hear from the baby's father? No.

What about your siblings? Yes. On and off.

Do your feet swell often? No.

Are you drinking enough water? How much is enough?

"Didn't that book you're reading help you?" I fussed.

"Yes, but—"

"The book should have told you to put your feet up," Marvina badgered, too. "Don't let your feet get this puffy again, you hear?"

"Yes, ma'am." Kerresha leaned back onto the bed while Marvina and I fussed at her and over her.

"You have to stay ahead of swelling," I informed her. Young folk don't know nothing about that, for the most part. "Be sure and tell the doctor about this when you see 'em."

Marvina turned her inquiry to me now. "Speaking of doctors and swelling, have you taken your medicine today, Rose?"

I didn't know she was monitoring me. I stammered, "N-no."

"You need to be taking care of yourself, too."

"I couldn't take it this morning. It makes me sleepy. We had stuff to do."

"While you're sitting there fussing at her, you need to be worrying about your own circulation. Go take it now. I'll clean up the kitchen."

Her pinched expression was both irritating and comforting. In the great tradition of women all over the world, wrong or right, worrying over somebody and fussing at them in that urgent, annoyed way is a universal sign of caring.

So I didn't push back. I left her to finish tending to Kerresha while I went to take my pill and lie in bed because it was only a matter of minutes before the drowsiness began.

Before my lids got heavy, I returned a generic text from David. He'd asked how things were going.

Not coming back to Dallas anytime soon. Marvina and I have to care for a girl. Pregnant.

David replied with a string of question marks. His name popped up on my screen as a caller before I could finish responding in writing.

"Hello?"

"What's going on, Rose? Are you hallucinating from your medicine?"

"I'm sleepy, not seeing things."

"But you said you were pregnant."

"I'm not pregnant. The *girl* is pregnant."

"What girl?"

"Listen," I began, and then I told him the whole story—the church Allies situation, the city's projected growth, Kerresha and the police officer, the discovery that Marvina was actually furious with me, Kerresha's mother. Took nearly ten minutes to catch him up to speed. "It's weird. I'm mad at Marvina about the forty dollars, which she doesn't care about anymore. But then she's mad at me for being a quote, 'deadbeat sister,' and I have no idea how she came to that conclusion."

"Did you ask her?"

"I keep trying, but it's like whenever we talk, both our tempers spike, and we just start going around and around in this argument-vortex. I think we both come out dizzy and even more confused than we were before we started talking."

"Rose." He paused for effect. "Did you get the recipe for the seasoning?"

His point-blank question made me remember why we married and why we split. On one hand, David's laser-sharp focus on what mattered most helped us prioritize. When it was time to save money for a large purchase, he axed all frivolous spending and made a plan with a timeline. We clipped coupons and took our lunches to work for months in order to take a cruise for our fifth anniversary.

On the other hand, once David said, "I'm sorry," for cheating and promised to try and stay faithful in the future. He honestly believed I should get over his philandering. Like those two words had the power to erase the past, to reset the balance to zero so we could start fresh.

He was real logical like that. Made sense for him to wonder how all this other mayhem took place when I embarked on the trip to Fork City for one reason alone.

"No. I have not gotten the recipe from Marvina yet. I told you, we've gotten ourselves into a guardianship arrangement with the police. I'm going to be here longer than I expected."

"Do you really think the officer will haul the girl away from Marvina if you leave? She's not a minor."

He sounded irritated.

"You all right?" I asked.

"Yes. I'm just trying to understand what's taking you so long to get the recipe and come back to Dallas." His voice reeked of concern.

I ventured, "David, is there something wrong?"

"No," he said, though the pitch of his voice contradicted his words. He finally confessed, "I'm worried about you. You're not usually gone out of town this long."

"Are you saying you miss me?" I asked incredulously.

"Guess so."

"You must be real single right now. All the times you've gone on a vacation or to a resort or to spend the holiday with your lady friends have been for far more days than this. You got some nerve to call yourself missing me."

"Is it a crime?"

"Yes. It's a bona fide crime—a felony, I think—to claim you miss somebody who's been gone for three days when you don't so much as send a text when you're gone for weeks sometimes when you're boo'd up."

"Do I detect jealousy in your voice?" he teased.

"Clean the wax out of your ears, David. There's no jealousy here. I'm just setting the record straight."

"Could have fooled me."

"You're fooling yourself. On purpose."

He chuckled.

I held back my giggle, lest he think I didn't mean what I said.

"Can you go get the mail from my house and keep it until I return?"

"I can, and I will."

"Thank you."

"You're welcome. And I hope you find what you're looking for in Fork City. However long it takes. I'll be here when you get back. Good night."

"Night."

I held no expectation of him holding up a banner to greet me upon my return, but I was too sleepy to argue with him. And my spirit was already tired from arguing with Marvina the past three days. When would it end?

A few weeks ago, my life had so little drama. I had a job, a quiet life, and an ex-husband who only occasionally, casually, tried to strike up the old flame again while he was between girlfriends.

Now I was laid up with a throbbing knee in Marvina's bedroom, with joint custody of a teenage pregnant girl, and David nursing new visions of an epic reunion.

The meds kicked in, sending me to the space between reality and dreamland. *Is this really my life?* Part of me wanted to wake up from it. But for real for real, a part of me was glad for the push and pull of human connection again.

Momma used to say it's not all-or-nothing in a relationship. You gotta leave room for people to be human beings.

Too bad she didn't apply that wisdom toward me.

CHAPTER 11
Rose

My sister sat at the kitchen table. From where I stood at the stove, I noticed she was starting on her third book since I got to town. The cover of this one showed a man and a woman holding hands, walking through a park. Another romance.

Marvina had already fixed herself a plate for breakfast. Extra bacon, eggs, and cinnamon toast lingered on a platter, presumably for me and Kerresha.

"Thank you for cooking breakfast."

She grunted in the I'm-busy-reading way.

I made a little saucer of food, poured a glass of juice, and joined her at the table.

Kerresha wasn't up yet, I gathered. She probably needed the rest. I heard people tell expectant mothers to get as much rest as possible before the baby arrived. The elders are also advised to sleep whenever the baby sleeps. Truth be told, I never understood either concept. Sleep can't be banked, and babies woke up every few hours, I was told. How could an adult survive on such a schedule?

There was so much I didn't know about babies, and so much

I avoided knowing because it hurt too much to think about their wrinkled toes, jelly rolls, and heavenly fresh scent.

I shifted my mentals back to Marvina. "What are you doing today?"

She waved her novel. Figures. When she wasn't at church, Marvina had her nose tucked between the pages of a book.

"They still got the Tuesday senior discount at Jefferson's General Store? I need a few odds and ends. My travel-size toiletries are running low."

"Jefferson's closed."

"What? When?"

"A few years back." She didn't look up from her book.

"Pixie's still here?"

"Thank the Lord, yes. I don't know where I'd get my paprika without them. We got a Dollar House now. Over where the Piggly Wiggly used to be. No discount on any day of the week."

"Huh." I chewed my toast, considering this news. It was one thing for Piggly Wiggly to close. If old Jefferson's General Store was gone, replaced by a national franchise, the town's flavor truly was changing. Might be good for businesses, but I had to admit to myself: I felt some kind of way about the store's closing, the opportunity to physically relive the nostalgia fading away like old ink on thin paper, so illegible it couldn't be delivered or returned.

Growing up, my mother used to take us to Jefferson's for everything from school supplies to fabric for making our dolls' clothes. She refused to purchase manufactured clothing for a doll; it didn't make sense to her to spend good, real money on accessories for a fake doll. But she did see how letting us design, cut patterns, glue, hand-sew, and embellish outfits for them sparked our creativity.

The memory brought a smile to my face. "You remember when Momma used to buy us fabric scraps to make clothes for our dolls?"

"Yes." Marvina looked up from her book, now. "We had the best-dressed dolls." She gave a tender smile, then returned her attention to the book again.

"I wonder if Momma knew how empowering that was for us."

"Of course she knew," Marvina said. "I'm surprised to hear you give her credit for doing something right."

Good Lord, I did not have the energy to argue with Marvina that morning. I filled my mouth with more toast, chewing on what she'd said. The fact that my sister and I were sitting there in our right minds could be construed as a testament to our good parenting.

In college, I heard horror stories about the things other people's parents had done to them. Beatings, violations, abandonments, and neglect. My freshman-year roommate, bless her heart, spent her leftover grant money on a cheap motel so she wouldn't have to go home over the holidays. She also spent a lot on marijuana, which is where I first realized some people use illegal drugs to keep from falling apart.

I didn't want to go home on most breaks, myself, but that was because, after months of college freedom, I didn't want to follow the rules or answer questions regarding my whereabouts at home. *Who you goin' with? What time you comin' home?* Regular parental pestering, but nothing I'd want to use *my* money to avoid.

My parents were not monsters. Momma and Daddy loved us. They had rules. They set boundaries. They rewarded us when we met the expectations. My biggest misgivings centered on how things went down when we fell short of the expectations.

"You don't think I loved Momma, too?" I asked Marvina,

hoping she wouldn't get all huffy like she'd done the night before when Kerresha was sitting at the table.

"I suppose you did. In your own fashion. But you had a funny way of showing it."

"What do you mean by that?" I pressed for answers I felt I deserved.

She laid her book flat on the table. Looked me square in the eyes. For some reason, I noticed her pores in that pose. Wide, shiny, pulling downward on her cheeks. Just like mine.

"You do realize you broke Momma's heart when you married David, right?"

"What was I supposed to do, Marvina? I was scared. And pregnant. And in love, according to my definition of love back then."

"In love with a married man," she jabbed.

That old rush of shame flooded over me instantly. I could feel the cortisol flowing and my stress level rising with this resurrected accusation. "He was not married when I got pregnant. Or when I married him."

"But he was when you *met* him."

"He was separated."

Marvina folded her hands under her ample bosom. "Still legally married. And everybody in town knew it, because his first wife's mother lived right over there in Daisy Falls. Momma could barely hold her head up at the regional church meetings. Folks whisperin' about her daughter behind her back. Saying you were a home-wrecker."

"Who said I was a home-wrecker—Momma or the church folk?"

"Both. And that's when Momma's health problems started."

"You blame me for Momma getting sick?"

"Put two and two together."

"That's not fair. Big Momma also had heart problems. Heredity plays a part in health. Lack of exercise. Environment, too. She perfected her seasoning with a whole lotta fried chicken, remember? So you can't pin Momma's health issues on me."

"Not entirely, but I can say without a doubt that her first emergency room visit occurred the day after you became Mrs. David Tillman."

This new information gave me pause. Then suspicion. "That doesn't sound right. Momma went to the emergency room once before. When I was in second grade. I remember it because Sister Higgens came and picked me up from school. You were with her. She said Momma had passed out from heat exhaustion and she was dehydrated. Sister Higgens took both of us home with her, and we stayed there until Daddy picked us up later that night."

"I don't remember that."

"You were in preschool. Of course you don't remember."

Marvina smacked her lips. "That's beside the point."

"No. That *is* the point. Momma…or you…or somebody is always trying to rewrite history and paint me as the villain."

"I'm only repeating what Momma told me."

I stopped short of calling our mother a liar. Marvina wouldn't stand for it, and I was raised to respect my elders at all times. I chose my words carefully. "I'm saying it seems like we have different memories about things. About Momma."

Marvina picked up her book again.

It took everything in me not to go there with Marvina. She was one of those black-and-white people. Once she made up her mind about right and wrong, that was it. And I was one of those people who always had to have the last word. I had no idea how we could move past our personality clashes. I only knew I didn't have it in me that morning to deal with her.

Maybe another day, but not then. Not with Kerresha in the house, and not coming off another pain pill a few hours earlier.

I finished my breakfast and left the house.

Instead of heading straight to Dollar House, I took a detour through my childhood neighborhood. Literally. Crossing the railroad tracks in Fork City, going from the east side of the city to the far west, a person might think they had entered another country altogether. Rougher, narrower streets. Rusty clunkers parked on lawns. Paint peeling from wood-framed houses. A stray dog searched for food in the gutter. Everything seemed so much smaller. And dirty.

When redlining confined Black folks to one section of town, we took a lot of pride in our neighborhood. Well, as much as we could. I remember Momma saying it was a challenge to keep the air clean when the city only sent the trash truck to the Black neighborhood once every two weeks, instead of once weekly like the white side of town. We also had to contend with frequent flooding, as the designated Black section of town came with the worst drainage system. City managers paid our complaints no mind.

But our parents and the other ones in the area made it a point to remain dignified despite the practices of that time. That's how I remembered my old neighborhood and my childhood home. Flowers and plants in front yards, men mowing the grass on weekends, dogs contained by intact fences. Proud, clean, and as well-kept as possible.

There was no glory left in the streets and run-down homes I passed by this morning. When I finally reached Momma's house, I parked across the street from the front door and evaluated the structure objectively. For a 1,300-square-foot house, the front seemed wider than I remembered, boasting four wide sets of windows, including bay windows for the kitchen. The roof sat low, in line with the homes of that decade. The bottom few feet, all the way around, was brick, while wood paneling comprised the majority of the exterior. Painted dark blue with light blue complementing the windows.

The yard had bald spots. Probably from abandoned cars sitting for months or years at a time. It's not how Momma would have kept it up. Then again, tenants were not beholden to the property. Thus, the "For Rent" sign in the middle of the yard, because the current occupant was moving out in a few days. Marvina took care of all that business.

The home's door itself had been upgraded a few months back. I knew this because, when Marvina sent me my portion of the rent income, she'd deducted half the cost of the new door from my cut. She also sent me the names and contact information anytime we got new tenants so that if something happened to her, I would know what the agreement was for rent and such.

I had no doubt there was a ledger somewhere showing exactly what had come in from the rental, the taxes and insurance, the repairs. Left up to me, I would have sold the house a long time ago. It's enough for me to keep up with my own finances, let alone another house and all the hassles that come with being a landlord.

Marvina was the "take care of business" type, which was how I knew she would have made a great business partner.

The new and improved front door of the house opened, and two children—a boy and a girl—came rushing out, racing to the mini-SUV parked under the carport. They were dressed up for something special, apparently, him in a suit and her in a poofy dress. *Christmas party? Award ceremony at school?*

Out came the mother, toting a baby carrier. Behind her, I saw into the hallways of the house and noted the brown boxes, packed for moving.

The screen door slammed, and I focused on the people again. The infant's tiny feet kicked frantically at the bottom of the pink blanket covering the carrier. I laughed, thinking to myself, "Somebody does not like that blanket!"

It was good to see the house still providing shelter for another family, but I don't think Momma would have approved of a single mother moving into her house. The only thing she would approve of is marriage, followed by children, 'til death did them part. No way she would have allowed Olivia Villegas and her three babies to move in six months ago, not without a husband to ensure the bills got paid.

Momma was old-school like that. She couldn't imagine a woman who didn't want a husband.

After strapping in all the kids, Olivia returned to the driver's door. She spotted me and paused for a moment. This was, after all, Fork City. Why would a strange woman be sitting in a parked car across from your home watching you and your children get in your vehicle unless she was some kind of stalker?

I gave a little wave, then held my phone to my ear and drove away, trying to create the illusion that I had been lost and pulled over to call someone for help. I drove down the street and waited for her to leave. When the coast was clear, I parked right in front of Momma's house this time.

Part of me wanted to go inside. To see if the wall inside the second bedroom still showed where Momma had marked off mine and Marvina's height every year on our birthdays.

Another part of me never wanted to go in the house again, in order to keep a vow I made to myself. When I thought of the bad days, I felt like this house could go, for all I cared. Were it not for our memories of cooking in the kitchen and dancing in the living room with Daddy... Well, there were more good memories than what came to mind at the moment. It was hard to convince myself one way or the other about my own feelings.

But the bad memories definitely made me want to sell and move on.

I opened the internet on my phone and looked up the property value of Momma's house. A nice, round number appeared on the screen. I couldn't imagine anyone paying that much for the structure. It was a step up from the surrounding homes, thanks to Marvina's resourcefulness, but one day it would be too much to maintain. If we sold now, we could have what I needed to start the business strong.

I doubted Marvina would see things my way.

I found what I needed at Dollar House. More lotion. Mouthwash. A nail file. With the buying power of a national chain, prices were comparatively lower than I remember them at Jefferson's. My wallet welcomed the switch, but my soul moaned sadly.

At the old store, the better-known brands sat on the right side of the shopping floor while the left side boasted locally made treats. Fresh canned preserves, handmade candles, specially for-mulated soaps, all bearing labels with family names I recognized from the teacher taking attendance in grade school. Whitehead, Smitherson, Farnsworth.

This new Dollar House had no character. Aisle after aisle of stuff made overseas. Socks…wait, socks? I needed some socks in Marvina's cool house. Especially at night.

I grabbed a pack of multicolored footies and rolled my basket to the checkout line. Lo and behold, I recognized the face on the other side of the scratched-up plexiglass.

"Earl? Earl Henderson?" I asked, narrowing my eyes to be sure of what I was seeing. Was this the same person who, circa 1978, cheated off my *Romeo and Juliet* test and got us both kicked out of the honors program?

"Yes, ma'am. The one and—" he stopped mid-cliché. "Well, I'll be. That you, Rose Dewberry?"

"Sure as the sun rises," I sang, glad to see an old acquaintance in this new store, even if he had negatively impacted my GPA. I didn't like *Romeo and Juliet* and all the stuffy old books we read in that class, anyway.

Earl stood up straighter, adding a few inches to his height, and smiled widely. I could see some of his side teeth were missing. My heart went out to him because, according to my personal theory: people with missing side teeth have lived a hard life. Front teeth are easily lost in accidents. Back teeth suffer by virtue of their placement in the mouth. But side teeth… You gotta miss a whole lot of dentist appointments to lose a side tooth.

Earl was one of those who had dropped out of school to start working to feed his younger brothers and sisters. A lot of the boys in my class made the same sacrifice. As soon as they could read and write well enough to get a basic job, they went from book reports to pulling levers in a factory overnight.

"You sure lookin' good, girl. You remarried?" He wasted no time.

"Just in town staying with my sister for a little while," I laughed.

"And no, I'm not remarried. Not looking to be married, either." I sat my items on the counter.

He swiped the toothpaste and stopped. He stepped from behind the clear barrier and leaned on the counter, bringing his face a few inches closer to mine. "Now why would you go and say a thing like that, Rose? A beautiful woman like you?"

"I'm sure you say that to all the women with five items or more."

He hooted. "You still sassy as ever!" He continued scanning my things.

Despite the fact he cheated off my test because he didn't have time to study, I remember Earl as smart, funny, and kind. He was the type of wholesome boy my mother would have wanted me to date, which immediately excluded him from my list of desired dates.

We made small talk. He asked about Marvina, I asked about his younger sister, Faye, who was the first Black majorette at Fork City high school. Everybody on our side of the tracks adored her. She probably got what she needed to try out and sustain her drill team career because Earl and the older working siblings brought money into their household.

Unlike most folks in Fork City, Marvina and I belonged to a small family. Our father was an only child, and our mother had only one brother, our late Uncle Cleo. Momma and Daddy were quiet, honest people. Daddy worked as much as he could; Momma raised us on the church pews by herself, for the most part.

Standing in Dollar House across from my old classmate, who looked ten years my senior, made me grateful. The lines deeply etched in his face, the cracked and dry hands, the sunken eyes confirmed my theory about his life's trajectory.

"Faye's good. She had a close call with her diabetes last year, but she pulled through, thank the Lord. You in Dallas, or was it Houston?"

"Dallas." It figures he knew my whereabouts. Word gets around a small town.

"They got any jobs up that way for an old fellow like me?"

"I have no idea," I said. "I just retired from the post office." The second I said the words, I regretted them. There he was probably working for minimum wage, at our age. I hoped he didn't think I was bragging.

"That so!" he piped up and gave a genuine, "Congratulations!"

I sighed. "Thank you."

He hung his head as he rang up the last few items. "I thought I'd be retired by now, but the way this economy is going, I don't see myself resting until the day I die. Cost of living is getting higher and higher and won't get no better once the expressway comes through here."

"That so?" I slipped into my native country dialect. Earl's position at this store likely put him in the know. Maybe even more than Pastor Pendleton. "You think Fork City's on the move?"

He muttered something that had a "shhh" sound in it. "I hear we're getting that fancy coffee shop. What is it—Starburst?"

"Starbucks," I corrected him gently. "What about the property values in our old neighborhood? Anybody making offers?"

He shook his head. "Got to wait and see. If so, I won't take the first offer. I'm gonna hold out until the last second and get the most for my momma's house!"

I didn't have the heart to tell him that's not exactly how it goes down. I'd seen the change-of-address requests and the certified letters going back and forth during a land takeover. When the first people sold their homes, the business venturers waited, strategically, and let their newly purchased properties rot in place. The vacant, untended houses brought in rats and stray cats and squatters. City services, in cahoots with the progressive investors, stopped tending to that section of town as earnestly because it had "fewer occupants." Eventually, conditions got to the point where the remaining homeowners could hardly stand living in their beloved neighborhood anymore. And that's the whole truth, from the post office point of view.

I winked at Earl. "Hope that plan to stay until the end works out well for you."

"Don't go winkin' and playin' with me, woman."

Flattered but not wavering, I shooed his flirtatious comment away.

"I know one thing. Investors been buying up a lot of the abandoned buildings just south of downtown. By the old skating rink. They must know something about the plans that we don't."

He read my total and waited for me to insert my credit card to complete the transaction.

The swiping machine was a good foot away from where I expected it to be, which sent my eyes searching. In that process, I spotted the funniest baby bib. It read: *Eat. Poop. Sleep. Repeat.*

Marvina probably wouldn't have approved, but it made me giggle. I grabbed the green cloth with white embroidery and asked, "Earl, can you add this to my total?"

"Sure thing. Somebody expecting?"

"Yes. You may know her. Kerresha. She's kin to the Redmonds."

His brows furrowed. "Don't ring no bells."

A new total popped on the screen. I did my part, and Earl finished bagging my items.

"Thank you, Earl. You take it easy, okay?"

"You do the same, Rose. Good seeing you, you hear?"

"Right back atcha."

I took the route past the old skating rink. Sure enough, the signs pointing to suburbanization hung behind the windows. It would not be long before this area paralleled any shopping center in the greater Dallas metro area. Places where you'd find a massage parlor, gourmet ice cream, a bookstore, and a smell-good store with soaps, lotions, and candles, all right next to each other.

I wrote down the developers' phone numbers, because I knew very well that, somewhere in the middle of all that shopping, people needed a good meal. That good meal could come from me and Marvina, laced with Momma's good seasoning. This time, this town, this opportunity was ripe for the picking.

CHAPTER 12
Rose

Earl was right about the hottest area for growth. It was easy enough to confirm his hunch when I clicked and scrolled through the city council meeting minutes online. Everything was right there in black and white—the investors, the zones, the plans, the timeline. The major developers and their brokers were listed as well, and I made two phone calls to Realtors, inquiring about a property I saw a block away from the projected busiest area of town. I left messages with both, because once the new gas station broke ground, Fork City would be more than a dot on the map, and everyone holding property or a business license stood to gain.

Pastor Pendleton must have known this, too, because he asked Marvina to clear out the kitchen in preparation for a renovation. "He said we're going to rent out the church for weddings and such," she told me one evening as we shared cleaning responsibilities in her home.

Marvina liked the smell of chemicals, so she cleaned the bathrooms. I liked to dust and vacuum. Something about clearing a wet path through light dust and making triangles on the carpet with the machine always satisfied me. It made sense to divvy up the work, since there was more to clean with me and Kerresha staying there.

The child tried to help, too, but we limited her cleaning to her own bedroom. No need to overexert herself.

I was all for cleaning up Marvina's home, but when she mentioned cleaning the church, I balked, "Don't y'all employ a janitorial service?"

"We used to. The budget got tight. We had to let them go. The church mothers took over the job."

"Figures," I said under my breath.

Marvina was getting used to me driving her around town. And I let her enjoy my taxi service because I wanted her to see what a good team we could be together, even if we fussed half the time. I still hadn't gotten the nerve to talk to her about the full business idea. When the right moment presented itself, I'd be ready.

We parked at the door nearest the church's kitchen and entered using Marvina's key. Pictures of Pastor Pendleton and the many men who led the church lined the back hallway. I found it ironic that there were no pictures of the women who cleaned the church, who put forth the love and smiling faces and interacted with congregants most intimately. The only pictures with women, halfway down the path, were when the women appeared with the groups they nurtured. Choirs, circles, supportive groups.

I couldn't get too mad at the church or my sister, though. Long live the patriarchy everywhere you go.

My sister didn't say much as we transferred flatware and cookware from cabinets to the cardboard boxes we'd assembled. I recognized two of Momma's tools right away. A sifter and a whisk with a bluebird perched at the end of the handle. I turned it over and rubbed my finger along the black groove created by the time I let that handle lean against the hot stovetop. I hadn't seen that whisk in more than thirty years.

I chuckled at the burn mark. "Why did you bring so much stuff to the church? No telling who was in and out of this kitchen. Not to mention letting kids use Momma's stuff."

Marvina didn't stop packing long enough to look at me. "What good is all this if no one gets to use it? Besides. Ain't you the one who damaged that whisk?"

My head shook involuntarily. "You remembered?"

"Of course I remember."

How she could remember that I burned a whisk but could not remember how Momma treated me when I got pregnant puzzled me. Classic case of selective memory.

A woman Marvina introduced as "Sister Eleanor" joined us in the kitchen a few minutes later. She, too, had come with an empty box to fill with personal belongings from the church kitchen. I listened as they talked around what was bothering them both, figuring they must have considered me an outsider. People might have all kinds of chaos going on just under the surface, but they always put on a good front with company in the room.

"Marvina tells me you're retired," Eleanor commented. She wore a long black skirt and a black knit sweater. Funeral-ready, she was.

"Yes. From the post office. Thirty-one years."

"That's a blessing. You and your sister both got it made in the shade."

I wasn't sure how to take her comment.

"It's by the grace of God," Marvina sighed.

Eleanor examined the bottom of a cast-iron skillet, then lay it into her box. "You moving back to Fork City?"

"No, I don't think so. My home is in Dallas."

"Uh-huh. Well, from the looks of it, they're trying to turn Fork City into Lil' Dallas."

"I know that's right," Marvina agreed. "I still can't believe we're moving out of this space. No more cooking here."

Marvina stood straight up, stretched her back. She wiped her eyes with the back of one hand. If it hadn't been so cold in the room, I might have thought she was sweating. But no, she was crying.

Eleanor wrapped an arm around Marvina's shoulders. "It's gonna be all right, sister. You've served well in this kitchen. Many, many hours. And touched many souls. Not to mention filled hungry stomachs!"

I stood on the other side of Marvina feeling awkward and unsure of my next move. While I felt sorry for her sadness, I did not feel sorry about the fact that we were removing our mothers' belongings from an organization that devalued Eleanor and Marvina's life's mission in the name of contemporary progress. Any hug I offered would be half-fake. *Should I try anyway? How would she react?* I patted Marvina's shoulder. "I know you. You'll find another way to serve."

"Or somewhere *else* to serve," Eleanor said under her breath.

Marvina's head snapped to the side to see her church sister head-on. "What you sayin'?"

"I said what I said. If Greater New Harvest don't want us to cook here, somebody else will."

"But Pastor said everything's changing. New city, new businesses, new families coming into town," Marvina recounted the sermon's highlights. "We have to adapt."

"You can adapt if you want to. My daughter lives in Daisy Falls. She's been asking me for months to move in with her and my son-in-law to help raise the kids. I ain't gettin' no younger. Might be time to move where I'm needed. Give my grandkids a great big hug and a hot meal every day." She shrugged.

Marvina nodded. "I'd miss you, but I understand. Sounds like a decent plan to me."

"You ever thought about leaving Fork City?" Eleanor asked.

"No. This is home for me," my sister said. "My first and last stop. This is where I've sown. Where my parents sowed. I shouldn't have to leave; I want to reap my harvest right here."

"Don't have to be your only option."

This conversation between Eleanor and Marvina was music to my ears. Finally, someone else was trying to convince my sister to get out of her comfort zone and try something new.

A tear fell from Marvina's eyes. "I don't know what to do with myself."

Yes! A window of opportunity flung open, and I attempted to ease into the space with, "You know, I was thinking—"

Suddenly, laughter floated into the room. We all stopped our packing and listened.

"They having a meeting?" Eleanor squawked. "Without me, the church secretary?"

"Sounds like it," Marvina said.

Eleanor dropped a spatula into her box and stomped off to the sanctuary. Marvina and I followed suit.

Right there in the main room sanctuary, Pastor Pendleton, two of the deacons, and two of the men from the Higher Works Alliance, all of whom I recognized from Sunday service, sat talking in the front rows and chairs.

They were so animated, so passionate that they didn't notice us at first. Their conversation about the need for a praise team instead of an old-fashioned choir came to a halt when they saw us. Pastor Pendleton said a little too loudly, "Eleanor! Marvina! And your sister, right? So good to see—"

Eleanor's scowl stopped him cold. "Is this an official meeting?" Marvina's eyes widened at her friend's demanding tone.

I wanted to pop some popcorn and watch this thing play out.

"No, no, no, no," he denied so hard his neck waddled. "We're only talking. Man talk." His face twitched nervously, like somebody was holding a gun to his back. "Right, Deacon Williams?"

"Man talk," he parroted.

"Seems to me, man talk ought to be conducted at home," Eleanor said, eyeing each of them individually.

Every last one of their lashes swept low, avoiding her gaze. They shifted in their seats. The creaking wood testified to their discomfort.

Pastor Pendleton straightened his glasses and cleared his throat. "Sister Eleanor, this is not official business. We don't need minutes for this conversation. I'm going to have to ask you to leave."

Her feet stayed stock-still. "You're telling me this is a private meeting. For men only. On church property. Our church lights. Our church heat." She shifted her weight to one side and crossed her arms on her chest.

The circle of us—Pastor Pendleton in the comfy chair usually reserved for missionaries, the deacons on their pew, the Alliance folks perched on the steps to the pulpit, and us three women—locked in a stand-off.

Deacon Williams lifted a brow and spoke. "As head of security, I have to ask. Why are you ladies here?"

"We're here to get dishes that belong to us from out of the kitchen," Marvina answered on our behalf.

The deacon stood, shoved his hands in his pockets, and rocked back and forth on his toes. "That's all good. After you finish collecting *only* what belongs to you, I'll take the church key off your hands."

Both Marvina and Eleanor puffed sharply.

A fist grabbed my heart.

"I beg your pardon?" from Eleanor.

"New people moving into town from the city will bring their big-city crime. We're proactively planning for new security procedures. A new alarm system and such," the Deacon said.

"And just so happens today is the day to repossess keys?" I asked. "They gotta come to you when they need access to clean the church, too?"

Marvina tapped my forearm softly, a warning for me to pipe down.

"We'll work through the details as we go," Pastor Pendleton answered. Then his face crinkled up like he just realized he didn't owe me any explanations. "I'll call a meeting of the church *members* later this week. Can you send out a message to see what's a good time for everyone, Eleanor?"

"Yes, I can. But I will not. I quit."

Before then, I didn't know it was possible to quit a job that didn't pay you, but Eleanor sure made a believer out of me. The way she threw her hands up in the air and zipped back to the kitchen, she might as well have sung "Take This Job and Shove It."

Marvina chased after her, and by default, I chased both of them back down the hallway to the kitchen.

"Eleanor! You can't—"

"I already did," she cut Marvina off. "Don't want to talk no more." Her voice shriveled to a sharp whisper.

Eleanor and Marvina sniffled and cried through the rest of the packing, with me feeling like a useless third wheel.

I helped them cart the boxes to our respective cars. Marvina and Eleanor hugged and said they'd talk later. Deacon Williams, who must have been watching us, came racing out of the building, waving his hand to stop us before we pulled out of our parking spot.

Marvina pressed the button to lower her window.

"Sister Marvina, I need your key to the building, please." His open hand rested on the car window frame.

I had to speak up. "You sat there and watched three women carry heavy boxes to their cars and did not lift one manly finger to help. But you wanna run out here now and collect a key?"

He ignored my scathing observation.

Marvina didn't fight his request. She maneuvered the key off her key ring and handed it to Deacon Williams.

"Thank you, Sister. Pastor will be in touch again when it's time to clean the church."

"You got the key. *You* and all those men inside can clean it up," I mouthed off. The nerve of him!

I expected Marvina to apologize to Deacon Williams for my behavior, but she didn't. She let me do my barking.

"Ladies. You have to understand. This is for your safety. We're about to go from a small, close community to a suburb. We can't have the mothers of our church coming in and out without notification. Supposed they're in here cleaning and a Dallas mugger comes in off the street and attacks them? The church might be liable for having people in here without proper security."

The funny thing about a lie is that the *best* lies almost sound like the truth. Or at least plausible enough for you to make you second-guess yourself. But I wasn't buying it. "If you're getting a new security system, it should be sophisticated enough to lock the door behind them when they come inside."

Deacon Williams clenched his jaw. "Goodbye, Sister Marvina. And what's your name, again?" he addressed me.

"Rose Dewberry-Tillman."

"Sister Rose. Have a good day."

I raised the window as he was speaking so he'd know I wasn't paying him no attention.

Once my sister and I were buckled into the car, I asked, "You all right, Marvina?"

"No."

"You ready to talk about it?"

She covered her face with both hands, and breathed into her palms twice. Then she slapped a hand on her thighs. "Just go ahead and say it, Rose."

"Say what?"

"That you think I'm a fool for my loyalty to the church. For staying here in Fork City all my life. For walking in Momma's footsteps and living a quiet, holy life, minding my own business, and helping out wherever I see a need."

"Your mind-reading skills get an F-minus."

"I have discernment," she stated.

"Your discernment is off. I respect your choices. They served you well in the past. But maybe it's time for a change." My heart raced as I danced dangerously close to the business partnership proposal again.

"How can you say this to me when you just retired after working thirty-something-odd years at the same job? You were comfortable, you stayed, you rode it out. And now you're ready to coast until the end doing something you want or doing nothing at all." Her voice began to crack. "But I wasn't ready to quit my cooking at the church. I feel like they just yanked the life right out of me. Through my nose."

"That's pretty graphic."

"That's exactly what it feels like. I can hardly breathe right now."

"Do I need to take you to the hospital?"

"No. It's anxiety. It will pass."

Hearing my sister's words, watching her face turn sour, jabbed my stomach. "I didn't know you suffered from anxiety."

"It's a late-breaking development. Not severe, but it happens sometimes. I just need a minute to breathe deeply. De-stress. Clear my mind. Pray."

Far be it from me to cause even more stress at the moment. I buttoned my lips and listened.

"If Momma were here, she'd know exactly how to keep the cooking going at church," Marvina said. "And if Pastor Pendleton's late wife, Vernetta, were here, none of this newfangled stuff would be happening. But everybody's gone now. Is this what growing old is supposed to be like? The older you get, the fewer people you have to enjoy life with?"

I swallowed hard, thinking of Marvina's despair and how much I could relate. I couldn't tell her about the business idea, but I could let her know she still had somebody in this world who cared about the way these folks were trampling on her purpose. "Not everyone is gone. I'm here."

Marvina slid her eyes over to me, giving me one of those you-really-shouldn't-have stares. "I know. Thank you. But you'll be leaving again, right?"

"Are you ready for me to go back to Dallas?"

She hesitated. "It's nice to have company. Sometimes. I don't know what I want right now."

I shrugged. "That's fair. We'll cross that bridge after Kerresha has the baby."

"Yeah. Sounds good."

CHAPTER 13

Kerresha had been with Marvina and Rose five days already, and she had said a few things that let Marvina know Kerresha had no shame about being a single mother. No religious regrets about intimacy with someone she wasn't married to. Lyla wasn't a shining role model, but…well… Marvina was raised different. As in get-married-and-be-stable-before-you-have-children different. That was Momma's expectation. Anything out of sequence, like what Rose had done when she got pregnant by David and then married the cheater, disturbed the order of things.

So when Kerresha told Marvina and Rose, over breakfast on a Wednesday morning, that she wanted to have a drive-by baby shower, Marvina nearly choked on her buttery biscuit.

"A baby shower?"

"A drive-by baby shower," Kerresha repeated. "It's where people come by your house and drop off gifts for the baby. You give them a thank-you party favor. They keep it moving. It started during the pandemic. I don't want a traditional shower. It would be too much to ask with all the decorations and party games."

Marvina's eyes darted to Rose, who didn't seem alarmed. She

just sat there chewing on her biscuit like there was no problem at all.

"Would it be okay to have it here?" Kerresha asked. "You won't have to do anything."

Marvina's sense of propriety tumbled out of her mouth. "I appreciate you thinking of us, not wanting to have a big party here. But a baby shower? In your...predicament?"

Kerresha searched their faces for a clue. "What predicament?"

Marvina took a breath. "Being pregnant. Out of wedlock."

"What is wedlock?" Kerresha asked.

"Wedlock means locked in a marriage," Rose clarified.

Marvina's fork clinked against her plate. She stuffed her face with another fork full of buttermilk pancakes.

Kerresha's face morphed to a mask of confusion. "I don't get what you're saying."

Rose translated. "She means she doesn't understand why you'd want to have a baby shower when you are having a baby without being married. You're supposed to go hide behind a rock, disappear from public view, and paint a red letter 'A' on your shirt like *The Scarlet Letter*. Did you read that in high school?"

"Stop, Rose," Marvina fussed. "That's not what I mean."

"It's *exactly* what you mean." Rose's flared nostrils betrayed her calm voice. "But I'm not gonna sit here and let you introduce shame into her life. I've been there and done that. Not happening on my watch."

Kerresha chuckled, "No one's in wedlock"—she air-quoted the word—"*before* they have a baby. Why would you get married when you don't know if you're going to be together forever?"

It finally registered in Marvina's mind that this concept was foreign to Kerresha. She wasn't being sarcastic or obtuse; she truly did not understand where Marvina was coming from. Marvina proceeded cautiously. "Well, when you find the right one and you've both committed to be there for one another and seal your deal in marriage, *then* you can bring a baby into a nurturing, stable environment so the child can blossom in the love of a mother and a father."

Kerresha shrugged. "That's cool and everything, but that's not my story. But what's that got to do with my baby shower? I mean, every baby needs bottles and diapers no matter if the parents are married or not."

And just like that, with Kerresha's simple matter-of-fact reasoning, Marvina's brain flipped. Every baby *does* need bottles and diapers, regardless of their parents' predicament. Absent the layer of judgment, the idea proved logical.

Marvina overlooked the smug look on Rose's face. "I do believe you're right, Kerresha."

"So, we're having the drive-by shower, then?" Kerresha asked, her face now beaming with excitement.

"Yes, young lady, we are," Marvina confirmed. No sooner than she spoke the words, doubtful thoughts swamped her mind. What would the other church mothers think of her celebrating this girl's baby? If Pastor Pendleton got wind of the shower, would he accuse her of celebrating sin? Of encouraging immorality in the young folk of the community?

Just as quickly, it occurred to Marvina that she didn't care what anyone at the church thought of her because, right about now, she was not on good terms with Greater New Harvest. The only thing that mattered was what God thought of her, and since He was the One who gave life and made babies, surely He understood that the baby needed stuff. It seemed right for those in the community to have an opportunity to help this homeless young woman—and of course, the baby.

"Let's go get some party favors," Marvina said. She got a kick out of Rose's astonished face.

"You serious?" Rose asked.

"As a heart attack," Marvina replied.

"Thank you! Thank you! Thank you!" Kerresha hug-attacked Marvina and Rose. "I'll build my wish list on Amazon and send invites on my cell phone. If you want, I can tell everybody to drive by the far curb, so they won't be all up under the car shed or on your grass."

"Sounds good to me." Marvina wondered who were all these people Kerresha planned to invite, and where they were when she was living out back in the guesthouse.

But instead of asking, she turned her attention to Rose. "I need a few more things so you can finally make your batch of seasoning, too."

"Thank God," Rose sighed. "I thought we'd never get around to it."

They all finished breakfast, cleared the dishes, and headed to the grocery store. On the way, the shopping list grew longer and the shopping map wider as Marvina interviewed Kerresha about her immediate maternity needs. Vitamins, no-slip socks, and a body pillow to get Kerresha through these final weeks were added to the list.

Rose helped Kerresha into and out of the car, Marvina pushed the basket, and Kerresha snapped pictures of them shopping together.

"Are you putting these pictures online?" Rose wanted to know.

"No. I'm going to print them and save them. I want my child to know who helped make things ready for the big entrance into this world."

Marvina and Rose sank into warm smiles.

"We're elated to be included in the baby's life," Marvina accepted the honor.

After that sweet moment, Marvina took charge of the grocery shopping. She ordered Rose and Kerresha around like a true Hollywood diva. Groceries, foil paper, parchment paper, all things cooking fell under her domain. "Reach me that." "Get the other size—this one's too small." "Not that brand!"

And for every order, Rose had a comeback. "Something wrong with your arms?" "You didn't specify." "I'm not a mind reader."

Kerresha interrupted their spat in the baking aisle. "On God, y'all stay crunk."

Rose and Marvina froze.

"What does that mean?" from Marvina.

"Both of y'all are on ten. For real for real," Kerresha tried to explain, which did not help.

Rose repeated, "On ten?"

"It means you two are always extra. Arguing."

Marvina finally understood the last word. She squinted her eyes. "I wouldn't exactly call it arguing."

"Whatever. You do you. I won't judge. I'm just saying."

Kerresha's observation quieted the sisters. Marvina was embarrassed at her behavior in front of this impressionable girl. Good thing she hadn't preached to her about following the Lord at this point; her witness might have damaged the invitation.

They made a second stop at Pixie's Market, the last family-owned shack. The sign on the white, partially unhinged door had so many different store hours written and then crossed off it was no longer clear what time Pixie's opened and closed. Someone had finally written in the widest, boldest Sharpie marker they could find, "If the light is on, we're open. If not, we're closed."

"That's different," Kerresha remarked as she read it, too.

It was a small price to pay for the freshest yellow onions and paprika peppers.

The third stop was at Dollar House to get the pillow and socks. Marvina also recognized Earl, though they only had a nodding acquaintance this whole time they'd both been living in Fork City.

Rose entertained his flirtatious words, to the point where Kerresha whispered in Marvina's ear, "Looks like Rose has an admirer."

"I'll say."

He struggled to find the tag on the oversized pillow, and Rose leaned every which way to help him locate the bar code. Her arm certainly grazed his more than once. All of it embarrassed Marvina again, her sister out here acting all desperate for male attention.

"Did you get a chance to check into the zoning and the revitalizing plans?" Earl asked Rose.

All of a sudden, Rose's body stiffened. Her voice rose an octave. "Oh, let's not talk about that now. How's your sister?"

Earl seemed confused. "Same as she was when we talked the other day. Nothing changes that fast around here, at least not until now. The Realtor lady came in here the other day. Told me about the zoning. You want me to put you in touch with her?"

Realtor? Why would Rose need a Realtor? And what was Earl talking about with the zoning plans and such? For the second time in a week, Marvina felt as though she'd stumbled into a conversation she wasn't meant to hear, but that ultimately affected her.

When Earl ducked below the counter to reload the cash register tape, Marvina asked Rose, "Is there something you need to tell me? You thinking about moving back for good?"

Rose dismissed the question with a roll of her eyes. "Earl and

I were just talking, that's all. Earl, you remember the time you cheated off my paper and we both got a zero on the test?"

He hee-hawed, letting Rose change the direction of the conversation. "I knew you'd bring it up sooner or later."

Kerresha asked for details, grinning alongside Rose and Earl as they replayed the decades-old scenario for her. And all the while, Marvina kept thinking it was mighty odd for Earl to mention about the Realtor, and even more odd for Rose to be flirting so hard with this man to avoid talking about a secret topic.

Earl wasn't even her sister's type. Rose liked 'em remarkably handsome. Like David. Even if it meant inevitable heartache, which, in Marvina's estimation, was more than likely with a good-looking man.

Marvina's late husband, Warren Sr., had been a solid five on a scale of ten. Nothing to write home about, nothing to attract a swarm of women at first glance. She had liked being her husband's prize. Momma always said, "Don't marry a man who's prettier than you."

Earl would never fit the bill for Rose. So why she has started trotting down memory lane with Earl all of a sudden made no sense.

Back in the car, Kerresha taunted Rose about the too-friendly encounter. "Did you give him the digits?"

"The what?" Rose exclaimed.

"Your phone number."

"No. What makes you think I'd want to?"

"Because you were cheesin' and showing all thirty-two of your teeth," Marvina jumped in on Kerresha's side of the claim.

"I don't want no Earl Henderson. He's just in the know about Fork City because of where he works. Folks don't have many places to shop, so I'm sure he sees a little bit of everybody and hears even more."

"Why you so concerned about Fork City?" Marvina's tone scraped away Rose's jovial demeanor.

"Nothing. It's nothing. I've got to get home. We've walked all around the grocery store and Pixie's and Dollar House. Need to rest my knee." Rose drove on, rubbing the knee with one hand, steering the wheel with the other.

"I'm 'bout sick of you and this knee. Every time I look around you're complaining or popping a pill. What else did the doctor tell you to do?" Marvina asked.

"So glad you care," Rose chided.

"If I didn't, I wouldn't be asking."

Over her shoulder, Marvina saw Kerresha push her earbuds in place.

Rose sighed. "I got pain medicine. And I'm doing exercises."

"I ain't seen you doing any exercises."

"I will."

"When?"

"Good Lord. You sound like David."

"Stop using the Lord's name in vain. And God forbid I sound like David!"

Rose scrunched her nose. "You do realize you just used the Lord's name in vain, right?"

"No, that wasn't in vain," Marvina insisted, "because I meant what I said. If I ever start sounding like your ex-husband, I want the Lord Himself to intervene, forbid it, and put an end to it."

"Can we please not talk about David or Earl or any of my other men?"

A laugh burst from Marvina's lips. "What other men?"

Rose laughed, too. "Look. I'm in pain right now. I can't go into details."

"The only thing you've ever been involved with outside of David was your work. I don't bit-mo believe you've had a boyfriend in all these years."

Rose flipped the spotlight. "What about you? You seen anyone since Warren Sr. died?"

Marvina shook her head. "Nobody in Fork City I'd be interested in. Small town. Everybody knows almost everybody. Too much room for gossip."

"Maybe you should have moved."

"I don't want another husband."

"Really?" Rose marveled. "I mean, let you and Momma tell it, a woman's life means nothing without a husband and children."

"Well, my life is the way God intended."

"I don't believe that," Rose stated.

"Suit yourself."

"Thank you. I will."

"All I know is, you'd better start doing these exercises. If you don't, you're gonna need that electric cart the next time we go to the store."

They returned home, and Kerresha got busy organizing and packing party favors for the drive-by baby shower guests.

Like clockwork, Rose and Marvina tied twine around the rosemary and thyme and hung them so they would dry out and be ready to create the seasoning later.

Next came splitting and removing the seeds from Pixie's paprika. This delicate task had taught them both persistence. Not one single seed left. Period.

Marvina took a misshapen pan from the lower shelf, and Rose gasped as the metal bottom hit the counter.

Gently, she placed her hand in the center of the pan. "Momma loved this pan."

"Sure did, all beat up and dinged everywhere."

"Bad pans, good food," they both recited one of Momma's chants, dipping their chins simultaneously as well to imitate Momma's deep voice. Laughter played between them, sweet and savory.

They set the opened paprika, insides facing up, on parchment paper to broil in the oven. A few minutes later, they removed the paprika and cut the peppers julienne style while the oven temperature decreased. The paprika would have to dehydrate on the lowest temperature for twelve hours to remove the rest of the moisture.

"Wonder why Momma didn't cut them up first before broiling them?" Rose asked for the first time.

Marvina cut her batch of paprika into slivers as well. "Never thought about it, but I reckon there's something to those burnt parts of the paprika that add more flavor." She pointed her knife at a slightly blackened portion of the pepper.

"I'm just saying. If we cut them—"

"Don't go messing with perfection, Rose."

"You ever heard the story of the woman whose great-grandmother cut off and discarded the ends of the ham?"

Marvina ignored her sister, slicing away as she had done for as long as she could remember. This was Momma's recipe. One wrong move could ruin an entire batch, which Rose should have known already given the fact that she sat up there and messed up her last one.

Rose ignored Marvina's ignoring and continued, "One day the great-granddaughter made her own ham the way she'd seen it made as a girl, but it turned out a little dry, like all the juices ran out when she cut it off. So she asked the great-grandmother one day how she managed to keep her ham moist despite cutting off the ends. And the grandmother said she only cut them off because the pan she had was too short. Her ham wasn't dry because she stuffed it all into that too-short pan, but the granddaughter's ham—"

"I get it, I get it," Marvina put a halt to the urban legend. "Now, first of all, whoever heard of a great-grandmother throwin' away good meat? If she had any sense, she would have used two pans and wrapped the two halves of ham in foil instead of cutting off the two ends."

Rose sassed, "You are ruining the metaphor."

"It's ridiculous."

Rose continued cutting her paprika. Then she snickered. "You're right. Most great-grandmommas were poor. And the ones who weren't had other folks working in the kitchen for them, so how would they know?"

"Right?" Marvina snickered, too. "Anyway, it takes time to properly prepare the ingredients for Momma's seasoning, especially since there was no sun outside to dry contents naturally. Besides, we do have some modern technology. We use a blender, and that's enough. Now, Let's finish these up and put them in the oven so we can work on you."

"Me?"

"Yes. Your exercises."

As soon as the trays of paprika were set in the warm oven, Marvina ordered Rose to start her exercises. "Bring me the papers so I can help you."

"No papers. It's on my phone."

"Fine."

Kerresha joined them in the living room, helping to gently stretch Rose's knee and calf, coaching Rose to breathe through the discomfort.

As she lay flat on her back, with Kerresha and Marvina pressing and pulling, Rose exclaimed, "I think physical therapy is legalized torture. Therapists got these exercise moves from the military's book of unauthorized ways to interrogate prisoners of war."

"No pain, no gain," Kerresha chanted.

Rose spouted off, "Remember that when you're in labor."

The exercise directions called for Marvina to press a spot on Rose's inner knee while rotating the joint slightly. This was hard work. Marvina felt the prickle of sweat already on her own forehead. It made her feel proud. Useful. She took a sip from her water bottle before proceeding. "Here we go." She assumed the position.

That rotation move made Rose's eyes bug out, and she literally cried, "Uncle! Uncle, uncle, uncle!"

Kerresha burst into laughter, which caused Marvina to spit out the swig of water she'd taken from her plastic bottle.

This, in turn, made Rose giggle so hard she nearly choked. "Y'all are trying to kill me!" she hollered between snorts.

Marvina pointed at Kerresha's belly, bouncing up and down with each laugh.

Rose yelled, "Your stomach looks like Santa Claus. Ho-ho-ho!"

And then another round of silly laughter ensued while Rose soothed her aching knee with a rubbing motion.

Marvina could not remember the last time she'd laughed so hard for so long. It felt good and right and long overdue. It brought to mind the feelings she had for Rose before David. Before the accident that took her sight in one eye. Back when Momma still upheld Rose as the perfect example of a "good girl," the model for Marvina to emulate.

Now, with Rose writhing on the floor in laughter, Kerresha chortling while her baby bump bounced, and tears of hilarity spilling from Marvina's own eyes, she suddenly felt like she'd been cheated of her sister. Maybe by David. Maybe by Momma. Maybe by her own judgments of Rose. She couldn't be sure, exactly.

What Marvina did know, however, was that as much as she missed the days when Momma, Rose, and Marvina created scrumptious meals in the kitchen, she had also missed seeing her sister like this. Free, open, and contagiously funny, funny, funny.

She had all but forgotten about this side of Rose.

CHAPTER 14

Rose

"Hi, Rose Tillman?"

"Yes."

"This is Elizabeth Maxwell from Countrywide Realty returning your call."

Any other time, I might have welcomed the call from this woman whose number I had gotten after making a call to Earl soon after Marvina, Kerresha, and I left the store. But now was terrible timing. I was still in the car with Marvina and Kerresha, headed to the obstetrician for a checkup.

"Can you hold for a second?"

"Sure thing!"

I muted the call and parked the car in the space next to the handicapped spot. "Y'all go on inside. I need to take this."

Marvina asked, "Everything okay?"

Her nose literally rose half an inch, like she'd smelled something rotten.

"Yes, I'm fine. I'll be in shortly."

She and Kerresha got out, and I gave my attention to Elizabeth again. "Sorry about that. I'm back."

"Oh, no problem," the woman sang with the enthusiasm of a possible sale ringing through her voice. "I'm here for you. How can I help you, Ms. Tillman?"

This would be my first time speaking the words out loud. I had given ideas thought, of course, but not voice. Those spiritual gurus on Oprah and in documentaries always talked about the creative power in every uttered word. I was about to find out if all their manifest mumbo-jumbo was true.

"I would like to lease?…or purchase?…the old Dairy Queen in Fork City."

"Wonderful! Are you obtaining it as a franchise for another Dairy Queen?"

"No. I want my own restaurant. Me and my sister. Southern cooking. With lots of love." The words dripped out of me as short sentences. My heart was beating so fast, proper businesslike syntax escaped me.

"Awesome. This city is primed for big changes. Having a traditional restaurant in the middle of newer developments will help the city retain some of its charm. Give the newcomers a taste of what they couldn't get in Dallas," she confirmed.

I wondered if she had a speech tailored to every potential sale. If I had been planning a toenail clipping store, would she encourage the futile idea just the same?

"Do you have a move-in date in mind?"

"A date?"

"Yes. A date. And a funding source lined up? Or are you using your own capital?"

Fear swooshed over me now that I was actually speaking my plans, using numbers, tying down the capricious concepts floating around my imagination. Who was I kidding? Momma was the best cook. If she hadn't opened a restaurant, what made me think I was capable? I was nothing but a retired postal worker. No entrepreneurial experience. No classes on advertising or marketing or bookkeeping. Shoot, I didn't even know what temperature to cook chicken, technically. I only knew in my gut when the grease was ready.

"Ummm…" I stumbled for an answer, feeling my ears burn with embarrassment and shame at having wasted Elizabeth's time. "I'm sorry. I haven't thought through all the details. I just wanted to know what it would cost to buy or rent the building."

"No problem, Ms. Tillman. Sounds like you're in the beginning phases of planning. I'm more than willing to help. Could you text me your email address? I'll send over the asking price and terms of lease and also share some resources to help you get a business plan together. Rent-to-own could be an option, too."

I released a pinned-up breath. "That'll be great, Elizabeth. I'm new at this."

"We all have to start somewhere," she said. "When I established my realty company seventeen years ago, I was a single mom of two school-aged kids. I knew absolutely nothing about real estate or running a business, but I was a really good listener and a fast learner. And I cared about people. I think if you've got that much going for you, the rest will follow."

At her encouragement, tears welled up in my eyes. It was like she had listened to my silence and knew exactly what I needed to hear. "Thank you, Elizabeth. I appreciate the information and the pep talk."

"This is why I do what I do. I'll send it right over, and I look forward to hearing from you soon, Ms. Tillman."

"Sure thing. And, uh. I have another question." Dread pooled in my stomach, and I readied my lips to betray Marvina. "If I give you an address of a property here in Fork City, can you give me an estimate of what it might actually sell for? I looked it up online, but I think the estimate was high."

"Yes. Absolutely. Is it a commercial or a residential property?"

"Residential."

"Do you own the property?"

"Jointly."

"Gotcha. Well, it's a seller's market right now. If you have one to sell and one to buy, you're in a perfect position to move forward. Text me the address, and I'll include an estimate and some comps. Might take me an hour or so. We can schedule a tour of the restaurant space when you're ready. Will that work for you?"

"Perfect." Seeing as I had no idea what "comps" were, I needed the time to google the definition. "Thank you again, Elizabeth."

"My pleasure. Have a good one."

"You, too."

I took a deep breath and stuffed the phone back into my purse. Today was a big day already, making moves for the business. Getting educated estimates on the value of Momma's house. Taking Kerresha to the doctor for the first time.

My life was changing before my very eyes. Finally, things were lining up for me to start the business that lay dormant in my dreams all these years. The fear, the adventure, the possibilities.

Again, my eyes overflowed. I felt like time had reversed and my chance at happiness swung within reach again. With a Realtor like Elizabeth and some help from a business adviser, there was no reason I couldn't be successful. No reason Marvina and I couldn't be successful.

I joined my sister and Kerresha in the clinic waiting room.

It smelled like someone had performed some old-school cleaning inside, to my great relief. Even with old furniture and out-
dated posters, the welcoming comfort of bleach and pine cleaner
prevailed.

Kerresha and Marvina must have already completed the
paperwork without me, because they were twiddling their thumbs
alongside five other big-bellied women. Three toddlers played in
a kiddie area, pushing toy trains and stacking blocks while their
mothers waited to be seen.

The only empty seat for me was to Kerresha's right. Marvina
was already at her left, so we sat with Kerresha sandwiched in the
middle and watched the children play. The innocence, the chubby
cheeks, the dimpled fingers all stoked the embers that never died
in me. *Babies.* Some women can have them; some women can't.

"Are you both going in with me?" Kerresha asked.

"I don't know," Marvina said. "The papers said only one person
could come in."

"I'm scared," Kerresha said. "I want you both in there with me.
What if…what if there's something wrong with my baby, since I
waited so long to make a doctor's appointment?"

Marvina patted Kerresha's thigh. "Hush up, now. Don't think
like that. Everything's gonna be all right."

Spoken like a woman who had never suffered a miscarriage.
Never canceled a baby shower. Never disassembled and donated
an unused baby crib.

Kerresha tilted her forehead, using the force of gravity to hold
back her tears.

"No matter what happens, we'll be here for you," I assured
Kerresha, because, in reality, life is so very fragile. She was right
to respect the uncertainty, in my jaded opinion.

The door beside the receptionist's window squeaked open.

"Rose and Marvina Dewberry! Shut yo' mouth!" Before I saw her face, I knew exactly who was calling our names. Age had given her voice a teetering quality, but the unmistakable cheerful soprano pitch remained.

"Sister Lillie!" Marvina rushed to hug the woman who had been our babysitter the few times Momma ever left us in someone else's care. Sister Lillie was a member of the same church we grew up in, and was, apparently, now some kind of office aide at this sliding-fee-scale county clinic.

She pinned her clipboard to her side with an elbow and held out her arms to embrace Marvina. Sister Lillie sported a short Afro, similar to mine. Her tiny frame still exuded tons of vibrant energy.

I hugged Sister Lillie as well, feeling the press of her warm chest against mine. It seemed odd to me that I was hugging this woman I had not seen in years, yet I still had not full-on hugged my sister since I'd been back in Fork City, almost a week at that point.

Sister Lillie's hooded eyes still twinkled as she spoke to us in the same manner she used when we were little girls. "I declare, you two are still as beautiful as ever. Looking just like your Momma, none other than Sister Alice Mae Dewberry, God rest her soul." Then she lowered her forehead and pulled us both into a circle. "It's nice to see you two talking again. Don't make no sense, sisters arguing and fussing the way y'all carried on all those years. Broke your Momma's heart seeing her only two children spatting. But look at you now, both of y'all. Here." She clasped her hands under her chin and gave an approving nod. "I'm sure your momma *and* Jesus and *all* the angels are rejoicing in heaven at this scene."

Then she switched to secular wisdom, snapping her fingers, swaying her hips, and singing the chorus to Peaches & Herb's "Reunited."

"Thank you, Sister Lillie," Marvina cut her off.

Wow. I had never witnessed my mother or any of her church friends move their hips in any sort of way.

Sister Lillie giggled. She whispered to us behind her hand, as though we were surrounded by nosy eavesdroppers. "Sometimes the music hits me. I listen to worldly music sometimes. Don't tell nobody, hear?"

"My lips are sealed," I assured her.

Sister Lillie looked past us at Kerresha. "This one of y'alls grandbabies? Your son get married?" She pointed her last question at Marvina.

"No ma'am. He's still out there. Single."

There was no mistaking the disappointment in Marvina's voice.

"Ooh! Then she must be yours." Sister Lillie pressed her hands against my cheeks. "Praise the Lord! He answered your mother's prayers and gave you a family after all. Ain't God good?"

My jaws went slack in her clutch.

"Yes, He is," Marvina said. "Kerresha is not blood kin. We've taken her in."

Sister Lillie, still holding my face, looked at the three of us individually. Her face whipped around so fast, stopping at each of us momentarily, she reminded me of a squirrel. I guess when it hit her that the Lord had not answered Momma's prayers—or mine—she released my head and backpedaled. "God is still good. All the time. Amen?"

I wish I had a dollar for every time a woman tried to convince me that, A: God would eventually give me a child like He did Hannah in the Bible (which they stopped saying after I turned forty); B: It was God's will for me to not have children; or C: Adoption was the answer for me. It always seemed silly to me that people had to come up with these simple, pleasant responses to my complex, painful situation. Why couldn't they just say, "This absolutely sucks, Rose, and I hate that you're going through this"?

I did not complete the chant with the expected reply: *And all the time, God is good.* Nor did I say Amen. This woman and all the women like her, my sister and my mother included, got on my last nerve with these empty clichés that make the rest of us feel like there was something wrong with us for not having it all figured out, for experiencing pain and getting mad at Him and being brave enough to say that to His face.

Marvina directed Sister Lillie's attention to Kerresha. "She's a smart one. Planned her own drive-by baby shower and everything."

"A drive-by shower, huh?"

They broke into casual conversation as I looked on. Third-wheeling it again.

Once they'd caught up, Sister Lillie asked questions and wrote Kerresha's answers on her clipboard.

Sister Lillie answered when one of her coworkers got her attention. "Looks like Dr. Wilhelm is ready for you now."

Kerresha stood and waddled toward the closed white door with the sign that read "Enter here for appointment."

She asked Sister Lillie, "Can I have both of them come with me?"

"Oh, no. I don't need to. Marvina, you go ahead," I tried to bow out. The last thing I needed was to be in a room with my sister and Sister Lillie when the doctor broadcast the baby's heartbeat for all to hear.

Kerresha desperately grabbed my wrist. "I need you with me."

Shocked by her statement, I could only swallow and agree, albeit with reservations. Why would she want me, a woman with no children at all, by her side?

Sister Lillie, in her glad manner, said she could make an exception this time. "Especially seeing as it's your first baby."

Dr. Wilhelm wore a tight-fitting tube dress underneath her white coat. I liked her from the moment she sauntered into the small but well-appointed examination room. She had her hair in a messy bun, pierced by what looked like chopsticks. Something about these unconventional millennials always sat well with me.

She greeted the three of us, asked Kerresha a few questions about how she'd been feeling, and congratulated her on the pregnancy.

There wasn't a seat for me, seeing as there wasn't supposed to be a second guest present, so I stood behind Marvina. Marvina rolled herself up right next to Kerresha and held her hand.

"Let me confirm," Dr. Wilhelm said. "You *do* want to know the baby's sex today?"

"Yes."

Marvina squeezed Kerresha's hand.

The doctor snapped on her blue latex gloves. "Works for me. Let's do this."

Anxiety ripped through me as Kerresha raised up her thin examination gown, exposing her round belly. Dr. Wilhelm pressed the sides of her belly. "Feel okay?"

"Yes, ma'am."

"Ma'am?" Dr. Wilhelm exclaimed. "I'm not *that* old."

Kerresha offered a nervous apology.

"Any complications? Bleeding? Swelling?"

Kerresha shook her head.

"Her feet swell up when she lets her legs dangle too long," Marvina interjected.

"Or when she walks too much," I brought up the rear.

Dr. Wilhelm chuckled. "Looks like you've got two mother hens over here taking good care of you."

Kerresha laughed, "They are."

When the doctor compressed the ultrasound gel from its bottle, swirling it around and around with the wand like she was filling an ice cream cone, my breathing nearly stopped. I hadn't seen this scene from above, like I was standing over Kerresha, now. But I had been the one lying on my back, feeling the cold gel squirt on my cone-shaped belly, anticipating the thump of a heartbeat, only to be met with a heartbreaking silence.

Marvina swiveled on her stool and looked me up and down. "You okay?"

I guessed I must have been fidgeting, moaning, sweating, or something that brought attention to myself. "I don't know."

Dr. Wilhelm dismissed my peril as jitters. "It's an exciting moment, I know."

The whoosh-whoosh of the baby's heartbeat came first, allowing me to release my own breath. My hands instinctively covered my trembling lips. Her baby was alive and well.

"We've got a strong, healthy heartbeat," Dr. Wilhelm announced.

I was so happy I clapped. My head ached with relief.

"Now, let's see if this little one is going to turn, so we can see if we're shopping for pink or blue." She floated the instrument around Kerresha's stomach.

No longer fearing the worst, I stepped to the side of Marvina, bringing the black and blue screen into view.

"Well," Dr. Wilhelm paused for effect, "looks like we've got ourselves a little boy."

Joy spread through me. Kind of surprised me, really, because since I lost my first one, I had never truly been excited about anyone else giving birth. It stung too bad. Like finding out there was an extravagant party that you weren't allowed to enter. You got the invitation all right, and you got all dressed up and went. Your friends were inside, your enemies were inside, your friends' enemies were inside, and they didn't even deserve to be there. But when *you* tried to open the door, it was triple-locked.

But sitting there with the joy of Kerresha's baby boy swirling around us, I felt something shift in me. I went from being an outsider to someone attached to the celebration. Like someone had opened the door to the party ever so slightly, given me a look inside. Let me enjoy the music a bit. Smell the aroma of the fresh flower arrangements on every table.

"What you gonna do with a hardheaded little boy?" Marvina teased.

A drop fell from Kerresha's eyes as she stared at the screen. "I'm going to love him."

"Awwww," I cooed. The love she had for this unborn child pinched my heart good. "You're going to be a wonderful mother, Kerresha."

"Thank you, Miss Rose."

The doctor finished her digital measurements, freezing the camera at certain points and making little noises like she was talking to an infant already. "Woooop! Femur. Shalllooo! Head circumference."

"Can you tell me my due date?" Kerresha asked. "I'm really not sure when my last period was. After the Supreme Court thing, everybody said we should ditch the period-tracking apps on our phones."

"Y'all got all your business up in the cloud these days," Marvina remarked.

Dr. Wilhelm pointed her pink, manicured nail at the screen. "You see that?"

Marvina and I leaned in closer.

Kerresha replied, "Mm-hmm."

"Shows the estimate right there. According to the measurements, you're at thirty-four weeks. The baby should be here in another six weeks. That makes your official due date January 27th."

"Ewww!" Kerresha snarled. "I was afraid it would be at the end of January. That's a terrible birth date."

I laughed. "What's wrong with January twenty-seventh?"

"When people tell you their birthday, they're like May 9th or October 4th. That's easy. But people with double-digit birth date numbers—nobody remembers them."

"Who told you that story?" Marvina asked.

"It's my theory."

"And quite a theory it is," I remarked. This child had some wild opinions, and I was glad for her. She reminded me of myself.

Dr. Wilhelm pronounced good health for mother and baby alike. "You'll need to come in every week from this point forward until the baby arrives." She held out her forearm for Kerresha to grab hold and lift to a sitting position.

"We'll be here," I obligated us all.

"Perfect. See you next week." The doctor dismissed herself from the room.

"A boy," Kerresha whispered. She swung her braids over her shoulder. "I'm glad it's not a girl. We're too hard."

Marvina warned, "Boys can be difficult, too."

This was the first I'd heard of her having issues with Warren Jr. From the way Momma talked, he was an angel.

We left Kerresha alone in the examination room so she could re-dress while we handled business at the appointment desk. There stood another young woman, full-bellied with a pair of flip-flops on her feet, in line ahead of us. From the looks of her swollen feet, she probably couldn't wear anything but flip-flops. Good thing for her it was a good fifty-five degrees outside.

Marvina pulled my arm, tucking us into a tiny corner beside the appointment desk window. "Listen. Before Kerresha comes out, I want to tell you something."

"What is it?"

"I...I know this was hard for you. I figured you stayed out in the car earlier for so long because the obstetrician's office is not a good place for you. And when you walked into the waiting room, I saw your red eyes. So, I wanted to say I'm sorry for your loss."

I replayed my mental tape because I didn't remember crying when—wait, yes, I *was* crying. But those were tears of joy, because Elizabeth had flung seeds of hope onto my heart about the business and selling Momma's house. Not tears of sadness over Kerresha's pregnancy. This wasn't the time to correct the error, though.

"Thank you."

"It's like Sister Lillie said. God is—"

"I really don't want to talk about God and me. If you want to talk about the blessing He's giving to Kerresha, that's fine. But this isn't about me."

Marvina cupped my shoulder. "Rose. I know He took your baby back to heaven with Him, but—"

"Bay-*bies*. Plural."

Horror skittered across her features too quickly for her to reel in her raw reaction. "How…how many?"

"Three. And I got the message loud and clear. I wasn't meant to be a mother."

"Rose. I'm so sorry. I didn't know. *Three.* Momma only told me about the one."

"Momma and I didn't talk much after I lost the first one." I stopped short of telling her why.

"I think Momma said y'all stopped talking because you married David."

"Momma had a way of remembering things her way. No disrespect. God rest her soul."

"Well, I'm sorry, anyway."

I should have said "thank you," but my throat felt like I'd swallowed a golf ball.

Kerresha rejoined us just as the appointment desk cleared of the previous patient. "Everything all right?"

Me and Marvina both slapped cheerful expressions on our faces, not wanting to talk about miscarriages or Momma drama in front of a hopeful, pregnant, first-time mother.

"Yes. It sure is," I said. "Let's get you set up for the rest of this pregnancy."

Marvina hung behind us. I could see her trying to wrestle with my words, reconcile her faith in God, her thoughts about our mother, her thoughts about me. It was about time.

CHAPTER 15

The second spare bedroom used to belong to Marvina's son, Warren Jr. From the time that boy turned twelve until he left for college, the room smelled like feet, sweat, and pizza no matter how many times Marvina threatened to rip everything out and make him sleep on a bare cot if he didn't clean up and bathe better.

When Marvina complained to her friends, the sisters at Greater New Harvest, about her son's lack of hygiene and his ever-funky bedroom, they assured her he was totally normal. "All boy," they had said, which always made Marvina feel good.

This room belonged to Kerresha, now. She'd share it with the baby, too, temporarily. The queen bed's old, wooden headboard had recently been painted white, minimizing the appearance of the giant "W" Warren Jr. had carved into the headboard with a fork the day after he learned to write the first letter of his name.

So many memories in that room. And so long since Warren Jr. had returned to Fork City. It was nice to have someone living in that space again. Someone to care for.

Rose had taken it upon herself to get a new comforter set for Kerresha, replacing the old-fashioned quilt Marvina had used in that bedroom until now. The only thing left to do before the baby got here was empty out the lower drawers in Warren Jr.'s bureau. Marvina hadn't done so before now, because, despite their stark disagreements, she never gave up on the idea that Warren Jr. might return home someday. When he came to his God-given senses.

But now that a blanket set and a baby manicure kit had been delivered to Marvina's house, it was time for the final clearance. With gifts already arriving from people who weren't going to be able to drive by on the designated day, they didn't have much time to get things in order.

Marvina unfolded the new blankets that had arrived in an Amazon box. She extracted the cardboard from between the layers. "I like the online gift registry and all, but it takes the surprise out of opening the gifts, huh?"

Kerresha responded in her nonchalant way, a quick tilt of the head with a shoulder bounce. "We're still opening a package and finding out what the gift is. There are no people around, but otherwise, isn't the outcome pretty much the same?"

"When you put it like that, I guess it is," Marvina had to agree. In fact, it shocked Marvina how often she agreed with Kerresha's unconventional perspectives. When Marvina gave the girl's ideas full consideration, they made common sense. Real sense. Not in the context of *ideal* life, but appropriate for Kerresha's *real* life. Was this child changing her? Was Marvina growing more compassionate? Was she too old to judge folks anymore? Or had her moral compass already become disoriented because she'd fallen out with her Pastor?

Either way, there was a lightness to how Kerresha moved in this world that Marvina secretly admired. Maybe it was better not to know what was required of you by the Lord, the church, and other decent folk in the community. If you didn't know, then you wouldn't have to worry so much about failing. You could just be you, take life as it comes. Like Kerresha did.

On the other hand, what became of people who had no morals? No care for what others thought of them or how they fit into society? No concern for the ways of a jealous God? Didn't anyone care about hell anymore?

Kerresha lowered herself in the rocking chair, something she had done three times in the past half hour to catch her breath. She swayed back and forth, palming both sides of her stomach.

"You all right?"

"It's these—" she froze. Her face wrinkled.

"Breathe," Marvina coached.

Kerresha inhaled. A second later, she was able to speak. "It's Braxton-Hicks contractions. I read about them in my pregnancy book. Sometimes I have to stop and catch my breath."

"Won't be too long, now," Marvina said. She leaned her behind against the dresser and crossed her arms, studying Kerresha's long braids. In just a few days, they had loosened at the roots. They were slipping because Kerresha had what people used to call "good hair," though Marvina always wondered what made hair that couldn't even hold a braid for a week so good.

Kerresha was such a beautiful young lady. Didn't girls these days know how to stay out of pregnancy trouble? Marvina decided to approach Kerresha's future plans indirectly. "Do you think your child's father will come to the drive-by? Or do you think he'll send a gift?"

"I don't know." She rubbed her fingertips along the widest part of her stomach. "He might. Might not. Depends."

"Depends on what?"

"I'm not ready to talk about it yet."

There it was. That bold, frank, unapologetic boundary all the commercials for empowering young women mentioned. Marvina had never fixed her mouth to tell someone she didn't want to answer their question. Especially not an elder. So it took a minute for Marvina to process Kerresha's decision, not to categorize it as rude or disrespectful. It was Kerresha's life, her decision to tell the story when and if she got good and ready.

Marvina loaded a stack of plastic diapers in the drawer, careful to double-check her placement with her hands, because, sometimes, her eyes saw something as straight when it was actually crooked.

"Miss Marvina. May I ask you a question?"

"Sure." Marvina hoped Kerresha would reciprocate question-answering soon. "Go ahead, sugar."

"Is there something going on with your eye?"

Marvina bit down on her bottom lip, shocked and shamed all at once. One of her biggest fears was coming true. If people knew she was partially blind, they'd start talking louder so she would hear. Enunciating. Insisting they knew best about her health because they had two working eyes over her one. They might also consider her ugly. Fear slammed into Marvina. Had Kerresha seen the slightest delay in the way her eye moved? If Kerresha saw it, could everyone else see it, too? "What makes you think there's something going on with my eye?"

"I can't tell by looking at you. But there's something in the way you tilt your head. How you position your body. And I watched you just now. When you slid the blanket into the drawer on the left, you had to turn and face it from a different direction to make sure it stayed smooth. Like, not the direction a normal person would have turned."

"I *am* normal," Marvina stated.

"I'm sorry. I mean...I was just asking. You don't have to explain if you don't want to. It's a free country."

Marvina sighed. "I lost sight in my left eye when I was sixteen years old." Marvina steeled herself for the dance of pity across Kerresha's face, but there was none. Only genuine curiosity.

"Was it, like, a disease?"

"No. An accident. I take the blame, though. I was doing something I had no business doing."

Kerresha said, "Did you mean to hurt yourself seriously?"

"Of course not."

"Then why do you blame yourself? I mean, who doesn't do stuff they're not supposed to be doing when they're sixteen? And who says you're not supposed to be doing whatever it was?"

"The law." Marvina quickly reclaimed her blame.

"Some laws are senseless." Kerresha shook her head. "I'm glad Martin Luther King Jr. and Rosa Parks didn't follow all the laws. We'd still be living in segregation."

Marvina touched her chin with a thumb as she studied Kerresha sitting in that rocking chair, philosophizing like she had the whole world figured out in her nineteen-year-old mind. "I should have followed the law, in my case. I was sixteen years old. I had just gotten accepted into the honors program at the high school, and Rose just passed her driver's license test. We thought it would be a good idea to drink some champagne to celebrate. One of her friends had given her a bottle. We snuck it into the house. Rose hid it under her bed."

"Under her bed?" Kerresha gawked, shaking her head.

"Where else were we gonna put it? In the refrigerator right next to the milk jug?"

"I guess it makes sense to a sixteen-year-old, or anyone who hadn't been around alcohol," Kerresha reasoned, giving Marvina and Rose grace anew.

It had been decades since Marvina told anyone the story. Yet, she remembered the details like yesterday. She remembered the mischievous smile on Rose's face, the feeling that she and Rose were in sync again, because, in the previous two years, Marvina had felt caught in the middle of Rose's and Momma's fights about Rose having a boyfriend, wearing a skirt too tight or a shirt cut too low. According to Momma, Rose was on her way to hell if she didn't start acting better.

But there, standing in the moonlight, her driver's license paper fresh off the printer and preparing to drink alcohol in Daddy's old shot glasses, Marvina understood why Rose rebelled. The champagne bottle seemed the perfect symbol of celebration, just like those special moments in the novels Marvina read. This would be fun. Adventurous. She and Rose together—never a dull moment. Even if Momma disapproved. Maybe *because* of Momma's disapproval. The thought was intoxicating, and she hadn't even taken a sip yet.

"So how did the champagne lead to the accident?"

"Well. We waited until our parents went to sleep, pulled the warm bottle out, shook it up—we didn't know no better. All we knew, from watching television, was that champagne was supposed to explode. We thought it was like a bottle of soda that needed shaking in order to make the explosion happen."

Kerresha's hands slapped the sides of her face.

"Rose tried to pop the top. The bottle was pointed at me. She made one quick move and next thing I know, I was on the floor, screaming. The cork hit me dead in my eye."

Kerresha's mouth dropped open. "Miss Marvina, that is a cray cray freak accident."

"Worse than cray cray. I was rolling around on the ground hollering. Rose dropped to the floor and rolled around with me. She clamped her hands over my mouth to keep our parents from hearing me scream. Trying to keep us out of trouble. It was a good hour before I stopped crying and Rose pried my hand off my face to get a look at my eye. She said it didn't look bad, but she said we should go ahead and tell Momma."

"Did you go to the hospital?"

"Goodness, no! We couldn't tell Momma we'd been trying to drink champagne! I swore Rose to secrecy because I never wanted to disappoint our mother."

"So you just went blind to avoid telling your mother you were blind? Didn't she know something had happened?"

All the lies came rushing back. In retrospect, the actual cork-explosion incident wasn't the worst of it. The time between the accident and her first visit to the doctor was the most ridiculous part.

"Oh, I made up some kind of lie about getting hit with a volleyball in gym class. My eye was red, but there wasn't a whole lot of swelling. Rose tended to me as best as an untrained seventeen-year-old could. She even saved her lunch money and bought me a hard eye patch to wear at night so I wouldn't accidentally roll over and put pressure on it when I went to sleep. One morning, Momma came in to wake us up. She saw the patch and asked for an explanation. We lied as long as we could, but our lies didn't add up. I finally told the whole truth.

"Momma took me to a doctor straight away, but there was nothing left for him to do. My retina had torn. The healing and scarring closed off any opportunity to regain sight in that eye.

"The doctor tried to comfort Momma by telling her that there was little chance they could have saved my sight, anyway. He tried to be compassionate, but Momma was inconsolable. Ooh, she cried and cried. And I think that was when things started getting bad between her and Rose.

"Poor Rose. She felt so bad. But she was just a child, too, I realize now."

"Right," Kerresha agreed. "And so were you. I mean, it made sense to both of you at the time. So don't blame yourself. Or Rose. Real talk: everybody I know snuck their first drink before seventh grade. We were, like twelve. Y'all were late!"

Marvina grimaced while chuckling sadly at the same time. "Chile! You and your friends were highly unsupervised."

"True that."

They sat in silence for a minute. Marvina filled her mind with thoughts of Kerresha's baby in order to drown the memory of her awful accident again. She lost more than her sight that night. She lost a sister. She lost the circle of womanhood in their small family.

"Also, you were both minors. Legally still children." Kerresha continued slathering grace all over the past, smothering it with empathy, as though she understood, at only nineteen years, what it was like to make a huge mistake.

It hit Marvina that, while Momma and all the other church folk she knew spent their time and energy learning how to avoid a moral lapse, errors, and sin, they did not have a plan for recovering from their mistakes. The only plan was "don't do it." Nothing for "but if you do, here's what you do after." There was only right and wrong. Black or white. No room for humanity or the gray nuances of life.

"Sooo, that takes care of my question about your eye. I have one more, about something I've noticed."

Marvina laughed. "Didn't know I was under surveillance."

"I'm not spying on you. I notice small things, that's all."

"Fire away," Marvina said.

"Okay. So, I've seen you stretching your hands. Your neck. What's up with that?"

Marvina felt like she'd been hit in the stomach with a fifteen-pound medicine ball. There was no denying Kerresha's eye for detail. Marvina contemplated how to answer the question, because, truth be told, Marvina hadn't accepted her medical diagnosis. She'd blocked it from her mind and thought she was doing a good job of hiding it until just now.

"If it's too personal, you don't have to tell me. Obviously," Kerresha laughed nervously.

Marvina exhaled. "I have multiple sclerosis. A mild case, thus far. In fact, it's called benign multiple sclerosis. Every now and then I have muscle spasms. Especially in my hands. Stretching helps."

"Have you told Rose?"

"No. And I don't want you telling her, either."

"But—"

"No buts, Kerresha. I don't want her or you or anybody else feeling sorry for me. That'd make it worse."

Kerresha raised her palms. "Okay, okay. I got it."

"Thank you."

Next, Kerresha asked, "What are you going to do with this room when I'm gone?"

Kerresha poked around Marvina's life all the more, without knowing it.

"I don't know. If my son ever comes back to visit Fork City, I hope he'll stay with me."

"Why wouldn't he?"

Marvina lifted off the dresser. A line throbbed across her backside from leaning too long. "We don't talk much. We don't agree about his lifestyle."

"Anything else you need to confess?" Kerresha laughed. "I'm a good listener."

"You sure are," Marvina conceded with a smile. "Well. Warren Jr. is…" Marvina softly uttered the word, "gay."

Kerresha nodded. "Why are you whispering the word?"

"First time I've said it out loud. About my son."

"Got it." Kerresha steadied herself with one arm and held the other one out straight to balance herself while she got up from the chair.

Marvina rushed over to help, pulling her forward, to a standing position. The move made Marvina's fingers cramp. She stretched them wide for relief.

Kerresha bent to her left, then her right. Stretching. Then she asked, "Does your son know you love him?"

The question stunned Marvina. *Did he?* After their last few hostile and hurtful conversations, he knew she struggled with the idea of him being gay, given what she had learned all her life in church. But did Warren Jr. actually know she still loved him? "I can't say," she answered honestly.

"Love seems like a good place to start."

Kerresha shuffled out of the room, mumbling about her weak bladder.

Dumbfounded, Marvina sat in the rocking chair now and let the phrase wash over her again.

Love seems like a good place to start.

CHAPTER 16

Rose

Elizabeth and I texted a few more times early that week. She even added me to her message group, where she shared an encouraging message every morning. Sometimes twice a day. The other people in the group, I gathered mostly women, replied with smiley faces and hearts and thanks. If I hung around that group long enough, I'd be a successful business owner, too.

Now that we had all the seasoning ingredients, and Marvina had Kerresha settled into her room good, my sister finally tapped on my door and asked if I was ready to re-create Momma's seasoning together. The Wednesday-morning invitation came unexpectedly. "You ready to prep the spices?"

I sat up in bed, closed out the card game I'd been playing on my phone. "We won't be done in time for you to go to church tonight." My sister was a midweek-service kind of chick, and, honestly, I was wondering when she'd start hounding me about going to church on Wednesday nights, too.

"I'm not going to church tonight." She offered no explanation, only a somber, tired expression. "You coming to the kitchen or not?"

"Yes, ma'am."

She left me to myself for a minute. As I stuffed my feet into a pair of fluffy, pink house shoes, I wondered if this was the end. Would she expect me to leave once I'd perfected the recipe again? Was she sharing this with me because she'd decided to leave the church for good? And if she was leaving Greater New Harvest, how would Marvina find her worth again?

Already, I heard cabinet doors opening and shutting, so I lifted off the bed, dropped my phone into my purse, and joined my sister in her kitchen. Seeing the strings of her threadbare apron disappear into the rolls of fat at her waist put me at ease. Reminded me of Momma. Plump and hot and working her magic in the kitchen.

I washed my hands in the sink and tied the second apron around myself as well. This one seemed newer; it hadn't seen nearly as many hours of work as Marvina's.

She rolled out a sheet of wax paper on a countertop. Four candy apple–shaped canisters stood at attention to witness the recipe come together. If these apples could talk, they'd sell Momma's recipe to the highest bidder.

"You remember what we start with?" she quizzed me.

I clicked my cheek at her kindergarten question. "With making the garlic powder, of course."

"Well, I'm glad you remember *something* of Momma's."

My fist propped on my hip. "I remember a lot about Momma. Different versions of the same stories, obviously."

Marvina stood to my left, giving her full view of the counter. She and I peeled the garlic, cut it into thin slivers, and laid them flat on a silicone mat on top of a cookie sheet. She slid the first batch of garlic into the oven.

"What exactly is your problem with Momma? Before the

adultery, before David, before you went to college, and even before my accident, you turned on her. What got into your mind, Rose? Every time I looked around, y'all were arguing. After all the years and times we spent cooking and laughing together. I never understood it."

I withheld a complete judgment of her narrative of my deteriorated relationship with Momma, willing myself to remain calm and hear this whole story out. But I felt the need to defend myself from this accusation. "For the record, I did not *turn* on Momma. You make it sound like I was a lion she'd raised as a pet, and then one day I reverted to my natural self and attacked her."

"People shouldn't keep lions as pets," Marvina deflected.

"Stay with me."

"Yes, I hear you." She laid out the next row of garlic slices.

"I loved Momma—no—*adored* Momma as much as you did when we were little. No way I could turn on my own flesh and blood."

"Glad to hear it."

Now that she'd backed off this idea of me turning, I skillfully whipped my knife through the garlic again, trying to remember where the fissure between me and Momma began. Marvina and I used to sit our bottoms on Momma's long, wide feet and hold on to her thick legs while she walked just because. And Daddy regularly gave spontaneous shoulder rides. We felt the safety, the marvel of sitting atop his strong frame. On top of the world.

I traced my emotions back to the first time I ever thought to myself, "Momma might not be right about this." Sitting in Marvina's question, with the smell of garlic whirling around us, muscle memory activated by slicing and laying out the garlic with my sister, the past came floating back easily. The earliest flash came in the summer before sixth grade. A young man at our church who had served in the military committed suicide. I said to Marvina, "I think maybe it started when James McHenry died. Momma didn't appreciate me questioning God's compassion."

"What did you say?" Marvina wanted to know.

I hoped I wasn't about to start World War III by sharing it with her. "Well, people were saying that suicide was an automatic ticket to hell. After the funeral, Momma had to drive home in a separate car because Daddy had to go do something with the elders. You were too little to go to the funeral, I think, so you were at school. That left me alone in the car with Momma after seeing James, so young and innocent-looking, in a casket. So I asked Momma if James was forever separated from God. She said 'yes.' And I was like, 'Why?' you know? Obviously, James must have been depressed. Mental illness, bullying, or some kind of abuse, because nobody says 'I can't wait to kill myself and go to hell' unless something is seriously going wrong. I basically asked her if God took everything a person had been through into account before He sentenced someone to hell.

"But Momma insisted James could not get into heaven because he had committed suicide, which meant he didn't have time to ask for forgiveness of his sin before he died. This was all too bad for him.

"So then I asked her, what if James had two seconds in between when he took the pills and when he fell asleep? Would God let him in then?

"Momma said no."

"Come on now, Rose. You know why she said that," my sister explained. "Momma was always scared. She probably wanted to scare you from any thoughts of suicide in the future."

Marvina held a PhD in excuse-ology.

"Be that as it may, there was no way for me to know that as a child. So then I asked her why God would do that to someone. She gave me some kind of roundabout answer. And then I asked her to show me in the Bible where it said people who ended their own life were going to hell, because, by that point, I had read a lot of the Bible and couldn't remember coming across anything like that—so heartless and unempathetic about God.

"Momma looked at me like I had grown another head. She stopped the car, pulled out that tube of roll-on blessed oil she carried everywhere, and prayed for me on the spot."

Marvina cackled loudly. "Oooh, Momma carried that oil everywhere, honey! Didn't leave home without it!"

"You ain't ever lied."

Though the spice ingredients had not all come together yet, their scents intermingled in the air. A prelude to glory.

"Well." My sister paused, laying out the final row of garlic. "I'm sorry Momma felt she had to scare you. It's hard being a parent. Sometimes you feel like fear is the only weapon at your disposal to save your children. It's a low blow, but sometimes it works. I mean, you're still here, right?"

"Once again, for the record, I was not suicidal. There was no immediate need for Momma to scare me straight."

Marvina giggled. "You always had a way with words. I always thought it was your sarcasm and dry humor that came between you and Momma."

"She didn't appreciate my wit, either. She slung oil on me for that, too."

This time, Marvina all-out guffawed. "Slung oil?!"

I threw my head back in laughter, too. "Wait a minute! You

remember the time Uncle Cleo asked Momma to anoint him with the oil so he could win on a slot machine in Vegas?"

We both hollered at the memory of Momma kicking her baby brother out of the house.

"I tell you what, though, I miss knowing Momma is praying for me," Marvina said. "I mean she prayed for us every single morning and night, without fail. And I'm not just talking about 'Lord, help my child have a good day.' She tarried over us. I'd hear her in the night crying and calling our names."

Though I had no relationship with my mother to speak of in her last years, I never doubted she still prayed for me. Even if I disagreed about the extra, unnecessary commentary that surely surrounded her prayers, my heart knew she still applied her faith to my life. Whether that had helped me or hindered me, I wasn't sure.

"All I know is Momma didn't appreciate me asking hard questions about God. When she faced me in that car, I saw the fear in her eyes at me making threatening inquiries about God or church or the rules she never was able to show me in the scriptures."

"Hmph," Marvina's voice thudded with consideration.

I added the second tray of garlic to the oven.

"You wanna do the peppers or the onion skins?" she asked me.

"I'll take the peppers." I repeated the same process to prepare the serrano peppers. Carefully, I removed the membrane and the seeds before slicing them, then started laying them on a rack I set inside a third pan.

Marvina peeled off the dry, cracked skins of onions. "I got another bone to pick with you."

"Shoot."

"My son didn't have an aunt. You missed out on him. And vice versa."

"I didn't think you wanted me there."

She slammed the wooden part of her knife on the counter. "Rose Yvette Dewberry-Tillman. Are you serious right now?"

I laid down my knife. "You and Momma kicked me out of your lives. And by default, your family, nephews included."

She shook her head in a way that let me know my narrative had been askew all this time, too. She picked up her knife again, carried on with the onions. "Warren Jr. missed you. He asked about you all the time. I told him what I knew. He was so proud of you. Told people he had an aunt who went to college and lived in Dallas. He wrote a paper about you. Third grade, if I remember correctly."

My face tingled. "How come you never told me?"

I made room in the oven for the peppers.

"Didn't think you cared. And I...I wasn't sure if you were... you know..."

"No. I don't know. Tell me."

"I didn't know if you were still living...in sin. I didn't want a bad influence in his life."

I spoke past the growing lump in my throat. "I'm not a monster. Just because I naively fell in love with a semi-divorced man doesn't mean I would have harmed your son. Jesus! You'd think I spent most of my life on death row by the way you talk about me when I've never seen the inside of a jail. Unlike Warren Sr.!"

To this day, I have no idea why I had to tack on that part about Marvina's deceased husband. It was petty, but seeing as we were already wallowing in the muddy puddles of our past, what difference did it make?

"He wasn't a jailbird," Marvina spat back. "He only went in once for a ticket he didn't pay before the deadline." She opened the oven and slid the onion skins inside next to the peppers.

"Don't I know this already. I hope the forty dollars of mine that you put toward his bail served the both of y'all well."

"Ow!" Marvina yelled. She shook her hand, then blew on it.

I dropped my knife on the counter, grabbed a plastic sandwich bag from the pantry, filled it with ice, and approached her. "Let me see."

A red welt, soon to be a blister, formed across the knuckle line. Gently, I pressed the ice on her hand.

She winced and her hand tensed.

"Shhh shhhhh." I rubbed her free thumb for what it was worth. Her hand relaxed at my touch. We stood still, the tenderness between us almost tangible. The scent of the spices, human empathy, and plain old muscle memory combined to re-create the gooey magnetism of being near Marvina again. Felt like macaroni and cheese—the kind with a bubbly brown crust on top—in my soul. Mmm mmm good.

"You'd think for as long as I've been blind in this eye, I'd have a handle on distance."

"Don't blame yourself."

"Funny you should say that," Marvina quipped. "You seem to blame me for so much."

"It all started with you spending that forty dollars the wrong way. Why'd you do that, Marvina? It was supposed to be the beginning of our business."

She yanked her hand from me. "Wasn't no *our* to it. When I got that paperwork, I saw where you'd named the restaurant after yourself." She looked over my shoulder as though reading a marquee shining in the middle of her kitchen. "The Southern Rose. Named by, for, and after you."

She refocused on me. "Naming our business venture after yourself wasn't no way to start a partnership. Pissed me off, quite frankly. And I felt like I had a right to do whatever I wanted to do with the money after you sat up there and single-handedly put your name right in the title."

First of all, I didn't even know the word "pissed" was in Marvina's vocabulary. Secondly, I don't remember naming the business without her permission. I don't remember having a discussion about it, but... *Did I really do that?* And if I did, why didn't she just say something? "All you had to do was give me a call. We could have discussed the name."

"Shouldn't have had to call and discuss the name of our business after you printed it on the registration forms."

Marvina blew cool air onto her knuckles.

I took her burned hand into mine again and re-applied the ice.

"Don't make no sense how you just did what you wanted to do with things," I reiterated.

"Aaah. So you *do* understand how I felt, then," Marvina played on my words.

Kerresha shuffled into the kitchen, fully dressed in a snug red fleece jumpsuit and Chuck Taylors.

"Wow! The kitchen smells delicious! What are y'all making?"

"The seasoning. We'll have fried chicken tonight," I told her.

Kerresha stopped in the center of the kitchen. "Wait. Y'all *make* the seasoning? From scratch?"

"Mostly," I told her. "Fresh spices make everything pop."

"Wow. That's some survival of the fittest skills."

She noticed the ice pack, now. "Are you all right, Miss Marvina?"

"Yeah. Top of the stove caught me."

Kerresha looked past us to the counter, where the ingredients still remained visible.

Soon as she started looking, me and Marvina slid in front of that counter like James Brown on the dance stage! "It's a family secret," I said.

Marvina added, "Our mother taught us. She told us to keep it between us."

Kerresha snapped her finger in a circle and gave us one of those go-on-girl grins. "I ain't mad at y'all. Gotta have something to pass down to the next generation."

"Thanks for understanding," I told her, hoping she'd take the hint and leave the kitchen.

"But. I'm not trying to be funny, and I don't mean to disrespect your family recipe. I'm just saying. It might go faster if y'all used a dehydrator."

All the muscles in my body went rigid. She might as well have slapped me. I was stunned. Appalled.

Marvina was disconcerted, too, judging from the tendons poking out the side of her neck.

I was the first to recover my powers of speech. "Really?"

"Yeah. A friend of mine uses it for…other purposes. But I don't know. Maybe give it a try."

Marvina's eyes narrowed. "Other purposes like what?"

Kerresha rolled her eyes playfully. "Marijuana."

"Huh."

"Sounds about right. Maybe we should invest in one," I said. "If Momma had known about them, she'd have tried it."

Marvina looked at me like I'd lost my mind. "Momma wasn't one for shortcuts."

I shrugged. "Well, it *does* take a full workday to make Momma's seasoning. If we could speed it up and maintain the quality and taste…" I stopped shy of saying anything about the restaurant.

One thing at a time. I still wasn't sure whether Marvina was offended by the child's suggestion or not.

"I'm just saying," Kerresha ended the conversation. "In other news, one of my classmates is home from college for Christmas break. We're going to lunch."

"That should be fun," Marvina encouraged with a sweet smile. "You go on and have a good time. Rose and I got our hands full with the seasoning. Like I said, we'll use it on our fried chicken tonight."

"Sounds good."

A horn honked, and Kerresha rushed to the door.

"Wait a minute," Marvina scurried after her, "who is this girl you runnin' around with?"

"It's just a friend. I gotta go. Bye."

Despite her bulging stomach, Kerresha had some moves of her own and got in a small green truck, old as Methuselah, before me and Marvina could write down the license plate or even make out a face behind the tinted windows. From the silhouette, it looked like a boy. Hard to tell these days, with so many girls wearing short styles, though.

We peeked out the window as they drove away.

"Reckon that's her baby daddy?" Marvina asked.

"Could be. Whoever it was, she didn't fancy us meetin' 'em."

Marvina said, "Wonder if it was a marijuana dealer."

"Sister. Please!"

"She *did* say her friend used a dehydrator for pot."

"Doesn't mean *Kerresha* is smoking weed."

"She might be."

"Can you blame her, with a mother like Lyla?"

Marvina clicked her cheek and released the window sheers.

"I'm gonna go read a book while the ingredients cook in our regular, old-fashioned gas oven, the same way Momma used to do it. I'm having second thoughts, now."

"About what?"

"Well," Marvina said, "I was thinking maybe, since the tenants in Momma's house will be leaving next week, maybe we could let Kerresha stay there while she's getting on her feet. I know she's tired of living with old biddies. Momma was such a giving person. She always said it was a blessing to be able to bless somebody else."

I did *not* see that coming. Her idea about letting Kerresha move into the house stunned me. I mean, everything she said about Momma was true. But I was thinking about *selling* the house, not using it for charity.

Marvina and I parted ways for most of the day. And then we came back together when it was time to crush the dried components and mix it all together. We unbound the thyme and rosemary and crushed them to tiny bits using a stone grinder. A cup of this, a dash of that, several teaspoons of the other. We sifted, ground, pounded, and pulverized. I made a mental note that Marvina seemed to be using more of those peppers than I remembered, in proportion to the garlic. It was these little things, these important ratios, that had faded from memory over time.

Marvina spooned out dry ingredients we weren't making from scratch, including maple syrup powder. Together, we combined all the spices, almost the way I remembered them, but I was off on the pepper, the ginger, and the maple syrup powder. Before I knew it—voilà. I had myself a homemade batch of Momma's seasoning again. We made enough for us both to have nice-sized containers full.

Even better, I freshened my memory in Marvina's presence. And we didn't even argue.

Seemed like the second after she dropped the last scoop into my airtight cylinder, my knee started throbbing from all the standing in the kitchen. I bent over to knead the sore spot.

"Hmph. That's funny," Rose said. "The whole time we were making Momma's recipe, your knee wasn't bothering you. You think that's a sign?"

I took a deep breath and let my eyes settle deep into hers. "I do."

By the time Kerresha got home, we were all good and ready for a nap. Afterward, Marvina and I fried the chicken, and, I tell you, all hell broke loose when Kerresha tasted the meat.

"Oh my God! Holy Jesus and Guadalupe Mary!"

Before Marvina could ask her to stop using the Lord's name in vain, Kerresha leaned back in her chair and feigned a heart attack. "Oh my God! Mmm, mmm mmmmm! Where? What kind of voodoo did you put in this chicken?"

"Ain't no voodoo here in this house," Marvina bucked.

"Yes! There is!" Kerresha licked her fingers. "I promise you. On God." She put a hand on her heart. "This chicken just took me back to the spiritual power of the ancestors."

Marvina was so flattered she couldn't be mad. We both looked at each other and laughed, because, truth be told, this was exactly the reaction people gave the first time they tasted Momma's seasoning on expertly fried chicken.

"Y'all." Kerresha raised both hands in the air like she was getting happy in a holiness church. "Is it the grease? The seasoning? Chickens raised by unicorns?"

"It's the seasoning," my sister and I said simultaneously.

Kerresha swallowed another bite. "Whatever y'all put in that seasoning is a miracle. A double miracle, since it also has the power to make y'all finally both agree on something."

CHAPTER 17

The December weather participated with the drive-by baby shower plans. It was sixty-seven degrees, clear blue sky, and no breeze. *Thank You, Lord.*

Kerresha got up and worked a miracle of her own. She took out her braids, flat-ironed her hair, and made herself up like a runway model. Marvina almost didn't know who Kerresha was when she came out of her room. She was beautiful, just like Lyla probably looked before life got ahold of her.

"Aww sookie sookie now!" Rose exclaimed when she beheld Kerresha emerging from the bedroom.

Kerresha wore a tight black dress—too tight in Marvina's opinion, considering they wore loose dresses to hide pregnancies back in Marvina's day. But these women of today ain't trying to hide what is and always has been obvious, even wearing a tentlike maternity dress: a woman's belly is big and round when she's pregnant. The more she hung around Kerresha, the more Marvina questioned everything she thought she knew about propriety.

And you best bet Kerresha ran the shower like a fast-food

restaurant drive-through, taking pictures with everybody and opening their gift right on the spot so she could oooh and aaah over it.

Marvina recorded the names of the people and what gift they gave for thank-you cards later. Rose stood a little farther down the street and handed them a baggy with candies and candles on their way out. They could have been a whole assembly line at General Motors.

Marvina thought she knew everybody and their cousins in Fork City. Wrong, wrong, wrong. Kerresha's crew, mostly people she went to high school with, consisted of a whole new batch of people Marvina had never heard of, whose folks she didn't know. More Hispanics than she realized were in the city. Good thing for a change. New people bring in new money, new ways of doing stuff. Kind of like Kerresha had done for her.

But Marvina swore, one particular carful of Kerresha's friends must have been in a different crowd altogether. One of 'em had blue hair; the other one had five or six spikes coming out of his face. And one of 'em had the thick painted-on eyebrows, looked like a math square root sign. Scary, when Marvina first laid eyes on them. But they hugged Kerresha and left her the cutest baby clothes. And when Marvina saw how they all posed together, she could see why there were so many different kinds of kids who liked Kerresha; she didn't see what Marvina saw—the odd hair, the spikes, the weird makeup. Kerresha saw people, and they saw her, too.

Soon as they left, Marvina finally encountered someone she knew. "Pauline Wilkerson! Is that you I see in this car?" She approached her window with pen and notebook in hand.

Pauline was Warren Sr.'s aunt. She and Marvina had a good

relationship that fizzled away after Marvina's husband passed. Although Pauline could be messy and petty, she and Marvina didn't have a particular falling-out. Just the business of life got in between them. Seeing Pauline again rewound time, especially with her wearing the same hairstyle she had since they'd first met. Finger wave in the front with about two inches of hair curled under at the back. The only difference was her waves showed more scalp than they used to.

"Hey there, Marvina!" Pauline put her car in park and hopped out to hug.

"It's so good to see you! You been taking care of yourself?" Marvina asked.

"Eatin' well. Too well," she laughed at herself. "My butt done got big as I don't know what."

She turned to the side. While Marvina could see the woman had gained weight, her behind was still flat. "Chile, I done seen more butt on a cigarette. You look perfectly fine to me."

Pauline laughed generously. Her gold front tooth glimmered in the sunlight. Then she hugged Kerresha and presented her with a plastic grocery store bag. "Sorry I didn't have a chance to wrap it."

Funny thing is, before Marvina's talk with Kerresha about the boxes, Marvina would have silently judged Pauline for showing up to a baby shower with a tacky gift presentation. But, for the first time, Marvina's heart truly believed the adage "it's the thought that counts."

"No worries." Kerresha took the bag and unlooped the knot. She squealed at the sight of the blue booties she'd placed on the registry list. "Thank you! Thank you! Thank you, Miss Pauline!"

"Small world. How do you two know each other?" As far as Marvina knew, Pauline had moved fifteen miles away from Fork City years ago. She must have had a strong connection, traveling all this far.

"Miss Pauline lived next door to one of my foster moms when I was in the system for a little while. We kept in touch."

The news shouldn't have been shocking, given what they knew about Lyla, but it was. And it hurt Marvina, for Kerresha's sake, to think she had once been in custody of the state.

"And how do you know Marvina?" Pauline asked.

"She and her sister, Rose, took me in. Until I have the baby and get settled."

"That don't surprise me about Marvina. She's always been a giver. It does surprise me about Rose, though. I thought y'all didn't get along because she is selfish and bougie and wild."

Kerresha's face widened.

Something bubbled up in Marvina to defend her sister. Even though Pauline was only repeating what Marvina had said, and it was true that Rose was selfish and bougie and wild, Pauline didn't have a right to say it. Marvina was the only person allowed to bad-mouth her sister. "Rose is doing well these days."

"Glad to hear it," Pauline backed away from the minefield that Marvina's face told her she was entering if she didn't lay off Rose.

Kerresha asked, "And how do you two know each other?"

"Everybody used to know everybody in Fork City, chile," Pauline laughed. "Marvina's husband was my nephew, rest his soul." Pauline did the sign of the cross on her chest even though she wasn't bit-mo Catholic.

"Wow. It really *is* a small world. And thank you again for the booties. They're so cute!"

Marvina jotted down the gift information while Kerresha posed for a picture. Pauline held the oversized, decorated picture frame, while Kerresha held the knitted socks between her and

Pauline. "Thank you for coming by. Rose will give you a party favor when you pull down the street."

As soon as Pauline drove off, Marvina's blood pressure returned to normal.

Kerresha rolled her lips between her teeth to keep from talking, but her eyes smiled. Marvina supposed it was amusing to see her standing up for Rose after all the arguing they did. Family was funny like that.

There was a lull about an hour into the party. Rose and Marvina snatched the time to transport gifts back up to the house. In Kerresha's room, they took a second look at all the gifts. They were both giddy with excitement. The baby was coming soon, and they'd be ready for him, thanks to the generosity of Kerresha's friends.

"Wonder why none of them would let Kerresha come and stay with them," Rose asked. "They all seemed nice enough."

"They're just babies, too."

"Hmph."

Marvina scooted the baby clothes hamper into a corner of the room. "This baby is loved already."

Tickled to laughter, Rose said, "And spoiled, too." She held a onesie to her chest. "I'm so happy for Kerresha."

"She's going to be a great mother."

"She sure will," Rose concurred. "You know something?"

Marvina stopped organizing and gave Rose her undivided attention. "What?"

"This is the first time I haven't been jealous of a pregnant woman. I'm simply happy for somebody else, without thinking about what I *didn't* have. Took almost thirty years, but it's here."

"Hmmm," Marvina reminisced. "You remember how Momma always said that cooking set her mind straight. Brought her peace?"

"She did, didn't she?"

"The other day, when we were making the spices together, and when Kerresha got all—what does she call it, crunk?—about the chicken?"

Rose laughed, "Yes, I think that's the word!"

"All crunked up," Marvina continued, "it made me think about how much healing there is in cutting up the garlic and the peppers and watching that chicken sizzle to a nice, deep brown in the grease. It's powerful, Rose. Heals the mind, heart, body, and soul."

Rose's eyes watered. She fixed her lips to say something but stopped.

"Go on. Say what you want to say," Marvina encouraged. Being around Kerresha had given Marvina new ears to listen, to be open to unfamiliar thoughts. It was nice to think those ears could be used with Rose and other people, too.

Rose hesitated a bit longer, massaging the onesie in her hands. "I was thinking...maybe it could heal our relationship, too."

"Stranger things have happened." Marvina made room for the possibility in her heart.

A loud muffler idled in the front yard. Marvina stepped to the curtain. The green truck was back with a short stocky boy leaning on the driver's door. "It's that same boy who took her to lunch. Now's our chance to get a peek at him. Might be the baby's father."

Rose punched the bedspread with a fist to help steady her rise from the bed.

Just then, Kerresha's loud voice careened through the closed window. "Go! Get away from here!"

Like the legend of the mother who lifted a car off her infant's trapped body, Rose defied the laws of kneecap flexibility logic. Supernatural maternal strength propelled her out of that room and

straight to the driveway with unbelievable speed. Whatever problems she had with her knee disappeared as she came to Kerresha's
rescue.

She was a good ten feet ahead when Marvina heard Rose say
in the Southern dialect she usually managed to hide, "No, sirree!
Not today you ain't!"

"Ma'am. With all due respect, this has nothing to do with you."

Judging by the light-green eyes, pronounced forehead, and his
attempt at manners, Marvina decided this short boy was somehow related to the Jefferson clan. Good people with reasonable
understanding. Church members, too. One phone call to Sister
Jefferson-Pope would bring an end to this show.

So long as Rose didn't escalate the situation with her dramatic
antics.

Rose took a step between Kerresha and the boy. "What concerns her concerns me, you hear?" She stuck her neck out like it
was a border he'd better not cross.

He must have seen the fire in Rose's eyes, because he backed
up. He pointed at Kerresha from a safe distance, as though he
realized Rose was liable to bite his fingers off if he got too close.

Again, those Jeffersons were fairly smart.

"This here is a drive-by baby shower. Your hands look mighty
empty," Marvina said.

Nostrils flared, he answered, "Ma'am, I didn't come here for
the shower. I came to talk to Kerresha."

Rose flapped her arms. "Do this look like the time or place to
be havin' a heart-to-heart?"

He ignored Rose's question and, instead, hurled forceful words
at Kerresha. "I *told* you we can work this out!"

"I can't! Leave me alone!"

Her high-pitched squeak moved Marvina to speak her brand of profanity. "You need to get your slue-footed self off my property, young man."

The boy narrowed his eyes like he wasn't sure what slue feet were. Nonetheless, he understood the message. He stomped back to the driver's side and slammed the door. Silly. He wasn't hurting nothing except the hinges on his hooptie.

Marvina and Rose wrapped arms around Kerresha as she sobbed into her steepled hands. Her perfect makeup slid down her face, ruining all her excellent cosmetic work.

Gently, Rose probed. "What was that all about?"

"I don't want to talk about it." Kerresha zoomed back into the house, leaving Marvina and Rose to greet and collect gifts from the last four cars in the drive-by caravan.

"I'm sorry, but she is not feeling well," Marvina told these kind strangers. She didn't bother to ask how they knew Kerresha or if they were from Fork City. One thing this drive-by had proven to Marvina was how out of touch she was with her city. So many new faces she couldn't match with family traits.

In previous generations, it was easier to tell who belonged to whom. Families were bigger—five, six, seven children. Same momma and daddy makes a whole lotta kids with the same marks. Big teeth, wide-set eyes, hooked noses—you see them so much at school, at church, you started to recognize them to the point where it was fairly clear when somebody was lying about who their baby's father was.

This array of folks come to support Kerresha and the baby scared Marvina. She had been so caught up in her church and reading her novels alone in her house tucked off the street, she didn't know her town anymore.

Pastor Pendleton was right, then. Things were changing. Perhaps they had already changed without her.

"Time's up. The shower is over," Rose called from her post. She grabbed the basket with the leftover party favors and walked toward Marvina. She was limping and breathing hard. "That was too much excitement in one day." She rubbed her knee and whistled with pain. "I need to go ice my knee. You gonna talk to Kerresha? I think one of us at a time is enough."

"Good point. If she's willing."

When Marvina tried to engage, Kerresha called out, "Please go away," behind her closed door.

"You sure? Talking usually helps you sort things out."

Stubborn silence.

"Okay. We can talk later. I'll leave the last of the gifts here in front of the door."

A loud sniffle ended their non-conversation.

Marvina checked in with Rose next. "What did she say?"

"Nothing except she doesn't want to talk."

She helped Rose stuff a pillow under her knee while Rose kept the ice pack in place.

Rose had moved the extra chair to an angle where Marvina's view of her sister was impossible, so Marvina repositioned the chair.

"What are you doing? I don't want to bump myself up against your chair on accident."

"I'm moving it. So I can see you."

"Oh."

Marvina sat, thinking how freeing it was to be able to tell someone the truth behind all the times she had to take initiative in order to see. Changing seats, walking a step behind, planning right-turn-only routes to suit her visual needs. Most often, Marvina was glad people didn't know she was visually impaired. Other times, she wondered if the outward declaration might bring preferred seating choices at a restaurant or an arm offered to help guide her through a dark movie theater.

"Sometimes I still can't believe that happened," Rose said.

"What?"

"The champagne. The cork. You losing your eyesight in one eye. It was the dumbest thing I ever did." Rose's eyes glazed over.

"I beg to differ. You *did* marry David."

"Really, Marvina? I'm apologizing to you and you bring up David?"

Marvina laughed uneasily. "I'm only trying to lighten the mood."

"Not necessary. I should have apologized a long time ago."

"You *did* apologize the night it happened," Marvina recalled.

"I apologized for opening the bottle so carelessly. Did you know the pressure of a corked wine bottle is two or three times the air pressure in a car tire?"

Of course, Marvina knew. She didn't need an external point of reference to know how forcefully she'd been hit in the eye. Tire pressure seemed mild compared to the pain she'd suffered. Yet, she answered with a lie, "No, I didn't know."

"Neither did I. And I didn't know a bottle of champagne should be cold before opening it. Putting it under my bed, shaking it, opening it warm, only made things worse."

This, too, Marvina knew by now. She had researched her injury numerous times on the internet in hopes of finding a surgeon, a discovery, a pharmaceutical company looking for a subject, a determined mad professor conducting a rogue study. When it became clear that no cavalry was coming for traumatic injuries like hers because too much time had passed, she'd googled for ways to live with the impairment.

Still, every time there was a breakthrough—robotic legs for paraplegics or an athlete with a torn ACL who returned to a professional sport—she hoped and googled "breakthrough in detached retina repair."

Nothing.

"What I need to apologize for now is not telling Momma," Rose acknowledged. "I know you made me promise not to say anything, but I should have. I'm the oldest. I should have known better than to conspire with you to hide a serious injury. I never forgot the sound you made when you let out that first cry. Gives me chills to this day. And I am so sorry I didn't respond differently."

Marvina gave a cleansing breath big enough for both of them. "We were young and foolish, Rose. At that age, you don't think anything bad can happen to you. Even if it does, you trust your body to heal fast, you think everything's gonna go back to normal eventually."

"I don't expect you to absolve me of my guilt. I needed to say it. I'm sorry, Marvina."

"I accept your apology."

"Thank you."

The sisters sat quietly again in each other's presence. Rose with an ice pack atop her wrapped knee. Marvina sitting with a storm of feelings swirling inside her, from head to toe. If she were a drinking woman, she'd have poured herself a full glass of alcohol to settle her thoughts.

Alas, Marvina rocked in Kerresha's new rocking chair and just let it all sink in. That apology from Rose had been a long time coming, and Marvina was glad about it.

CHAPTER 18
Rose

We were so busy planning for the drive-by shower Christmas Eve snuck up on us. Marvina had a tree in the living room, but there were no gifts under it.

When David and I were married, we stopped giving each other gifts for Christmas around year six. We bought everything we wanted or needed all year long. Plus, we'd lost two babies by then. Every Christmas reminded us—or at least me—that another year had passed without the gift I wanted most. A baby.

Now, there was a room full of baby gifts upstairs for Kerresha. Brought a smile to my face. So did watching David's Mercedes roll up Marvina's driveway. I'd asked him to bring me some things, and he had free time with it being the holidays and all.

Marvina looked up from her novel. "You expecting somebody?"

The chair's legs screeched against the floor as I pushed away from the breakfast table. "It's David."

She shook her head. "Would have been nice if you'd told me he was coming."

"For what? So you can shine up your boxing gloves?"

Contempt settled deep in her face. "I wouldn't waste my cleaning spray on David."

"Marvina!"

"Forgive me, Lord," she whispered.

"*This* is why I didn't tell you. You've got serious hate issues with him that you need to resolve if you plan on makin' it past your Pearly Gates."

"You're religious when it benefits you," she shot back.

"Don't you worry about me and my religion. I'm heading out with David today."

"To do what?"

"Nunya business."

David rapped the door three times.

I pinned Marvina with a stare. "Act like you've got some sense."

She shielded her face with the book. "I'll be busy reading."

"You sure you don't want to leave this room?"

"This is my house. I'm staying right here."

I walked to the door feeling like, despite these last few days of reconnecting, nothing sustainable had actually changed between me and my sister. The mention of one person—a person who wasn't even family, wasn't even a part of our everyday lives—had the power to punt me and Marvina back to the twentieth century. Make us quarrel like two angry birds fighting over an empty peanut shell.

When I opened the door, David leaned in for an embrace. I started to back away, but he said, "Merry Christmas." Who can refuse a Christmas hug?

"Same to you, David." His cologne, the hard-earned muscles, and his ever-towering height felt like warm tea on a cool morning.

I noticed two large Target bags on the porch. I'd asked him to bring a few things from my home, so I'd been expecting one tote. But two?

"I come bearing gifts." He lifted the handles and spread them apart, showcasing the beautifully wrapped boxes, all shiny with bows.

"You didn't have to do that! Thank you so much."

He yelled over my shoulder, "I've got something for you, too, Marvina. I see you over there."

"I see you, too, David."

David knew good and well that Marvina didn't like him. He always said it was because Marvina thought he'd stolen me from my family. His theory accounted for about 20 percent of the problem, but the rest lived with his unsettled marital status at the time he pursued me. Funny thing about David, though: he's real good at obscuring the past; he stuffs yesterdays into a shredder. Every day's a fresh start. And he moves like everyone else ought to do the same.

"You ready?" I asked him.

His gaze flicked over my bonnet, housecoat, and slippers. "I am," he replied without referencing my obvious state of unreadiness.

I took the sack from him.

"Oh. The envelope with the property information—"

"Wait for me in the car," I ordered. Couldn't discuss this within Marvina's earshot.

He nodded. Then he looked at Marvina again and prepped his lips to speak. I slammed the door.

I slid into the passenger's side of David's Benz, my backside savoring the heat from the seat. He must have warmed it for me in advance.

"You look good. Knee doing better?"

"Yes. Thank you."

"Where do you want to go first?" he asked.

I whipped the manila folder from the inside of my coat.

David laughed. "I take it you haven't told Marvina about the plans yet?"

"You worryin' about the wrong thing right now, David."

"You can't move forward without her consent."

"Please stop telling me things I already know."

He pressed a foot on the brake, a few hundred feet away from Marvina's driveway.

"Why are you stopping?"

"I want to try something new," he said.

"What?"

"How about we try regular, calm conversations? No sarcasm. No witty, cocky, sharp-tongued comebacks. No fight."

"I'm not fighting with you."

"I know you don't think you are, but you are."

"It takes two," I struck back.

"You're right. But I'm out. I hereby present a white flag." He waved an imaginary stick in the air. "Presume positive intent. Listen without formulating a comeback. This is something I need to work on, too. I'm seeing a therapist."

I twisted my body toward him and searched his face for sarcasm. "*You* have a *therapist*?"

"Not exactly." He pointed at the ceiling with an index finger. "I should say I'm *dating* a therapist."

"Figures." I flounced back toward the dashboard. "I hope she's billing you."

"Bill or not, I'm trying new things. Putting my sarcasm aside to just listen and talk. I gotta tell ya, it's much easier to engage in conversations, now. Don't have to spend so much mental energy trying to poke holes in whatever the other person is saying."

I quipped, "What if the other person says a bunch of holey stuff?"

"There. You just did it again. That fast." David said with a snap of his fingers.

"Did what?"

"Can you just say, 'yes, David. I will try'?"

"Why should I try? It's not like we're in a relationship together."

"Maybe not, but we're in this *car* together, and it looks like we'll be spending this *day* together. So can we both just…try?"

I exhaled.

He ran a hand over his head, and I knew then he was serious.

"Is this what you came out here for? To have an intervention for me?" I asked.

"I came to bring you what you asked for. And to look at the property with you. And I dreaded coming here the whole drive, because you and I go toe-to-toe almost every time we talk. It's what we have in common; it's what keeps us connected, even as exes. But we gettin' too old for this, now. It's time to give up the fight and enjoy life."

I squeezed my purse against my rumbling stomach. David could take this conversation and shove it. For one, this wasn't the first time he'd started dating someone new and then come to me to practice his new kumbaya attitude. Secondly, it suited him to let bygones be bygones; he hadn't lost anything precious in the past. See, when a man does wrong, he wants to apologize real fast and have everybody get over it real quick-like. Just hold a press conference and say, "I shouldn't have done that. I'll do better next time." Next thing you know, you're elected to office. Even if you get fired, the next man will hire you, because, hey, he doesn't want anyone digging up his past, either. They love short memories.

But the thing is: The past injuries live on until the one who committed the wrongs atones for it. You can't just break a woman's heart Monday, say "I'm sorry" on Tuesday with a teddy bear, and then expect her to wake up Wednesday morning and cook you a hearty breakfast. Not unless she's brainwashed. And numb. With no self-esteem and no options other than to lay up under your crusty behind.

At least that was my philosophy as I sat in the car with David, the wannabe Dr. Phil, just beyond Marvina's house.

"Can we go look at the property, now?"

He let out a puff of air and guided the sedan back onto the road.

I opened the folder and began analyzing the paperwork he'd printed. The value of Momma's house was about thirty thousand dollars below what it would cost to get a restaurant up and going. If I took out a home equity loan, I could get that money easily, but then I'd have another loan on my hands.

And all of these figures depended on Marvina saying "yes" to both selling Momma's house and shifting all the proceeds toward opening a business.

David drove another seven minutes to a small shopping center. Decades ago, there had been a movie theater, a Piggly Wiggly, and a Dairy Queen side by side. Now, there was a gun range with only a few cars in the lot and two vacancies for the grocery store and the abandoned restaurant.

"Looks deserted," David said, gliding carefully across the neglected, potholed parking lot.

"I checked the plans. There's gonna be a trampoline park there. That'll bring lots of families. And the gun range might be bought out by a nationwide bookstore chain, too. I think the mayor's gonna make that happen. Not a good look to have a gun range next to a kids' play place."

David nodded. "A smart mayor. A savvy city council can redraw boundaries to force the gun range out."

"Kind of sad they can shut down homes and business," I lamented.

"Welcome to America," David said. He held up a hand. "Wait. I'm sorry. That was sarcastic."

"The truth is sarcastic?" I asked.

"It can be."

"Now I know I can't agree with your new communication style. I'd have to be totally silent. Is that your master plan?"

He laughed. "I already told you. I'm not going there with you today, Rose Tillman."

"My goodness. Let's get out and look at the property. And my legal last name is Dewberry-Tillman."

David hustled around to my door and helped me out of the car.

I recognized Elizabeth from the giant advertisement stuck to the side of her van. She was a short, spiky-blond woman with a slightly startled expression, courtesy of Botox. The lines in her neck said she'd been through some rough times, but her too-perfect teeth said she was on the other side of the storms.

"Hello, Rose. It's nice to finally meet face-to-face."

"Same here."

"And David, right?"

"Yes. Nice to meet you as well."

We all shook hands, and Elizabeth walked us to the front

entrance of what would hopefully be my place of business, the old Dairy Queen. Elizabeth started her spiel while she was unlocking the doors. "There are plans to revive this entire strip, from the freeway to the end of the block. Prices are still reasonable now, but they won't stay that way for long."

"What's your definition of long?" David asked.

"A few months. Six, tops."

I looked up at him to discern how this news landed on his ears. He was biting his top lip. Thinking. Running figures in his head.

Elizabeth jiggled the contraption a few times and, finally, the door unlocked. David, always a gentleman, opened the door. The smell of stale grease and musty carpet instantly slapped us.

"It's been almost a year since it was used. So you'll want an updated inspection."

"Sellers paying?"

Elizabeth angled her forehead like she had to think about it. "We can certainly ask."

"We insist," David said.

I shut my mouth and let David do all the talking from that point on, because once he got that business computation expression on his face, his brilliance shined bright like a diamond.

We toured the whole building. The kitchen, electrical room, office, lobby, even the dumpster area out back. With each step, I heard the "cha-ching" sound as David and Elizabeth talked. Repair this, fix that, replace those, update this to meet new codes and people's expectations. Public Wi-Fi, family restrooms, a special food pickup window for app-based food delivery services—all things I hadn't considered. *Cha-ching, cha-ching, cha-ching.*

When we finished looking around, David inquired, "Do you have any other properties in better condition?"

"I do. But they're a pretty penny, even before the price increases expected in the next few months. I think this one's gonna end up being a steal once the surrounding venues are occupied and running."

He rubbed his chin. "Hmph."

Elizabeth turned to me. "What are your thoughts, Rose? You've been awfully quiet."

"Looks like a lot of work. But I didn't expect it to be easy. It's my dream. My mother's legacy."

She smiled, glad to have me back on her side. "Let's talk again later this week?"

"Sure thing."

Back in the car, David wasted no time telling me what I already knew he felt. "A year ago, it might have been a good deal. But now? I don't know. You and Marvina would need a lot of help getting this place up to speed. It's a big risk."

I couldn't help but think things would have been so much easier, so much simpler if we had done this back when I first tried to open a restaurant with my sister. Before I married David, when Momma would have gladly worked there for free. Also before I'd seen enough of life to become thoroughly indoctrinated in fear.

"But don't worry." David winked at me. "If it doesn't work out, you can always come back home to me."

I slammed the leather panel in front of me. "Drive the car, David. Jeez, Louise."

David laughed and followed my orders.

I laughed, too, because just when I thought he had turned into someone I didn't recognize, the old David showed up again. Snarky and dark-humored. Old habits die hard, to my great comfort.

Our next stop was Momma's house. Olivia was gone, so we

were free to look for areas of improvement we might want to tackle before selling. I'd contacted a local contractor to accompany David and I on the walk-through.

The contractor's yellow truck had a tent on top boasting its business name: "Regal Renovations." Reminded me of a pizza delivery vehicle, but I digress.

"Howdy," the contractor greeted David first. "Name's Mike."

"David."

"And hello to you, little lady." His western-movie mustache curled upward.

"Name's Rose. I'm the one who called you."

He paused. Smiled.

I didn't smile back.

"Rose it is, then. Let me get my tools and we can get 'er done." Mike walked back to his truck while David and I waited on the porch.

"Did you have to do that?" he asked.

"Do what?"

"Be so...hostile."

"All I did was ensure he gives me the same adult-level respect he gave you. How am I in the wrong?"

"Because he was only trying to be nice to you."

"By calling me 'little lady.'"

"Yes. In Fork City, Texas, 'little lady' is...nice."

"How would you feel if he called *you* 'little man.' In Fork City, Texas?"

He rolled his eyes, and I rolled mine, too, because he'd never understand what it means to meet with a contractor or a salesperson or a car repair shop owner without the benefit of being a man. It's scary and intimidating and patronizing. *Especially* in places like Fork City, Texas.

When Mike returned, I unlocked the door and stepped into my past. The last time I'd been in the house, Momma scalded me with words. Marvina avoided me. Daddy poked his head in to check on me, but didn't rescue me from the isolation.

David pressed his hand against my back to move me past the threshold. "You okay?" He whispered in my ear.

I took another step forward.

"Where do you want to start?" Mike asked.

To my left, the weathered kitchen and the revered primary bedroom. To my right, the wood-paneled living room and a hall-way leading to the other bedrooms, where Marvina and I slept as children. Newish carpet beneath my feet and a popcorn ceiling overhead.

"The kitchen," I said. The memories formed in that room made me happy. Greens, ham, potato salad, waffles, and the spices we cut and squashed to make the seasoning. Mike measured and wrote as David and I looked on.

"You okay?" David asked again.

I gave a tiny nod. Olivia must have been one cookin' chick, too, because the house kitchen bore the smell of hot grease.

"You looking to gut this and start over, right?" Mike asked. "New countertops, cabinets, everything?"

"Yes."

"Floors, too?"

"Yes."

"Great." He scratched on his notepad. "These improvements will fetch a handsome profit when you sell. What's next?"

I pointed toward my parents' old bedroom. As we walked down the hallway, a chill crawled up my arms and legs. My parents would not be on the other side of their bedroom door. This house was not the same, yet the memories returned clear as a bell. The cooking, the loving, the ridiculing. How could so many emotions be tied to one location?

Sorrow tumbled through me. "I need to step outside. Can you two finish without me? Just estimate everything. I'll choose what I want later."

"Okay," David covered for me.

I held my breath until I reached the fresh air outdoors. I'd be just fine if I never went in that house again.

David and Mike emerged a few minutes later. I was leaning against David's car, breathing deeply.

"I'll send you the numbers in email if that's okay," Mike said.

"Thank you," David replied for me.

"Was this your childhood home?" he asked.

"Yes."

"I understand." Mike rubbed his own skinny chest. "I renovated my parents' home after they passed. Cried every night throughout the whole project. It gets hard sometimes without your folks."

I wiped a tear from my eyes, thankful to hear Mike's story. "Sure does."

"Like I said, I'll send it through email. Give you a chance to recover and think through, when you're ready. The estimate stands for thirty days."

"Thank you."

David and I drove an hour outside of town, to Lone Creek, to have lunch. The sight of Starbucks, Target, and Taco Bell said we were closer to Dallas, more options for food, entertainment, shopping, health care. On the other hand, more traffic, higher prices, and no trees.

"That was rough for you."

"Yes," I agreed to the obvious. "I gotta eat my way out of it."

David laughed. "What do you have a taste for?"

"A good vegetable plate."

"Oh. Are you thinking of going vegan?"

"No. Do I have to be vegan to eat a vegetable plate?"

He shrugged. "No. You don't."

I waited a beat for his snappy comeback. Nothing. Sounded like he was going to let me have the last word, which I usually claimed, but not this easily. He was practicing his therapy homework on me, and I didn't appreciate it.

Over our meal, I let David do all the talking. He talked about his work, his sister's open-heart surgery, and even his girlfriend a little. Renita. Dr. Renita something, to be exact, but her "brand" was her title and her first name. When I asked David more about the "brand" thing, he gave me the 101 version of marketing.

"You're going to need branding for the restaurant," he said. "I can ask Renita to share the name of her marketing expert."

"No. I'll find my own. Don't want to be beholden to any of your ex-girlfriends."

"She's not my ex."

"She will be. Soon enough," I predicted.

"There you go again," he singsonged.

I set my fork down in my salad. "David. You've known me forty years. It's not fair of you to ask me to change who I am on account of girlfriend number four hundred and seventy-seven."

He took a sip of water. Ran his tongue along his teeth. "You're right. Change is a choice." And then he kept right on eating as though he hadn't just issued me a challenge.

Well, I wasn't going to sit up there and let him keep committing malpractice on me. I ate my food and asked him to take me back to Marvina's. With as few words as possible, we made it back to the house.

He didn't get out or walk me to the door. He just dropped me off like an ungentlemanly date, which was fine with me. I didn't want to bite my tongue anymore, and I didn't have the nerves to listen to him and Marvina argue if he came inside the house. That would be too much like...like me and Marvina.

Give up the fight.

A scary concept. Even when I was dead wrong, I still fought to hold my head up high, to keep my dignity. My pride. But what had it gotten me so far?

Plus, what happens when people give up too soon? Their dreams don't die; their dreams pick up daggers and chip away at the dreamers' hearts, right? I had to know, sooner than later, if Marvina was going in with me because this was all getting too real. Too, too real.

CHAPTER 19

The sight of Rose with David irked Marvina. Or maybe it was the sight of David, period. When Marvina was married to Warren Sr., she gave so much of herself to maintaining their home, raising their son, making sure her husband had everything he needed. She couldn't imagine what it felt like to have your husband leave you for another, younger woman the way David must have left his first wife for Rose.

Heartless.

Whatever gift that he'd brought, which Rose placed under the tree, was gonna get donated to charity.

With Rose out of the house and Kerresha resting in her room, Marvina decided to cook while reading a quick Christmas novel. She'd mastered the art of reading while cooking. And it was, after all, Christmas Eve. A house should be filled with the smells of cinnamon, sweet potatoes, and spices in the days leading up to Jesus's birthday party. At least that's what Momma used to say.

Since her husband and son left the house, Marvina had spent Christmas Eve at the church cooking for the community. Not this year. She hadn't talked to Pastor Pendleton or Eleanor since the unauthorized gathering of the deacons, so there was no chance to continue the tradition. The only place to cook was home.

This upcoming Sunday would be the day after Christmas. Marvina hadn't decided how to enter Greater New Harvest. How she'd feel, how to put the resistance to change aside long enough to receive the spiritual nourishment she needed in the sanctuary. Momma said going to church was like sitting a phone on the battery base. When your energy gets low, you need to get to the house of God and recharge.

Hmph. Momma used to say a lot of stuff. Marvina wondered what Momma would say about this overhaul at Greater New Harvest. About Marvina missing Wednesday night service. About Kerresha and her odd friends. About Rose and David's friendship after all these years, even after the divorce.

Cooking with Momma's spices helped Marvina process. Never mind she didn't have enough people in the house to eat everything she laid out for preparation. Several pies, pork chops, chicken, greens, macaroni and cheese, hot-water corn bread. She was just cookin' to be cookin'.

Then she thought about Kerresha's drive-by shower. That girl had practically arranged and thrown a whole party through her phone. Marvina followed her example and texted everyone she knew within a ten-mile radius. Giving away dinner plates tomorrow starting around noon until I run out. First come first serve. Merry Christmas!

Kerresha was the first to respond to the message. "It smells amazing in here already. What are you making?"

Marvina rattled off the menu.

"Can I be your official taste-tester?"

"Sure thing! You want to help?"

"Naaah. I'm not about that cooking life." Kerresha poured herself a glass of milk and stood by Marvina, observing as Marvina broke eggs for the pork chop coating.

Marvina reveled in the proximity, at the very staging—a youngster staring over her shoulder, taking in this tradition exactly the way she'd learned from Momma. The way she used to teach at the church.

"Listen here. You're about to be somebody's momma. What you gonna feed the baby if you don't learn how to cook?"

Kerresha twisted her lips. "I guess after he's finished breast-feeding, he'll eat what I usually eat. Hot dogs. Hamburgers. Chicken nuggets. Fries."

Marvina balked. "Concession stand food?"

"No. I mean…it's food, right?"

"Where's the dairy? The grains?"

Kerresha sat at the wood table, resting her glass on a coaster. "He could eat cereal, too."

"Honey, you're about to have a *boy*. Growing boys can eat a box of cereal in one sitting."

Shock engulfed her face. "Are you serious?"

"Yes, indeed. They will destroy your entire monthly food budget within one week, the way you're talking. Chicken nuggets and hamburgers." She tsked. "The key to keeping a family fed is casseroles. You throw in whatever you got, a little or as much meat, rice, and pasta. Dump in some cheese and seasoning. They won't know what it is, but they'll eat it and ask for more."

"Sounds gross."

Marvina laughed. "You taste it along the way to make sure it's good."

"Oh."

They continued, with Marvina doling out cooking and parenting advice, while Kerresha made several trips to the pantry for crackers. Then a granola bar. Back to the refrigerator for orange juice. Pickles. The baby had her eating all kinds of food that afternoon.

Rose let herself in with Marvina's spare key. She carried what appeared to be the same manila envelope David brought in the sack earlier. "Good afternoon."

"Afternoon," Marvina replied without looking up from the pot of macaroni she stirred.

"Hello," Kerresha chimed in cheerfully. "Have a good morning?"

"I did. Thank you. Yourself?"

"Yes. Miss Marvina's giving me cooking lessons."

"Is that so?"

Marvina cut her eyes at Kerresha, grinning. "I gave her a lecture on why she needs to *start* cooking. Haven't gotten her to wear an apron yet."

Kerresha pointed at Rose and Marvina. "You two are the ones who love cooking. Have y'all ever thought about opening a restaurant together?"

The kitchen froze from every angle, like a *Matrix* movie. Marvina's whisk landed at a forty-five-degree angle, her wrist perfectly still. Rose with a folder in one hand, the other balled in a fist at her side.

And Kerresha, wearing a tiny smile, waiting for one of them to respond. "Ummm...hello?" she checked to see if they'd heard her.

Marvina turned slightly to lock eyes with Rose.

Rose answered, cautiously, "We did consider it once. A long time ago."

"What happened?"

"We didn't do it," Marvina chopped the top off that conversation.

"Tragic," Kerresha proclaimed, shaking her head and poking her lips in a disapproving scowl. In the next breath, she asked, "So who was the guy in the Benz?"

Rose joined Kerresha at the table. "You spying on me?"

"Maybe."

"He's my ex-husband."

"Her *no-good* ex-husband."

"He must be *some* good. He rolled up in here with a bag full of gifts like he's straight outta the North Pole." Kerresha tilted her head toward the Christmas tree.

Marvina blew air between her lips, making a bubbling sound. "Guilt offerings."

"Wow," Kerresha said. "Never seen you hate on somebody like that, Miss Marvina."

Rose let out a high-pitched squeal.

Marvina opened her mouth to deny it but couldn't. There was no hiding how she felt about David. "I'll take this debate up with the Lord later."

"No. Not tonight," Rose said. "I saw an advertisement for the Christmas lights in Lone Creek. There's a whole new neighborhood they've decorated, and they're collecting money for a charity. I think we should go. Get out of the house."

"David talk you into this?" Marvina whined.

"No! David's gone back to Dallas to be with his woman. Dr. Renita."

Kerresha yowled like an agitated cat and clawed the air with her fingers.

"No ma'am. You don't ever have to worry about me fighting a woman over David. She can have him. Every time," Rose assured the girl. "This Christmas-light adventure would be just us. Starting something new. What do you say, Marvina?"

"I need to finish up cooking. I sent out a text for people to come by and get free dinners tomorrow."

"Here. I'll help you." Rose dropped the apron over her shoulders. "You in, Kerresha?"

"For the lights, yes. For the cooking, no. Isn't there a wise saying about how many people should be cooking at once?"

"Too many cooks in the kitchen?" Rose guessed.

"Yes, ma'am. Isn't that a scripture in the Bible?"

Marvina chuckled and replied, "No, darling. And I believe the saying pertains to too many *chefs* in the kitchen. Any number of people could be learning from the chef. Me and Rose and our Momma—three of us—worked together beautifully."

"We sure did."

An endearing gaze passed between Rose and Marvina.

"Awww," Kerresha cooed. "And look at y'all now. Still cooking together. In your olden years."

The sisters' necks swiveled toward Kerresha.

"I beg your pardon?" Marvina trilled.

Rose tacked on, "Watch it."

"I'm sorry. So very sorry," Kerresha apologized. She flattened her face and lay her hands on top of her stomach as though speaking at a somber event. "Let me rephrase. I mean in your elderly—"

"That's not better." Rose wagged a finger.

Kerresha's shoulders lifted. "In your cougar years?"

"Ooop!" Marvina hollered. "Kerresha!"

"Stop while you're ahead," Rose warned. "And after all these insults, you owe us at least half an hour's worth of work in this kitchen."

"Fine," Kerresha relented. "I'll drop a chop in grease. Just be sure and put extra seasoning on mine."

After they finished cooking, eating, packing, and refrigerating food for tomorrow's giveaway, Rose's knee started bothering her again. Kerresha and Marvina pressed and stretched that knee until Rose felt looser. She also took some ibuprofen to keep the inflammation in check.

This trip to Lone Creek was completely out of Marvina's comfort zone. Really, this seemed like white folks' stuff. Christmas caroling, roasting s'mores, loitering around outside. Black women's hair didn't fare well in all these outdoor activities. And Black folks standing around idle—not serving, not helping, not diverting eyes—in the presence of rich white folks felt dangerous. Still, she was going in order to be with her sister and experience this with Kerresha.

All the way to the ritzy neighborhood, Rose's phone kept dinging with text messages. Annoyed, Marvina asked about the sender. "Is it David?"

"No. I told you he's with his new woman."

"Well I hope whoever it is, you get back to them as soon as we stop. Or turn your phone off altogether."

"Are y'all going to argue all night?" Kerresha asked from the back seat.

"No," the sisters answered together.

Kerresha sighed. "Thank you."

The lights from the neighborhood lit the sky from a mile away, giving the area a blissful glow.

"Wow," Kerresha marveled as they approached the car line to enter the neighborhood. A warm, cozy feeling fogged Rose's Honda, the effect of Kerresha's childlike wonder.

This was Christmas. And family. And love.

Rose tapped Marvina's hand. "You remember the year Momma and Daddy bought us matching bikes?"

"Like yesterday. Worst Christmas gift ever."

"What?!" Rose exclaimed. "We *loved* those bikes!"

"*You* loved *your* new bike," Marvina said. "My bike was a hand-me-down. Had somebody else's name carved on the underside of the handlebars. *Jessica*."

"That's because you said you wanted that new banana seat bike at the last minute," Rose reminded her. "And they were all sold out. Momma found one at a garage sale and got it for you."

Marvina squinted. "How would you know?"

"Because I was there with her when she drove by it, turned the car around, and then bought it. She threatened to spank me if I told you."

"My, my, my," Marvina wondered out loud. Kerresha's favorite phrase now filled Marvina's mouth. "This is amazing."

"What?" Kerresha asked.

"So many of my childhood memories are just…wrong. All this time, I thought Momma bought me the cheap bike and got Rose the new, more expensive bike. Turns out, Momma jumped through hoops to get my bike after my late request. Huh. Paints the situation in a new light altogether. My memory was just wrong, wrong, wrong."

"Not wrong. It's just what you remember from your point of view," Kerresha said. "It's *your* truth, your interpretation of facts and events based on who you were at that time."

"You and my son… I don't understand the term 'truth' the way you young folk are using it. I mean, red is red. Black is black. A truth is true all over the world. When I'm speaking from my personal experience, my personal point of view, that's called an opinion. At least that's what they taught *us* in school."

"That is what they said. Fact and opinion. Black or white." Rose added. "Can't be both."

"Except there is this little color named gray. Ever heard of it?" Kerresha expanded the options sarcastically.

"Gray is too wishy-washy for me," Marvina said with an ardent headshake. "Too loosey-goosey."

Kerresha blinked. "I have no idea what you just said."

"I'm saying that's what's wrong with people today. Nobody wants to take a stand on one side or the other. Too much gray. Too much making excuses for their personal reasons and individual ways of thinking."

"What's wrong with, like, finding out the whole story, asking people for the whole context? What's the rush to categorize things as right or wrong, good or bad? For what? So we'll have an excuse to judge them quicker? Conserve our compassion for someone who deserves it more?"

"Mmph." Marvina's head swayed as though somebody hit her.

"I know that's right," Rose said. "Kerresha, you got a hat with you?"

"A hat?"

"Yeah. So we can pass it around and take up an offering because, chile, you preached a whole sermon."

Kerresha laughed. "I listen to a lot of really good podcasts. Plus, I just think y'all should be happy you have good *some* memories with your parents. Not everyone has those."

They paid the entry fee and joined the caravan coasting through the neighborhood, eyes gaping at the elaborate Nativity scenes, the giant inflated reindeer, the dancing fairy lights set to up-tempo Christmas music.

Marvina, look at that one!

Did you see this, Kerresha?

Slow down, Miss Rose, and watch the angel pop up again!

At one point, Rose, Kerresha, and Marvina's cheeks were side by side, their necks craning to get a look at Black baby Jesus.

"I can't believe it!" Marvina exclaimed. "They actually made Him Black!"

"That's because he *was* Black," Rose noted.

"You know what I'm saying. Folks don't hardly want to hear that, you know?"

"Looks like they do today," Kerresha said.

"Well, I'll be a monkey's uncle. Times really are changing," Marvina concluded.

The tour ended in the parking lot of a large church, with several vendors stationed in the parking lot. Dozens of people ambled around, patronizing and chatting. Rose found a spot. The three women bundled their coats tighter and got out to explore the grounds a bit.

They purchased hot chocolate to warm their insides against the cool, Christmas Eve winds. Kerresha frowned at the "First Christmas" ornaments with the year engraved on them. "Gotta wait another year before my baby can get one of these."

"You don't want him coming early," Rose said. "Let him stay in the oven as long as he needs to."

At a gift basket vendor's table, Kerresha spotted the back church entrance and went to use the restroom, a common occurrence for her now. She left her covered hot chocolate cup in Marvina's care.

This left Rose and Marvina to peruse the next few vendors in the row together.

"Thank you for bringing me here tonight."

"You're welcome," Rose said. "And I'm so glad Kerresha's here. Not only tonight, but…in our lives."

Marvina nodded. "Yes. She's good for us."

Rose held up an oven mitt that read: *Don't make me poison you.* They both giggled at the irreverent wording.

"My Lord. Momma would not have approved," Rose exhaled.

"Surely not." Marvina said. "What did Momma approve of?"

Rose placed the mitt back in its stack on the vendor's table. "I don't know. Momma had her own ways. She was a woman of her time. She did what she thought was right and…I don't know…I don't want to judge her. But I didn't agree with everything she said or did. I'm not her, and she's not me. She's not you, either."

Marvina was torn between respecting Momma and accepting Rose—flaws and all—back into her life. Gray, gray, gray. An area she'd always avoided. But at what cost?

"I gotta tell you something," she said, stepping away from the table, away from the cluster of shoppers.

Rose followed. "Yes."

"It's about Warren Jr. He's gay."

Rose's eyes widened. She blinked one time, slowly, presumably processing the news and all it meant for the relationship between Marvina and her son. "Really?"

"Yes. That's why he won't come home."

"He won't come back to Fork City because he's gay?"

"Not exactly," Marvina admitted. She pulled her sister's arm, bringing her in closer. "He knows how I feel about his lifestyle. So he won't visit. And he hasn't invited me to Washington State, either. But I miss my only child. He's my flesh and blood. We wanted him so much. And now he's gone."

"I see." Rose took a sip of her cocoa.

"So what should I do?"

"Talk to him."

"I don't know what to say. We just think so differently on the matter."

"Then *don't* talk to him and stay estranged," Rose said.

"Stop being so ornery!"

"I'm not!" Rose defended herself. "You just told me you miss Warren Jr., but you don't want to talk about the very thing that's separating you because y'all might not agree. What else can I say?"

Marvina's fear-filled eyes darted around like a mouse trying to find its next hiding place. "I don't want me and my son to go through what me and you went through. Being apart. With all our principles and hang-ups and ultimatums. Alone. Because the people you thought you'd replaced your family with turned out to not be your family at all." Marvina's heartbeat quickened, and she knew she was rambling, smushing Warren Jr., the church, and Rose all into one untidy analogy.

Rose squeezed Marvina's hand. "Listen. We don't have to solve all our problems tonight. It's Christmas Eve. Let's just enjoy."

"You sound like Kerresha."

"I'll take that as a compliment."

Kerresha rejoined them. "Thanks for holding my cocoa."

Marvina returned the white paper cup.

Kerresha cautiously took a sip. "This is good. But you know what it could use?"

"What?" Rose asked.

"Your mom's seasoning."

Tickled pink, Rose's and Marvina's eyes crinkled with their laughter.

"I'm so serious," Kerresha insisted. "Have you tried it in hot chocolate? That seasoning makes everything taste ten times better."

"I don't know about drinks," Rose said.

"Try it. I know y'all be trippin' on your mom, but she did at least three things right. You two. And that seasoning. One hundred!"

"Two hundred!" Rose yelled.

"Three hundred!" from Marvina.

Hot chocolate spewed from Kerresha's mouth. "I can't! Y'all are so goofy!"

CHAPTER 20

Rose

Christmas morning. My fifty-ninth one. I'd reunited with my sister, reignited my business dreams, and made it to the other side of my grief about never becoming a mother. When my eyes opened, I took account of how Marvina and I had opened up to each other and decided to give myself a deadline for a serious heart-to-heart with my sister. She was ready now. I had all the paperwork on Momma's house—how much it would take to repair, how much we'd list it for, the potential profit against what it would cost to open and run the restaurant in the red for six months or so. My self-imposed deadline to inform Marvina was January first.

Until I looked at my phone and saw the text from Elizabeth. Merry Christmas! Santa is busy today! Got an application for the Dairy Queen property late last night online. Are you going to apply? Eager sellers. Ready to list the other property yet? Let me know. Time is of the essence.

I called David.

"Merry Christmas," he whispered. "Is everything okay?"

Instantly, I pictured him sneaking out of bed to avoid waking Dr. Renita who, in my mind, slept in a white physician's coat. How and why I created these scenarios, I'll never understand.

"Yes." I matched his quiet voice, playing my part to keep him from getting busted for answering his ex's call on Christmas morning. Ridiculous. But I couldn't afford to get cut off from him under these circumstances. "Elizabeth says there's interest in the Dairy Queen property. Do you think I should apply now?"

"What does Marvina think?"

"The initial deposit is three thousand dollars. It wouldn't be her money."

"So you still haven't communicated your thoughts to Marvina."

"No. It's—I..." I tensed and pulled the covers up to my chin. "Things are going so well between us right now. I don't want to ruin it."

"I'm here. In the hall restroom," David's faded voice called out. Then he hissed, "Speaking of ruining things, I'm not going to ruin what I've got now with Renita. I have to go. Bye."

David hanging up on me wasn't a first. Him hanging up on me in order to tend to his lover? Also not new. But David leaving me to fend for myself? Brand spanking new. As quiet as it's kept, I think David liked being my rescuer. Him kicking me to the curb for Dr. Renita jabbed deep in my gut.

He really liked her. And the more I talked to him, the more I saw her rubbing off on his thinking. *You still haven't communicated your thoughts to Marvina*...not his native vernacular.

My phone dinged, and a smile curled inside me. I expected to see an apology from David.

I was wrong.

It was another text from Elizabeth. Two applications now. Please let me know your intent.

My entire life, it seemed, came down to this reply. Ten, fifteen years from now, I'd either be wishing I had said yes, glad I said yes, or regretting my "yes." One word. Three drastically different outcomes possible.

Three thousand dollars. Nonrefundable if I was awarded the contract and then reneged.

I typed the word "no." My thumb lingered over the send button as my life flashed before my eyes. Momma's love. Daddy's dancing. The guilt of Marvina's disability. Pride of graduating from college, hope of starting a business, the sense of betrayal at my sister derailing my plans. David. Momma's rejection. The angel babies. Thirty years at a job, numb to my desires and feelings, and all the ways my fears had disguised themselves as rational adult behavior.

If I hadn't already gone through menopause, I'd have guessed I was having a personal summer, the way my face blazed and tingled.

I backspaced. Yes. Send.

Elizabeth quickly replied. Great. Zelle me the deposit. I will submit the paperwork. Merry Christmas & Happy Business-owner Birthday! (Fingers crossed).

I lay in bed looking up at the ceiling fan, listening to the blood whoosh in my ears. It was exhilarating and terrifying at the same time. A dangerous adventure.

Probably should have just gone skydiving.

I swallowed. Breathed deep four times, pausing four seconds between each inhale and exhale. A tear rolled into my hairline. I closed my eyes and thought about praying, something I hadn't done in a long time. I never doubted God's existence. He and I disagreed on many topics, but I didn't doubt His involvement in the world in a general, good way.

And then I imagined Momma at God's side telling Him what to do, how to advise me in her fear.

Wait. Are people afraid in heaven? Does God take advice from overprotective, judgmental Mommas? Or did Mommas figure out when they got to heaven that nothing was ever in their control in the first place?

Kerresha's voice followed three knocks on my door. "You up, Miss Rose?"

"In a minute."

"Okay. I made breakfast. And we're ready to open the gifts."

From the unremarkable smell of my room, she hadn't made much. "Be right there."

When I stood, the first thing I noticed was the absence of pain in my knee. What a gift already. I received it as a good sign. After taking care of hygiene, I shuffled into the kitchen to eat the smell-less breakfast. Oatmeal.

"It's my favorite breakfast," Kerresha proudly ladled a lump into a bowl for me. "I've got brown sugar, almonds, and dried cranberries. Your choice."

"Tastes real good, Kerresha. This'll stick to your son's bones when he's older," Marvina exaggerated.

Oatmeal paled next to pancakes, waffles. But in the spirit of encouraging the next generation, I did my part to make Kerresha feel capable. I ate my oatmeal gratefully, determined to make this Christmas morning the wonderful first day of the rest of my amazing life that I should have had a long time ago.

"Let's open the gifts," Kerresha chirped.

Seeing her so chipper warmed me. I remembered how things were on Christmas mornings as a child. Marvina and I got up with the chickens and nearly knocked each other over to get to the tree, where all the gifts too big for wrapping awaited us. Dollhouses, wagons, Big Wheels. We'd shriek with delight. Daddy always looked so tired on Christmas morning. He must have been up all night assembling the gifts for us.

Momma made us pray before we touched anything. "Jesus is the reason for the season," she'd scold, as though we'd done something wrong for accepting His birthday gifts.

Despite the butterflies flapping in our stomachs, Momma made us bow our heads and thank God for our bountiful blessings. And then we'd dive onto the floor and tear into those presents like straight-up looters in a grab-all frenzy. Momma mixed up the name tags on purpose, so a box labeled for me might actually contain a pack of socks for somebody else.

"Those are for your Daddy," she'd giggle.

And I thought, "Thank God! I don't want no stupid socks for Christmas."

When the floor was thoroughly littered with ripped wrapping paper and bows, we'd bring our new dolls and gadgets with us to the kitchen, where Momma laid out a stupendous breakfast fit for a king. We'd pray again. Eat. And then Marvina and I played with our new toys the rest of the day.

This was Christmas growing up in the Dewberry household, and this was what I wanted again, fifty-something years later. Me and Marvina opening the gift of our new business. With gratitude. And shared butterflies about the days ahead.

In a more adult manner, we sat on the love seat and lounger and decided to open our gifts one at a time, one person at a time. Kerresha went first. She, of course, had received most of her gifts from the shower. And me and Marvina had picked up so many knickknacks for the baby in the previous few weeks, there was nothing left for the baby to desire.

I was glad to see Marvina had picked up something just for

Kerresha, not the baby. She got her a neck massager. "For when you're feeling stressed."

"Thank you, Miss Marvina."

Next, Kerresha opened my gift. Her eyes welled as she dangled the gold "Mom" necklace before her face. "I always wanted one of these. Thank you so much, Miss Rose."

I always wanted one, too.

"You're welcome."

David's gift gave Kerresha pause. She held it up for me and my sister to see. "It's a baby book." She slid a hand along the glossy cover. "I was thinking of getting one so I'd have a place to put his pictures. My mom got one of these for me."

"Ooooh, nice," Marvina gushed in a lilting, kindergarten-teacher voice.

"Not nice. She never wrote one word in it, which is why I was wondering whether or not to get a traditional baby book or just print everything out and put it in a binder."

"I'm so sorry about *your* baby book," I offered.

Kerresha smacked her lips. "My baby's gonna have a different story to tell. He's gonna know his first words, when he took his first steps, everything." She hugged David's gift to her chest. Then stuffed all her gifts into one of the boxes and asked, "Who's next? Miss Marvina?"

Marvina nodded. She had three gifts. One from me, one from Kerresha, and one from David. She opened Kerresha's gift bag first and fist-pumped to show her excitement about the bright red and white new apron that read: *Everything tastes better when Marvina makes it.* "I will wear this proudly! Thank you!"

"You're welcome."

Next up: David's gift.

Marvina rolled her eyes at me. Winked at Kerresha. "Let's see what I'm about to donate to Goodwill." She hacked through the paper, the box, the tape, and the packing noodles, finally producing a circular bronze sculpture of a woman laid back, reading a book.

Marvina's face glowed with undeniable admiration. "Well. Wow. Looky here."

"He remembered," I said, my heart warming at the same rate I'm sure Marvina's warmed as well. "I used to tell him all the time that you were a bookworm."

She carefully turned the sculpture around, examining it from various angles, to take in every detail. "This is beautiful."

"Too bad you've got to give it away," Kerresha teased.

Marvina hugged the sculpture to her stomach. "I repent. I'm keeping it."

Me and Kerresha fell over laughing at Marvina's sudden change of heart.

My sister swallowed her pride and said, "Please give me his address. I want to send David a thank-you note for this thoughtful gift."

"Will do."

All the polite talk and the perfect gifts made the morning truly feel like Christmas. With family. The way it's supposed to be.

Next up was my gift to Marvina. It was by far the biggest one under the tree. Marvina scooted the box between her knees and ripped through the paper, immediately revealing its contents.

"Oh…"

"Yes!" Kerresha hollered! "You got it!"

Marvina forced a smile. She finished unwrapping the full front. "It's the marijuana-making machine."

"It's not just for marijuana," I bristled. How perfectly like

Marvina to be ungrateful for progress. "The official title is food dehydrator. There's a separate compartment for drying, but you don't have to use it for drugs, thank you very much. I ordered it online right after Kerresha told us about it. Thought we'd try it together and see if it works."

"It's just so…big. And…"

I finished her sentence my way. "It's going to be way faster, for making the spices."

Kerresha struggled to get up from the sofa, turning left and right. She gave up. "Flip the box around so I can see the front, please."

Marvina obliged.

"Yes! High five, Miss Rose!"

She gave me an air-slap. Marvina's face still balked at the gift.

I gave her my resting don't-try-me face.

"I appreciate you going out of your way to get this for me, but…I prefer to do things the traditional way."

The traditional way? The slow way? The way that would block me from obtaining my goals?

"Fine. Don't open the box. I'll get a refund. Can you please pass me my gifts?"

Marvina slapped the top of the dehydrator box. "Rose. Come on—"

"Stop hitting the cardboard before you damage it and I can't get my money back."

"Ridiculous," Marvina clucked. She passed me two gifts. One from David. I wondered if, maybe, she and Kerresha had pitched in for the second gift.

I started with David's. It was a small, rectangular box. I guessed jewelry, and my guess was correct. He'd gotten me a silver bracelet with the words "Boss lady" engraved on a plate. A yellow sticky note tucked into the side read, in David's handwriting, *Here's to being your best boss!*

I quickly replaced the top on the box, keeping tears at bay. For as much as I wanted to rejoice over the gift, I couldn't let Marvina see the engraving. Not yet. She'd ask questions I wasn't ready to answer until she'd agreed to sell Momma's house, rent the Dairy Queen, and work with me.

Kerresha asked, "Are you going to show us?"

"It's a bracelet. A private bracelet." I pressed my closed box against my thigh and reached for the next gift.

Marvina said, "How is it gonna be private if it's on your wrist for all to see?"

"Maybe it's not for everyone's eyes," I extended the lie by omission.

"Well, that's stupid," Marvina snapped. "Why would he give you a private gift for Christmas? Y'all ain't a couple, and this ain't Valentine's Day."

I ignored her and kept digging through the tissue paper in my gift bag until I hit something solid. My fingers wrapped around a glass container. I pulled out a bright blue bottle of CBD oil. "Well, all righty then!"

"It's for your knee," Kerresha informed me. "People say it's amazing."

I twisted the bottle to read the label and instructions. "I can't wait to try it."

"My, my. Isn't this a very merry-juana Christmas," Marvina sassed. She put both hands on her knees and pushed to a standing position. "I'll be right back with my gift for you."

She left the room. Kerresha and I stifled giggles.

"This is too much weed atmosphere for her," I whispered.

"I didn't know you'd gotten her the machine."

"I understand. I'm just saying. We're pushing it."

Marvina reentered the living room with a gift basket wrapped in red and green cellophane.

"Ooooh!" Kerresha exclaimed. "What's the theme?"

Marvina plopped the basket on the coffee table. "The theme is retirement. Everything in here is for you to get somewhere and sit down. And quit chasing waterfalls."

Well, crap. She might as well have bopped me upside the head with a billy club.

Too stunned to speak, I went through the gift-opening motions. I pulled the bow off the top and mashed the cellophane to the table. Kerresha and Marvina acted as sports commentators while I lifted each item from the bed of shredded crinkle confetti. They named off the neck massager, bath bombs, fuzzy socks, and daily devotional, babbling with effervescent cheerfulness.

Kerresha clapped. "All of that plus the CBD oil. You'll be in heaven, Miss Rose!"

I tried to hoist a smile in place. Too slow.

"What's the matter?" Marvina barked.

Doubt, fear, and anger pinged through my body like a pinball game. *Tell her?* No. Not in front of Kerresha. *Lie?* No. I've done enough of that already.

I was gonna keep my true thoughts to myself, but Marvina kept peppering me with agitating comments. *You're retired, right? Almost sixty soon. You need to slow down.*

"I'm not ready to slow down in my life. I'm just getting started."

"So you don't appreciate my gift?"

"I didn't say that." Tears pricked my eyes as I realized that just like my knee slipped out from under me, just like my babies slipped out of my body, everything I'd been hoping for my future was slithering out of my grasp.

"Then what exactly are you saying, Rose?"

"I'm saying I don't want this life you're trying to force on me! I worked thirty years at a job I disliked. Now I want to live."

"*Me* force *you*? You got it all flipped around!"

"Oh my God! Stop it!" Kerresha yelled. "I mean, really. It's Christmas. Freakin'. Morning!"

Marvina and I both turned to stare at Kerresha. Tears spilled onto her cheeks, and her face reddened. Her bottom lip trembled as she spoke. "I don't know what happened to y'all. Who did what first or when. But you two need to squash it."

Marvina shushed her. "Now, Kerresha, you need to calm down. Don't get your pressure up on account of us. Why don't you sit back down?"

She scrunched up her nose in an ugly cry. "You two need to get over it. Family is everything. From what I can see, you two are the only ones left for each other in your family. I don't understand how y'all can't see what you have right in front of you."

I felt compelled to speak, because, while Kerresha might have understood the surface facts, she didn't know the whole story. "It's not as easy as it sounds. Takes time. A lot of time. Maybe."

Kerresha wiped her tears. "Yeah. Well, no disrespect and I'm not trying to be rude, but time's the one thing that's not on y'alls side. Why waste it?" She left me and my sister staring at each other. Marvina with the weed-baking machine and me with the leisure basket. Still huffing and puffing from our argument.

Marvina broke the heavy silence. "She's not completely wrong."

"She's also nineteen," I reminded my sister. "Optimistic."

"I've got a way to settle this gift debacle," Marvina said. "Let's switch gifts back. I'll take the relaxation basket, you take this here herb magic machine, and you take it back to Dallas and use it to make all the seasoning you want. How's that?"

"Works for me."

"Great."

"Good."

Despite what David had said—that I needed to give up the fight—I still couldn't let Marvina have the last word. "Fine."

CHAPTER 21

Rose

Well, Christmas morning had not gone as planned. Marvina and I traded back our Christmas gifts and went to boxing corners, our rooms, to regroup. Kerresha's words still rang in the air. *Time's the one thing that's not on y'alls side. It's stupid to waste it.*

The thing is, even though, mathematically, we'd passed the point where we had more time ahead of us than behind us, it's still each person's decision how they want to spend whatever time is left on the clock.

The first free-Christmas-meal knock at the door came around eleven, a full hour earlier than Marvina had announced. Through the wall, I heard her answer the door all chipper. "Well, hello, Officer McGillam! What a pleasure to see you here!"

I stopped playing solitaire on my phone and listened intently.

"Just stopping by to check on y'all," he said.

"Well, isn't that sweet of you. Merry Christmas!"

"Same to you. And, if I may say, your home smells exactly like my best Christmas memories."

I shook my head at this man standing outside, dry begging.

"Officer, you are in luck. Me and Rose and Kerresha prepared and boxed up as many meals as we could to give to the community today. You're our first customer."

Customer? Did she really just say *customer*? As though she were running a restaurant? The restaurant she refused to run with me?

The door hinge squeaked, and the floorboard creaked as he entered the house.

"So your sister, Rose, is still here helping you?"

"Oh, yes. She's resting in her room until the folks start coming. I told 'em noon. And as far as Kerresha, she's no trouble at all."

"Well…I've had a lot of second thoughts. But I'm glad it's working out. So far."

I didn't like the doubt in his tone, so I got out of bed and waltzed into the kitchen. Marvina was setting two covered dinner plates into a grocery bag.

I put on my fakest grin. "Merry Christmas."

"Oh! There she is!" He tipped his hat. I didn't know whether to be grateful that he was checking up on Marvina or angry that he didn't believe her when she told him how well things were going.

Kerresha came in carrying an empty cereal bowl and juice cup. "Hello again."

"Hello to you, young lady. So good to see you under better circumstances."

"True dat." She proceeded to rinse out her dishes and put them in the sink.

Officer McGillam crossed his arms, acting like he was really on duty in the middle of Marvina's kitchen collecting a free lunch. I wouldn't be surprised if someone had forwarded him the text about the free food and he showed up early to make sure he got a full plate.

Marvina double-tied the grocery bag and gave it to Officer

McGillam. "I put in two plates. Should be enough for several meals. I hope you enjoy it, for all your service to the community and whatnot."

"It's my honor and duty." He lolled the bag of food up and down, as though checking the weight. "You put quite a bit in here. Is there any way I can repay you? Leave a tip or something?"

Marvina threw her head back to say "no."

I jumped in with, "You sure can. We've got a tip jar right here." And I opened the pantry to retrieve an empty pickle jar I'd seen earlier. "Put 'er there."

His o-shaped mouth showed his surprise at me actually taking him up on the offer. "Glad to donate! You two are doing a service to our community as well. And I just wanted to be sure things were okay here."

I held out the pickle jar and he dropped a five-dollar bill inside.

"Thank you kindly," I said, screwing the lid back on.

Kerresha dried her hands on a cup towel. "It's awesome! These two." She grabbed Marvina's hand. She slid toward me and pulled me closer to the center of the kitchen. "They're just so...wonderful together. They're always laughing and hugging. I"—she gave an endearing smile—"I call them the hugging sisters. See?" Then she looked at us and ordered, "Watch 'em hug."

Marvina poked out her bottom lip.

I rolled my lips in.

Officer McGillam waited.

Kerresha nodded vigorously, wearing the widest grin.

I hadn't felt so put-on-the-spot since the time Momma and Daddy got a wild notion to make me and Marvina sing "This Little Light of Mine" a cappella at the family reunion.

Kerresha reached her arms out and scooched me and Marvina

closer together. "I don't know why they're acting so shy in front of you."

"Well, it was because of their relationship that I decided to leave you here."

Again, I didn't like that question in his tone. It implied a threat, in my opinion. I grabbed Marvina's neck, leaned into her, and bundled her up with a hug. "Oh, yes. My sister and I go waaaaay back."

My sister squeezed me, too, and, I swear, it felt just like Momma's embrace. Full and warm, seeping into every inch of my being. I couldn't remember the last time anyone had folded me in their arms.

So I pulled Marvina closer. So close I could feel her bra strap hooks on my fingertips. I shut my eyes and, somehow, my sister even smelled like Momma's light floral perfume coupled with the faint tang of garlic that always lingered in her clothes.

A deep groan escaped from my gut. Marvina hugged me tighter, if that were possible.

"Wow. They really are good at hugging," Officer McGillam's voice chopped through the moment.

Kerresha rubbed our arms. "Yes. They love each other. So much."

A scratchy voice came over the officer's walkie-talkie. "McGillam, you there? We've got a business alarm on Main Street."

"Probably just a stray dog too close to the perimeter," he commented to us. He answered the dispatcher's request in the affirmative. "Thank y'all again for the food. I've gotta head out."

Marvina returned to her erect, standing position. She wiped her eyes. "You're welcome."

Kerresha gave a sigh, as though her work was done, and dismissed herself.

My sister and I walked the policeman to the door.

He stopped at the threshold and whispered to us, "I'm so glad this is working out. But I just wanted to let y'all know there's a spot that opened up at the women's shelter over in Averton. In case, you know, things take a turn for the worse. We all know how teenagers can be."

"Oh, no," Marvina protested quietly, "I'm telling you, Kerresha is no trouble at all. In fact, she's quite helpful, even in her condition."

"Sure is," I hitched onto her words.

"Glad to hear it. But have you thought about what you'd like to do with her once the baby gets here?"

"*Do* with her?" I repeated.

"Oh, don't you worry about that," Marvina carried on, "Kerresha's becoming almost like family to us. In fact, I've been looking into her moving into our Momma's house pretty soon."

Irritation ran from my forehead down to my toes and back up again.

"Is that right?" Officer McGillam asked.

"Yes. So don't you worry about Kerresha no more. We've got her taken care of."

He winked at us both. "You two are saints. Again, Merry Christmas."

"Same to you," Marvina said. She closed the door behind him. "The nerve!"

"You read my mind," I said in a tone meant for her to question me, but my intent skipped over her.

That's when we heard the cry from Kerresha's room. "Wheeew!" We scrambled down the hallway to her door. "What's wrong?"

"Nothing," she said breathlessly, sitting on her bed and clutching her stomach. "More Braxton-Hicks contractions." She breathed short whistly, staccato breaths. *Whoo. Whoo. Whoo. Whoo.*

The way her face grimaced, I had to ask, "You sure you're not in *real* labor?"

"Believe me, she'll know when it's the real thing," Marvina answered.

I didn't appreciate my sister's undertone—intended or not—that I didn't understand real labor pains. "I'm. Asking. Kerresha."

"Well, clearly, she can't answer you because she's out of breath."

"She can speak."

"Yes, I can. And I want you both out!" Kerresha demanded, pointing past both of us to the door. Her arm shook with the extra effort.

My chest deflated. We'd done it again. My sister and I had managed to entangle ourselves in our wicked wrangle of words. The weird thing, however, was how it made me feel this time. Usually, I felt vindicated. Invigorated, even, after a battle of wits and words.

Back when David and I first divorced and my finances struggled, I looked forward to phone calls from bill collectors. We'd go back and forth with them telling me I was irresponsible, and I'd tell them how pitiful it was for them to have a job harassing people. We argued over which of us was the biggest loser. It gave me a chance to release my frustrations in a verbal boxing match. Fighting.

But I was tired of fighting. And now David's words made sense to me. *Give up the fight.* This wasn't working out between me and Marvina. She wanted to give everything away. Free, well-seasoned food to the neighborhood, free or next-to-nothing housing to Kerresha. We couldn't be further apart on how we moved in this world.

I shuffled back to my room and plopped on the bed. What was I going to do? I didn't want to lose my earnest money, but I also didn't want to throw good money after bad if I got the Dairy Queen contract. And Kerresha was a sweet girl, but she had no income now and no prospects for a steady, livable income after the baby was born, as far as I could see.

Nonetheless, if we disagreed already about Momma's house, there was no telling what else we'd disagree on. Marvina was an old soul. An old, country, Momma's-girl soul. And too optimistic. Always had been. She's the kind of person who'd mail a twenty-dollar bill in a thin white envelope. You just look at the sender's name and shake your head for 'em.

I should have known she'd want to operate as generously with Momma's house as with the food she'd planned to give away that morning.

Crap. What made me think I could go into business with Marvina? She'd give away the family farm if the opportunity presented itself.

I lifted my suitcase off the floor, unzipped it, and splayed it open on the bed. I removed a short stack of undergarments from the drawer and put them in the suitcase.

Marvina knocked and entered at the same time. She stepped inside and closed the door behind her. "I meant to tell you, I've done some more thinking about Kerresha moving into Momma's house. Thinking through the logistics. I'll forfeit my half of the rent and make sure you still get your half, seeing as you're on a fixed income now, in retirement and all."

She'd given this a lot of thought, apparently. Not only was she willing to give up the extra income, she was willing to sacrifice.

Marvina looked past me to the bed. "What's this? You packing?"

I smacked my lips. "Yep."

"Really?"

"Mm-hmm."

"So you're going to leave me here to play grandma all by my lonesome?"

I laughed to myself. "You've been a mother, remember? This should come easy to you."

Marvina sighed. "Listen, I didn't mean anything about the labor thing I said earlier. Sometimes I just forget..." she failed to finish the sentence, which I imagined as: *Sometimes I just forget you never gave birth to a child.*

"Must be nice to be able to forget something like that. What should we call it—mother privilege? Mommy bias?"

"Stop it, Rose. You heard Kerresha. We're bickerin' way too much. Stressing her out. Can we pull it together long enough for the baby to get here? He'll keep us busy for weeks. Kerresha will recover. Officer McGillam will stop poking around, looking for reasons to cart her way. And you can head back to Dallas afterward."

"I suppose if we stay out of each other's way, we might survive," I said. "But I want you to know. I'm considering your idea about Kerresha. I hope you'll consider my idea, too."

There! I did it...kind of.

"Your idea about what, Rose?"

Even though I already knew Marvina would reject my idea like an envelope with insufficient postage, I still needed to ask her. For the record. For my sanity.

My face grew hot in anticipation of her refusal. I blurted it out in one breath, "Will you consider opening a restaurant with me—"

"Nuh-uh."

"I didn't even finish the sentence!"

"No need." Marvina stepped back, holding up a hand like I was a robber trying to snatch her purse. "I'm not interested in opening no restaurant. It's too much work. Let it go, Rose."

I stood. "And what are we gonna do with Momma's seasoning recipe? Huh?" I slapped the back of my right hand into my left palm. "Where's it all gonna go when we die?"

Marvina shrugged. "Kerresha?"

"That gal is about as interested in cooking as I am interested in getting a motorcycle. You know this already."

"Maybe Warren Jr. would want it," she tried again.

Her sense of desperation fueled me now. "Have you asked him? 'Cause I ain't heard you talk to him none since I've been here."

Marvina's head turned to the side as though I'd physically slapped her.

I froze, unsure of exactly what I'd said to cause this reaction.

She made a fist and covered her mouth with it. "That was unnecessary. And I don't know why I gave you another chance. I should have known you came here for more than just Momma's recipe."

"I didn't—"

"I'll donate the spice recipe to the church if I have to," she fumed.

"Over my dead body," I stated blankly. "Besides, they don't want it."

A rapid knock on the front door reminded me that it was still Christmas morning, and Marvina had signed up this house for charity.

She straightened herself, putting on the good ol' Southern hospitality persona that wears a smile outside no matter what's happening behind closed doors. I swear both my sister and my momma could have smiled through a level-ten pain toothache.

Marvina lowered her chin. "I know they don't want Momma's recipe. And I agree. It would be a shame for Momma's seasoning recipe to die with us. I'll figure out something else."

Finally, she was talking proper sense...kind of.

"Maybe we could submit it to one of those Southern documentary societies. Or a Southern cookbook publication."

Houston, we still have a problem. No way was I going to publish Momma's secrets to the world.

"Ho! Ho! Ho! Merry Christmas in there!"

"That's Eleanor!" My sister's face lit up like a Christmas tree. "Come on! Help me start passing out these meals."

My sister skedaddled to the front door, leaving me alone in my room again.

Our conversation had ended prematurely, but maybe that was best given how Marvina had acted like bringing up Warren Jr.'s name was akin to blasphemy.

From my bedroom, I overheard her frantic conversation with Eleanor.

"Chile! Folks are lined up at the church to get your cookin'!"

"What?"

"You sent out the text sayin' to get free plates, and everybody thought you meant you were giving them away at the church, where they're used to getting plates from you. I passed by Greater New Harvest on my way to visit my aunt in the nursing home, and there was about half a dozen cars parked in the lot. So I got out and asked a few of them what they'd come for, and they said the free plate!"

Marvina giggled. "I guess we'd better get these plates up to the church, then. Let me go get my sister to help us."

I hid my reluctance when Marvina entered my room again

and asked if I'd come with them. "Yeah. Let me put on something warmer since we'll be outside. And I do want to talk some more about my idea, later."

"I don't. I'm done with it." She vanished from the doorframe.

My prediction was accurate, but my sense of hope had not completely died. Maybe if she saw what a good helper I was, how well we worked together, she might change her mind. She *had* to. Otherwise...no otherwise. I needed her to.

Clueless to the tension between my sister and I, Eleanor chirped her Christmas cheer, and Marvina gave sprightly laughs as we toted the plastic plates of food, wrapped in leftover grocery bags and placed into three large boxes, from the kitchen to the car.

Kerresha must have overheard their conversation to some extent because she came outside wearing a coat. "Merry Christmas, everybody. Let's do this."

CHAPTER 22
Rose

Eleanor didn't seem surprised to see our guest. Marvina must have told her all about our living situation. I wondered what else Marvina had told Eleanor about me being in town. Did she tell Eleanor about our two-person white elephant Christmas gift exchange?

I drove me, Kerresha, Marvina, and our boxes of food to the church. Eleanor followed. Sure enough, looked like about eight cars in the lot on a Christmas morning. We had roughly thirty meals packed.

I took one of the few parking spots left and popped my hatchback open. Folks unfolded and popped out of their cars like Santa himself had arrived, and Marvina morphed into her best self. Just talking and handing out plates. *Whoo! You sure lookin' good in that pretty coat!* And *Tell your momma I said she's doing a wonderful job raisin' you.* And *Hope to see y'all at church soon.* And *I'll keep you in my prayers. Let me know what you need.*

Basically, she and Eleanor loved on each and every one of them while feeding them at the same time. Watching them, especially my sister, in her element reminded me of one of those parts of the Bible—I don't memorize scriptures like some folks—where it says don't just tell people they will be fine, give them something to help them be fine, too. Like good food. Money. A place to stay or a contact to reach out to.

Two teenagers drove up in a beat-up Dodge. I stepped back, seeing as one of the wheels risked falling off at any moment. Out hopped a girl wearing black and fuchsia braids down to her behind and a boy with a neck full of tattoos. They clobbered my sister with hugs.

"Yes! Yes! Yes!" the girl screamed.

The boy added, "And you still smell like chicken grease, too!"

Marvina slapped his arm. "Oh, stop it."

She then introduced me to the teenagers, Sasha and Lil' Smoke, and I listened as they caught up.

"Where's Ta'riq?" Marvina asked.

Their eyes swept to the ground. "He's on house arrest, Miss Marvina. He can't be nowhere but in his house on evenings or weekends."

"What?! For what? Since when?" My sister's chest caved in as she processed the news.

"It's dumb," the boy said, shaking his head. "Last Saturday. He was hanging with the wrong people. I think he stole some shoes."

"He's not on house arrest for stealing shoes, fool." Sasha rolled her eyes at him. "He stole a car. And then he was stupid enough to go riding around Fork City in the stolen car."

We all shook our heads at the foolishness. I mean, if you're gonna steal a car from Fork City, at least go outside the city limits to joyride.

"We miss cooking with y'all," Sasha whined, pulling on Marvina's arm.

Marvina pacified them with, "God will work something out."

They grabbed their plates and left in high hopes.

Unbeknownst to us, Kerresha had brought the impromptu tip jar along. When the last of the original cars left, Marvina, Eleanor, and I were in position to see Kerresha holding the jar to a window as the driver exited the lot.

Marvina hollered out, "Come here!"

Kerresha walked as fast as she could to the back of my vehicle. The tip jar was halfway filled with greenbacks. No hard money.

"What in the world are you doing?"

"I'm accepting tips."

"I don't want no tips," Marvina fussed. "This is all free. From the goodness of our hearts."

Kerresha said, "They aren't paying for it. They're showing gratitude. Like the officer. That's fair."

Eleanor took the jar from Kerresha and held it up, counting the money through the glass. "Five, six, seven plus five. Twelve. Thirteen, fourteen. Ten! Twenty-three at least!"

"Not bad," I remarked.

Marvina's face screwed up into a tight wall of disgrace. "We don't want this money."

I don't know who she considered "we," but it certainly wasn't Eleanor because she said, "I'll take it."

"Eleanor! We never took money before!"

"Yes, we did. And people gladly paid whatever we charged, and then some. But we gave it all to the church."

Marvina retorted, "They paid for a good cause."

I drew an invisible circle between the four of us. "We are a good cause. Three on a fixed income. One with no income at all, and a baby on the way. That's as good a cause as a church."

The disagreement had barely started when Pastor Pendleton raced his big Lincoln into the lot and strategically screeched to a parking position that blocked off the entrance to the church property.

He got out of his vehicle, slamming the door and quickly busting up in our circle. "What in God's name are you all doing here?" His eyes settled on the tip jar in Eleanor's clutch. "Selling dinners despite my direct orders to cease and desist?"

Oh, the veins popping out of his man's forehead.

"Have we broken a law?" I charged him.

"You very might well might have. You're selling dinners, for profit, on the premises of a nonprofit organization." His face darkened with each word.

Marvina lowered her eyes. "I understand, Pastor. And us being here wasn't my doing. I sent a text—"

"Wait. We're not selling anything," Kerresha said. "These are tips."

"Tips. Are. Income." Each word pressed through his clenched teeth so hard that spittle escaped his control.

Eleanor reached into the jar and pulled out a five-dollar bill. "Here's your cut. Happy?"

Indignant, he hissed, "Why, Sister Eleanor. I never would have expected this behavior from you. God is not pleased."

But he did take the money and stuff it into his pocket.

"You know what else God ain't too happy about?" I informed the Pastor. "He's not happy that the youth my sister ministered to are now out on the streets getting into trouble."

"Their choice," he hissed.

"Your choice, too, to leave them to their own ill-equipped, ill-informed devices."

"Come through, Miss Rose!" Kerresha said.

I deduced "come through" must mean "I agree with you."

A black sedan slowed to a stop. The front bumpers nearly kissed the pastor's driver's-side panel. The driver's window lowered, revealing a silver-haired man with a red and white Santa hat. "Y'all giving away dinners today?"

"No. We are not," Pastor Pendleton barked.

The driver's face soured. "My wife sent me here. Said she got a message Miss Marvina was giving away food." His eyes traveled to the back of my car, where two bags sat ready for the next taker. He pointed at my car. "Y'all giving away somethin' else?"

"Those bags are filled with food," I said. "But Pastor Pendleton here doesn't want us giving them away," I informed the stranger, banking on his persistent personality.

"I'll pay for 'em, then. Don't matter to me so long as Miss Marvina cooked it, and I ain't got to go home empty-handed. My daughter-in-law's making Christmas dinner today. Terrible! Taste like hotel food and bad moonshine. No offense, Pastor." The man leaned to the side, reaching for his wallet. "How much?"

I blurted out, "Twelve dollars a plate. How many do you want?"

"Give me four."

Kerresha opened the tip jar.

Pastor Pendleton's lips tightened. "We are not selling or giving any food on this property."

"So, I can't pay you for the food?"

"No, sir."

The brother laughed, waving a folded fifty-dollar bill. "Well, this is a first. I've never known a pastor to turn down money."

Pastor Pendleton snarled like he just fell on a cactus. "This is a place of worship. Not a chicken shack."

He might as well have held out both arms, rotated in a circle, and slapped all four of us on our cheeks with that comment because even Marvina perked up with disdain, then.

"With all due respect, Pastor Pendleton, we're here to help the community in any way possible," she said. The word choice was kind, but she put a little bite in 'em.

I was proud of her.

Pastor crossed his arms. "You will no longer be able to purchase food on church grounds. Tell your wife, tell your daughter-in-law, tell everyone you know that Greater New Harvest is a state-of-the-art worship center."

The man looked right and left, then through his rearview mirror. He spoke directly to Kerresha. "Look here, young lady. I'm gonna pull up to the corner. I'mma give you this money—off church property"—he eyed Pastor Pendleton—"in exchange for the four plates." He backed out of the lot entrance and stopped at the mini-mart next door. Eleanor and Kerresha walked the fifteen feet to go give him the plates while Marvina and I stood at my car watching Pastor Pendleton seethe.

"Sister Marvina. This is highly unlike you to be so disobedient."

I said, "She's not a child."

He stamped the ground. "I am her shepherd. And right now, she's out of the fold of safety."

"Then go after her," I said. I stepped aside. "She's right here. Tell her how much she's missed, how much you love what she has to offer to the church, how she doesn't have to go looking for other places, other ways to serve the people of Fork City with her talents. Go on." I tapped Marvina's shoulder. "Here she go."

Marvina swiped my hand away. "That's enough, Rose."

"I have to agree," the pastor said.

I wrestled him with my icy stare until he broke eye contact.

Kerresha and Eleanor returned. President Grant sure looked stately on that fifty-dollar bill inside that old pickle bottle.

"He told us to keep the change," Kerresha said.

"Go home, ladies. Get the food off this property. And see to it that nothing like this ever happens again," he said to no one in particular. With that, Pastor Pendleton drove away.

We did as he said. Slowly. So slowly that we gave away six more dinners at the corner before we vacated the premises. And those two cars left tips, too. People tipped us about fifty dollars beyond the money from the man with the no-cooking daughter-in-law. We made a hundred bucks in a little more than an hour.

Eleanor broke the fifty-dollar bill so we could split all the money four ways. Cold hard cash slapping against our open palms, baby.

Eleanor stuffed her funds deep in her skirt pocket and hugged me, my sister, and Kerresha goodbye. "Pastor and the deacons are gonna give us a good tongue-lashing," she warned Marvina as she walked toward her vehicle.

"I know," was her only reply.

Marvina, Kerresha, and I piled into my car again. The warm air thawed us out from the Christmas cool.

"That was sooooo good," Kerresha cheered. "We helped people; people helped us. Total win-win. I told y'all you need to start a restaurant." She tossed her share of the money back into the jar and held it in the air like a daddy raising his firstborn to the skies. "Here's proof. People are willing to pay for what y'all have to offer."

I bit my tongue hard because I wanted to let Kerresha's words soak into Marvina's brain. Maybe, now, she could see things my way.

When we got back to the house, I couldn't wait to gloat about the situation with David, let him know that I had come one step closer to telling my sister about the master plan. So I texted him.

Hope you had a Merry Christmas. Everyone loved their gifts. Thank you! Very close to telling Marvina everything. Wish me luck. Or else I will have to take you up on the offer to move in with you. LOL! Never.

A few minutes later, David called me and said in a serious tone, "Rose. We need to talk."

"Oh? Is everything okay?" I sat up in the guest bed and laid my coloring book on the covers.

"I'm fine. But the passive-aggressive text message you just sent me is not."

"Excuse me?"

"I am your friend, Rose. That's it. I would not actually allow you to move in with me again."

"I do not actually want to move in with you again, either," I repeated in the same, flat tone he gave me. "And I do not appreciate you using me as your guinea pig to practice your new psychoanalytical vocabulary words on, you hear?"

"This is not practice."

"Well, if this is the real test, you've failed. The text I sent you was not passive-aggressive. What I sent is called joking. J-O-K-I-N-G. Look it up."

He sighed as though I was the one who had called him. If he didn't like my text, all he had to do was ignore it like I do his when I don't feel like talking.

"Rose. We really have to stop this. It's too much drama. And it's interfering with my relationship with Renita."

"That serious, huh?" I laughed.

He paused. "Yes. It is, Rose. I'm going to ask her to marry me."

Stars blinded my vision. "What?!"

"Soon."

"Now *you* are joking. You barely know her!" I argued.

"Life is short. And true love is obvious."

"True love? David, how—" I stopped myself before he misdiagnosed me again. "Good. If you're happy, I'm happy."

When he didn't reply for several seconds, I called his name.

"Yes, I'm here. Just waiting for your sarcastic footnote."

He was begging for me to give him a vivid description of where I wanted to put my foot, but I refused to give him the satisfaction. "I have no further comment. Enjoy the rest of your Christmas with your girlfriend, David. Goodbye."

"Goodbye to you, too, Rose."

CHAPTER 23

The Christmas Day run-in with Pastor Pendleton made for an awkward Sunday service. Even more awkward than making Rose and Kerresha get up and out of the house despite their obvious contempt for all things Greater New Harvest. Nonetheless, Marvina's promise that she would make sure every able-bodied person in her home went to church on Sunday morning was between her and God, not Pastor Pendleton. It was the Lord who let her be married to a lottery-playin' man and allowed them to hit the jackpot and buy the house. So there.

Throughout the service, Pastor Pendleton avoided eye contact with Marvina, Rose, and Kerresha. Marvina was not angled to see if he was doing the same to Eleanor, but she suspected he was. And, of course, his sermon, titled "My Sheep Hear My Voice," was all about being a responsive sheep. Not running away, making Jesus chase after you, and forcing Jesus to break your legs in order to teach you a lesson, then throw you over His shoulders to carry you, for your own good. According to Pastor Pendleton, this was an ancient practice shepherds employed to keep silly sheep from foolishly runnin' away from safety, toward dangerous wolves they had no idea existed.

Marvina had heard this sermon before, and it stirred up uncertainty in her chest. What if the Lord was getting ready to take her home, and closing down the church cooking was a part of His plan? What if God got so angry with her that he withdrew His hand of protection from her? Truth be told, Marvina always worried about whether or not God liked her. Especially since the accident that impaired her vision. She'd asked herself countless times: what had she done wrong to deserve the harsh sentence—blind in one eye for the rest of her life, with no chance of recovery?

When she couldn't fathom why, the obvious reasons surfaced: She shouldn't have been sneaking to drink liquor with Rose. Momma and Marvina's childhood church family always talked about staying in the "arc of safety," the place where God could protect you. Outside the arc, living in sin and disobedience, God either would not or could not override your will and continue to protect you. You were just out there, living on whatever grace and mercy happened to sprinkle on you in your state of sinfulness or ignorance.

Like being outside the sheep's pen.

If your parents and grandparents prayed hard enough, their prayers might float you until you got some sense.

The only part Marvina never could reconcile, the part that made her wonder if God actually liked her, was that Rose suffered no consequences, though it was her bright idea to drink the champagne. If God was righteously weighing sin, Rose should have been the one who lost her sight, not Marvina. This was a question she never brought to God or Momma. She never voiced it, never could understand it outside of her own internal rationale.

Which was why Pastor Pendleton's sermon seeped into Marvina's soul and rattled her sense of well-being. As much as

Marvina loved cooking with her mother's seasonings and passing her skills on to the next generation, she loved the Lord more. Feared Him more. Hadn't she learned her lesson the last time she teamed up with Rose to disobey God?

When the prayer line formed, Marvina made haste. When it was her turn to receive prayer, she raised both hands in surrender. Mother Butler, the oldest member of the church, stood behind Marvina for propriety's sake while Deacon Scott dabbed a cross of olive oil on Marvina's forehead. Pastor Pendleton beseeched the Lord on her behalf. He didn't ask for her request. He barreled ahead with, "Lord God, You know the rebellion in this sister's heart. But You also see her humility. Thank You for the years and years of service she put into this community with her whole heart, soul, body, and mind. You have seen her work alongside so many people, including my wife, God." His voice choked.

A tear ran down Marvina's face. She missed Vernetta something fierce, too.

"Now, Lord, watch over my dear sister. Lead her back into the fold before something terrible—"

"Something horrible!" Deacon Scott interjected directly into Marvina's right ear.

Pastor continued, "Before something bad happens to her. Have mercy, Lord. Don't break her legs, Lord."

Deacon Scott begged, "Don't do it, Lord. Please don't break 'em!"

So much for privacy in the prayer line.

"Honor her humbleness on this morning. Bring her home safe. In Jesus's name. Amen," Pastor Pendleton closed the prayer.

"Amen," Marvina echoed.

After church dismissed, Marvina made her rounds with the

congregation, expressing belated Christmas cheer and wishing everyone a Happy New Year, upcoming. A few of them leaned in closer, whispering whatever they'd heard about the Christmas Day chicken-selling tomfoolery. Either Pastor Pendleton had informed the deacons, or word got around town that you had to pull up to the next building in order to get a meal served. One way or another, people knew some version of what happened, they weren't happy about it, and several church members leaned in close to murmur their conspiratorial grievances.

"Just pray," Marvina said to each one, eager to de-escalate the situation. It was bad enough she'd stepped out of the arc. No need in encouraging others to become belligerent, too.

Back in Rose's car, Kerresha let out a loud roar as soon as all the doors shut and people couldn't hear her. "That! Was! Cray cray!"

Marvina buckled her seat belt and turned a full 180 degrees so she could read Kerresha's face. "What you talkin' 'bout, chile?"

Rose kept a blank expression and drove without comment, which meant she had an attitude about something, too.

"That whole sheep-with-the-broken-leg story," Kerresha said, shaking her head.

Marvina patted her purse. "Well. God knows what's best for us."

"No!" Kerresha tapped her phone and shoved it into Marvina's face. "I googled it while he was preaching. Look! It's all lies on top of myths. Shepherds don't break sheep's legs when they wander away. They'd lose money! Duh! Not to mention it's cruel. Can you imagine?"

Marvina held the phone at arm's length and read the first few sentences of the article posted on an international professional shepherds' website. She read the "Question and Answer" section

Kerresha had scrolled to. Question: Do shepherds break runaway sheep's legs and then carry them around? Answer: No. Shepherds are not cruel. And carrying around a hundred-and-something-odd-pound impaired lamb would slow the shepherd down, costing him money in the long run, especially if he had to haul several wayward sheep for weeks or months at a time while the bones healed.

This made sense, actually. And it made Pastor Pendleton's sermon null and void. She gave the phone back to Kerresha. "I'll have to look it up for myself."

Kerresha clicked her cheek. "It sounds like a cult to me. I can't come here every Sunday and let him pump all this fear into me week after week, like I'm living life with Michael Myers chasing me 24/7. Whew! I'm shook. I can't with you people. I'm tired. I'm taking a nap as soon as we get home. I hope my baby didn't hear all this."

Rose poked out her lips as she rolled onto the main street. Still, she kept quiet. Marvina knew her sister wasn't a big churchgoer, probably because of guilt. But she grew up in the scriptures just as Rose did. So Marvina asked, "What do you think, Rose? You don't believe in God's wrath?"

"Doesn't matter what *I* believe. What do *you* believe?" she reversed the question.

Marvina sat still the rest of the way home. She'd heard the broken-leg parable before. She honestly thought it was true. But if it wasn't—and she was fairly convinced this was a falsehood, from the website—then maybe what happened to her wasn't wrath. It was just something bad that happened. Rare, but it happened. Like when she won the lottery, only it was good.

Just life.

And if that were the case, she couldn't blame Rose anymore.

And maybe God had been there through it all. Not to punish her or elevate her, but to walk with her through it all the days of her life, in love.

In Kerresha's words, Marvina was too "shook" to get out of the car and turn down the roast when they got home. She charged Kerresha with the responsibility instead, hoping the task would also endear Kerresha to cooking a teensy bit more.

"Where are we going?" Rose asked.

"I didn't want to say anything while Kerresha was in the car, but we're going to Momma's house. With the baby due at the end of next month, we don't have much time to get repairs done. I want to surprise her by getting this home on the approved county housing list and choosing her as our tenant."

Rose held up a hand when she should have been using that hand to shift into drive. "Wait a minute, Marvina. We need to talk. I'd like to have a say about Momma's house."

"A say? No, ma'am. *I'm* the one who has taken care of Momma's house all these years. Protesting the tax appraisal, doing the insurance paperwork, calling the repairman in the middle of the night, serving eviction notices, interviewing the lease applicants, and mailing you a check every quarter. I've never charged you a red dime for all my administrative work, for postage, for gas money. Nothing extra."

Marvina could see the angry ridges in Rose's face flatten as she considered, probably for the first time, what a hassle it had been to take care of Momma's property all these years. She started the drive to Momma's house.

The nerve of Rose to take interest in Momma's house now.

All this time, Marvina had handled things with no help from Rose. Not to mention how little she helped when their mother took sick. It was typical of people who haven't been there all along to try to come in at the last minute and tell everybody else what to do.

The very nerve!

As far as Marvina was concerned, Rose had no moral right to tell Marvina what to do with Momma's house. Left up to Rose, the house would have caved in on itself a long time ago, and they'd have nothing but a half an acre of rotten wood and broken bricks to their family name right now.

Rose parked the car in Momma's driveway. The contractor's black, rusty truck was nestled next to the mailbox.

"It's all fine and good that you've taken care of Momma's house. I appreciate it. But—"

"No buts."

"But," Rose repeated forcefully, "the house is in both our names."

"You know from the checks I send you, it's not worth much," Marvina said.

"It's worth *something*."

"Definitely, to someone like Kerresha who has *nothing*. I mean, it's small. And old." A thought occurred to Marvina. "Wait. Are you trying to move into the house?"

"No ma'am," Rose insisted. "I'm saying. The market is in sellers' favor right now."

Marvina gasped. "Are you talkin' about selling Momma's house?"

"We ain't gettin' no younger, Marvina. And you just rattled off a list of reasons why this house is way too much for you to manage," she twisted Marvina's intentions masterfully.

"I was only telling you those things in hopes that you'd show some gratitude for all my unnoticed hard work," Marvina stated with a huff.

"Well. I do thank you very much, Marvina, for your kind service. I have never been a landlord. I did not know what the job entailed."

"Of course you don't. And you're welcome. But you can kill the idea of selling Momma's house." Marvina made the universal throat-cutting gesture, running a stiff hand under her chin.

"You don't have to be so violent," Rose chided.

Nonetheless, Marvina got out of Rose's SUV. She stepped toward the home's entrance, waiting for both Rose and the contractor to catch up. She shivered in the cold winds as she stood on the porch, large and in charge.

"Marvina Nash?"

"Yes. You must be Charles?"

The balding man pushed the large glasses up the slope of his nose, then shook her hand. "Yes, ma'am. Thanks so much for calling."

"And thanks for coming on a Sunday. It's not usual for me. But when you suggested it, I figured why not," she said, almost apologetically. Sunday was still the sabbath, after all. "This here is my sister, Rose."

"Nice to meet you both." He shook Rose's hand. "And thanks for the opportunity. I'm not new to construction, but I am new to Marion County. So I'll take every chance I can to get my team's name and good reputation established in this community."

"Perfect. Let's go inside."

"I'll wait out here," Rose said.

"Don't be silly."

Fear stamped across Rose's features, and Marvina rushed to her sister. Grabbed her hand. "It's okay. We're together."

Marvina unlocked the door and led them all inside, where memories met her instantly. Time slowed, the air stilled. Nostalgia crept up Marvina's nostrils and down into her chest, spreading a pleasant affection throughout her body and limbs. She hummed with the pleasant feeling. "Home, sweet home."

How could Rose consider selling?

"Nothing like it," Rose responded in a way that let Marvina know she felt the undeniable connection to this almost sacred space. In fact, the reason Marvina had waited so long to replace the kitchen cabinetry was because nearly every ding, every splotch, every scratch in the wood had a story.

Marvina stepped to the edge of the soon-to-be replaced kitchen cabinet. "You remember when Momma smacked the corner of this cabinet with the cast-iron skillet?"

Rose covered her mouth with a hand. "That was the biggest, hairiest spider I ever saw in person in my entire life!"

"I thought Daddy was playing a trick on us," Marvina recalled. "But the way those eight legs moved when Momma raised the pan...nuh-uh!"

"Sounds like you all had a close encounter with a Texas brown tarantula," Charles inched his way into the conversation. He tapped and swiped on his large electronic tablet, readying for the estimate.

So as not to take up too much of his time on a Sunday, Marvina said, "The kitchen is my main concern. The sooner we get an estimate, the better. Are you familiar with city and county requirements for low-income housing?"

Rose's face shriveled into a giant question mark. "County requirements?"

Marvina swiveled to face her sister. "Yes. We gotta get certified through the system or we won't meet the county housing standards."

"Yes, ma'am. I am familiar with the requirements," Charles answered the original question.

"Since when did we make the decision to let Kerresha move in?"

"Don't you remember? Kerresha said she'd applied, but they won't give her the voucher until the baby gets here and she has a dependent she can't provide for. Ain't that something? It's like you gotta have a baby out of wedlock to get help."

"Whoa. Wait. You said you were *thinking* about letting Kerresha move into the house."

"I *am* thinking about it."

"Looks to me like you've already planned for it."

"Do I need to…step outside?" Charles asked shyly.

Marvina said, "No."

Rose said, "Yes."

For a second, Charles stood there confused. Then, he suggested, "Why don't I just get the measurements, then I'll open up my app, input the numbers, and it'll kick out an estimate. You two can figure out the rest later. What do you say?"

Without a word, the two sisters watched him stretch the aluminum tape measure across the cabinets, drawers, countertops, and floors, jotting down numbers on a traditional sketchpad. They fumed all the while, waiting for him to finish his job so they could finish this conversation away from company.

When he finished gathering information manually, he tapped into his tablet again and took a few pictures. Then his brows wrinkled in confusion. Charles glanced at his screen again. "Well, Miss Marvina. It seems…hmmm…"

"What?"

"Looks like we've already done an estimate here," Charles stated with a question in his tone.

A small, unintelligible sound came from Rose, but she clamped her mouth shut.

Marvina asked, "An estimate from who?"

"My colleague, Mike, was out here not too long ago. I'm merging with Regan Renovation soon. We're sharing our database. He did an estimate for a…let's see here…" He flicked a finger on the screen. "Do you know an R. Dewberry?"

Marvina crossed her arms against her chest. "Sure do. She's standin' right here."

CHAPTER 24

Rose

With a town as small as Fork City, I should have known all the contractors were in cahoots. But when the man's work truck didn't bear the same sign as the one who'd come when I requested the quote, I thought the secret of my previous estimate was safe.

Wrong. A sour feeling wormed through my body, like the expiration date on all my internal organs suddenly passed.

Charles's eyes toggled back and forth between mine and Marvina's. "The estimate on file is good for thirty days."

Marvina pursed her lips and spoke with her gaze deadlocked on mine. "How old is the estimate, Charles?"

He searched the machine.

"You don't have to answer her," I told him.

"Yes, you do," Marvina countered.

He gulped.

"And don't listen to R. Dewberry. She's from Dallas. She's not in a position to bring you future business here in East Texas like me."

"Yes ma'am." His eyes fell to the tablet again. "You've got three weeks left."

A smirk curled across Marvina's face. "Thank you, Charles."

"You're welcome, ma'am," he said to her. Then he said to me, "I'm sorry, ma'am. It's business."

I ignored him.

With her eyes still on me, Marvina asked, "Mr. Charles. I'm sorry to impose, but could you possibly drive me back to my home on Wilkerson Road because I do not wish to ride home with my conniving sister."

He started to say yes, but I cut him off.

"I'm not the only one conniving here. Sounds like you've also done some homework yourself with the county welfare department."

"I made one phone call. And here you are, getting estimates on Momma's house so you can sell it!"

"What do you call *him*?!" I pointed at Charles.

His eyes widened. He stuttered, "I-I-I'm really not—"

Marvina yanked a thumb toward Charles. "Leave him out of this!"

"Ladies, I'm gonna be at my c-c-car when you come to a decision." He ran out of the house as fast as James Brown skidding across a dance floor.

That left me and Marvina alone in Momma's kitchen, surrounded by the essence of her presence despite I-don't-know-how-many tenants that had come and gone. The air, the wood, the linoleum still rang with her old energy. But would those old ties be strong enough to bind me and my sister together again?

"Marvina. Listen. We both know it's time to make renovations to the house. Once we do that, it won't be the same. All our memories will live on in our minds, but they won't be in this house anymore once we tear this kitchen down to the studs," I dramatized the cabinet overhaul because, well, the kitchen was tiny, thus the majority of the cooking took place in a small area—the exact area we both wanted to renovate. "Besides, after the kitchen comes bathrooms. Bedrooms. In a matter of time, the house will be foreign."

When Marvina didn't respond, I reached into my purse with what I imagined was the caution of a cashier pulling money out of a register for a two-bit robber. Slow and easy, no sudden moves, I extracted the manila envelope and offered it to Marvina.

Her hands didn't budge from under her bosom.

Struggling to keep my tone steady and optimistic, I proposed, "I got a Realtor. This is the comparative market analysis for the house."

"A Realtor. You don't say?" She flipped up the tip of the envelope and began pulling the stack of papers out of the envelope.

I continued, "And behind that is the start-up cost for the restaurant."

"The restaurant?" She shoved the papers back inside and thrust the package back into my hands. "Are you still playing that fairy tale in your mind, Rose?"

"Yes," I came very close to yelling. "Marvina. This is our chance to get back what we lost." I wanted to say what *you* lost us, what *you* stole from me. The whole honey-vinegar thing, however, caused me to hold my words. "Can you please… I just want to start over again."

"You do realize you're making the same mistake again." Marvina cut her eyes at the envelope.

"What do you mean?"

"You're making moves, making major decisions without me, just like you did forty years ago when you single-handedly ratified the restaurant name without me. This is the very reason I wouldn't go into business with you then, and it's the reason I won't now, either."

"But, I—"

"That's the problem!" She threw her hands in the air. "You! It's always about you, Rose! This is all about you! Not Momma's seasoning, not her legacy, not me, not even *us*. It's you! You have the big ideas, you make the plans, they always crumble, and I'm always the one who suffers for them!"

"What in the world are you talking about, Marvina?"

She grabbed the envelope from me, ripped the entire package in half, papers and all, and threw it to the floor.

Watching her tear through the folder and its contents then disregard them like trash unleashed a torrent of anger through my system. This was it. For all her sanctimonious churchgoing, judgmental, self-righteousness, for her to sit up there and so violently, so cold-bloodedly destroy my last hope without even reading the papers…a before-and-after line hacked across my heart.

I was done with her.

My whole body went numb. Time stopped, and I realized that the last time I'd felt my entire system shut down like that was the day I knew my marriage was over. In fact, the horrible flashback came into complete view again.

David had come in from a late night "at work" with the smell of perfume on his shirt. Classic. Pathetic. Like he wasn't even trying to cover his tracks anymore.

I was sitting on the couch watching old reruns. He bent over me and kissed my forehead. "I told you not to wait up."

The flowery smell, different from the one he'd wafted in with last month, had a sweet quality. Not cheap, this one. "She has good taste."

His walk to our bedroom stiffened, but he didn't stop. Didn't deny my accusation. It occurred to me, in that moment, that we were settling into a routine. He cheated. I complained. He stopped for a little while until someone else caught his eye. Rinse and repeat.

I loved David. He loved me, to the best of his limited, squirrelly ability. But it wasn't enough love in return to sustain a marriage. Something clicked in me, like a definitive switch, and turned off all hope of renewal. Shut down my emotions and made my next moves a matter of factual processes only, devoid of all feelings. Numb.

File the paperwork, check.

Pack bags, check.

Find another place, check.

Move, check.

I cleared my throat before Marvina now. "I guess that's it, then."

Marvina took in a breath through her nose. "Guess so. 'Cause I'm not putting Momma's house on the market under no circumstances. And I don't appreciate you getting possible selling prices without talking to me about it first. You just proved to me all over again that I can't trust you."

Shame struck me so hard, my eyes averted hers. I let her win the staring match. "Well, I don't want to be around you if you think I'm a crook. I'll get out of your house. Call me when Kerresha's about to have the baby. I'll bring her back to Dallas with me for a while or…we can take turns or…whatever. We can figure it out later."

"Fine."

"Fine."

I gathered the pieces of my paperwork off the floor and left Momma's house. But my shield of numbness crumbled as soon as I left the porch. Tears streamed down my face so quickly, and the cold wind made the tear trails on my cheeks feel like streaks of ice.

Charles nodded his head at me as though he were a spectator watching the family walk down the center aisle of a loved one's funeral. Somber and respectful. Appropriate.

I drove back to Marvina's house, my heart throbbing inside my chest. Crying. No, slobbering. It was over. Me chasing my dreams, trying to remember Momma in a good way, considering a reconciliation with Marvina. It all came crashing down, landing on my now-pounding chest.

Feeling faint, I reminded myself to breathe. But I couldn't breathe for the weight of sorrow sitting on my chest. My only option was to part my lips half an inch and take in shallow sips or air, panting through the pain of my sister's rejection, through the massive, overwhelming return of guilt and shame that had barred me from Fork City all these years in the first place.

I shouldn't have come back here.

Salty tears slipped into my mouth. I licked them away. It had been a while since I let myself feel so deeply, and it hurt so bad, so tangibly, I could not imagine why I had ever opened myself up to this kind of pain again. For as much as it felt good to laugh with Marvina and remember Daddy's dancing with her, I'd forgotten how bad she could hurt me, how unsafe vulnerability and relationships could be.

I'm not putting myself through this again. Forget David's and Dr. Renita's stupid advice. I refused delivery. The fight to protect myself was on again. Now and forever.

When I reached Marvina's house, I left my purse in the

passenger's seat of my vehicle; it didn't make sense to bring in a bag when my goal was to bring all my bags out and drive away.

I opened the front door of her house, removed her key from my key ring, and set it on the closest end table.

With all the blood rushing wildly through my veins, my knee fussed a bit as I started packing.

Marvina thanked and said goodbye to Charles, then came inside and went straight to her bedroom, slamming the bedroom door.

"I don't care," I mumbled to myself. "Go on and slam your little funky bedroom door. Go on and bury your head in your little novel and escape your little sad reality with your…your little kicked-you-out cult church and your little I-don't-wanna-see-you-because-you're-gay son. Mm-hmm. Talkin' about how *I* need to give up on *my* dreams when *you* the one who needs to *get* a dream, my dear."

I punched my clothes into the carriers, stuffed my toiletries into the cases, talking to myself, pumping my mind with defensive fighting words because, at that point, I was the only one who had my back. And according to Beyoncé, in the end, all you got is yourself.

The last thing I took from the house was my fresh batch of seasoning, which I carefully sealed at the top with plastic wrap and placed on the floorboard right next to the dehydration machine and the second bag of clothing David brought me, most of which I hadn't even worn yet. What a wasted trip for him. For me. This entire excursion was a bust.

Except for Kerresha, whose questioning face met me in the living room when I came back inside. This wasn't the setting I had envisioned. She was supposed to be in her bedroom, lying in bed, barely awake when I told her I was leaving. In that case, she might not have the wherewithal to ask any of her astute questions.

Shoot, I had a few astute questions for her behind, come to think of it. Like, who is your baby daddy? Did you really plan to squat out a baby while squattin' in a guesthouse? Do you have any freaking idea what a blessing it is to give birth? And if you do, please plan better in the future!

"Miss Rose? Where are you going?"

I held on to the doorknob as though it were holding the only thing supporting me. "I'm leaving. Heading back to Dallas."

Instantly, her eyes filled with tears. "What? I mean, why? And were you not going to tell me?"

"Yes. Later. I thought you were still asleep. Didn't want to wake you before necessary," I explained.

She pointed toward the couch. "You want to sit down and talk?"

"No. I need to leave. But I'll be back. As soon as you go into labor, Marvina will let me know. And I'll be here for the baby's birth."

Kerresha didn't try to stop herself from crying. Her nose turned red and began dripping. "And then what? You'll be gone again?"

"That is not my plan." I pulled her shivering body into a hug. "Kerresha. I know we haven't known each other long, but I adore you, young lady. You've got a way with words and a way with people that…makes me want to be a part of your life for as long as you and little man will have me. So that won't change. But me and Marvina…we simply don't get along. Do you understand what I'm saying?"

I felt her head tilt up and down against my shoulder.

Knowing Kerresha, I expected her to say something like "but you could if you tried." She didn't. And the fact that she didn't hurt me all over again, because if Kerresha had given up on me and my sister, if there were no wise words left from the one who had been trying to patch us up all along, then Marvina and I were stick-a-fork-in-it done.

She pushed away from our embrace and mopped her face with her sweatshirt's sleeve, sniffing to clear her nose. "How often will you come back to Fork City?"

I lifted my shoulders. "As often as you need me. You're welcome to come to Dallas if you'd like. Lots more job opportunities. There's always steady city and county work. I could put in a word for you at the post office."

Kerresha grinned and shook her head. "No offense, Miss Rose, but I don't want a job."

I blinked hard because I didn't think I'd heard her correctly. "Come again?"

The grin stayed in place. "I know, I know. My baby will need food and shelter. And that takes money. But…it's like you said Christmas morning. You worked for all those years doing something you didn't really like. You put your life on hold and now here you are…"

She didn't finish the sentence.

I quickly turned away and opened the front door fully. "Didn't mean to do the whole reverse-inspiration thing, but okey-dokey."

"Miss Rose, wait. It's not too late for you to live your life," Kerresha said.

"Maybe not. But I need to go lick my wounds right now."

"What?"

"I need to pout."

She nodded. "Okay. That's real."

"Thank you."

"I love you," she said.

At those three words, I whirled around and faced her head-on. And I wanted to hug her again, bring her back to my bosom the way a mother does her child. But it occurred to me that loving Kerresha meant she, too, possessed the power and position to hurt me the same as Marvina, my Momma, and everyone else I'd ever held so close. It hurt more to lose people than to be alone.

"I said I love you," she repeated. "The way you stood up to the officer for me that first night... I'll never forget it. And the way you keep it real. I mean, no disrespect to Ms. Marvina. She's a sweetheart. But me and you." She wagged her index and middle finger in the shape of a V, back and forth between us. "We keep it one hundred. That's why I love you, Miss Rose."

"That's really sweet of you," I said, rubbing her arm. I didn't have the heart to tell her how foolish she was for loving someone so easily. Hadn't she learned that lesson from her own mother? Instead, I said, "You take it easy until the baby gets here. I'll look for the call from Marvina next month when you go into labor."

She cupped a hand over mine, pressing my palm onto her elbow. "I know, like, seventy-five percent is the best you can do right now, Miss Rose. It's okay. It's enough. Thank you."

I kissed her cheek and walked out of my sister's home, into my car, and started the loneliest, emptiest drive back to Dallas from my hometown. I listened to the saddest music on my playlist once I got a reliable signal on the highway, crying and slobbing and thinking and yelling and fussing. All of the above. Marvina, Momma, Daddy, David, Kerresha, Dr. Renita, Officer McGillam—I loved or liked and despised them all for different reasons. Well, maybe not Kerresha so much with the despising part, but she was a character in this god-awful movie, too. And speaking of God, He had a terrible starring role as well, one for which He would win no Oscar. As far as I could tell, He had been mostly off-screen.

Thankfully, I had left early enough to make the trip back to Dallas before sunset. It was bad enough the tears blurred my vision. I couldn't imagine what would happen with nightfall on top of my smudgy eyesight.

Halfway home, I reached for my phone to call David. But I changed my mind after the first ring. For all I knew he might have been engaged to Dr. Renita already.

My phone dinged with a text.

I quelled a smile, thinking David had probably seen my name pop up on the screen and was texting me just to make sure I hadn't needed him.

But when I glanced down, it was a message from Elizabeth. Congrats! You got it!

And just like that, I was broker by three thousand dollars, on top of everything else.

"That's the icing on my moldy cake!"

I put the phone on silent and turned it face down on the seat.

CHAPTER 25

Marvina held her breath as she listened to Rose's SUV crawl over the gravel. The snap and crackle of rocks under wheels provided the perfect soundtrack for Marvina's crumpling heart. All her life, people had told Marvina that she was too gullible. She loved too easily, gave too much, and others would take advantage of her kindness. "Others," as it turned out, was family. Her own sister.

Pressing her fingertips against her puffy eyelids, Marvina exhaled. As the air left her lungs, she felt as though someone was extracting the life out of her. She breathed in again, but the intake was short-lived, as the pulling sensation returned. A tug-of-war for her breath. She recognized this as the beginning of an anxiety attack.

Marvina forced herself to pull on her side of the rope, to breathe deeply. To pray and remind herself that this would pass. *I'm not dying.*

"Miss Marvina," Kerresha said before she knocked on the door.

Marvina couldn't respond. It was all she could do to breathe. She stayed sitting upright on the foot of her bed, just allowing the oxygen to pass through her system.

"Miss Marvina, you in there? Are you okay?" A few seconds later, Kerresha cracked the door open.

Just having someone else present provided some relief. Marvina croaked, "Yes."

Kerresha came closer. Visually inspected Marvina's o-shaped lips. "You don't look okay."

"It's anxiety."

"Oh. I'll be right back."

Marvina focused on the photo of herself, Warren Sr., and Warren Jr. sitting atop her gilded antique dresser. Family used to make her happy. Family was everything at one point in her life. Family and church.

Looking at the picture wasn't helping. She closed her eyes. Kept breathing.

"Here." Kerresha entered again with a brown, glass bottle with a ring of colorful beads on top. Looked like something straight out of witch doctor's medicine bag. "Hold this to your nose."

Marvina waved the bottle away. "I don't mess with new age, psychedelic stuff. I stick with God."

"It's lavender. I'm pretty sure God made it."

Kerresha twisted the top off the bottle and held it under Marvina's nose.

The scent, deep, calming, and pure, filled her the same way she imagined her body would feel if somebody poured the color purple all through her soul.

A minute later, the anxiety level had gone from a 7 down to a 2. "Thank you."

"I'll leave this bottle on your nightstand in case you need it again. I have another one of my own." Kerresha let herself out again.

All Marvina could do was sit there and laugh. *This girl, this child, and her ways.*

Marvina's phone dinged with a text message. In a flash, she grabbed her phone, half-hoping it was from Rose.

But it wasn't.

Pastor wants to meet with us. Can you come to the church now?

But she and Eleanor were used to these spur-of-the-moment calls on behalf of the church. Someone might need a witness for a notary signature or a letter typed up for funeral resolutions. Pastor knew he could rely on them. Up until now, Marvina had been glad to be counted with the faithful.

Nonetheless, Marvina texted: Be right there.

Still wearing her church clothes, Marvina regrouped and prepared for Pastor's reprimand. "I'm heading out for a bit," she told Kerresha in passing.

Kerresha's baby bump was protruding so much it nearly hung off the edge of the couch as she lay on her side watching television. Seemed like that baby gained a pound at day, here lately.

With great effort, she raised her body upright and said, "Miss Rose is gone back to Dallas."

"I know."

"You going after her?"

"No. And I'm sorry she left you, but…my sister just—"

"It's both of you," Kerresha opined. "You know that, right?"

Kerresha might know about social media and lavender, but she didn't know everything. "Maybe we can talk about it later."

Eleanor's car was already parked near the church's back door, the one they used to enter the kitchen. Marvina pulled up parallel and parked. She felt like an outsider when she had to knock on wood to enter this house of worship that she had made so many sacrifices for, like a wife without a key to her own house.

"Hello, Sister," Eleanor, who was also still wearing her black tutu and pink cashmere cardigan with her white blouse from the Sunday morning service, greeted Marvina with a kiss that left a cinnamon smell on her cheek. "Pastor's waiting."

They strode a few steps then made a quick turn down the hallway leading to Pastor Pendleton's office. The building was so quiet, Marvina didn't have an opportunity to pre-brief with Eleanor without the risk of their voices carrying like two teenage girls whispering during a pop quiz.

"Welcome," Pastor Pendleton said. His reddened eyes bespoke weariness and his face had lost that haughty Higher Works Alliance glow. "Please have a seat."

Marvina and Eleanor took turns returning his greeting and took their seats, albeit cautiously.

Pastor plopped into his chair. He swiveled around to the picture of him with Vernetta as though silently consulting with her. With his back turned to them, Marvina examined his desk, which seemed to have twice the amount of clutter as the last time she'd visited his office.

Pastor quickly pivoted forward again and faced the two women in his office. His cheeks filled with air as though playing a saxophone. Then he sighed. "I'm just gonna come out and say it. Our collaboration with Higher Works Alliance has come to an impasse."

"A what?" Eleanor asked.

"It's a point where they can't move forward," Marvina translated, trying to keep sparkles of joy from tinkling into her voice.

"You don't say," Eleanor remarked in a flat tone that could be interpreted as sarcasm and nonchalance.

"They want me posting online three, four, five times a day," he remarked, holding up all ten fingers on his skinny hands. "And doing these email swaps. I told 'em that I'm used to working together for revivals, not social media blitzes."

Eleanor poked out her duck lips and tilted her neck to the side.

The way Eleanor sat there animating her feelings, Marvina wished she'd just come out and say, "I told you so."

"What's your plan, Pastor?" Marvina asked.

"I gotta find something in the middle," he said. "Where we can keep our hometown feel, our traditional ways, and add things to our plates gradually. As we see fit."

Marvina had to know. "Does that mean we might be able to use the kitchen to minister again?"

"Possibly," he said with an encouraging lilt.

Anything was better than a no. Marvina enthused, "Pastor, I'm so glad you're reconsidering."

Eleanor kept her gaze on Pastor Pendleton while laying a hand on Marvina's bouncing knee. "Not so fast. What about all the other auxiliaries?"

"I think we need to sit down and come up with a customized vision for our church in light of the changes around the city. Once we get that in place, we reevaluate each auxiliary, each group, and see if it aligns with our new vision," he said.

"And we'll do all this *together*?" Marvina asked, finally catching on to Eleanor's master plan.

"Yes. Together," Pastor agreed.

"Then let's get to it," Eleanor said. "I'll check your calendar, set up a meeting, and send out the emails."

"Thank you, Sister Eleanor," Pastor said, standing to shake hers and Marvina's hands.

In the droop of his tired eyes, Marvina also saw another reason for his change of heart. Pastor just wasn't up to starting over. She completely understood how he felt. She wished Rose could have been there to witness the death of Pastor's go-gettin' ways. She could use a little tempering, too.

Eleanor tucked her small purse underneath her armpit. "I've gotta run. Need to get back home to my cookin'." She beat Pastor and Marvina back down the corridor and to the parking lot.

Pastor Pendleton kindly walked Marvina to her car and thanked her for coming on such short notice. Again.

"It's my pleasure, Pastor."

"Well, you know if you ever need anything, Sister Marvina, I'm here for you. I'm not one for all these platform-building schemes, you know? I love shepherding God's people, you know?"

Marvina thought about the lamb-leg-breaking sermon. Whether that leg-breaking was true or false made no difference for her. She wasn't the wandering type. And she appreciated a loyal, dedicated pastor despite whatever Kerresha scrounged up online.

In fact, now that Pastor Pendleton was back to himself, she needed his guidance. On Rose, Kerresha, Warren Jr. Since her son had known the Pastor throughout his childhood, Marvina thought it best to start with him. She stopped short of unlocking her driver's-side door and turned to face Pastor Pendleton.

The same winds that had swirled around her only a few hours ago when she and Rose stood outside with Charles the contractor still chilled the air. Marvina pulled her coat tighter. If Eleanor hadn't been in the office, she would have talked to him under warmer conditions. But there was no turning back, now.

"Pastor, I need to talk to you about something. *About someone*." She bit her lip.

"Go 'head," he gently prodded.

"My son. Warren Jr. We haven't spoken in months because. He said he's…" She had to say it. "He's gay."

Pastor's eyes stayed level. In fact, nothing on his face twitched or flipped. Like maybe he wasn't surprised. "I'm glad he told you."

"What? You knew?" Marvina asked.

"Not exactly. Warren Jr., was a fine youth in our programs. When he was in high school, one day he came to talk to me."

Horrified, Marvina asked, "What did he say?"

"Well, I can tell you what I said. I said that I loved him, that God loved him, and I'd be praying for him just like I pray for all my kids."

Marvina let the information swirl around her brain. "Thank you, Pastor. I'm going to reach out to him as soon as I get home."

Marvina rehearsed her lines all the way home. "I love you, Warren Jr. Always have and always will." Or maybe, "Son, there's nothing keeping us from loving one another." Between those phrases, she should be able to come up with something reasonable.

And she planned to make good on that promise to call her son immediately, but when she walked into the house and saw Kerresha's clenched jaws and the sweat forming on the girl's forehead, Marvina's plans quickly changed course.

CHAPTER 26
Rose

My phone vibrated two more times back-to-back, but after losing three grand, I was in no mood to talk to Elizabeth or David or whoever else wanted to harass me. Count me out for any more lectures, therapy sessions, guilt trips, or business motivational speeches. I just wanted to get home, get out of those church clothes, elevate my knee, sprinkle some of Momma's seasoning inside a bag of family-sized tortilla chips, and eat the entire bag as though there was a magic happiness-genie at the bottom of the sack.

A steel anvil thunked onto my chest, pinning me to a realization I needed to accept: I would never give birth to anything. Not a child. Not a good idea. Not a business. My life began and ended with me. Period. I needed to dig a hole, throw my ambitions inside the hole, and shovel dirt on top.

I pulled off the highway, switched my gear to park, turned on my hazard lights, and cried all over my steering wheel.

Cars flew by me, shaking my vehicle a little each time. I wanted to pull myself together, but I couldn't. Not with my chest heaving up and down.

So I waited, the same way I'd always waited when I had a

meltdown. I waited for the hurt and pain to transform into an anger that would pick me up, refuel me, and drive me back to… back to what? Not back to work, where I could drown myself in busyness. I was retired. Maybe I could get a hobby. Make new friends.

Who was I kidding? I didn't want new friends. I wanted my sister. And Kerresha. And the baby. But even that seemed to be slipping away because Marvina and I stayed arguing.

I waited some more. The anger didn't come. Sadness and grief came, but I was all out of fight.

The third time the phone began its vibrations, I answered without even looking because, really, did it matter? "Hello?"

"Rose. It's me," my sister's voice rang with concern.

"What is it? I told you not to call me until next month."

"No. You said to call you when Kerresha went into labor."

It took me a minute to register what she was saying. "What?"

"Her water broke."

"Is she contracting?"

"Well. She's uncomfortable," Marvina said. "We've put in a call to Dr. Wilhelm to see what she wants us to do."

"Aren't you supposed to go in when your water breaks?" I asked.

"That's what I thought, too," Marvina said in whisper, "but Kerresha's know-it-all book said you don't always have to. And she wants to wait until the last possible minute so they don't drug her up and make the baby drowsy. She reads too much, if you ask me."

"I agree. This ain't no time for Dr. YouTube."

In the background, I heard Kerresha's moan. Instantly, all my feelings got shoved clear to the back burner of my brain. I punched the gas pedal and signaled right to get off on the next exit. "I'm on my way back to Fork City."

Only the likes of Albert Einstein and the laws of physics or quantum leaps could explain how fast I made it back to Fork City. I turned my phone back on to answer three calls along the way. Two from Marvina giving me updates. Kerresha's contractions were mild, but definitely beyond the Braxton-Hicks category.

"I think we've got some time," she said calmly.

And I replied as though we hadn't been in an argument only hours before. "All right. I'll be there shortly."

We knew from experience that we could draw on a reservoir of emergency partnership when needed. Like robots. Back when Momma first got sick, I used my vacation to come back to Fork City and help get her settled. My sister and I took care of the cooking, the laundry, getting the hospital bed, getting the home health care arranged, the medications lined up, the right doctors, the right Medicare, the right Medicaid. We started out as a team, but when it comes to stuff like that, messages get crossed and balls get dropped when there are two different points of contact. Marvina was the best choice to handle things long-term since she lived in Fork City. But when we were getting it all set up, initially, the two of us put our differences aside and worked together.

Momma didn't say much, but Daddy told us both, "Your momma's been praying for you two to reconcile. Maybe her getting sick and bringing you two together was the answer. I guess she should have been more careful of what she prayed for, huh?"

Marvina had repeated the age-old cliché, "God does work in mysterious ways."

I despised the saying because, in my experience, people quoted it when they didn't have answers. Church folk blamed everything on God, good or bad.

The three of us were in the living room, out of Momma's hearing distance. Marvina and I were folding clothes while Daddy watched a football game. I was divorced from David by then. Marvina was married and had come over late that evening after taking care of everything she needed to handle with her own household.

As us two girls folded clothes while our Daddy did absolutely nothing, I wondered who in the world, who in past generations, created this dynamic where women did all the domestic work and men did so little around the house.

Alas, it wasn't the day to rewrite the history of humanity right there in our parents' living room with the velvet portrait of Jesus and the disciples looking on.

"You think you can come back on the regular, Rose?" Daddy asked me. "You don't have to be a stranger once your mother gets better."

I paused and looked up at Marvina, realizing instantly that she hadn't told Daddy everything the doctor said about Momma's condition.

Marvina threatened me with a don't-say-nothing glare.

I snapped a bath towel, then smoothed it into a rectangle and set it on top of the tower of towels. "I can't say, Daddy."

Marvina moved my towel from the top of the pile and used it to start a new pile. Now that Momma was incapacitated, it was clear to me Marvina had taken up the mantle of coming behind me to let me know I was doing things incorrectly in this world.

"I'm sure your Momma would love to see your face more."

I replied, "We're headed into the Christmas season. My work gets extremely busy at the post office."

"Hmph. That's convenient," Marvina said under her breath.

She tucked two socks into one another and threw them into Daddy's pile.

I glared at her and hissed, "What do you want me to do? Quit my job?"

Daddy leaned over in his easy chair and looked at us. "Huh?"

"Nothing, Daddy." She glared back at me.

The chair groaned as his attention returned to football.

"You've already made your choices," she whispered.

"I'm helping as much as I can," I grunted.

"I don't need you to help me take care of Momma. You *help* someone when it's *their* responsibility. I don't want your *help*. I want us to be *jointly responsible*. Together."

"You know I can't. I don't live here."

"Again. A convenient choice." She flapped a sheet straight and raised her hands high to spread it wide, putting a physical barrier between us for the moment.

Yes, Marvina and I were well-versed in putting our disagreements, our anger, our truths aside in order to deal with the current crisis.

We could perform as emergency sisters when necessary. Like now, when a woman was in labor, one of the biggest emergencies known to mankind.

The third phone call I received on my turnaround trip to Fork City was from David, checking on the nature of my previously abandoned call, as I suspected he would. "I can't talk now. Kerresha's about to have the baby."

"Wonderful! Keep me posted."

I swear, the way he left the conversation so open for me to attack him—it's like he laid down on railroad tracks so I could roll over him with, "Oh, are you sure it's okay for me to call you? I don't want to *interfere* with you and Dr. Renita."

But I held back because, truth be told, it's no fun fighting with somebody who won't return the punches.

"I'll let you know as soon as the baby gets here. Bye."

Wow. That felt different. Civil. I wondered if that was how David and Dr. Renita "communicated." And if they used big words all the time.

When I was ten miles from the house, I called Marvina again to let her know I was close.

"Girl! You flyin'!" she laughed nervously. She called to Kerresha, "Breathe through. Rose is almost here."

My heart raced for a different cause, pumping with a renewed excitement now. *A baby.* Tiny chin, mouth full of gums. Swirls of feathery hair at the temples and the heavenly smell of newborn life tucked between their neck rolls.

"Mmm, mmmph, mmph," I said to myself. If we could bottle that smell up and sell it…

"Naaah," I laughed to myself, thinking it was too sacred to sell. That would be like selling hugs. Selling love. Impossible.

It struck me, then, that must have been how Marvina felt about Momma's seasoning recipe. Not that I agreed with her, but I understood her better, now. Once you put a price on something priceless, it feels cheap.

My knee cooperated, stretching and carrying my weight back into Marvina's house. I flew past my sister and dashed to Kerresha's side as she lay on the couch with her shoulders propped against the armrest. Awkward angle aside, Marvina had been correct when she described Kerresha's appearance as "uncomfortable."

Her brows furrowed, her nostrils flared slightly, and her forehead glowed with dampness. "Agitated" might have been an even better word.

I clasped her hand. "You ready to go to the hospital yet?"

"No. I want to wait until the contractions are five minutes apart."

"How far apart are they now?"

"Last one was nine minutes," Marvina replied, flashing a timer on her phone.

Our eyes met, silently registering the temporary truce.

"Oooooh!" Kerresha unleashed a deep groan. "How many minutes this time?"

Marvina touched her phone screen. "Seven."

"Nuh-uh. I'm not gonna make it to five," Kerresha cried. "I can't do this. I can't have this baby."

I squeezed her arm. "Yes, you can, Kerresha."

"But his father. I don't know…"

"Now is not the time, sweetheart." I shook my head.

Marvina stood behind me and pressed a hand on my shoulder. Strength radiated from her straight into me, and I hoped from me straight into Kerresha. I spoke with a newfound courage. "Listen to me. We are going to the hospital. And you are going to have a beautiful baby boy today. We are with you, and every woman who ever came before us is with you."

Marvina added, "You're surrounded by nothing but love."

Eyes filled with fright, tears, and gratitude, Kerresha said, "Okay. Yes, ma'am. Let's go before another contraction comes."

Marvina grabbed the hospital bag, and I wrapped Kerresha's arm around my neck to help her to the car, but we didn't make it before another contraction hit. The way her face screwed up, I prayed, "Lord, have mercy," as she bellowed through the pain. I had seen labor in movies and read it in books, but to be there and feel the intensity, the energy of it all was another thing altogether.

Knee don't fail me now.

Marvina came along her other side and helped her stay upright while the contraction passed by. "Keep breathing, Kerresha. Just keep breathing."

I took my sister's cue to keep calm, but I swear I almost burst out crying from the pity over her pain, and maybe even my own helplessness to relieve her agony.

Kerresha whooshed oxygen through her lungs, one forceful breath after another. I mimicked her actions, like I was the one ready to give birth. Marvina looked at me like I was off my rocker, but I ignored her curious gaze.

We made it to the car and strapped Kerresha into the front seat. Marvina had barely closed the back door before I burned rubber, racing to the hospital. Between contractions, Marvina cheered Kerresha on. When the pains hit, Kerresha grabbed the door handles and squeezed for dear life while we all took deep breaths in unison.

My sister tried humming gospel hymns as though the flat blues notes could possibly comfort Kerresha during this time of turmoil and tribulation.

Kerresha shot me a horrified look.

I ordered, "Marvina. Scrap the Mahalia Jackson concert."

She stopped mid-croon. Cleared her throat. "I'm only asking the Lord to help."

"He heard your plain words the first time," I assured her.

Thankfully, we reached the hospital before the fourth contraction, not that being in the facility meant anything for the birthing process. Kerresha's body kept right on going through the motions, and the nurses, as sweet as they were, did their job before and after the contractions.

"I know you filled out paperwork with your doctor, but I have to ask a few questions for the record. What's your full name, sweetheart?"

"Go ahead and change into these as soon as you get past the next one."

"Verify your wristband when you get a moment, okay love?"

I imagined when you see women in labor every day, you must become immune to seeing them struggle through the pain in order to do your job, just like an emergency room physician who has to assess a patient's injuries before administering any pain medication.

Once Kerresha was in her hospital gown and had all her paperwork squared away, the baby's heart monitor was put in place, and the nurse determined Kerresha's cervix was five centimeters dilated. At this rate, we had several more hours. I wasn't sure if I could take it, and it wasn't even my body going through these sudden dramatic changes. So I asked, "When can she get her epidural?"

Kerresha shook her head. "I don't want one."

After which I nearly passed out because, at that point, I darn near needed an epidural on her behalf. My body ached with apprehension.

Marvina asked, "You sure you don't want anesthesia?"

"No. It slows the labor. And it might make the baby drowsy."

"He's gonna sleep all day anyway," Marvina reasoned.

The attending nurse intervened, "Kerresha, it's your choice. We have some mothers who give birth naturally, with no anesthesia, and some who choose to have the anesthesia. And some who change their minds as the labor progresses. It's totally up to you."

"Thank you."

Marvina's face pinched tighter. My stomach flipped, worried because this child was only at the halfway mark, yet she looked like the winner of the Boston Marathon after every contraction—bowed over, breathless, and spent.

For the next hour, she soldiered through, alternating between misery and recovery. At one point, Kerresha let out a yelp that pierced through my soul. I stood up and walked to the window.

Thankfully, it was Marvina's turn to coax Kerresha through. When it was over, Marvina got all in my ear and chastised me between gritted teeth, "Pull yourself together, Rose. Kerresha needs both of us to be strong. You cannot fall apart."

"I know," I wiped my eyes with shaking fingertips, thankful Marvina's body shielded me from Kerresha's view. "I know, but this is too much for me."

"Rose. Look at me."

I faced my sister. Noticed her trembling lips, her brimming lids. "You are the strongest, bravest woman I know." She bunched her lips tight, inhaled, and shook her head slowly.

I had never seen my little sister look at me with such pride.

My heart swelled with overwhelming gratitude. I had not been the recipient of that "look at my baby" expression in a very long time.

"Ain't nobody else I know who can set out to do the things you've done with nobody in your corner except you and still succeed in life. Without losing your sanity. I'm just sorry you had to do it alone. I'm sorry, Rose," she squeaked out the apology softly, in the corner of the hospital room, between the two of us alone.

Ooh wee, a dam broke in my soul and a flood of pinned-up emotions released all through my spirit. I fell into Marvina's arms for the cling of a lifetime. And I felt her heart thumping wild next to mine. I imagine I felt like a butterfly when it comes out of cocoon, how it sits there for a second, gets its bearings, and then realizes: I'm gonna be different from this moment on.

"She's about six centimeters," a cheerful, heavily tattooed nurse called from across the room.

Marvina and I jumped. We hadn't heard her enter to check Kerresha's progress.

"What are y'all over there doing? The patient is *here*?" she barely disguised her sarcasm.

"Yes ma'am," Marvina smiled at me.

"We're on it."

We shuffled back to Kerresha's bedside. But suddenly, the nurse's face turned sour when she scanned one of the monitors. She pressed her palm against the Doppler, encased in a thick belt contraption around Kerresha's stomach.

"What is it?" I asked.

"The baby's heart rate is lower than expected," she said in a deliberately calm way, like an airline attendant who'd been trained to tell everyone to stay in their seats while the plane was losing altitude. "I'm going to get the doctor."

The nurse's quick feet told a different story than her mouth.

"What's happening?" Kerresha whined. "This wasn't in my books."

Instinctively, I patted Kerresha's forearm. "We'll get this baby here safely in a little bit."

The nurse returned with the on-call doctor, a bear of a man with hands so large I couldn't imagine him touching any woman's delicate parts, and a second nurse. Almost in unison, they jumped into action. Nurses pulled up the rails and cinched the IV cord. "The baby is in distress. We need to intervene. Ladies, can you move back, please?" The older, curly-haired nurse addressed me and Marvina.

We took exactly two steps back, allowing them room to attend to Kerresha while letting her know we hadn't left her side. The nurses helped Kerresha roll onto her left side in hopes that would get more oxygen to the baby.

When that didn't work, they had her drink more water to increase her fluid levels.

Marvina nodded faithfully, keeping everyone's spirits optimistic.

Two contractions came and went while they were trying to figure it all out, and both times the baby's heart rate dipped lower and lower, to the point where I could tell the doctor was getting antsy, by the sweat on his forehead.

And Kerresha, bless her heart, was crying and asking questions none of them would answer directly. Just more airline-attendant talk.

This wasn't her regular doctor—the one we'd seen at the clinic. We'd gotten the person on call. Dr. Wilhelm was out of the country on holiday vacation. No one expected the baby this soon, so we were all out of sorts.

Anyway, my nerves were already shot, and my impatience grew with every contraction. And then I started thinking about Serena Williams and how she was in tip-top physical condition with all the money in the world when she gave birth, but yet and still, she almost died because her doctor didn't take her medical symptoms seriously. All of this taken with the fact that Kerresha's water had broken four weeks too early made me feel like something might go wrong if we didn't get this baby out soon. So I said, "Y'all got to do something different 'cause this ain't workin'."

And that older nurse—the one who was about my age—stared at me with relief, like thank-God-somebody-said-it.

The doctor, though annoyed, spoke some kind of jargon. Next

thing I knew, the nurses grabbed the rails, unlocked the bed wheels, and prepared to take Kerresha for a C-section. "Which one of you will go with her?"

Marvina said without hesitation, "You go, Rose."

I'd never been so terrified yet so determined to be somewhere at the same time. I wasn't about to leave Kerresha without an advocate, with her regular doctor being gone. "Okay. I will."

I grabbed Kerresha's hand, and together we rolled with the team to the emergency operating room. Everything happened so fast. A nurse scrubbed me in and draped me in sterile clothes and a hat. They gave Kerresha anesthesia, threw a little dividing cloth up so we wouldn't see too much of the surgery party. Put an oxygen mask over her mouth and nose. She started crying so hard she fogged up the oxygen mask.

I held back tears for her sake. "You're about to be a mother, Kerresha. It's the greatest gift. Let's do this, girl."

"I need you, Miss Rose!" She squeezed my arm.

"I'm right here!"

"We're all right here, and you're doing great," the older nurse said with a wink.

A few twists and pulls later, the baby boy's cry filled the room. The bundle of joy appeared above the blanket, brand spanking new life. A real, precious, dropped-from-the-heavens baby.

He cried, all wrinkled and surprised at this whole new world.

We all cheered as the doctor held him by his behind and his neck for all to see. Once I got past the sheer miracle of watching his first moments, it took everything in me to keep my voice eventoned when I fully registered his features. 'Cause let me tell you, I was not expecting that widow's peak, blond hair, and those clear blue eyes, but there they were staring right out at us!

"He is beautiful!" I exclaimed because he truly was. *A baby.*

Kerresha laughed and cried and smiled at her baby boy, like she couldn't believe she'd just made a life.

The nurse placed his little wiggling body on Kerresha's chest for skin-to-skin contact. Kerresha had showed me this ancient bonding technique in her book, actually. It was even more beautiful than the illustrations, watching a mother bond with her baby, and watching the newborn instinctively root around for her breast. It amazed me all over again, the way a tiny baby is born already knowing where to search for food.

I bent down and kissed Kerresha's forehead. "You done good, girl."

She stared at her baby and sobbed. "Oh my God. He's finally here."

"He sure is. And he brought a whole lotta love with him." I allowed myself to cry with her this time. In that moment, nothing mattered more than this new life. Being there for the new beginning, for birth, filled me with a thousand balloons. I could have floated away. Even though I wasn't the mother, I had been a witness. And doing so made me feel better than I'd felt in a long, long time.

CHAPTER 27

If she'd had some candles and a prayer shawl, she would have made an altar right there in the hospital lobby as she waited for news of Kerresha's labor. The wait was excruciating.

Marvina played the mental sport she read once in a book titled *Pollyanna*. In the book, the main character played a game where she found one good thing to be thankful for in every bad situation. Matter of fact, a church song about gratefulness in that same vein came to mind, too. Something about being happy for your shabby shoes because there was someone else who didn't have feet.

Try as she might, she couldn't think of anything good that might come of Kerresha losing this baby, especially not with Rose in the room. Might send Rose over the edge. She'd already given birth to her own deceased infant. What irreparable damage would witnessing a second stillborn baby do?

"Lord, what was I thinking?" she asked herself out loud, pacing the white-tiled floor, wringing her hands. The empty space where Kerresha's bed had been now haunted Marvina. For the first time in days, she was alone again. The reunion with Rose, while sweet, didn't equate to Rose moving back to Fork City or Kerresha turning down an invitation to Dallas. A young new mother might prefer the conveniences of city life for the baby, much like Greater New Harvest preferred life groups and praise teams over community cooking classes and choirs with three-part harmonies.

All this progress pushed Marvina into the margins. The reality plunged and sank into the depths of her stomach like a stone. Heavy, heavy, heavy.

Too much to think about.

Marvina searched through her purse looking for a book to read. But she couldn't remember where she'd placed her book in all the excitement around Kerresha going into labor. Clearly, it wasn't in her purse.

No book to read, only her troubling thoughts.

Adding to her anguish was the antiseptic smell of this hospital. She couldn't stand it. The same scent had filled the air when she'd lost Warren Sr., right at the beginning of the pandemic, before anyone knew what was happening, when doctors' only diagnosis was severe pneumonia.

She'd also lost Daddy at this hospital. This building had imprinted itself on final memories of Momma, too, before they sent her home for hospice care because Momma refused to spend her last days getting poked and prodded by doctors.

Marvina hoped today would be the day that this place brought a new feel. Life. A baby.

And then, suddenly, she remembered what she was supposed to do before she found Kerresha in labor. She had meant to call Warren Jr. And now, with nothing but time on her hands, she could make good on what she'd told Pastor Pendleton.

But first she had to get Warren's number. Thankfully, in a small town like Fork City, that came easily. She knew the mothers of many children Warren Jr., went to school with. A few minutes later, Marvina found herself with a phone in one hand and a shaking slip of paper in her left.

Nervousness washed over her as his phone rang. "Hello?"

His voice sounded so grown-up. And city proper. "Hi, Warren Jr. It's me. Your mother."

"Oh. Hi, Mom."

His attempt to sound unflappable was ruined by Marvina's heightened sense of hearing. He was glad to hear from her and she knew it.

"I just wanted to tell you that I love you," Marvina spoke honestly. Plainly. Well, as plainly as one can speak while crying.

"I love you, too, Momma."

Silence.

"Is that it?" he asked.

"Yes. That's the whole message."

"I think—like—Thank youuuu?" he dragged out the last vowel sound with uncertainty.

"You're welcome." She bit back the urge to ask him a thousand questions. *How are you? Where are you living? Are you okay? Have you made friends? Do you still insist that everyone pronounce the "Junior" part of your name? Do you ever miss me?* She wanted to unleash all the questions but knew doing so would flood him like a tsunami.

"Ummm…I'm headed to a meeting. But I guess I'll…call you another time?"

"That would be perfect, Warren Jr."

Hearing her son's voice again made her eyelids press together. She squeezed tears past them, thankful because Marvina had never imagined that the squatter in her guesthouse would be the one to lead her back to her son. Back to love.

Sometimes, God is full of surprises, and here came another one.

Lyla stumbled into the room and visually searched the entire space before her eyes, smudged with yesterday's black eyeliner and mascara, landed on Marvina as a last resort. She pressed her lips together and sighed, obviously reluctant to deal with Marvina. "Where's my baby?"

"Hello to you, too, Lyla. I'm fine, thank you."

"This ain't no etiquette class. Kerresha give birth yet?" She tossed her mangy hair over to one side. She smelled of cigarettes, but not liquor.

A muscle twitched under Marvina's eye. She tried to think of how Rose would have answered the question. Something brilliant and cutting. Marvina didn't have it in her, though. "I don't know."

"Well, where is she?"

"She had a complication. They took her to the delivery room."

Lyla hugged herself. As she did, her oversized sweater cinched up, exposing a hole in her tights. "She gonna be okay?"

Marvina was now thankful she hadn't said anything snarky to Lyla. The woman was afraid, as any mother would be. "I believe so."

Lyla laughed deeply. "Your belief won't get us far."

"You never know," Marvina replied. She pointed to the only comfortable chair. "You want a seat?"

"No. I didn't come here to wait."

Marvina remained frozen in place, waiting for Lyla's next move. All the while wondering who comes to visit a woman in labor without expecting to tarry.

Lyla's fake leather boot tapped against the floor. She unwound her arms from her body. "Tell Kerresha I came."

"Can you stay until we get news?"

"No. This is frustrating. I need something to calm my nerves."

"You've been here less than two minutes," Marvina stated.

Lyla snapped, "At least I came."

"Coming here and *staying* here is two different things." Marvina wanted to say more, but she stopped as she watched the progression of emotions play across Lyla's face. Guilt, hurt, defensiveness, and then self-protective anger.

"You have no place judging me, Marvina Dewberry-Nash. Word around town is, you and your sister been up at the church stealing Christmas dinner money."

Marvina's mouth fell open.

Lyla grinned. "I knew that would shut you up."

The sound of the room's door squeaking came next, with Rose's voice booming over Lyla's shoulder, "Whoever told you that fake news lied with a capital L. Me and my sister ain't got no reason to steal nothin' from nobody.

"And congratulations, Grandma. It's a boy."

"Thank you, Jesus!" Marvina hollered. She and Rose hugged and laughed like they had just finished the climb up Mount Kilimanjaro together.

"I didn't think I was gonna make it, Marvina."

"I knew you could. You strong, I told you."

"But Kerresha was stronger," Rose rambled on proudly. "I am so proud of her. And the baby—ooh!—he's beautiful. Healthy. Ten fingers, ten toes. The nurses are helping him latch on for his first feeding. And Kerresha is so patient."

Lyla stood by. Stewing. She crossed her arms. "*I* am the grandmother. Shouldn't you be telling *me* this information?"

Rose stepped to the side, breaking her embrace with Marvina.

Marvina squeezed Rose's arm, blocking the upcoming tirade.

"Come on in here and get a hug, too, Lyla." Marvina opened her free arm, welcoming Lyla into the ring of love.

Shock covered Lyla's face. A silent protest threatened to come forth, but the longing in her eyes spoke what her mouth would not.

Marvina dug a nail into Rose's elbow, and Rose raised her free arm, too.

"Now Lyla," Rose warned, "I don't know about you, but I went a long time without somebody offering me a happy, free hug. No strings attached. You want some of this love or not?" Rose sweetened the invitation by beckoning Lyla with wiggling fingertips.

Lyla's face melted, her shoulders dipped in surrender, and she eagerly widened their circle. She lay her head on Marvina's shoulder and closed her eyes. "Thank y'all."

"You're welcome," Rose answered. "Kerresha is a wonderful young lady."

The three women leaned in for an encore hug.

Then Rose cleared her throat. "There's something I need to tell y'all, though."

Marvina and Lyla stiffened.

Rose quickly said, "He's healthy. And Kerresha's fine. I'm just saying. He looks white."

"White?" Lyla repeated. "I had a cousin who was albino."

"No, not that kind of white. Like *plain old* white," Rose clarified. "Blond hair and blue eyes white."

"Uu-uuuuuu-uuum," Marvina and Lyla's voices climbed and fell in unison.

"So the baby's mixed," Marvina said.

"Biracial," Rose updated them.

"Are his ears—"

Rose cut off the question of potential for additional melanin with a shake of her head. "No. I checked his ears and his fingertips. He gon' be white. For life."

"Huh," Marvina said and huffed at the same time. She turned to Lyla. "Did you know?"

"No clue. She didn't tell y'all?"

"Nope," Rose said.

Lyla shrugged. "Probably better. Sometimes, naming the daddy slows down the benefits paperwork, you know?"

Marvina nodded as though this fact might come in handy someday. "I was not aware."

"Mmm hmm," Lyla confirmed with confidence. "When can we see the baby?"

"Soon as they move Kerresha to recovery, she can take visitors," Rose replied.

Lyla dropped her arms and broke the circle. "She probably won't want me there."

"Au contraire," Rose replied with a smart laugh. "Proud as she is of that baby boy, she'll want everybody to see his cute little face."

As it turned out, Rose was right. When Lyla shuffled in, cautiously, beside Rose and Marvina, Kerresha had welcomed her. "Momma!"

Instead of being angry for all the times her momma hadn't been there, she gave her credit for this one time she did show up. Kerresha's innocence, her ability to forgive after so many years of neglect… It was maybe the most Christian thing Marvina had seen in a long time. Like the prodigal son. In reverse. With a daughter and mother.

Lyla insisted they give her a gown so she could hold the baby, which was a good idea, given the smoke smell and all. And the nurse acted fine about it, as though Lyla wasn't the first or the last family member to come into the ward with tobacco trapped in the fibers of their clothing. She whipped a blue gown and a disposable, elastic-lined bonnet out of the closet lickety-split. And just like that, Lyla was ready for Kerresha's camera—she even had the appearance of someone who had been on the scene at the crucial moment.

Once Lyla was suited up, the nurse left the room.

The two adopted great-aunts, grandmother, and mother passed the baby around. Lyla and Rose stood with him while Marvina stuffed herself in a chair securely before holding him. Kerresha snapped photos, capturing the moment for his baby book. He slept soundly in a classic hospital-issue pink and white striped blanket and head warmer, unaware of all the love being showered over his tiny self.

"What's his name?" Lyla asked.

"I don't know yet," Kerresha answered. "I thought I'd wait until I saw him. Do y'all mind if I put a few of these pictures on the 'gram?"

"The what?" Rose asked.

"Instagram. Social media."

"I don't want him all over the internet yet. Let him get a social security number first," Marvina balked.

"I agree," from Lyla.

Rose cooed, "How can she not? Look how cute he is?! I smile every time I see a baby in my feed."

Both Marvina and Lyla had to agree.

"Okay. Just one. With only his hand or his foot showing," Kerresha compromised.

"Here. Take this one," Lyla said, turning the baby sideways and holding his hand close to her cheek. "I'm gonna show everybody at the club."

Lyla flicked her lashes at us in a moment of hesitation.

Marvina covered her midsection with clasped hands. Given all her years as a dutiful daughter, she would not impose on this moment.

Rose stuffed her hands in her pocket.

Kerresha paused, lowering her camera. "Can I get all three of you with him?"

Lyla tilted her head, inviting Rose and Marvina into their relationship. "Wasn't for y'all, he might not even be here. Come on."

Snap!

They continued raving over the baby. Rose and Marvina leaned toward the traditional comments. *He's gonna be a heartbreaker* and *Long fingers! Might play the piano.*

Lyla pulled the mother card and pried, "I gather his daddy is white?"

Kerresha nodded slowly.

Her mother dug deeper, "Where is he?"

"Not here."

"Duh." Her eyes scraped up and down Kerresha, and the mood in the room shifted from jubilee to judgment.

The funny thing about dramatic folk is they don't know how to act when stuff is peaceful. They always have to ruin it, make some kind of conflict where there is none.

Marvina took it upon herself to ease the tension. "Why don't we give Kerresha some time to rest, now?"

"I'm not leaving until—"

"We're leaving *now*," Rose stated forcefully.

Lyla gently set the baby on Kerresha's chest. "You done lost your mind, yelling at me."

"Ain't nobody yelling at you," Rose said.

"You did raise your voice a little," Marvina commentated.

Rose passed a brief scowl at Marvina, then returned her gaze to Lyla. She set her lips in that familiar I'm-about-to-give-you-a-piece-of-my-mind posture, but froze. Thinking. And then she bowed out of the fight with, "Marvina and I are going home to get a few things. We left so quickly, we forgot our overnight bags."

"That's what I thought," Lyla antagonized. "Can't nobody tell me when I gotta leave my own—"

"Stop it, Momma." Kerresha whispered forcefully. "Just stop."

They all gave attention to her desperate plea. Her lips pressed against the baby's forehead and a tear fell from her eye to his cheek. "This isn't what I want for him. Momma, I'll always love you. But I grew up with so much fighting and arguing and screaming and conflict. And I was so scared. *Always* afraid. I don't want that for him." Kerresha caressed his soft spot with her pinky finger. "I want him to grow up brave. But he can't do that if he's constantly surrounded by angry outbursts and judgment and always feeling like he doesn't have a safe place to be."

"There is no safe place," Lyla said in a slow, low tone.

"Yes. There is," Kerresha pushed back. "For him, that place is right here in my arms. With me. And for me, it's with Rose and Marvina. I hope you find your safe place, too, Momma. I really do."

Lyla snatched the sterile gown off her body and the scrub bonnet off her head. "I can tell when I'm not wanted." She balled up the lightweight gear and threw it in the trash.

And then she sashayed out, swinging her arms like she was the queen of the room, without so much as a wave goodbye to the peasants.

Marvina and Rose stood dumbfounded for a moment. What happened? One minute Lyla was taking pictures with her grandson for display at the club. And the next, she was leaving without a word for her recovering daughter.

Kerresha never took her eyes off the baby throughout her mother's theatrics. She smiled at him when she left and whispered, "Little brave one, that was your grandmother. Her name is Lyla. She's sad. So we have to send her beautiful thoughts. But you won't be like her. You have so much love." Her voice quavered, and she kissed his sleeping face again.

Rose and Marvina draped Kerresha's sides and hugged her as she stifled a whimper. Then she chuckled softly. "That's my momma for you."

"Well," Rose said, "you have to come to terms with the fact that your momma is a fallible human being. We all are."

Marvina quickly added, "But they do the best they know to do at any given time. Just so happens, most of them are pretty young and still wet behind their own ears when they're raising kids." Marvina swiped behind Kerresha's ear. "Like you."

Kerresha cradled her stomach. "Don't make me laugh."

"I'm sorry."

"And please. I know you mean well, Miss Marvina. Don't make excuses for her, though. I know people do the best they know. But at some point, people either refuse to learn better or they make bad choices even when they do know better. That's different. It sucks. Period. No excuses needed."

Marvina made duck lips. Nodded. "Okay. I agree."

"Ha. Lay. Loooo," Rose said. "And please do not laugh, Kerresha, but I mean that. Call a spade a spade and move on. Cause this little man here. Hmph." Rose's eyes crinkled again as she stared into his face. "He's coming into a world with a Momma who's a truth teller for *real* for real."

A nurse gingerly entered the room and asked how mother and baby were doing.

Sleep began its restorative work on Kerresha by weighing down her eyelids. "Can he stay here next to me?"

"Of course," the nurse assured.

Marvina told Kerresha and the nurse they'd be back in a few hours to settle in for the night with her and the baby.

"Great. She should be in a regular room by then."

Rose and Marvina tucked Kerresha and the baby in, then tip-toed out of the room together. They walked down the hallway, arm in arm, feet in sync, savoring the tenderness between them.

"That was amazing," Marvina said. "Kerresha's gonna be a wonderful mother."

"Yep. She's an old head on young shoulders. I'm glad she came into our lives. And I'm glad we did this fill-in grandma thing together."

They took a few more steps, then Marvina asked, "You think she's gonna give the baby one of those noun names, like Stone or Buckle?"

"What the hell?" Rose jerked away from Marvina.

They both laughed as Rose pressed the elevator to return to the ground floor. "I hope not. Can't tell these days. We'll see."

The evening chill met them outside, and Rose quickly switched the heat to full blast in the SUV. When there was enough warmth to be comfortable, Rose resumed their conversation. "I never asked if she planned to have him circumcised."

"Oh, I'm sure she will. Ain't it nasty if you don't? Harder to keep hygiene?"

Rose shrugged. "I don't think so. Not from what I can tell."

Marvina gasped. "Are you...wait...what are you saying?"

"I'm saying. From my own personal experience," Rose eyed her sister playfully, "circumcision is not necessary."

"I swear, Rose Yvette Dewberry-Tillman," Marvina taunted. "How many men have you been with?!"

Rose raised one hand off the steering wheel and twirled it in the air. "Enough to know they ain't all the same!" She laughed. "I mean. I was married at one point. So I knew what I was missing when I divorced. Can't close Pandora's box once it's open. Don't you miss making love since Warren Sr., passed away?"

Marvina missed Warren Sr. every day—especially their intimacy—since he passed away. And, for once, she had someone to tell. "Ooh, yesssss, Rose. Something fierce! That man used to kiss me every day like a soldier returning home from war." The words spewed out of her like hot lava from a volcano. Felt good to share her feelings without worrying about somebody judging her. Tsking her because she was being inappropriate. It might have been inappropriate to discuss sex with most people. But your big sister was different. And safe.

She missed Rose, too.

"Well. I'm glad you had a good time with your husband. I worried about you," Rose said. "Momma always made it seem like sex was dirty and wrong, and something women did to please men. I didn't know any different until I found a copy of *Bronze Thrills* magazine stuffed at the bottom of the youth choir robe closet. Like way down at the bottom. I have no idea who brought it, but I stole it and kept it in—"

Marvina inhaled sharply.

"What?" Rose asked.

"The magazine. It was mine."

"Yours?!"

"Yes!" Rose hollered as her sister confessed, "I got it from a girl at school. I can't remember her name. But she sold it to me for a dollar, and I read it from cover to cover for months. Then I took it to church to let that fast Metford girl borrow it. But she claimed she lost it. And I was sweating bullets for weeks, hoping nobody found it."

"Well, somebody did! Me!" Rose exclaimed, still laughing.

"Anyway. The damage was done—Momma never could convince me sex was bad after I read that magazine. Not to mention my novels. I swear, I could not wait to get married and see what the fuss was all about. And it was true. Every bit of it."

"Marvina Yvonne Dewberry-Nash. Do you know how hard I tried to hide that magazine from you? To keep you from its detrimental contents? And you had already read it many times over—before me!"

Marvina had never told anyone except Sue Metford about the magazine, and that was only because Sue had already admitted to having sex. When they went to youth group and the mothers preached how awful life would be after losing your virginity, Sue popped her gum and sat there like "oh well." She'd already done it and was still breathing—still had good grades, had enough sense to use a condom, and apparently enjoyed the act. According to Sue, the only drawback was that, once the boys learned you were "putting out," they only wanted you for one thing.

These thoughts, these silly memories hadn't entered Marvina's mind in years. She felt light and easy in Rose's presence, now. Sure, they were both rounding the corner to sixty years old. Health not the best. But they still had a lot of good memories and good laughs left to share between them, and Marvina didn't want to miss out.

As they reached Marvina's house, she noticed the reflection

of red lights from an idling car standing where Rose should have been able to park in the driveway.

A lone driver sat up straight. As Rose got closer, she noticed a chunk of metal missing from the passenger's door panel. She remembered the raggedy car from the drive-by. Kerresha had taken a gift from that person. Quietly. And she'd instructed Marvina to write "F.J." for the name instead of a full name like everybody else.

"You sure you gonna remember him?" Marvina had asked. And Kerresha had rolled her eyes like she was annoyed, though it wasn't clear if she was annoyed with Marvina or the person behind the wheel.

"Somebody you know?" Rose asked Marvina as they approached the beat-up car.

"The car rings a bell. From Kerresha's shower."

Rose speculated, "Wonder if they brought another gift?"

"Maybe so," Marvina said.

Rose parked so that the visitor could leave without having to car-shuffle. She and Marvina climbed out of Rose's car, and the driver of the other car got out as well.

One look at his face, his hairline, and his eyes cleared up the mystery.

Marvina reached out to shake his hand. "Congratulations. It's a boy."

CHAPTER 28

Rose

Hmph. There he was. The baby's father, by all appearances—and I do mean *all* appearances. From the pinched nose to the wide ears, the Cupid's-bow lips, and that point of hair at the top of his forehead, I'd bet the entire farm he was the unnamed father of Kerresha's unnamed baby. Marvina and I both saw it, which is why she greeted him accordingly.

He grinned wide, and his face flushed red. "You think so?"

"Unless you've got an identical twin brother," I said.

He lifted a foot off the ground as he celebrated in his own countrified way. He waved a pretend lasso and turned a full 360-degree circle. "Whooop! Whoop! Yes! Yes!" After his second rotation, he bum-rushed me and Marvina into a bear hug.

"Oh my," she managed to remark despite him squeezing the air out of us. "I can't breathe."

"Oh sorry! Of course." He set us free.

He'd ruffled us so thoroughly, Marvina and I had to pull our coats back down to normal position.

"I'm sorry. It's just...I couldn't tell from the 'gram pic if he was mine. From the camera angle. I only saw the baby's hand, I mean."

I nodded because he was right about that photo, on account of Marvina not wanting the baby all on the World Wide Web yet.

But now that this boy had finished his jig, I had some questions for him. "So, where have you been these past nine months, son?"

A cold breeze kicked up his blond mop of hair and snuck up my coat.

"And make it snappy," I added for good measure.

He closed his eyes and shook his head. "It's a long, stupid story, ma'am."

"Did you hit her?" I wanted to know because, in my book, all relationship conversation ceases at that point.

His brows shot up. "No! No, ma'am! There was no abuse between us. I don't hit or talk down to women."

"Good," Marvina said. "So what's the problem?"

He resumed his sorry stance. "Doesn't make sense no matter what angle I tell it from. But the short version is: We had an argument, and we stopped talking. Like that was really gonna help solve it."

We stared at him 'cause Lord knows Marvina and I also owned that same T-shirt.

He hung his head. "I know. I know. It's ludicrous. Especially since we're family, now."

"No truer words have been spoken," Marvina whisper-coughed to me.

I wanted to be angry with him, but like I said—I'd fallen out with my sister over forty dollars for forty years. Who was I to judge him for running away from a disagreement? At some level, I felt him. On the other hand, it's different when there's a child involved. "Young man, what's your name?"

"Falcon."

"Ain't that a bird?" Marvina asked.

"Yes. A fighter."

Marvina had to ask, "You wasn't planning on naming him Falcon Jr., were you?"

His face perked up at her suggestion.

"Because I don't believe in naming children after animals. Or cars. Or household items," Marvina lectured. "Makes the child's life harder, you understand."

He looked at me like I was supposed to save him from my sister's opinion.

"It's your child. He's your family," I tried.

"You're right. He is family. And that's...you know what I'm gonna do? I'm going to fight for my family. I love Kerresha!" He declared it like someone had passed him a bullhorn at a pep rally.

My eyes popped wide open. So did Marvina's.

I cupped his hand. "Slow down, Falcon. Fold your wing flaps. Tap your talons on a tree limb for a second, okay? First thing you need to do is go to the hospital and ask the nurse to let Kerresha know you'd like to meet your son."

"I was gonna do that when I saw the post, but I wasn't sure she'd let me. That's why I came here first. To ask you if you'd ask for me. Please?" He petitioned me, not knowing Marvina was his best bet for mercy.

"I got a problem with men who wait until a baby is born to show their faces. Being a father is not an event; it's a lifelong commitment," I said. "And what we don't need is you parading yourself up to the hospital for the birthday party, then running off next week or next month when fatherhood becomes inconvenient. If that's your plan, you can keep stepping."

"What my sister means is—"

I held up my hand to stop Marvina from painting over my words with her magic kindness brush. "I said what I mean."

Falcon nodded so hard his thin, pink lips shook. "Yes, ma'am. Me and my dad have a great relationship. I want the same for my son. And Kerresha. To have a family."

"The family part will be up to her," I made clear. "But I'll ask her about seeing the baby on your behalf."

What did I say that for? He went to grab me again. I stepped back, "Enough. You don't know me like that."

"Oh. Okay. I'm excited is all."

He gave me his number, said he'd be waiting for my call, then left.

Marvina and I hustled inside to the warmth, took off our coats, and plopped down on the love seat, side by side, despite the available couch on the other side of the coffee table.

What a day it had been. What a week, a month.

Marvina and I sat there a moment, processing. Tired.

Her living room decor felt like 1985. Simpler times. Slower times.

"You remember when Momma and Daddy bought us that matching twin bed set?" Marvina asked.

Visions of pink eyelet lace and white headboards came to mind. "I think so."

"I remember it 'cause Momma fussed at me. Even though they had sacrificed to get us two of everything for that set, I'd climb into your bed in the middle of the night. Momma said, 'Marvina, children all over the world are sleeping four and five to a bed—or on the floor! And here you are, with your own bed, still climbing into your sister's bed. What's wrong with you?'"

I leaned into her side, into a nook that seemed created for me.

She continued, "And I told Momma that I was sleeping next to you because you made me have good dreams."

I brushed her arm. "It's good to have a sister again."

"Sure is."

We sat in silence, letting the words curl around us, surrendering our hearts to the healing. Cuddling next to each other on that small couch like we'd done when we chose to share a twin bed.

I went ahead and composed the message to Kerresha while Marvina and I caught our breath. Marvina insisted on proofing the text. "I wanna make sure you're saying it in a hopeful way."

"It is what it is," I fussed, tilting my phone so she could read my point-blank language: Falcon came by. He wants to see the baby. Okay?

"No!" Marvina recoiled. "You have to say it gently." She patted the air to demonstrate the word "gently" as if I didn't already have a working definition. "And start with a greeting."

I huffed dramatically. But instead of the usual defenses that reared up in me when she and I disagreed, I only felt a soft, mild irritation, like when a mosquito bites you while you're outside on the porch eating ice cream. It's annoying, but it comes with the territory.

Obediently, I added the words "Good evening, Kerresha" at the beginning of the text.

"GIN-TULL!" Marvina repeated.

"Here," I dropped the phone on her lap. She tapped away, then gave it back to me. I read.

Good evening, Kerresha. I hope you are recovering well. A young man named Falcon came by. He would like to visit you two at the hospital soon. Will that be fine? Please let us know so we can text him back.

"This sounds nothing like me. Why don't you send it yourself?"

"Nah. He asked *you*. But what we can do is put both our names at the end of it. So she'll know we put our heads together and wrote it."

I added a dash to the text along with our names, though I had no doubt Kerresha would recognize Marvina's voice alone.

Before I pressed the send arrow, Marvina asked, "And do you want to add anything about when she should respond? So she won't keep the young man waiting? He's so happy about the baby. Did you see him light up like a firefly's behind?"

"I did, but I most certainly will not put pressure on Kerresha. She will see the message whenever she wakes up from her well-deserved rest, and she can reply when she gets good and ready. For all we know, Falcon could be lying through his beak-teeth." I hurled the message into cyberspace before Marvina could suggest another people-pleasing move.

I sat back again, thinking that this compromise—the lengthier response from Marvina, my refusal to push Kerresha on the time frame—served as a good model for how we might move forward. A little of her, a little of me.

Awkwardly, I initiated what I hoped would be an end to our fussing about how to remember Momma. "Marvina, I know you had a special relationship with Momma. I don't want to tarnish your memories of her. I just want you to know that I remember her differently than you do. She taught us how to cook. She gave us her spice recipe. She cared for us and did what she thought was best. We can leave it at that."

"We could," she said. "But I would like to know what happened between you and Momma, other than David."

I shook my head, stalling. I needed to weigh the benefit of telling her the whole truth versus letting our mother's saintly memory live on in my sister's mind. What good would it do now to speak ill of Momma?

"Please tell me. The more I know, the more I can make sense of what happened. Might help me understand how to reconnect with Warren Jr., too. I don't want what happened to me and you to happen with me and him."

"Fine," I relented. And then I took a deep breath and told her my grown-woman story; the story of how I came to view life the way I do, how I came to be up until now. Every woman has one. It was time my only sister knew mine.

Somehow, staring out of Marvina's window instead of staring into her face let me speak more freely. If I was looking at the beautiful evergreens just beyond the glass, not the potential judgment in her eyes, I could get through my story.

"When I first met David, it's true that he was married. He said he was in the process of divorcing his wife. Said the only reason he married Anne was for the money she and her family offered. See, David grew up poor."

"We were poor," Marvina butted into my story.

"No. We were not poor. You just said we had matching twin bedroom sets."

"Felt poor."

"That's because all the Black folks got squished into one corner of town with the redlining. But no. When I say David was poor, he was po'. Like, he never owned new clothes. Made his toys from empty water jugs."

"Guess that *is* another level of po'," she mumbled agreement.

"Anne's parents owned a restaurant and a nightclub. According to David, from the first time he met them, they promised him a stake in their businesses if he joined the family. He'd be the son they never had. David's parents never owned a house, a car, let alone a business. So he married Anne in order to become a part of something bigger."

"Did he love her?"

"No. He loved the opportunity and the money she presented more than anything. But once he got a peek into how businesses worked, how money worked, he saved and invested and bought his first few properties. He got in early on some profitable internet deals and made good for himself. He didn't need Anne's family anymore; he had his own."

Marvina said, "He don't sound like a victim to me."

"He wasn't. But you couldn't tell me that when I was nineteen. All I saw was this fine-looking slightly older man who had pulled himself up from poverty by marrying for the wrong reasons. And I let myself believe that whatever happened between Anne and David couldn't happen between *me* and David because we had *true* love. We'd last forever."

She laughed.

"I know. Anyway, somebody at the church told Momma a dramatized version of my relationship with David. And Momma told me I was a fool for believing I was the answer to David's problems."

Even as I replayed the past for Marvina, I saw Momma's face in my memory, standing over me as I sat on my bed, telling me that David's problem wasn't growing up poor or Anne or anybody else. She told me he was a no-good lying, cheating man who had used up his first wife and would use me, too—if he in fact was actually divorcing her.

"Anyway, long story short, when I told Momma I wasn't going to stop seeing David, Momma dubbed me a fool for believing he was actually going to leave his wife and a home-wrecker, the villain of all things godly, for being his other woman. She told me to take my butt on back to Dallas if I was gonna be whoring. So I moved into one of David's properties. I got pregnant, and I think that forced his hand. He divorced his wife and married me the following month. And we lived somewhat happily for a little while."

"So that's why you left?" Marvina asked.

"Yeah."

"I thought you left because you were mad at me for not starting the business."

I admitted, "That, too. When you didn't register the business and didn't want to venture with me, we started playing the silent game. I didn't have a plan B for my life. And then, I think it was maybe a week later, Momma heard something about David at church, and her antagonizing started. I felt lost in my own home and in my own town. So I left.

"I thought Momma's anger toward me would soften when I told her I was pregnant. Wrong. Momma burst out crying, saying she couldn't believe her first grandchild was going to be the product of an affair. I was like 'Momma, David and I are married, now,' and she was like 'Not in the eyes of the Lord! David's covenant with Anne is the only one written in heaven's books! You ever thought about his *true* wife's feelings? That poor woman must be beside herself wondering what she did wrong. Ain't nothin' wrong but you and David trampling all over her heart! And now with a baby! You mark my words. God is not pleased. Nothing good will come of this.'"

Marvina said, "Stop right here. Baby aside, Momma had a point. About the other woman, I mean."

"I already told you—I know that *now*, but I didn't know it then. I felt like Momma was trying to suck all the joy and happiness from my life. Plus, I really liked sex, the thing Momma always depicted as a horrible, terrible thing before marriage, and an unpleasant wifely duty afterward—right up there with the joy of folding clothes. I figured if she had already been wrong about David actually divorcing and marrying me and about something as wonderful as making love, she'd been fooling me my whole life."

"Huh," Marvina said. "So that was the real trouble with you and Momma?"

"No. Rock bottom came when I suffered my first miscarriage. You remember David brought me from Dallas to Momma's house to recover in her care? Back then, he traveled a lot for business; he couldn't take off work. So, out of need, I spent the week at Momma's house. You remember?"

"Yes," Marvina said with a question in her tone. "But I was busy in love with Warren. I remember you being in the guest bedroom. That's about it."

Satisfied with Marvina's recollection, I continued, "I was so happy to be home. I needed Momma's embrace. I needed her to love me back to health. Back to myself. But that's not what happened. That very first night, Momma stood right over me and said that David and I deserved what we got because God don't like ugly. I was broken. Bleeding. Had lost my baby. And all she could do was curse me even more. I vowed not to set foot in her house again."

Marvina sniffed. "That wasn't right."

"I know," I said. "Of course, I attributed the miscarriage to simply a quirk. But the second one. And the third one, which ended in a fully formed little boy who never took his first breath. Seeing my baby born sleeping was a sight that never left my mind."

"Rose, I'm so sorry you went through that alone."

"Yeah. Well. After that, I felt so ashamed. Alone. Unloved.

And then when I heard about you having a child…and it seemed like you had a great life without a jinx like me in it. I decided we were both better off without each other."

"That was the worst story ever," Marvina ranted. "I know Momma had her convictions, but I didn't know she had hurt you with them. I believe all babies are a blessing. They're God's way of letting us know He hasn't given up on humanity. I'm sorry Momma didn't see it that way, too. Sorry your life took such a terrible turn."

"Yeah. Well. Thank you. I've moved on. It hasn't been *all* terrible, even with the divorce. I still had a job. I had a best friend. We went to concerts. To Vegas. A lot of fun stuff before she died. I just…never got the chance to shine."

Marvina wrung her hands. "For what it's worth, I'm sorry I misdirected the business registration money. I think you would have been a great business owner. I'm sorry I ruined your dream."

"No, Marvina." I raised up and looked at her squarely. "Now that I've heard your side of the story, I can see why you acted the way you did. Bottom line, it takes two. We should have talked it out. But it was my dream. I shouldn't have stopped on account of you."

"I did like the dream, too. So it was ours," Marvina said.

"Yeah, but I—"

"Stop it, Rose. Stop acting like you some kind of lone, cold maverick out tromping in the woods, bucking at anybody who tries to wrap their arms around you. It would have taken both of us to make it work. So lay your head back down. We're having a precious moment here." She pushed my head down again.

With my temple pressed against Marvina's soft, warm upper arm, I let go of the anger. It slipped away like dirty water draining from a tub.

Marvina made a clicking noise with her cheeks. "Well, no one is blameless here. When I was a child, I had to do what my mother said. Like any good daughter, I listened to her wisdom. She said hanging around you would corrupt me. And she said any time I doubted her words, all I had to do was remember what happened to my eye."

A pang of guilt shot through me.

"But when I got older, I realized that either Momma was using what happened with my eye to make me afraid of everything, or she was afraid of everything because of what happened to my eye."

"Probably the latter," I gave Momma the benefit of the doubt. "As much as I don't like what happened to our relationship, I don't think Momma ever meant any harm. She did love us in her own way."

"I agree. She did."

That truth hung in the air, unquestioned.

"The thing is, I have no excuse for why I chose the easy way out once I realized that Momma was so full of anxiety, bless her heart. Instead of reaching out to you myself, I chose to do things Momma's way. It was easier. Kept the peace back here in Fork City. This is where I gotta live, you know, so it was easier to hide behind Momma's anxiety than to face my own fears."

"What are you afraid of?" I asked, leaning up so I could match her nonverbal expressions with her words and perceive my sister's feelings completely.

"Afraid of trying new things. Change. Afraid that when I really need something, one day, I won't have it." Her face bobbed up and down slowly. "Yep. There it all is, on the table."

"What do you mean you won't have what you need? I mean, you did win the lottery."

"Yeah. I had a nice-sized nest egg. But we used most of it putting Warren Jr., through rehabs only to find out his real problem was using drugs to stuff down his internal conflicts about being gay, especially with the way we raised him. Not so much Warren Sr., as it was me. And Momma, you know. My son said his truth was he didn't want to disappoint us, but he didn't know another way to handle his feelings. Got so bad at one point, he considered taking his own life."

Listening to Marvina, I understood for the first time that her simple life in Fork City hadn't been as simple as I imagined. She'd had to juggle my departure, Momma's fears, motherhood, marriage, and a child whose struggles to align with his mother's belief system nearly led him to suicide.

That's a lot for anyone to handle. But it had to be doubly hard on Marvina, seeing as she thinks it's her holy responsibility to make sure no one around her feels pain.

"Listen," I told her, "it's time for you to do something for yourself, Marvina."

She tilted her head to glare. "Are you talking about the restaurant? 'Cause the answer is still no." There was no mistaking the resolve in her eyes.

"No. Not altogether."

She sighed.

"For real, Vina."

She gasped. "You haven't called me that in years."

My lips floated up into a smile. "It came back to me, I guess."

"I missed it. You want me to call you Rosie again?"

"No ma'am. Rose will do."

A giggle passed between us.

"Seriously," I continued my thought. Our faces couldn't have been more than six inches apart. The perfect proximity to speak what I'd been thinking, and the perfect distance for her to take it straight, no chaser. "You and Momma picked up a terrible habit of taking on extra worries so other people won't have to. But where did that leave y'all? Always worried, always scared, always putting everybody else's needs before your own. You need to learn how to expect less from yourself and more from other people. Otherwise, you just gonna end up worrying yourself sick, and nobody else ever learns how to think for themselves 'cause you got it in your mind you're supposed to be the worry-savior."

Marvina protested with her hand up like a stop sign. "This is what women do, Rose. We're the workhorses of the world. And some of us like it. I know everybody's on the 'make yourself happy first' kick, but that ain't for me. Some of us are proud of helping others. Don't try to—what's the word folks use these days?—shame us, make us feel like we're less than y'all go-gettin' types because we have the God-given gift of hospitality. Like singing or drawing—hospitality is something born in us."

"Well, I can't say if it's a God-given gift or not, 'cause, unlike singing and drawing, somehow the women seem to be the only ones gettin' this particular gift," I stated.

She raised her chin in defiance.

I brought simple math into the conversation with, "What percentage of the men you know caught the gift of hospitality?"

She lowered her hand to her lap because she knows nine times out of ten, it's a woman in charge of making sure everyone else is comfortable. In a house, at a job, in a church, a family reunion, a hotel, on vacation, wherever and all over the world. It be us.

"I rest my case. Anyhow. All I'm saying is, you can't keep the peace for other people while tearing yourself up inside."

"Mmmph," she let out one of those groans you give when a preacher says something that sounds like he's got a secret camera installed in your house, because it's exactly what you needed to hear.

This time, Marvina leaned into me, with her face resting on my sleeve.

"Rose. There's something I need to tell you. So I won't be worrying about it by myself." She sniffled.

I stayed still so she could get it all out before I reacted because, Lord knows, if my sister was fixing to tell me she had cancer, I was about to fall out on the floor.

"They say I got benign multiple sclerosis."

She stopped talking.

I stopped breathing while a thousand questions raced through my mind, starting with why hadn't she told me. But I already knew the answer. She was the worry-savior. So instead of demanding answers that served me, I asked, "What does this mean for you?"

"Don't know, rightly. It comes and goes. Tingling. Numbness. Muscle spasms. Might have symptoms for a few weeks, then they go away for a while. That's why I sat in the chair before I held the baby earlier today. I didn't want to put him at risk, in case my muscles started acting up without notice."

Suddenly, snapshots of Marvina awkwardly leaning her weight against a counter or stretching her fingers came to mind. I realized she'd been making certain moves not out of habit or because she was blind in one eye, but because she was silently living with a form of MS.

"It's not too bad, overall. I try not to think about it, not let it get me down, you know. Doctor says so far, my case is mild. That's why they call it benign."

"Is this the real reason you won't open the restaurant with me?" I asked.

"Partly," she admitted. "But I didn't say anything because I didn't—"

"Want me to worry," I finished the sentence with her. "Jeez, Marvina. I'm not a robot. I have a heart. Could have saved me three thousand dollars," I joked to keep myself from crying. All the while, the cushions of her couch seemed to give way as I sank deeper into the moment, deeper into the understanding that my sister needed me as much as I needed her.

"What you spend three thousand dollars on?"

"Bidding for the old Dairy Queen. They offered the contract, but I'm gonna have to text the lady and let her know we're not moving forward."

"Hmph. Well, if you would have told me you were gonna bid, I certainly would have told you about my medical diagnosis to keep you from burning money. But you didn't tell me. So, like you said, I ain't gonna take on something that ain't my fault. You like how fast I learned?"

"Oh, *now* you wanna learn fast?" I clucked, and we both laughed at her smart-aleck response.

She lay her head back on my arm.

Me and my sister. Together again. We still had some healing to do, but we'd gotten to the point where we weren't cutting each other anymore. We had a scab. And if we let time and nature do its work, the scab would fall off, leaving us with a healed-up scar to remember the lesson of what happened without feeling the hurt all over again.

CHAPTER 29

Marvina and Rose dozed off right there on the couch together, and they both jumped when Marvina's phone rang.

"Hello?" Marvina answered, rising to her feet to stretch.

"Hi. It's Kerresha. Sorry. I had to call you from the hospital phone. Are y'all coming back?"

"Oh yes, honey." Marvina motioned for Rose to get up, too.

Rose hoisted to a standing position and shuffled to the restroom.

"Me and Rose sat down and started talking and, I guess we were so tired, we both fell asleep."

"Am I on speaker?" Kerresha asked.

Marvina pressed the phone tightly to her ear. "No."

"Did you tell her about the diagnosis?" Kerresha asked.

"Yes. I did. You been a momma less than twenty-four hours, and you already tryna tell everybody what to do," Marvina teased. "We headin' back up there. Did you get the text about Falcon?"

"Yes. He's here."

Marvina's chest fluttered to full attention. Kerresha and Falcon's potential reunion reminded her of a storyline in one of her romance novels. "Is everything okay between you two? No problems?"

"No ma'am. We're talking." She paused. "Oh, and he said thank you and Miss Rose for sending the message."

"Tell him I said he's welcome. We only want what's best for you and the baby."

"Thank you. And Miss Marvina, could you bring me my charger? And something to eat from your kitchen? The food here is horrible."

The request for food never landed on better ears. "You got it."

Marvina whipped up a batch of chicken salad using some of the chicken breast from the Christmas meal surplus. After peeling off the crispy fried skin, the tender meat made for a perfect light sandwich filling. But just in case Kerresha wanted the extra seasoning flavor, Marvina grabbed her container of seasoning, wrapped sandwiches, a bag of chips, and napkins to take back to the hospital.

She made enough chicken salad sandwiches to feed all four of them, including Falcon, as well as anyone else who might want a taste 'cause that's what folks with the gift of hospitality do. Rose didn't understand it. Wasn't in her mindset, and that would have to be okay with Marvina. In order for them to get along, all that judgment had to go. They might not ever understand each other "one hundred," as Kerresha would say, but they could still love one another. And she could focus on love in order to rebuild the relationship with Warren Jr., too. Baby steps.

At the hospital, Marvina and Rose slipped into Kerresha's darkened room. The baby was asleep in his transparent bassinet. Falcon had built himself a temporary bed with hospital blankets and a pillow in the lounge chair. He hopped to attention as they entered.

A groggy Kerresha turned her head and smiled. "Thank God. I almost starved."

They all greeted one another properly again, which seemed right because this day alone felt like seventy-two hours had passed.

Marvina served the sandwiches and chips on napkins. Falcon offered to get everyone cold drinks from the vending machine.

While he was out, Marvina initiated the check on Kerresha's mental health. "You and Falcon getting along?"

"Yes, ma'am."

"He's not bothering you, is he?" Rose double-checked.

"No. Everything is fine. I'm just glad this whole…situation is over, now that the baby is here." She tipped her head toward her son.

"Don't leave us hanging," Rose eased into it. "What *was* the situation, exactly?"

Kerresha didn't wait for the drink. She took her first bite of chicken sandwich. Chewed and swallowed. Marvina noticed the furl in her brow.

"Okay. Here it is. I wasn't sure who the father was. I was with Falcon. Until the night I met his parents and they… Let's just say they were fine with him dating a Black girl, but they weren't okay with us getting serious. And Falcon wasn't standing up for me. For us. So I broke up with him and had this…I guess it was a rebound with—"

"The slue-footed Jefferson boy with the green truck!" Marvina exclaimed like a game show contestant.

"Calm down, Marvina," Rose said.

"I'm sorry, it's just I read a lot of novels."

"Okaaaay. Anyway. Yes. Him. His name is Drey. He said no matter whose child it was, he'd raise it as his own so he and I could be together. I couldn't make a decision one way or another until the baby got here."

"And now you know who to give a second chance," Marvina surmised, "for your son's sake."

"She don't have to be with either one of them," Rose fussed.

"Drey's a nice guy, but I don't really want to be with him. We talked. He deserves to be with someone who is into him, which is one of our mutual friends, as it turns out."

"I've seen that happen, too," Marvina said.

"I really want to be with Falcon. But he has to stand up to his parents for us. I get it. It's hard to go against what your parents believe. He doesn't have a choice at this point, though."

Here again, Marvina and Rose could relate.

"Y'all got to find your own way," Marvina advised. "Is this baby their first grandchild?"

"Yes."

"Well. Whether y'all stay together or not, one look at this little angel will give them a reason to reconsider."

The baby squirmed with the beginnings of hunger. Together, Rose and Marvina helped Kerresha sit up a few more degrees so she could nurse the baby comfortably. Rose helped hold the baby's head in place for latching on while Marvina coached them through the process.

By the time Falcon returned, his son was busy getting nourishment from Kerresha. He made quite the suckling noises for a newborn.

Afterward, Falcon burped the baby. Marvina changed his diaper, and the little man returned to his slumber.

Falcon finally got a chance to eat his sandwich. "This is amazing," Falcon eked out between bites and sloppy, ravenous chewing.

"I told you. Whatever comes from these two is gold," Kerresha said.

Kerresha asked for half of a second sandwich just as hospital staff brought in the facility-prepared dinner.

When the staff left, Kerresha lifted the silver lid off the plastic molded plate. Salisbury steak with gravy, mashed potatoes, and greens.

"Don't look half bad," Marvina. "I'm sure your body will welcome the vegetables."

Kerresha gave her an are-you-serious-right-now glance at first. But then she picked up a fork and tried to ingest the greens. She swallowed and made a disgusted face. "Tastes like food they'd serve in a reform school."

"Oh come on," Falcon said. He picked up Kerresha's fork and gave it a taste as though he was trying to get a two-year-old to eat something green.

Rose beat Marvina laughing when his face soured, too. He fussed, "Tastes like food made for sick people."

"Well, this is a hospital," Marvina said. "They have to make it bland to meet all the dietary restrictions. Here." She reached into the bottom of the oversized recyclable bag she'd used to pack the food. "I brought some of my Momma's seasoning." She sprinkled a few granules on the greens, stirred it with Kerresha's spoon, and asked her to see if it tasted any better.

Kerresha gave it a try. Her entire countenance brightened. "Now we're talking. Babe. Here." She offered a forkful to Falcon.

Marvina and Rose eyed each other at the word "babe." Fodder for later conversation, surely.

"Snap! This is, like, before and after." He took another bite.

"Hey!" Kerresha snatched the bowl from him.

"What's in the seasoning? It's, like, magic!"

Marvina sat in the extra chair, gloating. "I told you. It's my mother's seasoning."

"Can you put it on the mashed potatoes, too?"

"Sure can."

"Wait!" Kerresha said. "Let's do a video."

How in the world this girl wanted to post a video right after giving birth to a baby, Marvina would never know. She supposed the anesthesia from the cesarean was still working. Or maybe just the fact she was nineteen made her body up to the challenge.

Within a minute, those two made an impromptu video of him taking a bite of the potatoes bland. Then adding the seasoning, the tasting afterward and his genuine response to the improvement. "I swear. This stuff changes everything for the better. Just like you, Babe."

Then he twisted the camera on himself and Kerresha and bent to kiss her forehead.

"No," Kerresha pushed him away playfully. "I just had a baby."

"I know. But I'm sayin'. Wait." He sprinkled seasoning in his hand, licked his lips, dipped his lips in the seasoning, then leaned toward her again.

Kerresha gave a weary smile. "Can't resist now." And she kissed him.

Marvina rolled her eyes at their corny courtship. Definitely something from the sweet romance category.

Next thing we knew, Kerresha's phone dinged six times in a row. She looked at Marvina. Then at Rose. "I know y'all are not going to open a restaurant. But the question in the comments is: Do you sell the seasoning?"

CHAPTER 30

Rose

Me and Marvina locked eyes as an invisible charge passed between us.

"A restaurant is too much, but..." Marvina started.

I finished, "But the seasoning—just the mix—would be the perfect product. Enough to keep Momma's memory alive, but not too much work for us to enjoy our lives."

We replied to Kerresha in unison, "Yes."

Fireworks and confetti popped off inside me as I hugged my sister.

"We can do this," Marvina power-whispered, trying not to rouse the baby. Tears filled her eyes.

"We sure can. And people all over the world will be serving their friends and family with all the love that Momma gave us."

"Amen and amen," Marvina rejoiced. "All things work together for good."

Though we disagreed on all the religious details, I had to agree with her this time.

Little Falcon Jr., or whatever his name would be, wasn't the only birth in the family that day.

Kerresha stayed in the hospital a few extra days because she got a fever and needed antibiotics to fight infection. When we finally got her home, a bad winter storm hit most of northeast Texas and knocked out the power for a day. We all bundled up in Marvina's bedroom close to the fireplace eating ice cream and other foods we didn't want to go bad or melt. The baby slept twenty-three hours a day, thankfully, and Kerresha's strength began to return. She walked every few hours and did all she could to help her body heal, with Marvina and me watching her like two hawks to ensure she got enough rest.

In between baby and baby-momma shifts, I researched benign multiple sclerosis to make sure I was getting the entire story, because I didn't trust that Marvina thought I could handle everything. Once I was fairly certain my sister wasn't suffering needlessly and there wasn't a doctor or a treatment her insurance had denied her, I freed my mind to consider the other door Kerresha had kicked open with her social media stunt.

The restaurant deal was off, and I had lost money.

But the seasoning business, which had a far lower start-up sticker tag, had just begun.

When I finally got a moment to talk to David about it, I holed up in my room at Marvina's house and called him. But after our hellos, he seemed preoccupied.

"I'm sorry," I said after I'd asked him twice if he heard me. "Are you busy?"

"Oh. Did you say something?"

"We're on the phone. Of *course* I said something. I said *a lot* of things."

"You're right. I'm not giving you my undivided attention. I apologize. I don't have the headspace for this conversation."

There he went again with his psychological lingo. "You want to call me later?"

"No."

I wasn't sure how to respond. "Okaaay. Then how do we talk if you don't want to talk now or later?"

"Rose, I need to speak to you in person. Sooner than later."

Fearful scenarios played through my head. Was David sick, too? Dying? Was he broke or had he just broken up with Dr. Renita and wanted my compassion?

"Do you think I could come see the baby?"

"I—I guess," the words bumbled out of me. "What's this about?"

"It's a conversation better endured face-to-face."

Endured? Honestly, I never thought there would come a day when David and I would say a final goodbye. Not even if he remarried. But if he wanted to sever all ties, I had to respect his decision.

"Fine. When are you coming?"

"Let's get past the New Year."

If I remembered correctly, he was to propose to Dr. Renita before then. Maybe he wanted to cease communication, officially, now that he had secured the prospect for his third wife for real for real.

Whatever.

"Works for me. But can you reel in your brain for a second and listen to the ideas about selling the seasonings alone?"

This time he heard me. "Wow. That's brilliant. Wish I had thought of it. And I'm glad y'all came to a sustainable concept."

"Me, too."

His quick, positive response gave the confirmation I needed

to move forward. We were a disaster as a couple, but I always respected David's business acumen. His hustle.

"I'll see you next week, then?"

"Yeah. And I'll shoot you the names of some branding experts who can help y'all launch. If you want me to."

"Sure. We'll take all the help you're willing to give. And thank you."

"You're welcome."

Silence.

"That was good," David broke the lull.

"What?"

"Us. Talking. Even when I told you I wasn't paying attention, we didn't argue."

"Hmmm." I tried to remember the last time I'd bickered with Marvina. Or anyone. "Shoot, my sister and I have been so busy with the baby, he's the only one allowed to fuss around here!"

"Keeping y'all busy, huh?"

"He sure is."

"Did she come up with a name?"

"Yeah. Jasiri."

"Ja-who?"

"Ja-si-ri."

David questioned, "She named him after Siri? Like on your iPhone?"

"No! Jasiri is the Swahili word for brave."

"Oh. I feel better about it, now."

I laughed at David, sounding like Marvina with her bougie name requirements.

"So, I'll see you next week?"

"Yes. I'll call first."

I went on with the duties at hand, washing dishes and dusting around the house. My mind wandered back to the conversation with David. No fighting or arguing might mean no us. Who was noncombative David, anyway? The "fight" in David was what made him such a successful businessman. Was he learning how to turn his fight on and off? For different purposes?

Then my phone lit up and I saw David's name again, only he was requesting a video call this time. "Hello?"

"Never mind. Let's talk now. Okay?"

I dried my hands and went back to the bedroom. "Yes. I was going to worry about it until you got here. Is everything okay?" I winced at myself. Now David and I both sounded like Marvina.

"Here goes, Rosey-Posey." He blew air through his lips so hard they made a bubbling sound. "I asked Renita to marry me."

I forced my eyebrows to lift high. "Congratulations! Y'all set a date?"

David blinked. "She said 'no.'"

My eyes stayed fixed, in shock, for real for real, now. "What? Why? I thought you two were certain. Racing against time."

He sighed. "She said no because she thinks I haven't processed my feelings for you. Or our marriage. The deaths of our babies. Our divorce."

With each topic, my brain popped louder. Me. Marriage. Babies we never really talked about. The end of our marriage. The muscles in my face automatically mimicked David's concern. "I'm sorry she..." I paused, looking for a kind word. "Declined. This time. Maybe she'll reconsider once you've worked through the issues."

"I need your help."

Well, I'll be. Four words I don't think I'd ever heard from David. Dr. Renita, the master magician, struck again.

"I'm glad you're working through. What do you need me for?"

"Couples therapy?"

"We're not a couple."

"But I'm still stuck there, Rose. And I still want to be married to you."

The phone camera showed my mouth wide open. "Hmmm."

My doubtful tone crushed his smooth skin into wrinkles of despair.

What would Marvina say? What would Marvina say?

"David. We love each other. Deeply. That said, we both know I'm not in love with you. You are not in love with me. And you're probably not in love with Renita—even though I think she's fabulous for what she's teaching you."

He nodded in agreement.

"But the whole truth, David, is that you. Love. The. Chase. You're ambitious. You're a hunter. You like excitement and adventure, and that's why you have trouble with committed, long-term relationships. Knowing all this, give me one reason why I should reenter a romantic relationship with you."

He laughed. "I guess 'cause I'm getting too old for the chase."

"What makes you think I want you, now, after you're all washed up like an old, faded T-shirt?"

"You see these muscles?" He flashed his arms, Popeye style.

"I do. But you still need counseling."

"Renita also said my proposal was all wrong."

I rolled my eyes. "Good Lord, David, what did you say?"

"I told her what I thought every woman wants to hear: I love you; I can't live without you. You make me a better man, and I want to spend the rest of my life with you."

I slapped my forehead. "No. You didn't."

"Yes. I did tell her all those wonderful things, and she said I needed her too much."

"Hello! All your reasons for wanting to be with her are about how she benefits you. Especially the part about her making you a better man. You might as well have printed out a middle school worksheet packet and given it to her. No woman wants the homework of making a man better. That was your momma's job, not Renita's."

David stared to his right. "Got it. I wish she had explained what she meant instead of sneaking out of bed and leaving."

"Well. Nobody's perfect. Just because she can diagnose other folks don't mean she can do it for herself. I hope she stays in counseling, too."

"What about you, Rose? And Marvina?"

I twisted my lips in thought. "Nah. Right now, me and my sister are just learning to connect again. Plus, I don't know about all these popular methods for counseling. Gotta go back and dredge up everything that ever happened between you and your parents. I don't think the healing is in analyzing the past. Rather spend my time building the future. Until they figure out a better way to treat people than re-traumatizing them with all those questions about the past."

David peered at me. "You serious? I mean, these are researched methods. With empirical data."

"I'm sure the psychiatrists had empirical evidence when they performed lobotomies, too."

"Touché. So what's your plan?"

"Don't have one. I'm just gonna reconnect with Marvina, start this spice company, and enjoy life between here and Dallas. With Jasiri. He is such a sweet baby."

"I can't wait to see him."

"Oh. You're still coming?"

"Why wouldn't I?"

I shrugged. "Thought you wanted to have the heart-to-heart. Which we just concluded."

"I still want to see the baby. And I do miss you. Friend."

"You are always welcome in Fork City. Friend," I singsonged.

"Thanks, Rose. Talk to you later."

"Bye, David." I tapped the screen and blackness appeared. I placed the phone against my heart.

David, David, David.

He deserved a wonderful relationship with the right person. Not me. Somebody who liked being chased, maybe?

Shoot, I couldn't figure out his drama. I had enough relationship work to do on my own. Starting with baby Jasiri, who was hollering for his milk.

"Hold your wing flaps, little Falcon," I teased, my voice echoing throughout the west side of Marvina's house.

Marvina appeared out of nowhere. "Sure taking your time with these chores."

"I'm on my way to warm it."

"Get a move on. Jasiri's turning red."

"That ain't hard for him. He's white."

Despite the annoyance pinching her face, Marvina and I laughed at my revelation.

"What am I going to do with you, Rose Yvette Dewberry-Tillman?"

"Keep on keepin' on. Together. That's what we're gonna do."

She threw an arm around my shoulder, and we headed back to the kitchen.

EPILOGUE

Baby Jasiri was finally asleep. He was barely three months old and was already trying to fight sleep, like he knew he'd be missing something important if he shut his blue eyes. On this occasion, he might have been right. It was an especially important day for Rose and Marvina. Kerresha had presented a business plan for their new seasoning business alongside comparisons to other brands and projections and budding ideas. There was only so far that she could go, however, without an actual brand name.

"Okay. I've gathered some ideas." Kerresha clapped her hands once before turning her laptop screen to face Rose and Marvina at the kitchen table.

Over these past several months, this heavy, steady wood table had witnessed negotiations with local police, a decades-old recipe revised with technology, and a heavy burden between sisters buried within twenty feet of where it sat.

And now, it would witness the birth of a business, assuming Rose and Marvina could agree on some basics.

Kerresha cleared her throat and threw her shoulders back as though she were sitting in the boardroom of a Fortune 500 company, button-down black shirt with black slacks and all.

Rose and Marvina smiled at her, proud of all the hard work Kerresha had put in to make their mother's seasoning business a reality. With the way the sisters had grown attached to Jasiri, Kerresha might as well be family at this point.

"I've prepared a slide deck with mock-ups so you can see what the business name might look like on an actual bottle, sitting on a table next to a bunch of fresh collard greens, as though it were in an advertisement. We're going to examine ten brandable business names."

Marvina raised a finger. "What does that mean?"

"It means people would be able to easily remember the name, and when they hear it, it will evoke a feeling. We have to manufacture that feeling over time, but it helps to start with a good, fresh name in the first place. You ready?"

Rose nodded.

Marvina raised an eyebrow like she wasn't sure about all of this. "I thought we were just gonna call it Our Momma's Seasoning."

Kerresha gave a swift, decisive headshake. "No, ma'am."

"Fine," Marvina mumbled.

"Let the girl speak, please," from Rose.

"Focus," Kerresha commanded with another clap of her hands. "Now. For this first time through the deck, all you need to say is yes or no. Two nos means it's automatically out of the contest. Two yeses, and it becomes an automatic finalist. We'll discuss the names you disagree on. Got it?"

Both sisters echoed her words.

Kerresha pressed the arrow key on her laptop and the first name flashed across the screen. She read it out loud like a newscaster. "Love Spice."

"I like that one," Rose exclaimed, sitting back in the rickety chair, popping her fingers and moving her neck side to side like she was grooving at a club. "That name is tha bomb!"

"Number one—one vote for yes. And, for the record, no one's saying 'the bomb' anymore." Kerresha placed a check mark in the "yes" column of her printed chart. "Miss Marvina, what do you think?"

Marvina said, "no," which immediately stopped Rose's giggling. "Why not?"

Marvina raised the tip of her nose. "It sounds like a sex toy."

"What?" Kerresha shrilled. "A sex toy?"

"It does, to me," Marvina stood her ground. "And I'm not gonna shame the folks of Fork City or Greater New Harvest with such perversity."

Kerresha and Rose howled in laughter, but Marvina wasn't having it.

"One vote for yes, one for no. Got it," Kerresha said, gathering her composure. "Next up. Zesty Spice."

Both sisters hemmed and hawed a bit, so Kerresha marked it a "no."

"Next up is Spice & Honey."

"Awwww, that's cute!" Rose squealed. "Like I'm the spice, and Marvina is the honey."

"Ain't no honey in Momma's recipe," Marvina objected. "Plus that sounds like an old wives' tale recipe for curing a rash."

Kerresha laughed again, this time with Marvina.

"Well, you never know," Rose giggled. "Momma's recipe healed us. Might be good for healing more stuff. Add some lavender?"

Marvina reached across the table and tapped the corner of Kerresha's paper. "Mark that one as a 'no' for me."

The next idea, Rezesty, was a solid no from both sisters, and Kerresha had to agree that it wasn't exactly one of her favorites, either. But since she wasn't the target audience, she still wanted to run it by Rose and Marvina.

Ours to Tango? Yes, but nothing to get excited about.

SoulSpice? split vote. Marvina said "yes" because it made her think of Jesus. Rose said "no" because it sounded too much like the word "hospice," and she didn't want that association.

Bakedish? No.

Munchlift. The ninth name evoked a jowl-shaking "no" from Rose and a grave "when hell freezes over" from Marvina.

Kerresha's jaw dropped. "No? Really? I liked this one!"

"Munch. Lift?" Rose broke it into two words.

"No. Munchlift," Kerresha said it quickly, as though that would make it sound better.

"That sounds like something that big blue Cookie Monster came up with. Not for *my* momma's seasoning."

"No, sirree," Marvina agreed.

Kerresha tapped her pen on the chart quickly. "We only have one more name."

Rose covered Kerresha's hand. "Listen. My sister and I can come up with a good name. Together. Right, Marvina?"

"Yes."

"Might not be brandable, though," Kerresha said, her voice tinged with despair.

"Sweetheart, how did you come up with these names?" Marvina asked.

"From a website. Artificial Intelligence that takes your keywords and suggests ideas based on the brand names, online purchasing, marketing jargon, algorithms."

"Fine. You give us the website, show us how to use it, and we'll share what we find with you. How's that?"

Kerresha's gaze ping-ponged between them. "I really wanted to help."

"You *did* help," Marvina said, scooting the laptop closer to Rose. "And we appreciate it."

"They talked about this in my class," Kerresha said. "Gen Xers and baby boomers always think they know best."

"Well, sometimes we do," Rose said. "But we are taking advice from you by using this here computer program instead of running through ten sheets of paper the old-fashioned way. Right?"

Kerresha rolled her eyes. "I suppose. But whatever names you come up with, I have to research them and analyze their overall marketability, okay?"

"Okay, sugar," Marvina said in her soothing tone. "Now, show us what to do."

After a short tutorial, Rose and Marvina shooed Kerresha out of the room to get to their baby boomin' know-it-all work. The entry fields on the website asked for key words, then the next tab asked whether they wanted one- or two-word results. Did they want exact matches or random surprises? It was a lot to require, but the sisters sat and fussed and clicked and snipped at each other for at least half an hour, and still no solid results. *Spice, fresh, sisters, mother, recipe, good food, good taste.* Whether one word, a phrase, or a compound word, no combination seemed to yield just the right result.

Exhausted and at their wits' end, Rose pushed the computer away from her body. "I need a break. My eyes are crossing. This is nerve-racking."

"Sure is. Whatever happened to the days when somebody just came up with a name that sounded good to their ears and that was it?"

"The baby boomers probably took all the good names." Rose's humor lightened the mood.

Marvina took the reins of the laptop, bringing it closer to her side. "Wait. We got one word we didn't try. Love."

"Love? How's that gonna fix the problem?"

"I don't know, but we can't do no worse than Nosesoul," she pointed at the ridiculous name suggestion on the screen.

Rose sighed. "Go for it."

Marvina typed in the word "love" and refreshed the results.

There, front and center, popped up a name that made both of them gasp with pleasure. They faced each other and simultaneously exclaimed, "Vine and Rose!" They slammed into each other with a tight cling that sealed their deal, screaming like they had been called to contestants' row on *The Price Is Right*.

Their cries brought Kerresha running from her bedroom. "What's going on?"

Marvina sang, "We got it!"

"What is it?"

Rose gave the countdown from three, and they declared, "Vine and Rose."

Kerresha beamed. "I love it! Vine says fresh ingredients; Rose says fragrant. And taste is all about the combination of smells. Plus it's kind of a combination of your names."

"Yes, all we needed was to add love, and it generated the perfect solution!" Rose explained.

Kerresha smiled. "Sounds about right for you two."

"3. 2. 1. Action."

Rose pursed her lips and spoke into the camera, also known

as Kerresha's iPhone, surrounded by a bright, circular light. The ocean waves whispered over Rose's shoulder, and Marvina gave Rose a thumbs-up as she spoke her lines. "Hey y'all. Thanks for joining us. This week we're on a cruise. Can you believe it? Water, dancing, live shows. Me and my sister are here with our Momma's seasoning." She held the shiny red cylindrical container front and center so everyone could read their brand name: Vine & Rose.

Marvina spoke next. "Shout out to my church home, Greater New Harvest in Fork City, Texas. We used to cook every weekend, but now we figured it out to where we doin' it once a month. Which worked out, 'cause I got to be available to do stuff like this here on the weekends. But shout out to my church.

"Anyway, last night, we spiced up the meatloaf they served at dinner. I'd say it was a little…"

"Unsouthern," Rose said. "No shade to the cruise chef. There's folk from all over the world on this ship. He can't please everybody."

"And," Marvina added, "you know they got restrictions on heat and grease and such on a cruise ship. Keeping everybody safe."

"Right," Rose said. "Safety first. No kind of fires we can't extinguish."

"So," Marvina continued, "We put some Vine & Rose on that meatloaf. Bay-bee boom!"

Rose covered her mouth so she wouldn't appear like a gaping fish on video. But Marvina's expression was hilarious. And true. "Everybody at our table eating meatloaf asked for some, and they all fared much better with Vine & Rose."

"Mm-hmm," Rose agreed. "So today, we've found ourselves a little alcove on the deck, and we're enjoying a cruise ship pizza. 'Cause the truth is, as much as me and my sister love to fry foods with Momma's seasoning, we can't be eating fried foods every day."

"Shole can't," Marvina warned. "Arteries be all clogged up for real!"

"So try Vine & Rose with some other dishes. I've put it on salads and plenty of vegetables. Now we're putting it on pizza. Hit me up, Vina."

Marvina christened the pizza with Momma's seasoning. "You know we always pray before we take a bite. So let's do it. Lord, thank You for this food we're about to eat. Bless the hands that prepared it. And bless everyone who eats Momma's seasoning to feel her generous love. Amen."

"Amen."

Together, the sisters repeated their now nearly IG famous taste test, culminating with their signature Mo' Betta Love score.

"On a scale of one to five, the Mo' Betta Love score is three," Rose threw out the arbitrary number, which had become part of their brand.

"How you figure three? I give it five. This pizza tasted like wax until we seasoned it."

"Wax! How you know what wax tastes like?" Rose fussed.

"I tasted a beautiful pink candle once," Marvina admitted. "Didn't you ever get curious?"

"Ain't that much curiosity in the world," Rose said. Then she looked directly at the iPhone. "And now, everyone knows who the *real* daredevil in this family is."

"Don't put my name and devil in the same sentence, hear?" Marvina snapped.

"I never said your name."

"Well, you talkin' like me and him are besties."

"You goin' too far," Rose said.

Behind the camera, Kerresha stifled a laugh. She twirled her finger, signaling for them to continue the banter. Viewers loved it almost as much as they loved Vine & Rose. Marvina's and Rose's friendly nips had become their brand as well.

"Put some in this drink. It needs a kick," Rose said. She sipped. "Mo' betta Love score of two. Y'all ought to try it!" She held up the glass as though toasting the hundreds of people who had joined their live broadcasts.

This entire marketing plan had been Kerresha's idea. It was part of a project she undertook for a program she'd enrolled in online. Rose and Marvina hired her part-time to handle the social media, which turned out to be half the battle of business. And it was working beautifully.

Plus with the tax expert David referred, part of the outings could be counted as tax expenses, so long as they kept making advertising videos. They added Vine & Rose to movie theater popcorn, boiled Easter eggs, carrot cake, and even sweet potato pie. Sometimes it was Mo' Betta. Sometimes it was No Betta. People tuned in to watch Rose and Marvina eat, fuss, and wish them all the love they could stand. All the while, they bought Vine & Rose as though Momma herself came through the bottle and pulled them into a hug.

Kerresha planned the content. She'd even helped them get makeovers which, according to David, made Rose look like she did the day he first met her.

David could often be found on set with Kerresha, Jasiri, Marvina, and Rose, because Jasiri took to David like a long-lost grandpa.

He'd stayed in Fork City that weekend to help Falcon with Jasiri, in fact, so Kerresha could get footage without interruption.

As soon as they wrapped on the cruise, adding Vine & Rose to at least four dishes and lightly fussing with each other the whole time, Marvina said she couldn't wait to remove her makeup. "Got me lookin' like a clown in all this paint."

"You look marvelous. Might fool around and catch a man," Rose teased.

"I'll catch a cramp in my leg before I catch a man," Marvina laughed.

"You said a mouthful, honey!" Rose cackled.

The more time she spent with Marvina in Fork City—which had increased significantly with their business and their continued reconciliation—that Southern accent and those country clichés seeped back into her language.

"We've got more than enough for our summer ads," Kerresha said. She tapped away at her phone, doing whatever she did to organize and promote their videos at the right time, in the right way. "I'm gonna go back to my room so I can call Jasiri."

This being her first time away from the baby, she stayed checking on him throughout the duration of the short cruise.

That left Rose and Marvina to reconnect. Talk. Argue. Compare more memories, rewrite old stories.

And it felt good. Felt real, real good.

Acknowledgments

I'm forever thankful to God for the gift of writing. I'm not sure where I would be without it. In fact, I'm quite sure writing was poured into my blood from the beginning. Thank you!

Thank you to Cassie McLaughlin for helping me think through plot points. To my online writing crew headed by fellow authors from Sisters of Faith, meeting with you all monthly helped hone this book, and I appreciate you! Shout out to Vanessa Riley, Vanessa Miller, Rhonda McKnight, and Michelle Lindo-Rice, especially, for chiming in on key turns throughout this novel. To the face-to-face writing team, headed by Becky Wade and Lynne Gentry, I appreciate you all letting me kick the dust off my writing boots in this group. Best to you all!

To this book's technical advisers: Thank you, Uncle Kenneth Williams, for the information about the United States Post Office. Thanks, Teressa Music, for teaching me all I needed to know about frying chicken like a boss (at least theoretically). Thanks, Shaundale (Stoney) Rhodes, for reading my synopsis and giving feedback. Thanks, Dr. Penny Gamez and Rebecca Music, RN, for the medical advice I needed to make sure my imagination aligned with reality.

Thank you to my journaling sisters who remind me that God has great plans for me. Right back atcha!

And thank you to my agent, Emily Sylvan Kim. I appreciate you helping me make it through these transitions as a writer. To my editor, Deb Werksman, at Sourcebooks, thank you for embracing me, these characters, and my vision to bring this story to life.

Finally, to my readers. Oooh, some of us have been together for twenty years now! Can you believe it? I still can't. I'm so grateful to be your literary sister, and I hope we'll hang in there together for another twenty years. I appreciate you!

About the Author

Michelle Stimpson has had a distinguished traditional publishing career writing Christian and inspirational contemporary romance fiction. She has won an Emma Award, two Christian Literary Awards, and Best Feature Film at CapCity Black Film Festival. She lives in Dallas, Texas.

Visit Michelle online at michellestimpson.com.